In the murky darkness Braille could make out a wide stairway. The stairwell was packed with bodies. There was no place to walk, no place to put his feet, and worse: the bodies were stirring, coming to life.

Braille began running up the street. The creatures were wide awake now. Many were standing on the street, others were coming out of buildings. Something slashed out at him, clawing his shirt. He kept on going. Another one leaped at him, trying to tear out his throat. Braille rammed his fingers into its temple, continuing to wade through the mob. A female tried to sink her claw-like nails into his throat, hissing and squalling like an evil cat . . .

He had come to Seattle knowing the city was in trouble, but never in his wildest dreams had he envisioned there would be so many of the creatures.

Hundreds. Maybe thousands.

With luck, maybe the soldiers could keep the New Ones confined to the center of the city for a couple of nights, but that would be it. Eventually the soldiers would get overrun and then they would become part of what they were fighting. They would become vampires.

Say good-bye to the world as you know it, Braille thought, and welcome to hell on earth. . . .

Books by Patrick Whalen

Monastery
Night Thirst
Out of the Night

Published by POCKET BOOKS

05 - 20 - 91

NO. 1.7.84

04 *   * 4.46   TM
                * 0.32   TX
                * 4.78
                * 2 0.78 CA
2 CL   * 16.00   CG_TND_TL

7'11.1' NO.
TM 12.-33.

NIGHT THIRST

PATRICK WHALEN

POCKET BOOKS

New York   London   Toronto   Sydney   Tokyo   Singapore

"Self-Control," words and music by Steve Piccolo, Raffaele Riefoli, Giancarlo Bigazzi. Copyright © 1984 Editiones Sugarmusic, controlled in the United States and Canada by Edition Sunrise Publishing, Inc. International copyright secured. All rights reserved. Used by permission.

An *Original* Publication of POCKET BOOKS

POCKET BOOKS, a division of Simon & Schuster Inc.
1230 Avenue of the Americas, New York, NY 10020

Copyright © 1991 by Patrick Whalen

ISBN: 0-671-70654-3

First Pocket Books printing June 1991

10 9 8 7 6 5 4 3 2 1

POCKET and colophon are registered trademarks of Simon & Schuster Inc.

Cover art by Gary Smith

Printed in the U.S.A.

I know the night is not as it would seem.

. . . I live among the creatures of the night.

—from "Self-Control,"
sung by Laura Brannigan,
lyrics by Steve Piccolo

NIGHT THIRST

THE ASPHALT FREEWAY STRETCHED OUT ACROSS THE CENTRAL Washington State desert like an endless black ribbon. The driver of the two-year-old station wagon was bored. He lit a cigarette, adjusted his sunglasses and glanced disinterestedly to his right. The sun-scorched desert seemed to go on forever, and he shook his head at the contrast. Five hours earlier he had left a rain-soaked Seattle and now he was rolling through a desert that made Death Valley look like a rain forest.

The driver shifted in his seat as he spotted something small perched on the shoulder of the road just ahead. He smiled, tapped the gas pedal and aimed the car at the shoulder. The station wagon's four-hundred-horsepower turbocharged motor roared to life and a steel-belted bullet-proof Michelin tire squashed a surprised jackrabbit into an obscene stain that immediately began to evaporate in the December heat. Stupid jackrabbits, the driver thought, guiding the heavy armor-plated vehicle back on the road. A thousand square miles of desert to play in, and they pick a road to sun themselves on. Cute or not, anything that dumb didn't deserve to exist.

A half hour later the town of Arron Lake came into view. Blistered, sprawling, most of its weathered buildings in need of repair, the town was as ugly as the desert. The freeway skirted the town, and as the driver started back into the desert, he caught sight of a boarded-up building buried under a mountain of tumbleweeds. A faded sign on the building's roof said: Valhalla Bar. The driver's eyes flicked to the speedometer. He memorized the mileage reading and exactly 14.5 miles later turned on to a dirt road. The road was strewn with rocks and tumbleweeds and appeared to be as fragile as a dried up creekbed. Yet the driver knew that just inches below the dirt there existed a well-maintained cement roadway strong enough to support a convoy of tanks. Twelve miles later the driver pulled to a stop in front of a twelve-foot-high cyclone fence topped with concertina wire. It seemed like an insurmountable barrier; there was no sign of a gate, just a steel fence stretching across the road and the desert for as far as the eye could see. The driver pulled out a small remote control device, aimed it at the fence, pushed a button and immediately a fifteen-foot-wide section of fence began to sink into the ground as if the road were made of quicksand. A moment later he drove on, glancing into his rearview mirror, his view of the gate being pushed back into position by a set of underground hydraulic motors obscured by a cloud of dust trailing out from behind the station wagon.

He came to a second fence and repeated the same procedure. A few miles later he came to a third fence. Unlike the first two, this one had a gate and an air-conditioned guardhouse. Two guards emerged from the hut. While one opened the gate, the other motioned him to continue on, saying, "Nice to see you back, Dr. Cutter."

As he drove on to the abandoned Air Force base, Dr. Hargrave Cutter made a mental note to have the guards reprimanded. They should have done an electronic palm scan or a retina check. Cutter briefly considered Greenland for the guards—or the Aleutians—but then changed his mind. The men couldn't do worse than where they were right now. The average summertime temperature was a hundred and eighteen. The winters were just as ugly with drifting snow, chronic winds, and a noontime temperature that rarely exceeded twenty degrees. Harsh, barren, isolated, home to rattlesnakes and ticks, the desert resembled an endless lunar landscape. No, Hargrave Cutter thought, he would not have the men transferred. Instead, he would have the guards' pay cut and have them assigned to one of the ancient un-air-conditioned watchtowers that surrounded the old base.

The desert was reclaiming the abandoned Air Force base. Sagebrush and clumpy undergrowth had heaved the sidewalks and split the roads. Most of the wooden barracks had collapsed. Several blocks of brick houses, once home to officers and their families, now resembled a deserted ghost town. The wind had leveled the USO club.

Cutter drove past several dilapidated control towers and pulled out onto the base's huge network of runways. Wind and sand buffeted the station wagon as Cutter drove across the runways, heading towards one of the largest manmade structures in the world. Twenty years earlier the giant airplane hangar had been the focus of massive activity because of its ability to shelter large numbers of B-52 bombers at one time. But now it stood alone in the sun, a rusty metal mountain of a building so vast it seemed to block out the horizon. As he neared the structure, two huge doors, each one four stories tall, began to part like massive metal curtains.

It was like watching the gates to hell open up, Cutter thought.

He drove into the black opening, parked and got out. It was quiet and cold in the hangar. Halogen lights mounted on the girders supporting the roof cast out an eerie orange light. Cutter craned his head back and studied the large cement building rising up from the hangar floor like a huge stone monolith. Windowless and seven stories tall, the structure resembled a giant tombstone. The building was a far cry from the small laboratory he'd started out in after being recruited by the National Security Agency a dozen years earlier.

Leaving the station wagon behind, Dr. Hargrave Cutter, the Director of the Office of Strategic Medical Studies, walked slowly towards the building, thinking back to how all this had come to pass.

Thirteen years earlier the NSA had created the Office of Strategic Medical Studies with the idea of taking the rapidly advancing technologies in the field of medicine and turning these advances into covert weapons. Specifically, they were interested in the development of substances which could kill yet resemble a natural death. The NSA recruited Hargrave Cutter to head up the project. He was a physician specializing in internal medicine, a gifted scientist in the field of medical research, and his psychological profile revealed that Cutter did not have a conscience. To him, other humans were simply stage props that served to enhance the existence of only one person in the world—himself.

In the beginning, he and his staff worked out of a small laboratory on the East Coast. After an inauspicious start, Cutter and his people managed to mutate a simple form of airborne bacteria with radiation. Prior to having its genetic structure altered, the bacteria had been harmless; afterwards it was as deadly as cyanide gas—at least to laboratory animals. An operational field test followed. The mutated bacteria was released into the cooling system of a hotel's air-conditioning system. Twenty-nine hotel guests died. The press called the outbreak "Legionnaire's Disease."

In 1980 the OSMS discovered a synthetic hormone similar to epinephrine, which is produced when an individual encounters an emergency. When man lived in caves, faced with daily fight-or-flight encounters, the energy produced by the hormone was useful. In modern man, the hormone is unnecessary but is still produced in times of crisis. Often after being produced, the hormone stays in the body, causing jitters and a *highly* elevated cholesterol level for several hours. The synthetic hormone the OSMS developed was identical to epinephrine except in two respects: it was hundreds of times more powerful than the human hormone, and a few hours after it was introduced into a warm environment, it broke down into untraceable elements. It also had one other unique property: it was readily absorbed by the skin. This meant it could be induced into a subject by means of an aerosol hairspray, hand cream, Chapstick, or toothpaste. Once absorbed into the body, the victim's cholesterol level went off the chart. Within minutes tiny deposits of fat would begin to clog the heart. Some hours later the hormone began to break down in the warm environment of the blood stream. Eighteen to twenty-four hours later the subject was dead, an apparent victim of an undiagnosed heart condition.

In 1985 the NSA decided to relocate the Office of Strategic Medical Studies. The move was obligatory. The OSMS employed over three hundred and fifty people and by now they had begun to do research into such forbidden areas as the creation of manmade strains of bacteria and viruses, epidemiology, and Recombinant DNA experiments. It was the NSA that came up with the idea of moving the OSMS from the East Coast to an abandoned Air Force base in the middle of Washington State. It was also their idea to build Cutter's laboratory and hospital within the confines of a giant hangar. They also built a second building for the OSMS staff beneath the roof of another hangar a mile away, and connected the two structures by means of a large underground tunnel.

It was the perfect place. The massive airplane hangars camouflaged the newly built buildings from the prying eyes of overhead aircraft and surveillance spy satellites. The isolated location, coupled with the desert environment, three security fences, and an army of security guards ensured no one would ever get onto the base and discover what was really going on. Air traffic in and out of the old base was kept to a minimum with take-offs and landings occurring only at night.

As head of the OSMS, Cutter could've commanded a Lear jet or a helicopter, but as always he chose to drive his specially built high-powered two-year-old station wagon. The drive to the base added an element of drama to his life and also gave him a feeling of humility, a feeling he was immensely proud of. He was the head of an organization that one day would discover a weapon that would allow the United States to rule the world, and yet he was not above driving to work in a station wagon. He liked himself very much for that.

Aware he was being monitored by television cameras, he mounted the steps, pushed open a heavy security door, and entered a large room furnished with plastic and chrome furniture. Immediately his eyes were drawn to a large picture window that looked out upon a spectacular desert. Cactus flourished in abundance in the red sand. Off in the distance, beyond a wall of cliffs, an ominous bank of clouds rolled towards him. Lightning flashed within the clouds, and he could hear the muted rumble of thunder. The curtains on both sides of the window billowed out in response to the ever-growing wind.

Cutter had been away for six weeks, and as always it took him a moment to realize the desert he was looking at was not the one he had just driven through. It was an Arizona desert, he decided, or perhaps a desert in Utah. Still, it didn't matter because what he was looking at was a motion picture. The window was a screen, and the unseen projector behind it was showing a film of a desert on it. Everything was fake. The curtains were responding to air vents controlled by a computer to enhance the illusion that there really was a desert outside the building, complete with storms, lightning, and a growing wind. As Cutter smiled at the illusion and continued to stare at the oncoming storm, unseen speakers in the room's ceiling reverberated with the sounds of close thunder.

His interest in the storm faded when the assistant director of the OSMS entered the room. "Welcome back, sir," Dr. John Riddick said, shaking Cutter's hand vigorously. "How were things in Washington, D.C.?"

Cutter made a face. "Boring and humid." He forced himself not to frown as he noticed Riddick's blotchy complexion. He hadn't seen Riddick in six weeks, yet it seemed that during that time the network of veins in the man's cheeks and nose had become redder, more pronounced. Obviously Riddick was drinking again, but this was not the time to bring it up. "How's our man doing?"

Riddick smiled. "Incredible. He's surpassed our wildest expectations. The reports are in my office, if you care to see them."

"That's why I came back early," Cutter said with a mounting sense of excitement. He walked with Riddick down a corridor, moving past his office and into Riddick's. While his assistant worked the combination of the wall safe, Cutter glanced out the window behind Riddick's desk. The storm had passed and a rainbow bracketed the distant cliffs.

Riddick handed him a metal file thick with reports. "The tests and narratives are in chronological order." Cutter sat down on a couch, lit a cigarette, and read in silence. When he finished, he fixed his eyes on Riddick. "What's our man's current status?"

"He hasn't eaten food in forty-six days and hasn't said a word to us in just about that long." Riddick lit a pipe and waved the smoke away from his face. "We're sustaining him with forceful injections of human blood every eight hours. We tried to go the intravenous route, but he kept tearing out the needles."

"Who's giving him the injections?"

Riddick smiled. "Golem. It's the only thing that has the strength to deal with him. It's not in the reports, but two weeks ago he almost pulled Johnson through the bars."

"I thought our man was chained up," Cutter said.

"He was, but he broke one of the chains and grabbed Johnson by the arm. It was Johnson's fault. He was prodding our man with a broom handle."

"How's Johnson?" Cutter asked.

"Broken arm, dislocated shoulder, broken collarbone, cracked sternum. Still, he's lucky he's not dead . . . or worse."

Cutter glanced down at the file in his lap, then back at Riddick. "Do you realize what we have on our hands? Do you realize what our man's been through with no side effects? We've injected him with almost every disease known to man, along with massive injections of living cancerous cells from every type of cancer known to exist. The list of what we've done to this man goes on forever and our man still shows no side effects from anything we've done to him. No side effects whatsoever. God, do you realize how incredible that is?"

Riddick started to respond, but Cutter cut him off. "There wasn't anything in your notes about what happened to the men who volunteered to take injections of our man's blood."

"I thought it best not to put that in writing," Riddick said, studying his pipe.

"What happened to them?"

"They're all dead," Riddick said softly. "All died within forty-eight hours of receiving our subject's blood. They all went violently insane and then died. Within moments after their deaths their bodies disintegrated into ashes." Riddick shuddered. "I've never seen anything like it. We have their deaths and disintegrations on videotape, if you care to see them."

"Later. Right now I want to go over everything we know about this man and what he and the other survivors said about what happened on that island."

Riddick began to recite a strange litany from memory. "About ten weeks ago a nuclear power plant on a tourist island up in Puget Sound exploded. The resulting cloud of radioactivity killed everyone on Chinook Island, but five people escaped in a boat just before the power plant exploded. They were Dr. Lewis Radcliff and his wife, Jade, and a woman named Leslie Chapel, who's a talk show hostess for a religious station in Seattle, a three-year-old girl whose parents died on the island, a man named Braille, and an old dog."

At the mention of the strange name, both men stirred uncomfortably. Cutter lit a cigarette; Riddick relit his pipe and continued. "After these five escaped from the island, they headed for the mainland and came ashore on the outskirts of a town called Bellingham. After they arrived, Chapel called the local hospital and asked for an ambulance, because Radcliff had been hurt during their escape. The hospital naturally contacted the police, the police contacted the feds, and about every government agency you can think of sent people out to meet this launch, not only because a nuclear power plant had exploded, but nobody'd heard anything from this island for weeks; even the ferry that took the tourists out to the island hadn't been heard from. So everybody converged on the wharf where the boat was tied up. While the attendants were carrying the doctor off to the ambulance, the police and feds started to question Chapel, but she wouldn't answer them. She was worried about Braille. He was still out in the launch and wouldn't come ashore. Then, all of a sudden, he started the launch. She ran out to the end of the pier and talked to him, but he left anyway.

"Later, just before they put her in the ambulance, one of the NRC men asked Chapel where the guy was going, and she said he was going back to his home on the island. The

NRC man couldn't believe it. Because of the explosion, the island had been saturated with enough radioactivity to kill anyone who would get near it for the next fifty years.

"Everyone figured the guy who went back to the island—Braille—was as good as dead. But nine hours later a Navy destroyer out searching for survivors found a man floating in the water just off the island. They took him aboard. The ship's surgeon examined him and thought the man was dead. He had third-degree burns over ninety percent of his body, his lungs were filled with water, 'bout every bone in his body was broken, and he had a body temperature in the low sixties. The doctor thought it was a waste of time to work on the guy, but he went through the motions anyway. Nothing worked. Then, just to complete the procedure, he gives the guy plasma and—wham! Instant miracle! The guy comes back to life and, more than that, his injuries start healing at an incredible rate. Within minutes the man's broken bones begin knitting and the burns disappear. When his patient finally comes to, the doctor tries to get him to talk, but he won't. He just stares at the doctor as if he resents the doctor bringing him back to life. Well this is way out of the doctor's league and he orders a helicopter to transfer the man from the ship back to Bellingham."

"Didn't this man say something to the doctor?" Cutter asked, even though he'd read the reports and knew the story by heart.

"Yeah." Riddick stared down at his pipe, then slowly raised his eyes to Cutter's. "He told the doctor he was a vampire and begged to be put over the side. The doctor almost did. Hell, who can blame him. His patient had literally come back to life after receiving blood. Anyway, after the man had been lifted off the destroyer, the doctor called Bellingham Hospital and talked to some of the doctors. The word got out about this guy thinking he was a vampire and how he was resurrected after receiving a dose of plasma. So when he was finally admitted to the hospital, the physicians put him in isolation. At the same time, we heard the story about Braille. The National Security Agency came in with a containment team to handle the press and the hospital employees and within twenty-four hours, the girl and dog were shuttled off to a foster home in Tacoma and the four adult survivors were sedated, then Airvac'd here." Riddick gestured at Cutter with his pipe. "You want me to go on? You were here when we began interviewing the survivors. You know the story they had to tell about what happened on the island *before* the power plant exploded."

"I know," Cutter said. "And if it hadn't been for the NSA calling me back to Washington, I would've been here through the whole process. Anyway, I want to hear the story again. From the beginning."

Riddick stared at the wall just above Cutter's head, trying to collect his thoughts, trying to figure out a way he could tell the strangest story he'd ever heard in his life. Then he began.

"A few months after World War I ended, the Church in Europe built a huge fortress-like monastery on what was then a deserted island located off the coast of Washington State. Then they entombed coffins in a special vault in a subterranean chamber below the monastery. These coffins contained the withered remains of Ancients. To really understand what the Church was doing, you have to understand that vampirism existed in Europe, especially during the Middle Ages. And there's a strong possibility that there was never any such thing as the Black Plague. What actually happened was a massive epidemic of vampirism wiped out most of the population of fourteenth-century Europe. Now, the Church was instrumental in exterminating the vampires. They killed most, but not all. A few surviving vampires had changed. They had become more human and regained their memories of what they were like when they were human. Because of the continued ingestion of blood, their bodies changed and they became extremely powerful and immortal. Disease had no effect on them. They didn't age. If wounded, their bodies could heal at an incredible rate. They *were* immortal. But because of what they were, the Church continued to hunt them, and though we don't have a specific date, we do know that at some point an army of priests trapped these Ancients in the Ural Mountains and used special rituals and the powers of their Deity to immobilize them, literally turning them into withered, dehydrated husks.

"They entombed the Ancients in an abbey in France, but

during World War I the abbey was damaged by artillery fire. The Ancients didn't escape, but it was close, and this frightened the Church so much they decided to build a monastery on a deserted island and entomb the Ancients there. As a kind of added insurance, the Church assigned priests to look after the monastery. Two priests would come to the island, guard the monastery for ten years, and on the night the old priests left, two new ones would arrive to take their place. There was no problem for about sixty years. Then in 1981 two recently arrived priests both died on the same night. We now think that one had a heart attack and the other was killed in a car wreck while driving into town for medical help. Now, if the island had still been deserted, this wouldn't have been a problem. But everything had changed since the Church first built the monastery. Over the years the island had become a popular tourist attraction with a modern resort town, though, oddly, the only way you could get to the island was by ferry.

"The monastery stood deserted for some years, then some college students got into the monastery, broke into the vault where the Ancients were entombed, found the coffins, opened them, and were killed and turned into vampires— New Ones—by the Ancients who needed their blood to return to life.

"That night or the next, the leader of the Ancients, a nine-hundred-year-old vampire named Gregory, decided he would turn the island into a kingdom for his kind. Somehow he managed to set a fire that destroyed every boat in the resort town's harbor, including the ferry. That act, coupled with a week of freakish windstorms, isolated the island, cutting it completely off from the mainland twenty-six miles away.

"Then, to put it bluntly, all hell broke loose as vampirism began to spread over the island.

"Our man Braille lived on the island, in an old lighthouse he was restoring. When he found out what was happening he went into town to see if he could help and ended up taking fourteen people back to his lighthouse. Among the people he rescued were the little girl, Lewis and Jade Radcliff, and Leslie Chapel. In the days that followed, it was a matter of staying hidden and hoping the vampires on the island wouldn't find out where they were. We think it was then that Braille and Chapel began to fall in love. On several occasions Braille was forced to make daylight trips to town for supplies. On one of those trips he came face to face with Gregory; the encounter was no accident. Gregory had seen Braille kill one of the vampires in town using his martial arts skills. Gregory was intrigued by the style of fighting and purposely trapped Braille in a park so he could talk to him and find out more about this strange style of fighting.

"Oddly, a strange friendship began to form between these two, a kind of adversarial friendship based on their respect for each other's killing skills and powers. This friendship took on other dimensions when Gregory saved Braille's life when a pack of vampires attacked Braille in the park. Shortly after that, when some of the Ancients Gregory had been entombed with in the monastery wandered too close to the island's nuclear power plant, they died and literally dissolved. This rocked Gregory to his core. He didn't understand why the other Ancients had died and could barely believe it had happened. After all, Ancients like him were supposedly immortal. It was Braille who finally explained to Gregory what nuclear radiation is and suggested that maybe Gregory and his kind had no tolerance for even minuscule doses of radiation. Some hours later, when Gregory's woman was trapped by five looters who wanted to kill her, oddly enough, it was Braille who intervened and saved Clementina's life. Like Gregory, Clementina was an Ancient, and she and Gregory had been together as lovers for over five hundred years. This was the first time a human had ever helped an Ancient, and in this case, he killed five of his own kind to save Clementina's life. This left Gregory shouldered with an enormous obligation. He paid off his debt by leading Braille to the only boat not destroyed in the harbor fire. The boat was on the beach about seven miles from Braille's lighthouse and because it was close to sundown, Braille couldn't get the other humans out of the lighthouse and down to the boat. Consequently, they were forced to spend one more night in hiding. And it was that night when the vampires on the island finally discovered where the last remaining humans were. Hundreds of them attacked the lighthouse, and in the end the vampires began to overrun the walls built around Braille's lighthouse. Braille knew the only way they could survive was to escape in cars, trying to make it to the boat and leave the island.

"Only, something odd happened. There was a man out at the lighthouse named James Warren. He had been a nuclear safety engineer at a power plant in Oregon. During the fight with the vampires, Warren's autistic son was bitten by one and this pushed Warren over the edge. Just as the others were about to escape from the lighthouse, Warren decided he was going to take his son, drive to the nuclear power plant, blow it up, and let the resulting cloud of radiation destroy all the vampires on the island. A couple of people tried to get Braille to stop Warren, but after talking to Warren and finding out that Warren planned to blow up the power plant a couple hours after sunrise when Braille and the others would be in the boat and well away from the island, Braille decided to help Warren. He even gave Warren a hundred pounds of plastic explosives to help him blow up the plant. Then Braille and most of the survivors took off in a car, hoping to get to the boat on the beach. Warren and his son headed off to the power plant.

"Braille and the four remaining survivors managed to get to the boat and they were getting ready to shove off, when Gregory and Clementina showed up on the beach. Gregory had been watching the humans and had figured out what was going on; he knew that someone out at the power plant was going to blow it up and destroy the New Ones and the last of the Ancients with radioactivity. He demanded the boat back from Braille. Braille refused, and a fight that had been a long time in coming finally occurred. It was one hell of a fight. They fought for almost an hour, and in the end, Gregory finally beat Braille. Braille was blinded in one eye, had a shattered arm, and a massive concussion.

"Just as Gregory was getting ready to kill Braille, Clementina came between the two and said that if living on through eternity meant killing the one human who had become their friend and had helped them, then she didn't want to continue on this way. She didn't want to live eternally. We don't know a lot about this Clementina, but because of what she did say to Gregory, we know that she was probably tired of her eternal existence, tired of taking blood so she could live forever. What she wanted to do was to die. She wanted the peace and nothingness that the other Ancients who had been killed by the power plant now had. She tried to talk Gregory into staying on the island and going back to the church they had taken over as their home, but Gregory would have no part of it. In the end she simply turned around and walked away from a man she had loved for five hundred years. We also don't know what went through Gregory's mind at that moment, but apparently he finally came to realize how much he loved his woman and how lonely his existence would be without her. He gave Braille back the boat, even helped him to launch it, and the last time Braille and the others saw him, Gregory was walking down the beach, heading towards the resort town and the church where his woman was waiting for her own death.

"True to plan, Warren blew up the power plant a couple hours after sunrise, and the resulting radioactive cloud destroyed everything on the island.

"Braille and the other survivors were several miles from the island when the plant exploded, and they weren't hurt. But it was while they were on their way to the mainland that Braille's injuries began to heal at a phenomenal rate. The side effects from the concussion disappeared. His arm healed and his sight returned. For a while he was baffled by what was going on. Then he noticed some puncture wounds in the heel of his hand. That's when he realized that during the fight with Gregory he had hit the Ancient in the mouth with his hand, and now he was contaminated.

"He was becoming a vampire.

"So that's why after everyone was safe on the mainland, he turned the boat around and went back to the island to die. He didn't think he could control what he was becoming and he didn't want to start an epidemic of vampirism on the mainland. He wanted to die. He wanted the radiation to kill him. But that didn't happen and you know the rest of the story."

Cutter shook his head in disbelief. "Jesus Christ, we have a real, living vampire in the laboratory of this hospital." He shook his head again. "What do we know about Braille before all this happened to him?"

"His parents died in a nightclub fire when he was young. Some years later he was adopted by an older Oriental couple from Japan. We suspect they were the ones who taught him his martial arts skills, and by the way, Braille has master instructor status in Tae Kwon Do and Akaido and is also a fifth Dan in Shinto Ryu Karatedo. The man is skilled, formidable, and deadly."

"What else do we know?" Cutter asked.

"We know he spent time in Vietnam, was a Green Beret, a Ranger, and a paratrooper, and we think he did a lot of work for a certain Colonel D. W. McKlean as a behind the lines enemy assassin. The same sources who gave us this information also said Braille was the best killer McKlean had in his unit.

"It was while he was on one of those missions for McKlean that he was wounded behind enemy lines, captured and tortured for almost three years in a North Vietnamese POW camp. After his release from North Vietnam, Braille spent almost a year convalescing at Madigan Army Hospital in Tacoma, then dropped out of sight for a year, then resurfaced on Chinook Island where he bought a dilapidated lighthouse and set out to restore it. A year or so later he started his own business. He built some greenhouses next to the lighthouse, began to raise rare ferns, and eventually began selling them to exotic plant wholesalers all over the world."

Riddick fixed his eyes on Cutter and lowered his voice. "We made some inquiries. Seems he was paying almost twenty thousand dollars a year in property taxes and insurance on that place of his. In addition, it cost him almost three hundred thousand dollars to restore the lighthouse. In all cases he paid in cash. Braille didn't make much more than twenty thousand dollars a year off his ferns, so the question is, Where did the money to buy the lighthouse, restore it, and pay the property taxes on it come from? We did some checking around and found out he had a savings account in a bank in Seattle and a second one in Canada. He had about twenty-five thousand dollars in savings in the Seattle account."

Cutter shrugged. "So what?"

Riddick smiled. "And a little over four hundred thousand dollars in the Canadian bank. He told the Canadian banker the money was from a trust account his dead parents set up for him, but we checked. His natural parents didn't leave him a penny; his adoptive parents left him a small ranch in Washington. But after they were killed in a car crash, he sold the ranch and turned everything over to charity."

"So where did he get all the money?" Cutter asked.

"Good question. Since we were running into a blank wall, I went ahead and asked the NSA to check this out also."

"And?"

"This'll blow your socks off. Remember when I mentioned Braille worked for a man named McKlean in Vietnam? Well, the NSA thinks McKlean may have set up a similar operation in Atlanta. They think he hired some of the men who worked for him in Nam and put them back to work doing what they did in Nam—killing people. Only, now they do it for money. It's only speculation, but the NSA suspects McKlean functions as an agent. People contact him about someone they want killed. He checks out the situation, gathers the details, then farms out the hit to someone in his organization."

"You saying Braille's a hit man?" Cutter asked. Riddick nodded. Cutter lit a cigarette. "A professional killer? Christ, that's incredible."

Cutter took a drag off his cigarette and exhaled thoughtfully. "As I recall, the survivors from the island said that after someone was bitten by a vampire, they would go crazy and get caught up in a kind of bloodlusting frenzy."

Riddick nodded. "And the survivors also said that if these newly contaminated humans didn't get blood within a matter of hours, they died and their bodies disintegrated."

"So is that what happened to the people we injected with Braille's blood?" Cutter asked.

"Technically, yes. They went through the same thing that the people on the island went through. They lost their human personalities and turned into rabid animals. Every one of them would've killed their own mother for a mouthful of blood."

"They're all dead?"

"All died within forty-eight hours of receiving an injection of Braille's blood . . . except one."

"He didn't die?"

"Actually, he did die, but he didn't die because he couldn't get blood. See, we took that one out into the sun as kind of an experiment. He lasted maybe two minutes, and it was pretty bad." Riddick shrugged and made a face. "We have all the deaths on videotape."

"What I don't understand," Cutter said, "is if all those people went crazy and died after being contaminated, how come Braille didn't go crazy and die? Your reports indicate that from the very beginning he was calm, rational, and logical."

"I have a couple of theories about that," Riddick remarked. "Braille did receive plasma on the destroyer and later he received more plasma at the Bellingham Hospital. After we brought him here, we took him off plasma and put him on whole human blood. Now that explains why he didn't die. As to why he didn't go crazy or get caught up in that bloodlusting madness, I'd say that was due to the internal strength of the man. He's intelligent and has an incredible amount of mental self-discipline as a result of his involvement and dedication to the martial arts. Consequently, he overcame the madness, and if you ask me, I'd say he's becoming an Ancient or may already be one. His own internal strength helped him bypass or speed up the evolutionary process that normally occurs when one of these New Ones finally becomes an Ancient."

"What are your thoughts about Gregory, the leader of the Ancients?"

Riddick took a long moment to collect his thoughts. "Nine hundred years old, powerful beyond our imagination, cunning, immortal, and capable of immense love. He gave up eternity so he could die with his woman."

"I noticed in one of your reports that just before he stopped talking to us, Braille said he thought Gregory was still alive."

Riddick nodded. "Just after the helicopter lifted him off

the destroyer, Braille thought he heard Gregory cry out. Personally, I think Braille was having a nightmare. The copter was ten miles from the island and Braille was in shock. It was just his imagination but Braille's not sure. He thinks that Clementina died in that radioactive cloud, but somehow Gregory didn't. In my opinion, nothing could have survived that nuclear holocaust. *Nothing."*

"How goes the research on developing vaccines from Braille's blood?"

"Not well. Whatever's in his blood that makes him immune to all those diseases and heal so rapidly breaks down the minute we take a sample. Hell, we can't even get a specimen under the microscope."

Cutter scowled. "That man holds the key to vaccines that would put an end to every major disease in the world, including cancer. There's also an equally strong possibility that there's a substance in Braille's blood that would retard the aging process. If we could isolate whatever he got when Gregory contaminated him and modify it so people wouldn't go crazy or die when we injected them with it, the sky would be the limit for us. We couldn't even imagine the amount of money we would come into. Think of it, John. Braille's living proof that there's a substance in this world with the properties to end every major disease we know about, make the body heal at an incredible rate, and might even end the aging process."

Riddick tried to hide his confusion. The development of a vaccine had not been Cutter's original objective for Braille six weeks earlier. "What about your initial goal to create a race of superior human beings with Braille's strength and ability to heal rapidly?"

Cutter glowered at Riddick. "You're misquoting me. I never used the word *create* and I never used the word *race*. My original plan for Braille was to endow a few chosen individuals with Braille's strength, stamina, and healing powers. Think of it—a group of men with inhuman strength and the ability to recover from wounds within moments! The possibilities are unlimited! They could be sent out on assassination missions. They would be fearless in hostage rescue situations. They could go aboard a hijacked jet and concentrate on the mission because they wouldn't have to worry about dying themselves. That was my original plan for Braille's blood, but while I was in Washington, I had a chance to think about it and develop other possibilities. I would still like to see the original plan put into effect, but the other plan, the plan to end aging and disease, has more merit. And it would be more lucrative." He stubbed out his cigarette and got to his feet. "I think we've talked enough. I want to see Braille now."

Both men walked down a long corridor to an elevator. The door opened automatically, the men entered, and the elevator descended sixty feet below the hospital's main floor. After it stopped, Riddick placed the palm of his hand on what looked like a small TV screen built into the side of the elevator. The screen glowed briefly and went out. Then Cutter put his hand on the screen. Again the screen flickered as it checked Cutter's palm print, then an overhead metallic voice with feminine qualities said: "Access approved." The elevator door opened and the men stepped into a large foyer. Two heavily armed guards stood up, stiffly acknowledged the doctors' presence, then one of the guards walked over to a large metal door, unlocked it with a key, and slowly pulled it open.

Riddick and Cutter entered a dimly lit large room that resembled something out of a science fiction movie. The wall to their left was lined with a vast array of high-tech computers and computer consoles. A series of stainless steel laboratory tables supporting a wide variety of scientific equipment and sophisticated medical monitoring machines lined another wall.

A tall, powerfully built man in his mid-thirties hurried over to greet them. His name was Alan Kendricks. He stood six feet seven inches tall, and because he'd worked out fanatically with weights most of his life, he had a body an Olympic weightlifter would envy. Yet, oddly, he had feminine facial features. It was something most people could never quite get used to. The man had a face of a pretty twelve-year-old choirgirl and a body that resembled the missing link. Cutter knew Kendricks' odd appearance was the result of a glandular disorder, but the hormonal imbalance and massive slabs of muscle didn't bother Cutter. Kendricks was intelligent and his advanced degrees in biology, nursing, and robotics made him the perfect man to oversee the lower-level laboratories. His job duties were wide-ranging. He supervised many of the research experiments, monitored the staff and security, and looked after Braille. Cutter had stolen Kendricks away from NASA six years earlier and was fond of the fellow. Kendricks was loyal and followed orders without question. He was also a sadist. He enjoyed inflicting pain on animals and humans, and since pain and death were integral components of many of the OSMS experiments, Kendricks was the perfect man for the job.

Kendricks shook Cutter's hand enthusiastically. The man had a powerful grip and baby-soft skin. "How are things going?" Cutter asked.

"Not too well, I'm afraid. Chromosome analysis, tissue cultures, amino acid studies and blood work-ups are almost impossible to perform."

"Why?" Cutter asked, even though Riddick had already explained some of the problems earlier.

"The samples break down almost the moment we take them," Kendricks explained. "If you care to look, I'll show you what I'm talking about." Kendricks led Cutter over to a table, prepared two slides, and slipped one under the microscope. Then he motioned to Cutter. "See for yourself."

After bringing the powerful microscope into focus, Cutter had the impression he was looking into a drop of sterilized distilled water. He straightened up and Kendricks inserted the second slide. This time Cutter had the feeling he was examining a highly magnified dried leaf. Confused, he glanced at Kendricks.

"The first slide is a sample of Braille's blood," Kendricks explained. "We took the sample earlier this afternoon then went through the standard preservative processes."

Cutter shook his head. "Christ, there isn't a trace of corpuscles."

"I know." Kendricks gestured at the microscope. "The second slide is a tissue section. We took that sample at the same time we took the blood. Golem passed it through the bars and we had it in the freezer in thirty seconds. You just saw me make up the slide. It didn't take more than ten seconds and yet all we got is something that looks like parchment. We've tried every means we know to preserve the samples we take from this man. Nothing works. Everything we take breaks down into nothing within seconds." Before Cutter could respond, Kendricks' wristwatch beeped. "Eight p.m.," he observed. "Feeding time." He glanced at Cutter. "You might be interested in this. We've made some modifications in Golem."

"Modifications?" Cutter asked.

Kendricks smiled. "We improved his hydraulics, modified his auditory receiver, and enhanced his program. He now has the capacity to respond to sixty-one commands and thirty-six multiple word directives. If he keeps learning at this rate, he'll replace Dr. Riddick in six months." Kendricks smiled at Riddick. Riddick looked away.

"Bring him out," Cutter said.

Kendricks pulled a radio transmitter out of his pocket and lifted it to his mouth. "Come, Golem."

Cutter heard a soft mechanical whirring sound behind him. He turned towards the noise and felt a chill move up his spine as a huge alien-shaped mass emerged from a dark corner.

Golem was a robot. Part of his design had come from NASA. The rest was pure OSMS. From a distance Golem resembled a horrible blend of man and machine. Where there should have been legs, instead were rubber-encased treads similar to tank treads. The torso, rising up from a platform above the treads, resembled a huge stainless-steel barrel and was home to Golem's brain, a sophisticated HK-II computer. Golem's head consisted of two video cameras capable of working in unison like human eyes. A large round bowl of clear bulletproof mylocene plastic protected the cameras the same way a human skull protects the brain. More than once when both cameras had focused down on Cutter, he'd had the feeling he was looking up into the mechanical face of something almost human. Disturbing as that was, the most chilling part of Golem was its arms and hands. Constructed from solid rods of titanium steel, the metal bones making up Golem's hands and arms were identical to the hands and arms of a human skeleton. A complicated system of metal cables and miniature hydraulics served as tendons and muscles, while sophisticated cartilages constructed from myfel plastic held everything in place.

Cutter encountered Golem almost every day, but he had never grown accustomed to a six-foot-five-inch, four-thousand-pound machine with the giant arms and hands of a skeleton. Even now, as Golem rolled towards him, Cutter felt his stomach roil at the sight of the macabre appendages that had the power to crush metal to dust or pick up the most fragile of test tubes.

Golem rolled to a quiet stop on its rubber treads and its fishbowl-like head turned slightly until the eyes were focused on Kendricks. The lab technician gestured at Cutter. "Say hello." The torso rotated slightly and the camera eyes focused in on Riddick. Golem consulted its memory banks, then the torso turned a bit more until the cameras locked in on Cutter's face. "Hel-lo Doc-tor Cut-ter," it said, extending a bony hand. Cutter had no choice. The staff was watching. He shook Golem's huge grotesque hand. The machine's grip was cold but gentle. After a moment Golem released him, but continued to stare at him expectantly.

"Interested in watching Golem feed Braille?" Kendricks asked.

With Golem trailing along behind, Kendricks returned to the refrigerator. When he finally closed the door and turned around, he was holding a large syringe with an eight-inch-long sixteen-gauge needle. He held the syringe up for Cutter's inspection.

"Six fluid ounces of blood—it doesn't matter what type —every six hours. Less than that and our man's vital signs begin to fluctuate. More than that and he gets feisty. He was on twelve ounces of blood every six hours when he broke the chain and pulled Johnson through the bars."

"You make him sound like blood turns him into a superman," Cutter remarked dryly.

Kendricks shrugged. "Before a transfusion he's dangerous. After one . . . well, let's just say that big as I am, I'd hate to be around if he ever escaped after receiving an injection of blood."

"What would you do if he ever escaped?"

"Let Golem take care of him."

"Golem can fight?" Cutter asked skeptically.

"We got some videotapes. They're training films actually, put out by the Israeli Army of some of their hand-to-hand combat instructors in action. Golem's been viewing the tapes and committing the moves to memory. Would you care for a demonstration?"

"Maybe later." He gestured at the syringe Kendricks was still holding. "Is that the only way to feed him?"

"Let's just say it's the safest way to feed him. We tried intravenous feeding and he tore the tubes out. We considered administering the fluid orally, but he won't open his mouth. I could probably get Golem to pry his jaw open, but if he were to fight it and Golem applied full pressure, Golem would tear his jaws apart to complete the command. This is the best way. It's fast and safe and it doesn't matter where the needle goes. The man's gonna heal in minutes anyway."

Kendricks motioned to a lab tech. She pushed a button near the door and the back wall of the laboratory began to slide to one side as the hinged room divider folded away like an accordion. Cutter's attention was drawn to a raised twenty-foot-square platform extending out from the lab's back wall. The platform was surrounded on all sides by a floor-to-ceiling iron bar fence. A lone man knelt against the back wall on the far side of the bars. Aside from a toilet and small wash basin protruding out from the wall, the enclosed platform was barren. "What happened to his chair and mattress?" Cutter asked.

"He broke up the chair and tried to use one of the legs as a club. Couple days later we caught him trying to make a rope out of the mattress pad, so that was taken away."

Riddick, who'd been standing around looking useless, spoke. "After Johnson got hurt, I had the engineers extend those bars all the way up to the ceiling. By the way, we're especially proud of our new chain system."

Cutter studied the four lengths of chain emerging from

small holes in the metal wall, connecting to the bands wrapped around their prisoner's wrists and ankles. "They look like the old chains."

"They aren't," Kendricks informed. "They've been redesigned along the lines of a car's seat belt. As long as our man moves slowly, the chains will play out and give him some room to roam. But if he makes a quick move, tries to grab one of us, the system snaps back and jerks him back against the wall. Dr. Riddick helped with the design," Kendricks added charitably. "Clever, don't you think?"

Suddenly preoccupied with the lone man on the platform, Cutter didn't respond.

The man he was looking at was about six feet two, with broad shoulders. He was dressed in tan boots, jeans, and a faded shirt blotched with blood and perspiration stains. The man had a strong body, but he didn't have the slabs of muscle and fireplug-shaped physique Kendricks had. Braille's body was sleeker, with the smooth, elongated muscles of a swimmer. His prisoner was handsome in a rugged way. He had craggy features, a wind- and sunburned complexion, collar-length hair, and brooding dark brown eyes. In spite of all he'd been through since being brought here, the man still had enough self-discipline to look after himself. His hair was obviously clean and he'd shaved earlier in the day. Cutter liked the man for that, but there were changes Cutter did not like. There was more gray in Braille's hair, and deep lines around the outsides of his eyes. Captivity and the experiments had taken a toll on Braille, Cutter decided, but he didn't care. Flanked by Riddick and Kendricks, with Golem rolling along behind, Cutter walked up to the fence of heavy metal bars and stopped. "How are you feeling, Braille?" he asked pleasantly.

The man hunkering down on the platform stirred. He lifted his head, fixing cold eyes on the director of the OSMS. Then he looked away.

Cutter felt as if he had just been dismissed. "I asked you a question. Answer it."

The man in the cage continued to treat Cutter as if he did not exist.

"My staff tells me you have not been cooperating with them. But now that I'm back, I intend to deal with these

24

stubborn behaviors of yours. From this moment on, you'll answer all questions about your condition, willingly submit to any tests my staff wishes to perform on you, and you will not hurt anyone who works for me. Understood?"

Braille's silence was as loud as the hard edge creeping into Cutter's voice. "I don't have the patience that Kendricks and Riddick have, and I'm not nearly as pleasant. So if you don't begin cooperating here and now, I'll enlist your support through other means. Do you understand?"

Silence.

Unused to insolence and defiance, Cutter gritted his teeth. "I think I should point out to you that three of your friends are living quite comfortably seven stories above you. Your failure to cooperate could make their lives very uncomfortable."

Continued silence.

"Talk to me, Braille. I resent your silence."

Again silence.

"I'm not in the mood to appreciate your stubborn streak. I don't have the time to put up with it." The director of the OSMS turned to Kendricks. "Take three of your staff and go up to the seventh floor. When you return, bring me one of Dr. Radcliff's fingers, one of his wife's nipples, and one of Ms. Chapel's teeth—preferably a molar. Perhaps a visual display of our intentions will bring Mr. Braille around."

Riddick paled. Kendricks smiled and started to walk away.

"Sweet Jesus," Braille said in horror, slowly rising to his feet.

"The man can speak," Cutter proclaimed triumphantly. Kendricks motioned for several men to follow him, then continued towards the lab door.

"Call him off," Braille shouted, "and I'll do anything you want."

"Mr. Kendricks," Cutter called out, "stand by for a moment." Cutter looked up into the face of the man on the platform. "No more games?"

"No games," Braille promised.

"You'll cooperate, no matter what you're asked to do, and you won't harm my staff?"

"I won't touch them. Now call off your ape," Braille

pleaded. Kendricks reacted as if he'd just been slapped. He put his hands on his hips and glared at Braille.

Still staring up at Braille, Cutter raised his voice. "Kendricks, just bring me one of Radcliff's fingers. I want Braille to know I'm fully capable of following through with my promise to hurt or kill his friends."

If there had been a way, Braille would have torn Cutter's throat out, but he was weak and bound by chains, and there was a wall of heavy metal bars between him and the director. "Don't do this," he whispered. "I said I'd cooperate."

"Mr. Kendricks," Cutter bellowed. Kendricks stopped just inches from the laboratory door and gave Cutter a crestfallen look. "I'm impressed with the sincerity in our man's voice. I think we'll let Dr. Radcliff keep his finger for the time being. Now, I think I would like to see Golem feed our friend. I'm curious as to what you've done with your robot over the past few weeks."

The prospect of showing off Golem brightened Kendricks' mood considerably. He returned to the table and picked up the large syringe of human blood, handing it to Golem as he whispered some commands no one else in the room could hear. Golem's metal torso immediately rotated a hundred and eighty degrees and stopped as its camera eyes focused in on Braille. At the same moment several wall-mounted television monitors blinked on. The image on the TV screens was a close-up of Braille's face.

"Golem's camera eyes are tied into the television monitors," Kendricks explained. "You're seeing what he's seeing."

At the same moment, Golem began rolling across the room, the stainless-steel torso appearing to float as the rubber treads propelled the robot forward. Golem stopped exactly two feet in front of the gate of vertical iron bars. The image on the monitor screen split in two as one camera remained on Braille's face and the other camera panned down to focus in on the gate's electronic lock. Kendricks pulled out a small transmitter and aimed it at the gate. He pressed a button and the gate swung open. Golem rolled through the opening and mounted the platform as if it weren't there. The machine stopped eighteen inches from Braille.

"One-twelfth power," Kendricks said into a radio transmitter on his wrist. Immediately, Golem made a whirring sound like a car's transmission gearing down. Kendricks turned to Cutter. "Golem is twelve to fourteen times stronger than your average human. Essentially I just asked him to cut his power so he wouldn't hurt Braille. Without this reduction, he could crush a human while carrying out a task and never realize it."

Braille glared at Golem, and the overhead monitors captured his expression. "Easy," Cutter said. "Resisting Golem is the same thing as resisting me. I suggest you relax and cooperate. If you don't, your friends will pay the price."

Braille relaxed visibly, then turned his face away from Golem's all-seeing camera eyes. With his head turned away, no one in the room saw Braille's eyes begin to glow red with hate. Suddenly Golem slammed a huge metal hand against Braille's chest, pinning him against the wall. While one camera eye stared hard at Braille, the other eye of the robot focused in on the syringe it was holding like a competent nurse. It seemed to study the syringe for a moment, then before Braille could brace himself, it plunged the eight-inch-long sixteen-gauge needle into Braille's abdomen.

"Impressive," Cutter murmured after Golem rolled off the platform and out of the cage. "Very impressive. Now I'd like to spend a few minutes with our other guests from the island." He turned and walked briskly out of the laboratory with Riddick and Kendricks trailing behind.

Braille glared with hellishly red eyes at the men leaving the laboratory, vowing to kill all three. They had lied to him, broken their promises, and experimented on him. They had injected him with diseases, cut him open, and shot him in the thigh so they could time and videotape the healing process. They had chained him up, put him behind bars, and given him forced injections of blood to keep him in good condition for the next experiment.

And now they had come horrifyingly close to mutilating the three people who had escaped from the island with him. It was beyond Braille's comprehension. Dr. Lewis Radcliff was a gentle middle-aged orthopedic surgeon who'd never harmed anyone in his life, and his young wife, Jade, was just as harmless.

Then there was Leslie Chapel. They had become lovers on the island. And after their escape she had remained at his side while he fought the changes overtaking his mind and body, changes brought on because he'd been contaminated by Gregory, the Master Ancient. It had been a hideous time for him. He'd been delirious, feverish. His body had felt like it was on fire. Only the night brought peace . . . the need to hunt . . . and kill . . . and take blood. It was as if he had been giving birth to something inside him . . . something that had the power to take him over . . . something that was an animal. But he had fought the changing and tried not to give in to its animal urges and appetites, because during that time Leslie had stayed with him, holding his hand, and all the while it would have been so easy to tear out her throat and drink her blood.

But he hadn't. He had fought the monster he was, and he might have beaten it. But then Cutter and his organization had come in and taken over. They had lied to him and the others, then sedated them, bringing them here as prisoners.

Then they had fed the monster that was inside him with human blood. Now he was everything he fought against. He was a vampire. An Ancient. Cutter and his people had helped create the beast that he was.

Braille could feel his body grow warm as hate raged through him. He clenched his fists and would have screamed out, but in that instant he caught a glimpse of himself on an overhead television monitor. His eyes were glowing like liquid steel. His teeth were longer. Hate had contorted his face into something unrecognizable. Except Braille recognized the face. It was the face of an animal . . . the face of a blood beast. It was *his* face.

He tore his eyes away from the screen and looked through the bars at the source of the television picture. Golem was staring at him as if it didn't quite understand what Braille was all about but was working on it.

"Don't you ever blink?" Braille whispered. Then he looked away and pushed Golem out of his mind. He missed Leslie and the thought that Cutter and his staff might hurt her curdled his guts. He had been alone for most of his life, and had thought that no one would ever become important to him, but somehow, this woman had. He missed her, missed her terribly, and not for the first time since arriving at the OSMS, he knew he was in love with her. Deeply in love with her.

2

THE SEVENTH FLOOR OF THE OSMS RESEARCH FACILITY HAD been turned into a series of spacious well-designed apartments furnished with expensive furniture, widescreen television sets, and well-stocked wet bars. Only a few inconveniences detracted from the luxurious condo-like atmosphere. None of the apartments had windows, telephones, or doorknobs. And there was an armed guard sitting next to the elevator at the far end of the hallway twenty-four hours a day.

Cutter, Riddick, and Kendricks stepped out of the elevator and moved past the guard. As they started down the corridor, Cutter said to Riddick, "There's no sense in meeting these people individually. Go get the Radcliffs and bring them to Chapel's apartment." Riddick hurried away as Cutter and Kendricks stopped in front of the first door they came to. While Cutter knocked politely, Kendricks pulled out a small transmitter, aimed it at the door, and pushed a button. The door's electric lock slid out of position and the door opened automatically.

A beautiful blond-haired, brown-eyed woman was standing just inside the doorway. She glared at Kendricks. "I don't know why you bother to knock. You know I can't open the door unless you push your magic button." Then she noticed Cutter, and her expression hardened. "Well, as I live and breathe, it's the director of this goddamn place."

Leslie Chapel's outburst irritated Cutter, and he elbowed

his way past her, heading for the wet bar at the other end of the living room.

"Why don't you come in and make yourself at home?" Chapel grumbled.

"I just did, Ms. Chapel." Cutter walked behind the bar. He took a glass from a mirrored mantel and poured himself a Scotch. "How are you, Leslie?"

Chapel's brown eyes narrowed. "Is that a sincere question or just more of your PR bullshit?"

"Sincere question. I am interested in how you are." And he was. Leslie Chapel was one of the most beautiful women he'd ever seen.

"Then I'll tell you. These fancy apartments are nothing but jail cells. There's no windows. No phones and the doors won't open unless you have one of those fancy electronic thingamajigs. Our meals are delivered. Nobody answers our questions, there's an armed guard out in the hallway. And what the hell have you done with Braille? Where is he? Why can't I see him?"

Cutter raised his hand, hoping to calm her down. It didn't work.

"I don't know who you are or what your agency is all about, but you were supposed to help us, and make Braille better. But instead you took him away and locked us up. If you think you can get away with it, you've got another thing coming. I've got friends and influence. So does Dr. Radcliff. Eventually we'll get outta here, and when we do, we'll go straight to the media and blow this fucking organization of yours right out of the water. You understand me, Dr. Cutter? Right out of the fucking water!"

"My sentiments exactly," Lewis Radcliff said as he, his wife, and Riddick entered Chapel's apartment. "I don't know what kind of power you think you have, but heading up a government agency doesn't give you the right to treat people the way you've treated us. One of these days you're going to have to let us go, and when that happens, I intend to bring this agency to the attention of the media and some influential politicians who just happen to be my patients."

Jade Radcliff, Dr. Radcliff's young wife, took her husband's arm and nodded in fierce agreement.

"I came up here hoping to have a pleasant conversation,"

Cutter sighed. "Obviously, that's not possible at this point. Perhaps later." He started towards the door.

"Wait!" Radcliff called. "I think it's high time you tell us when we're getting out of here." Cutter merely kept on walking. "Dammit, when are you going to let us go?"

Kendricks and Riddick walked out into the hallway. Cutter paused in the doorway, looking back at the trio. "Perhaps you'll be more agreeable to a calm and rational conversation in a few days. Until then—" He pulled the door closed.

Radcliff started to say something, but Leslie Chapel hushed him with a finger. She snatched a glass off the bar, dashing across the living room to the door. She put the rim of the glass flat against the door, then glanced at the Radcliffs. "It works in the movies," she whispered. She pushed her ear tightly against the glass and listened intently to the muted conversation she could hear on the other side of the door.

"They're absolutely right," Cutter was saying. "They can blow us out of the water. I think we'd better start making plans to dispose of them."

Leslie gasped and almost dropped the glass. She repositioned it against the door in time to hear Cutter say, "Personally, I like the idea of an airplane accident. A fiery midair explosion over the desert wouldn't leave much in the way of evidence and all we'd see in the newspapers would be 'Jet Goes Down with Chinook Island Survivors Aboard.' Of course, we'll need a look-alike for Braille, and the accident'll cost us one of our licensed pilots, but it's better than being blown out of the water. I'll see to the pilot. John, start looking for a male who could pass for Braille if he were burned beyond recognition."

"We won't be able to continue experimenting on Braille if he knows his friends are dead," Riddick pointed out. "He won't cooperate with us."

"He won't know," Cutter said. "We'll bluff."

"It could take as long as a year to figure out Braille's physical chemistry."

"Then we'll bluff for a year, longer if necessary. You saw the way he reacted tonight. All I had to do was threaten to hurt his friends and he turned into a puppy dog. Hell, we don't have to prove his friends are alive. All we have to do is keep his hopes up and he'll let us do anything we want to him.

"Now, about that plane crash. There'll have to be lots of fuel on board and some sort of remote control device. Alan, how difficult . . ." Their voices faded away as the men began walking down the corridor.

Stunned, Leslie turned away from the door and looked at the Radcliffs. "Dear God," she whispered, her face ashen.

"What'd you hear?" Jade asked.

"They're planning on killing us and they're doing horrible medical things to Braille."

Lewis Radcliff clenched his fists. "I should've known, should've realized. All this prisoner crap. All the secrecy. Christ, I thought agencies like this only existed in spy movies." He looked down at his fists, then raised his eyes to Leslie's. "They're going to kill us?"

She nodded, and wiped her face with the back of her hand. "Some sort of airplane crash. Cutter talked about us as if we were . . . were dogs he wanted put to sleep."

"What're we going to do?" Jade asked in a worried tone.

"We get Braille. Then we get out of this place," Leslie said.

"Just like that?" Jade looked at Leslie, then at her husband. "This place has more armed guards than an Army post."

Leslie took Jade's hand. "We don't have a choice. They're planning to kill us. We've got to try."

Jade shook her head violently. "It won't work. We're locked in. There's armed guards all over the place."

Lewis rubbed his chin thoughtfully. "We do have a couple of things going for us. We've been here almost two months and haven't tried anything. My guess is they've gotten used to taking us for granted. And they won't expect trouble from two women and a middle-aged doctor. If we did come up with a plan and acted on it, we'd shock their socks off and we might just have a chance of succeeding."

"But we don't have a plan," Jade wailed.

Leslie smiled. "Yes we do." The Radcliffs looked at Leslie quizzically as she continued to smile. "Cutter likes me. To put it bluntly, he has a hard-on for me. I think I can use that hard-on to our advantage." She explained her plan to the Radcliffs. "Let me also show you what I've been saving up for a rainy day." She led them over to the living room couch, tossing aside a pillow. She reached into a crack and pulled out three sharp steak knifes with serrated edges.

"You were right, Lewis, when you said they were getting overconfident about us. For the first month the man who brought us our meals counted the utensils when he came back to pick up the dishes. Then he stopped. When I realized he wasn't checking anymore, I started collecting steak knives." She handed two of the knives to the Radcliffs.

Lewis Radcliff slipped his knife inside his shirt. "When?"

"Now," Leslie answered without hesitation.

She pushed a button on the intercom system next to her apartment door. When the guard in the hallway responded, she said, "The Radcliffs are ready to go back to their apartment. Push the button, Max." The guard, whose name was not Max, sighed audibly and pushed a button which activated the electric lock on Chapel's door.

"Good luck," Lewis whispered as he and his wife walked out into the hallway. The door closed automatically behind them.

Leslie waited a couple of minutes then pushed the intercom button. "I need to talk to Dr. Cutter. Tell him it's an emergency." The guard grumbled something about it being late and not wanting to bother the Director.

"Listen, buster, when your boss finds out I tried to get ahold of him and you didn't bother to pass on the message, he'll hang you up by the balls." She released the button and glanced at her wristwatch. It was a little after nine in the evening. She folded her arms and waited.

Five minutes later Cutter's voice came through the intercom speaker. "What is it?"

She stepped up close to the speaker. "I want to apologize for the way I treated you earlier. I was in a bad mood and I took it out on you. I'm sorry."

"The guard said it was an emergency."

Chapel took a deep breath and hoped Cutter wouldn't hear the tension in her voice. "My emergency is I hate to drink alone. After you left I went to work on the Scotch you opened up, but drinking alone isn't the same as drinking

33

with company. I thought maybe you'd like to come back up and help me kill off this bottle. You might even want to bring along another one since there's not much left in this one."

"I spent most of the day on the road, Leslie. I'm tired. Maybe we could have that drink tomorrow."

"I'm not used to being turned down. I won't extend the invitation again."

"Like I said, Leslie, I spent the whole day driving—"

"Fine. Good night, Dr. Cutter." Leslie released the button with an audible click, then glanced at her watch and gave him ten seconds to get back to her. Five seconds later Cutter's voice came through the speaker. "I'll be up in a few minutes."

While Leslie waited, she checked her makeup, brushed her hair, then looked over the selection of clothes the agency had provided for her weeks earlier. There wasn't a sexy outfit in the bunch. She finally decided on heels, skintight jeans, and a loosely fitting white silk blouse. After dressing, she studied herself in the mirror. On impulse she took off the blouse, removed her bra and put the blouse back on, stepping back in front of the mirror. It was obvious she wasn't wearing a bra. The blouse clung to her full breasts and her dark arcolas were visible through the thin material. She knew she was beautiful, and if her face didn't distract Hargrave Cutter, then the sight of her breasts swaying under the blouse would.

She returned to the living room, picked up the steak knife, and slipped it into the wasteband of her jeans. She was fluffing out the back of her blouse to hide the handle when she heard a knock on her door. An instant later the door opened and the Director of the OSMS entered her apartment.

It was easy to see what Hargrave Cutter had in mind. He was wearing loafers, slacks, a white shirt, and an ascot. He had a bottle of Scotch in each hand, and as he walked over to the bar, the heavy odor of his after-shave assaulted Leslie's nostrils.

After putting the bottles down, Cutter leaned back against the bar. "I'm glad I accepted your invitation," he said, his eyes drifting from her face to her breasts. With effort, he lifted his eyes back to her face. "God, you're a beautiful woman."

"I'm glad you came." She gestured at the bottles of Scotch behind him. "Why don't you pour us a drink? There's some ice in the bowl on the other side of the bar."

He smiled, turned, and leaned over the top of the bar, reaching for the bowl of ice with both hands.

Leslie pulled out the knife, moving in behind Hargrave Cutter. Just as he was straightening up she stabbed him in the back. Cutter squealed, dropped the bowl, and whirled around to face her.

Holding the knife in both hands, Leslie jabbed the tip against his cheekbone. "Scream or move, and I'll stab you in the eye." Cutter's eyes darted from the blade to the apartment door. "And if you try and run," she hissed, "I'll stab you in the back of the head."

"You stabbed me!" Cutter squealed. "Why?"

"To let you know I'm not bluffing. I'll do it again if you don't do everything I say."

"Wha-what do you want?"

"You're going to help me and the Radcliffs get Braille out of this place. I know what you're doing to him."

"Leslie, I don't know—"

"Shut up, you son-of-a-bitch. I know what's going on, and I don't have time to argue. Now you're going to help us set Braille free."

In spite of his pain, Cutter seemed to smile. "There's guards all over the place, security checks everywhere. You'll never make it."

"Then neither will you," Leslie said. "I overheard that conversation you had in the hall. I know what you're planning for the Radcliffs and me. We don't have anything to lose. But you do. So here's the deal. Help the four of us get out of here and you'll live. Fuck it up, and you'll be the first one to die. Understand?"

Cutter understood. And he cooperated. He freed the Radcliffs from their apartment and said nothing while all of them walked down the hallway towards the elevator and the armed guard.

The guard got to his feet, nodding to Cutter. Cutter

glanced at the guard's name tag. "Johnson, I want you to give Dr. Radcliff your weapon." Johnson started to open his mouth. "Don't argue with me," Cutter snarled. "These people'll kill us if you don't do what I say. Now give him your pistol." The guard gave Lewis Radcliff his .357 Magnum Smith & Wesson combat revolver.

"Push the button, Max," Leslie said, glaring at the guard.

Johnson pushed the elevator button. He was turning back to look at Cutter when Lewis hit him in the head with the barrel of the heavy pistol. The guard went down like a sack of wet cement.

"Jesus Christ, you split his head open," Cutter wailed.

Lewis glanced at Leslie and shrugged. "Hell, I don't know how to knock a man out." He shrugged again.

"You did fine, Lewis," Leslie said as the elevator doors opened.

The doors shut. Cutter pushed a button and the elevator dropped to the basement and stopped.

"Why don't the doors open?" Jade asked.

"Good question," Leslie noted, nudging Cutter with the knife. "What's going on?"

"I don't know. A malfunction maybe?"

Lewis Radcliff shook his head. "Malfunction, hell." He pointed at the glass screen built into the wall of the elevator. "That's a palm scan machine. The door won't open unless Cutter puts his hand on the screen."

"Two choices, Dr. Cutter," Leslie hissed. "You put your hand on the screen, or I cut it off and I put your hand on the screen."

Cutter put his palm on the screen.

Nothing happened.

"What's wrong?" Leslie demanded.

Cutter sighed. "We're on a restricted floor. The computer knows there's more than just me in the elevator."

"It's hopeless," Jade sobbed.

Leslie shook her head. "No, it's not. Cutter, you tell that damn machine of yours that we're your guests." Cutter started to argue. "No arguments. Do it or die. Just lie to it the way you've lied to us. It'll believe you. You're a master at lying."

"This is Hargrave Cutter, the Director. Do a voice

check." A moment later a mechanical voice said: "Identity confirmed."

"I'm requesting a security override for VIP guests. Respond to access entrance code H . . . C . . . two five two four nine."

A moment later the elevator doors opened.

They entered a small foyer. The two guards standing by the metal door to the lab looked at Cutter expectantly. Cutter gestured at the others. "Visitors from Washington."

At that moment Lewis Radcliff pulled out the security guard's pistol. He pointed it at the guards. "Give us your weapons." One guard froze. The other began reaching for his pistol.

"Don't do it," Cutter screamed. "They'll kill me."

"He's right," Lewis Radcliff said, stepping up to the man. "Now give me your gun." The guard did. Jade took the pistol from the other guard.

With Cutter and the two guards walking ahead of them, Leslie and the Radcliffs burst into the large underground laboratory.

It was late. There were only three other technicians in the room. And Alan Kendricks. All spun around in surprise at the abrupt entrance of five people.

"What do you want?" Kendricks shouted.

"We want Braille," Leslie demanded, pushing Cutter ahead of her. Then she froze. At the far end of the room she saw Braille. He was standing on a platform, chained to a metal wall. She was horrified by what she saw. He was battered and bloody, and it looked like the only thing that kept him up were the chains. "Sweet Mother of God, what have you done to him?"

"It's not as bad as it looks," Cutter said.

"Braille!" she screamed. Leslie whirled on Cutter. "Unlock that cell and those chains, damn you. Do it or you'll die right now."

"Kendricks," Cutter shouted. "Unlock everything."

Braille had heard the familiar voice. He lifted his head and looked down between the bars. She stood out like a marble statue in a dark room. Golden hair, wide, brown, madonna-like eyes. God she was beautiful. "Leslie?" he said, his voice weak and far away.

"We're coming. We'll get you out of here."

Braille could feel energy and adrenaline starting to surge through his body. The woman he loved was here. He recognized Lewis and Jade Radcliff and blessed them for what they were trying to do. But he knew it was hopeless.

"Don't get killed because of me. In two minutes this place'll be swarming with guards. Get out of here—now!"

Lewis waved at him with one of his pistols. "No way. We're in this together." He gave one of his pistols to Leslie, pointing the other one at Kendricks. "Unlock the door like your good Director says."

Kendricks' eyes darted from Cutter to Braille. "But if he gets loose, he'll kill us!"

"Unlock the gate," Cutter snarled.

Kendricks pulled out a radio transmitter, but instead of aiming it at the gate he brought it to his lips. "Golem. Intruders . . . destroy."

"What's that!!" Jade Radcliff screamed, pointing her pistol at a huge mass coming out of a dark corner.

"Jesus Christ," Lewis Radcliff shouted. "Move, Jade, it's coming for you!"

And it was. Golem had scanned the lab with its camera eyes, and within a microsecond had compared the faces of everyone in the room to the faces of the OSMS employees in its memory banks. And it now knew that Leslie Chapel and the Radcliffs were the intruders. Holding its macabre arms out in front of it like a zombie from a horror movie, it rolled across the room, heading for Jade Radcliff.

"Move! Get out of the way!" Lewis Radcliff screamed at his wife. Golem was almost on her. Then it *was* on her, and with one swing of its metallic arm it sent her crashing across the room.

"You son-of-a-bitch," Radcliff snarled. He aimed his pistol at Golem's glass skull and the twin cameras visible inside the bowl, firing three times. The slugs glanced off the bulletproof plastic and ricocheted around the room.

Unharmed, Golem calmly turned its attention on Lewis Radcliff. At the same time, Kendricks spoke into his transmitter. "Escalate. Golem, full power."

As the giant machine turned and started towards the doctor, Chapel hefted up the automatic pistol Radcliff had given her and hit Cutter on the head. The Director of the OSMS went down on his hands and knees.

Up on the platform, Braille was going wild. His adrenaline was working at a feverish pitch and the muscles and tendons in his arms and neck had turned to cables as he struggled with the chains holding him to the wall. Jade Radcliff was down. The machine was heading for Lewis, and Leslie was next unless he could stop the robot. Suddenly the chain binding his right arm to the wall shattered. His eyes were glowing like flares as he whirled and grabbed the chain on his left arm. An instant later a second chain snapped. He reached for one of the chains binding his legs.

Radcliff fired another shot at Golem, then bolted to get out of the machine's path. A titanium skeleton arm struck him a glancing blow on the shoulder and sent him skidding across the floor, crashing into a wall thirty feet away.

Leaning over, Braille grasped the last chain with both hands and snapped it.

He was free. A bloodcurdling snarl broke from Braille's throat as he charged the iron fence twelve feet away. Running full out, he leapt from the platform and threw his body against the bars. The iron bars bent, and the footings in the floor and ceiling shuddered, but the fence held.

"Braille!" Leslie screamed.

"Jesus!" Lewis Radcliff shouted as he watched Golem come for him again. The robot was working on full force now and the machine swung at Lewis while he scrambled to get out of the way. A metal fist crashed into a cement wall just behind him. The wall exploded, and when Golem pulled its fist back, there was a hole in the cement the size of a coffee can.

"Jesus!" Lewis murmured again, looking back over his shoulder.

With a final terrifying scream, Braille savagely attacked the fence again with a running dive. He hit it hard, slamming into it with his shoulder and forearms like a football tackle. The fence bent outwards, then, with an explosive shriek, it collapsed.

Kendricks whirled towards the commotion, realizing Braille was free. "Golem, destroy Braille." Immediately the machine turned away from Radcliff. Motors whined and whirred as Golem's torso spun around and the cameras zoomed in on Braille.

Braille got to his feet and took several steps towards Golem. He knew how powerful this monster was, what kind of strength those arms possessed and he wondered if he could deal with it. He was weak. His struggle with the chains and fences had drained him of what strength he had. He glanced over at Leslie, then back at the monster and knew he had no choice.

"Come to me," he murmured.

Golem rolled straight for him. Then the machine was on him, towering over him like a colossal tin man. A shiny skeleton fist came out of nowhere. The blow caught Braille in the middle of his chest and sent him flying twenty feet across the room. Leslie screamed. Braille hit, rolled, and came up on his feet as he saw Golem coming for him again.

How do you fight something that's half steam shovel, half tank? he wondered, backing away from Golem. Then he noticed a large metal table lying on its side. You cheat, he decided.

Steel arms closed in on the space of air where Braille had been a heartbeat earlier. After ducking Golem, Braille ran to the table and savagely ripped off one of its legs. Now he had a weapon. Yet it wasn't much—just a three-foot-long section of a metal table leg. He hoped it would work. Golem was almost on him again when Braille sidestepped the monster, dropping to one knee and wedging the section of pipe under the monster's tread. A giant metal hand grabbed Braille by the back of the neck and started to haul him to his feet. At the same time, Braille grabbed the pipe he'd pushed under Golem's tread with both hands, and with all his strength he began to lift it upwards.

Before Kendricks or Golem realized what was happening, one of the robot's treads was off the floor and the huge monster was beginning to tip precariously, like a giant tree in a windstorm.

Then, with a final burst of strength, Braille angled the pipe higher, and Golem crashed over on its side, its free hand flailing out for him like the skeleton arm of a mindless cadaver.

Kendricks scrambled over to the gun Jade Radcliff had

dropped. He whirled around and fired at Braille twenty feet away. The bullet slammed into Braille's arm and he staggered backwards under the impact. Leslie screamed and threw her knife at Kendricks, missing. At the same moment, Lewis Radcliff fired his last round at Kendricks and missed.

Kendricks made a decision. He turned, cocked the pistol, and aimed it at Lewis Radcliff, starting to squeeze the trigger. Jade Radcliff threw herself on Kendricks, draping herself over his shoulder like a shawl. She flailed out with one hand and caught Kendricks in the face with her fingernails. He shrugged her off, and as she landed on the floor, he shot her at point-blank range.

Lewis Radcliff didn't move or make a sound. He just stood there and stared at his wife's still form.

Braille bellowed savagely and charged Kendricks. As he rushed past the prostrate body of Golem, the metal machine clamped a bony steel fist around Braille's ankle. Braille went down hard and kicked out at the monster's hand with his free leg. The robot held him firm and began to pull him closer. Golem was lying on its side, its own massive weight pinning its other arm against the floor, but as it dragged Braille closer, the trapped arm began to emerge from beneath the metal body and reach for Braille. Braille kicked at the hand and clawed at the floor, trying frantically to break free of Golem's inhuman grip.

Lewis Radcliff finally tore his eyes away from his wife's unmoving body and fixed his terrible gaze on Kendricks. Without a word he began walking slowly towards the man who had just shot his wife. Kendricks glanced at Braille, saw he was trapped, and turned his attention to Radcliff. He waited until the middle-aged doctor was almost on him, then shot him. Lewis Radcliff staggered backwards. Kendricks smiled, then shot the man again. Lewis Radcliff collapsed a few feet from his wife.

The cold-blooded act flooded Braille's body with hate and fury. He tore his leg free of Golem's fingers, leaving behind bloody chunks of flesh and muscle from his calf.

Moving almost like a robot herself, Leslie Chapel slowly crossed the room and stopped five feet from Kendricks. Kendricks turned in time to see her aiming the automatic pistol at his forehead.

Leslie pulled the trigger—nothing happened.

The look of shock on Kendricks' face twisted into a smile. "Should'a jacked a round into the chamber," he whispered. "Now it's my turn."

He started to take aim at Leslie, then realized Braille had escaped from Golem and was slowly limping across the room towards him. Fear dissolved Kendricks' smile. He backhanded Chapel with the pistol and ran over to Cutter, who was getting to his feet. Both men stumbled across the room to a small metal door twenty feet to the right of the main entrance to the lab. While Kendricks fumbled for his key to the door, Braille hobbled over to Leslie.

"Kill 'em," she whispered.

Braille tried. Gritting his teeth, he started for Kendricks and Cutter. As Braille closed on them, Kendricks finally unlocked the door, pulled it open, then followed Cutter into the opening. Moving as fast as he could on his bad leg, Braille threw himself at the men in a desperate dive. Cutter screamed. Kendricks jerked the heavy lead-lined door closed, and Braille crashed into it.

After a long moment Braille got to his feet and surveyed his surroundings. The lab looked as if it had been through an earthquake. The heavy iron bar fence was down. Tables were overturned. Exotic medical equipment lay strewn across the floor. Some of the animals had escaped from their cages. Golem lay on its side, its treads turning, its free arm clawing the air, its eyes still focused on Braille.

Out in the middle of the floor, Leslie Chapel was kneeling beside the quiet forms of Jade and Lewis Radcliff. Braille closed his eyes. They were hurt—badly hurt—because of him.

Braille limped over to Leslie and knelt down beside her. She was holding Jade Radcliff's head in her lap. The woman was alive and looking up at the ceiling with wide bewildered eyes. Close beside her, Lewis Radcliff lay on his back, one hand covering one of the two large wounds he had in his chest, the other holding his wife's hand. Lewis focused his eyes on Braille. "My wife okay?"

Braille looked at Jade Radcliff. The bullet from Kendricks' powerful pistol had caught her in the center of her throat. She wasn't okay, she was dying. Braille shook his head sadly. Leslie began to cry.

"Can she hear me?" Lewis asked in a whisper.

Jade's eyes were open. She looked at peace and nodded weakly.

Braille put his hand on Lewis Radcliff's arm. "She can hear you."

Lewis started to say something, then coughed and made a quiet gurgling sound. Braille leaned close, close enough to hear Lewis Radcliff whisper, "Tell her I love her. Tell her she's my life."

Braille turned back to Jade. She smiled and nodded as if she'd heard what her husband had said. Then she died.

Braille looked down into the eyes of Lewis Radcliff. "I know," Radcliff said, closing his eyes. "I know she heard what I said. That's good." Then Lewis Radcliff sighed and joined his wife.

Braille looked at his friends with haunted eyes. They'd tried to help him, and now they were dead. A hideous secret government agency no one had ever heard of had shot them down in cold blood. It was senseless, beyond his comprehension. He vowed to the couple—the gentle middle-aged doctor and his wife—that one day he would return to this place and deal with Cutter and Riddick and Kendricks. And when he would be done, when he would finally walk away, their agency would be in ruins and the men responsible for this madness on their way to hell.

He reached out and touched Leslie. She was still cradling Jade Radcliff's head in her lap, still crying. She shook her head as if she needed a moment longer to say good-bye.

Braille got to his feet. The leg Golem had eviscerated had healed. The miracle didn't surprise Braille, not after everything the OSMS had put him through. He picked up Radcliff's pistol and the weapon Kendricks had dropped when he'd run out of the room. He checked both, saw they were empty, and walked over to a guard cowering under a table.

"Please . . . please don't kill me," the guard whimpered.

Braille was carrying two Smith and Wesson combat magnums with eight-inch barrels. He held one up for the guard to see. "You got extra ammunition for this?" The man ripped off his pistol belt and handed it up to Braille. As he began inserting fresh cartridges into the cylinders of the weapons, Braille gestured towards the door Kendricks and Cutter had gone through. "What's behind that door?"

"It's a storage area for radioactive material," the guard said, his eyes locked on the weapons in Braille's hand.

"Is there a way out?"

"Yeah. There's a stairway leading up to the first floor."

Braille walked back to Leslie and knelt down beside her. "We've got to leave now. Cutter and Kendricks got out. They'll be waiting for us. This whole agency'll be waiting for us. The less time we give them to get organized, the better our chances of getting out of here."

Leslie sniffed and nodded, allowing Braille to pull her to her feet. She walked beside him as he moved out of the lab, past the guard station, and into the open elevator.

The elevator was still responding to Cutter's earlier directive. Sounding like a stuck record, a mechanical voice coming from an unseen speaker continually repeated without emotion: "H.C. directive. Open access. H.C. directive. Open—" Braille pushed a button, the doors closed, and the elevator began to rise.

"What now?" Leslie asked.

"Now we blast our way out of this place and head for the desert."

The elevator arrived at the first floor. Braille pushed the button that kept the doors from opening. "You know we don't have much of a chance." Leslie nodded. Braille leaned over and kissed her gently on the lips, then took his finger off the button. The elevator doors opened. Braille cocked both pistols, stepped out into a long empty hallway, and, with Leslie behind, began moving towards the lobby at the far end.

They came to a set of closed doors at the end of the lobby. "Stay here," he whispered, pushing her against a wall next to the doors. "Don't come out no matter what you hear. When it's right, I'll come for you."

Braille edged out of the hospital doors. The floodlights mounted on the roof of the hangar had been turned off. It was close to pitch black in the hangar, yet Braille could see perfectly with eyes that were no longer human. He spotted two men high up in the girders that supported the hangar's roof. Off in the distance, two hundred yards away, a half a dozen guards crouched down beside some military-type vehicles and four large helicopters. At that moment he would've given a testicle for a high-powered sniper rifle. Still, he'd always been good with weapons of any type. The magnums he was carrying had eight-inch barrels, and he knew that in his hands the revolvers were almost as good as rifles.

Suddenly he heard a faint whistling sound and noticed a red dot, no bigger than the head of a pencil, sliding across the front of his shirt. Laserscope, he thought. One of the men in the girders had a laserscope mounted on his rifle. Braille bolted to his left, spotted the man with the laser rifle ten stories above him, sighted and fired. The sniper slipped from the girder and screamed as he fell over three hundred feet to the cement floor below.

A second sniper activated his laserscope and Braille fired again. As before, the man screamed all the way to the floor.

Gunfire erupted from the men hiding behind the jeeps and helicopters.

Braille snapped off several shots. The guards ducked down. He stepped back into the building and grabbed Leslie. "We go."

They darted down the steps, out onto the hangar floor, and began running hard towards the hangar's huge partly open doors.

The men over by the helicopters began opening up with automatic weapons. Braille pulled Leslie up close to his left side to shield her from the bullets. The hangar doors were still forty yards away. It would be the longest run of their lives.

A bullet grazed Braille's back. A second creased his neck. He ran on. A high-powered slug caught him in the shoulder, ripping away a chunk of muscle. He gasped, faltered, and continued on. More bullets. More automatic fire. Someone cut loose with an M-60 machine gun. The gunfire, magnified by the corrugated walls, made it seem as if World War II had just broken out in the hangar.

They arrived at the hangar doors and Braille offered up

thanks to the idiot who'd planned this ambush. Had the lights been on, he and Leslie would have been cut to pieces by the bullets the moment they headed out of the building.

"Turn on the goddamn lights," someone shouted.

"Shit," Braille grumbled. "Knew it was too good to last." As they worked their way alongside the hangar door, someone again opened up with the M-60 machine gun, stitching a long line of bullet holes in the corrugated metal beside them. Instantly bright, dusty moonlight flooded in through the holes. Braille swore again. Why did there have to be a full moon tonight?

They came to the end of the massive sliding door, and Braille stared at the four-foot wide opening between the two doors, deciding he didn't like it. Either Cutter and his crew didn't have time to close the huge doors or Cutter was going to spring another trap on them once they stepped out in the moonlight. The M-60 put more holes in the side of the building and Braille decided it didn't matter. They were dead if they stayed inside. And maybe dead if they went out the door.

Go with the maybe, he thought.

He crouched down and pulled Leslie down with him. "We're going out on our bellies," he said. She nodded and got down on the floor. "Stay close," he whispered as he squirmed around the edge of the door and low-crawled out into the moonlight.

There were three jeeps parked fifteen yards away in a half circle in front of the open doors. Behind each was a man holding a machine gun. For one brief moment Braille wondered why they hadn't opened fire; then he realized the men had expected their targets to come running out of the building, not crawling out on the pavement.

Braille discarded the empty pistol, pulling the other one from his belt. He didn't have much in the way of targets. He'd have to make do. From his position on the ground he fired three times, aiming at the guards' boots, visible under the jeeps. All three went down with shattered ankles. As they began screaming and writhing on the asphalt, Braille fired three more times, silencing the screams.

He got to his feet and pulled Leslie up. Suddenly all the floodlights in the huge hangar flared on, casting a thick shaft of bright light out the open doors and onto the runway. Braille dragged Leslie around behind the jeeps. "Stay here," he shouted.

He picked up a dead guard's machine gun and slung it over his shoulder. Then he leaned into the cab of one of the jeeps and levered the gearshift into neutral. He gripped the steering wheel with both hands and began pushing the jeep towards the hangar. As he nosed the jeep into the light flooding out of the open doors, the men inside the hangar cut loose with a fierce barrage of gunfire. Bullets thunked into the hood of the jeep and shattered the windshield, ripping through the front seats and kicking tufts of upholstery stuffing into the air.

When the heavy vehicle finally entered the opening, Braille jerked on the hand brake and backed away, unslinging the machine gun. As he continued to back away, he opened up the weapon, focusing his fire on the back of the jeep and the gas tank. The stream of bullets ripped the gas tank apart, then sparks from slugs glancing off metal ignited the volatile liquid. The jeep exploded with a loud whump. Suddenly Braille's view into the interior of the hangar was obscured by a shimmering wall of flames.

He ran back to Leslie, who was crouching behind the second jeep. "Get in," he ordered. While she clambered into the passenger seat, he got in behind the wheel. It didn't surprise him to see the ignition key missing. Hoping to hotwire the jeep, he reached under the dash, but his access to the ignition wires was blocked by a thick steel plate bolted to the underside of the dash. He looked at Leslie. "Looks like we walk."

She pointed at a dozen men carrying rifles and flashlights coming around the far end of the hangar two hundred yards away.

"Looks like we run!" she exclaimed.

Holding hands, they took off running across the runway, not knowing or caring where they were going, just running as hard and as fast as they could.

Braille heard two jeeps start up behind them. Gripping Leslie's hand tightly, Braille forced himself to run even faster. As he did, he marveled at Leslie's quiet courage. He was crushing her hand and dragging her across the runway, and she wasn't making a sound. Moments later two sets of headlights engulfed them. Braille glanced back. Two jeeps were racing to overtake them.

He skidded to a stop and told Leslie to keep running. He turned on the vehicles, bellowing, "Leave us alone!" He began raking the lead jeep with machine gun fire. The bullets shattered the windshield and killed the driver and passengers.

At close to seventy miles an hour, the jeep drifted to the left and headed out across the endless runway.

The other vehicle was almost on top of Braille. He trained the machine gun on it and pulled the trigger. Nothing. Empty. The driver of the jeep sensed Braille's plight and aimed the speeding vehicle at Braille, intending to run him down. As the other guards rose up in their seats and began firing over the top of the windshield, Braille hefted the machine gun up over his shoulder as if it were a javelin and drew back his right arm. In that instant the driver realized what Braille was up to. He frantically cranked the wheel to the right, but it was too late. As the jeep started to cut away, Braille threw the machine gun like a spear. The heavy weapon pierced both the windshield and the driver. The jeep screamed out of control.

Braille caught a brief glimpse of the other passengers grabbing the steering wheel, trying desperately to wrench it free from the dead driver's grip. Then the jeep hit a rut in the runway and flipped into the air, throwing bodies out into the night like a trampoline. The vehicle came down on its top and exploded in a fountain of flames.

Braille ran over to the burning wreckage. Spotting one of the dead men's weapons lying on the ground, he snatched it up. It was a Heckler and Koch assault rifle, capable of firing six hundred .308 caliber rounds per minute. It had been keyed to automatic fire and still had a full clip in it. Braille smiled.

Leslie came out of the darkness. "Don't you ever duck?" she asked, a worried expression of anger on her face. Braille gave her a sheepish smile, and her expression softened. She hooked her arm around his elbow. "What now, my love?"

Braille didn't know where they were, or which way the

nearest town was, so any direction would do as long as it didn't lead them back to that massive ancient hangar. He shrugged. "Pick a direction. Your choice."

"Really?" she giggled. He smiled and nodded, marveling at the way her brown eyes shined like burnished copper under the light of the moon. "That way," she said, pointing a finger straight out in front of her.

They set out again, running until she couldn't run anymore, then walking, then running again. Uncomplaining, she tried to keep up with Braille, but it was impossible. He scooped her up in his arms like a baby and continued on. She protested. "I weigh too much." He smiled, started to agree, noticed the way she was looking at him and then thought better of it.

They had put about five miles between themselves and the burning jeep when Braille looked at the woman he was carrying in his arms. "Did I thank you for breaking me out of that place?"

"No," she answered.

"Thank you."

"Welcome," she said. "Now put me down."

Braille slowed the pace to an easy walk. As they continued on across the flat hard blackness, and the moonlight bathed them in a blue-white light, she said, "Did I ever tell you that I loved you?"

"I think so." His voice was raspy with his own labored breathing.

"You don't remember?" she asked, mustering up the energy to sound irritated.

"Things were pretty hectic. We'd finally gotten to the mainland and I was changing, becoming something different. But it seems to me you said something along those lines—"

With a display of strength that surprised them both, she stopped abruptly and spun him around so she could see his face. "Let's get this real clear. I love you. I love you very much, Braille."

Braille's throat tightened. He looked at her and felt the same feelings for her. But words came hard for him.

She sensed how difficult it was for him to voice what he

was feeling and she took his hand. "That's okay. We got the rest of our lives for you to get over this thing you have about expressing emotions."

He looked at her intently. "But you know how I feel?"

She smiled. "I know. Now we better get moving."

They finally came to the end of the asphalt and started out across the rocky, flat desert. A half a mile later a faint humming noise distracted Braille, and he stopped. It was an alien sound, a bothersome incessant humming that reminded him of the noise flies made when they hovered around something dead.

Braille unslung the rifle, and with Leslie moved towards the ominous noise. A hundred yards later Braille spotted a dilapidated watchtower and ten yards beyond that, the source of the sound: a twelve-foot-high cyclone fence so charged with electricity it hummed like a giant transformer.

He turned to Leslie. "Stay here. I'm going to check it out. If it's safe I'll motion to you." Before she could respond, he was gone.

Keeping low, he loped across the blighted landscape, stopping finally behind a clump of sagebrush not far from a fence. Crouching down, he studied the three story tall lookout tower. It was old and so dilapidated it swayed back and forth in the wind like a stalk of wheat. Braille's eyes told him the tower was empty, but to be sure he picked up a rock and hurled it at the lookout tower. He heard the rock strike the corrugated roof and clatter off it. Braille waited, staring up at the tower expectantly. Nothing.

He walked over to the fence. There was no way of knowing how much electricity was running through the wires, but the current had to be lethal. The ground along the bottom of the fence was littered with the blackened skeletons of rabbits and other animals. Deciding he could short-circuit the fence using his rifle and some of the old boards and coils of rusty barbed wire scattered on the ground near the base of the lookout tower, Braille started back towards Leslie, motioning for her to come ahead and meet him halfway. It was safe. Wherever Cutter's men were, they weren't in this area.

* * *

A hundred yards away a security guard climbed up out of a shallow ravine and stopped on a small barren knoll. It's them, the guard thought. Stunned, he turned on the infrared laserscope mounted on his AR-15. He hefted the rifle to his shoulder and peered through the scope. Greenish images of two people came into focus. The wind was kicking up a lot of dust, making it difficult to prioritize his targets. Finally he decided he'd take out the one on the left first. Then the other. He didn't feel squeamish about killing two people in cold blood. The orders coming over his radio had been specific: "Terminate without hesitation. Couple armed and dangerous." With the rifle braced against his shoulder, he turned on the laser sighting device. At one hundred yards, with equipment such as this, he couldn't miss.

Leslie was thirty feet from Braille when she asked, "What now?"

Braille smiled as he continued to walk towards his woman. He tried to sound hopeful. "We hotwire the fence, take on the desert, then it's just you and me."

"You and me," she mused, looking away. Then she stopped, and slowly raised her eyes to his face. "Like for a long time . . . just you and me?"

"Like you and me forever, if you want it that way."

She returned his smile. It was a gentle lyrical smile and he could see there were tears in her eyes. "A day. A year. Forever. I'll take whatever time we have and be grateful for it." She opened her arms to him.

She was close now, not more than ten feet away. He started to reach for her.

Too late—he saw the red disc of light materialize in the middle of her white blouse.

The universe seemed to go into slow motion. He saw the red dot, started to scream a warning . . . started to run for her.

Then he heard the rifle crack and saw her lurch backwards. The smile on her face changed to shock as the red circle of light became a circle of blood. Leslie staggered backwards, looking down at her chest with a puzzled expression.

He tried to reach for her before she fell. Then, to his horror, he saw the red laser dot reappear on her blouse inches above the first wound. As he dove for her the dot of light exploded into a smear of blood. He grabbed her by the shoulders but she slipped away, crumpling to the ground. Braille screamed out in anguish, and as he screamed, he jerked up the HK-91, whirled, and fired blindly from the hip. The bullets raked across the desert, up the knoll and into the security guard. A withering hailstorm of .308-caliber bullets ripped into the man. The bullets almost cut him in two, lifted him up, and threw him backwards off the knoll.

Braille's world was still playing out like a film in slow motion. He saw the guard go down, feeling the rifle slip from his hands. Turning away, he knelt down beside Leslie's unmoving form, cradling her head in his arms.

"I just got shot, didn't I?" she whispered.

Braille tried to say something, but no words came.

She touched the wounds in her chest, then looked up at him. "You'll have to leave now. Somebody will've heard all that noise. They'll come for you. Trap you."

Braille touched her forehead with his. "Doesn't matter. Nothing matters."

"I'm too tired to argue," she said faintly. "If you're not going to leave, then hold me. It doesn't hurt. So hold me."

Braille took her into his arms, kissing her cheeks and her closed eyes, burying his face in her hair as he held her close.

And he continued to hold her . . . long after she stopped breathing.

It was only when her warmth began slipping away that he lowered her to the ground. Her eyes were closed. She looked as though she were sleeping. He sat beside her and brushed a strand of hair away from her face. Then he kissed her once and got to his feet.

It was hard to see, hard to breathe. He felt numb inside, empty and dead. Off in the distance he heard the sounds of helicopters coming his way and he didn't care. He was out in the open, easy to spot, and he didn't care.

Two miles away a fleet of helicopters, their searchlights turning the black runway white, moved towards him. If there had been a way, he would have signaled them and screamed out his position. He wanted to die. Nothing had worked so far. Maybe the firepower from a half-dozen gunships would bring him peace. But as the hate continued to burn inside him, he realized he didn't want peace. He wanted vengeance. He wanted to obliterate Cutter and the OSMS. Vengeance first, then peace, he thought. If peace were possible.

He wanted to look down at Leslie a final time, but didn't have the strength. He knew the sight of her lying there on the ground would drive him to his knees and he would never be able to get up again. Braille walked away. And he never once looked back.

3

THE SOUNDS OF HELICOPTERS BORE DOWN ON BRAILLE, GROWING loud all around him. As he approached the watchtower, a Huey gunship dropped down out of the sky, its prop wash kicking up billowing clouds of dust and sand, the floodlight under its belly turning the desert a vivid white. It hovered briefly over Leslie's body, then the body of the dead guard. Then, like a great predatory monster, it slowly rotated in the air until its huge Plexiglas eye was looking at Braille.

Braille started to run for the fence. Behind him the ever-closing helicopter opened up with twin M-60 machine guns. Bullets splattered the soil, kicking up huge plumes of dust. Braille ran on. The fence loomed up in front of him—a twelve-foot-high metal barrier charged with enough electricity to take out an army. While he ran, Braille wondered if he would survive the fence. He had lived through everything the OSMS had done to him. But electricity? This much electricity?

He leaped high into the air, reaching up with both hands, anticipating the pain . . . anticipating the lightning-like surge that would surely end his life.

He slammed into the cyclone fence, his hands gripping the thick metal wires as his world exploded in a fiery shower of sparks and pain.

In a brilliant flash of energy the fence short-circuited itself in an explosion of sparks. The brilliant white flashes momentarily blinded the pilot of the helicopter hovering directly overhead. After his night vision returned, he scanned the area for a moment, then spoke into his headset. "Where'd he go?"

The fence and the sagebrush growing on either side of its border were burning now. The observer leaned forward and peered out of the Plexiglas window. "What'd you mean, 'where'd he go?' He tried to climb the fence and got zapped by two hundred thousand volts of electricity."

"Maybe so," the pilot said. "But I still don't see him."

Leaning out the door as far as his safety harness would allow, the gunner checked the area. "He's down there," he shouted into his headset, his words obscured by the Huey's engine. "It's just that he's been burned to a crisp. Remember the guard that bumped the fence with his rifle? The guy looked like a piece of fudge. Our man's down there. We just can't see'im cuz the ground's all black and burning and so's our man."

The pilot shook his head. "Maybe, but I'm not about to set this bird down so we can search the area. I saw what he did to those jeeps. There's no way I'm landing when I can't see a body. I'm going to radio this in to Cutter. Let him send out a search party. Maybe they can find the body."

Cutter took the pilot's call over the shortwave radio in his office. After listening to the pilot's assessment, Cutter ordered the four OSMS helicopters to continue the search out beyond the fence.

"You think the man's still alive?" the pilot's voice crackled over the radio.

"Just continue the search," Cutter said politely. He put the microphone down and turned to Riddick and Kendricks. For a man who had just had a research laboratory trashed, three vehicles destroyed, and who had lost upwards of a dozen men, he was remarkably composed. He motioned at the radio. "Incredible. Our man came into contact with enough volts of electricity to wipe out half the state, and he survived." Cutter sounded almost elated. Kendricks and Riddick looked at one another questioningly. Maybe the strain of Braille's escape had been too much for the Director.

Cutter continued. "The Radcliffs are dead. Leslie Chapel is dead. And Braille's gone. You know what that means?" Kendricks and Riddick shook their heads in unison. Cutter smiled. "It means that someday Braille'll come back here. Not today or tomorrow, but one day he will come back."

"Why would he ever come back here after all we did to him?" Kendricks asked, genuinely puzzled.

Cutter shrugged. "We killed his friends . . . and his woman. He'll come back to square the account. He'll come back to kill us."

Kendricks paled. Riddick looked sick. Cutter's smile broadened. "When he does, we'll be ready for him."

"But look what he just did to us," Riddick pointed out.

"A case of underestimation. I underestimated both Braille and his friends. Next time I won't. Next time we'll be ready."

A lone figure stood on top of a cliff, watching four helicopters flying in a sweep search formation, all heading in his direction.

A mile from the cliff they broke formation. Three of the Hueys veered away and headed off in different directions. The fourth one continued to close on him, its searchlights raking the desert floor sixty feet below its belly. The pilot slowed his gunship as the copter approached the base of the cliff. More searchlights came on. Hovering in the air, the copter turned slowly in one direction, then the other, then began to rise straight up in the air, the painted tips of its rotor blades cutting a bright circle in the night not more than twenty feet away from the face of the sheer cliff.

Braille looked down at the machine coming up towards him. He was exhausted, and in agony. He'd been hit several times by bullets during his run for the fence, and the electricity in the fence had seared the flesh off the palms of his hands and chest. The pain was incredible, but even worse was the agony of the healing process. At first there had been nothing but numbness. The nerves and synapses had been smashed to pulp by the bullets and burned to nothingness by the electricity. But with the healing—with the resurrection of flesh—came newly developed nerves capable of transmitting the pain of the injury and the pain of regrowth. It was the genesis of agony.

Braille glared at the helicopter hovering up the side of the cliff below him. He knew he couldn't outrun the Huey. There was no place to go. No place to hide. "No more," he whispered, his words drowned out by the whine of the copter's motor.

As the helicopter cleared the upper face of the cliff, the gunner leaned out of the doorway, his handheld floodlight illuminating the flat table of rocks coming into view . . . and the man who was standing on the rim of the cliff not more than twenty feet away—a man who was slowly hefting a rock the size of a watermelon up over his head with both hands.

The gunner shouted a warning.

The observer turned in his seat, saw what the gunner saw, and screamed. "Get outta here! Get us the fuck outta here!!"

Braille threw the rock. It crashed into the helicopter's tail rotor, shattering the machine's directional controls.

The observer screamed. The pilot fought to control his ship as it began to pitch and yaw and spin out of control. Shuddering violently, the gunship whipped around in a careening circle, then veered violently to the right.

"Watch out for the cliff!" shouted the observer. The pilot pulled back on the controls. The copter rose a few feet higher and continued to slide to its right. Braille watched the helicopter lurch and shudder in his direction. At the last moment he dropped to the ground, and the copter's runners cleared the top of the cliff and his body by inches.

The pilot jerked hard on the stick, almost ripping it out of the floor in a final desperate bid to gain altitude. But he knew it was hopeless. "That's all she wrote," he said softly.

Canted at an angle, the helicopter slammed into the earth forty feet behind Braille, its rotor blades hitting first, digging up chunks of rock and earth as the blades whipped into the ground. Then the body hit. The blades snapped and flew into the air like huge chunks of shrapnel. The plexiglass front shattered. The motor tore loose and the huge metal body rolled over in a maelstrom of debris and flying metal parts.

In the awesome silence that followed, Braille got to his feet and started for the stricken craft. The gunner was lying on his back. Part of the tail assembly covered his legs. The man was looking up at the night sky through a shattered visor. He heard Braille coming and turned his head slightly, looking at the man standing over him. "Can you help me, Mister? I can't feel anything. I can't move anything."

Braille stepped over the gunner and checked the inside of the helicopter. The pilot and observer were dead. He walked back to the gunner, the man following him with his eyes. "All I can move is my head," he whispered, "but you know what bothers me? It bothers me that I'm going to die with this stupid helmet on."

Braille knelt down and gently removed the gunner's helmet.

"Jeez, that's better," the gunner said. "Know what else bothers me?" Braille remained motionless. "It bothers me that I can't feel anything and maybe I won't die."

"Don't worry," Braille said softly. "You're going to die."

The gunner seemed to brighten at the prospect. "Jeez, do you really think so? I'd hate to go through life like a mannequin, not feeling anything, not able to move."

"Believe me, you're going to die," Braille said. "Now close your eyes."

In shock, close to death, the man smiled and closed his eyes.

Braille snapped his neck like a twig. Then he took the man's blood.

Nine hundred miles away, on an island twenty-six miles off the coast of Washington State, a creature with an appetite similar to Braille's was also trying to take blood. But it was impossible. It was trying to extract blood from the dehydrated torso of a human being that had days earlier

PATRICK WHALEN

been drained of blood. The creature gave up, threw the corpse down, and began to pace around in the room like a caged animal. The steel floor of the thirty-foot-square room resembled the lair of a predatory flesh-eating animal. In a way, that's exactly what it was.

Eight weeks earlier the huge bank vault had served as a daylight haven to a large group of creatures exactly like the one now pacing its floor. Eight weeks earlier the vault had been the perfect resting place for newly bitten vampires. Sunlight could not pierce its steel walls, and as long as the creatures had been satiated on blood, they did not attack one another, but rather gathered together out of an instinctual fear of the sun and to await the coming of the next night.

But then something happened. They had come together and begun to dream the black dreamless sleep when suddenly the earth shook and rolled under them. Some stirred. Others woke up. The vault door was closed. The tremors ceased. Not knowing that a nuclear power plant had exploded and that the resulting radioactive cloud had killed thousands of their own kind and contaminated the island, the New Ones drifted back to sleep.

Prompted by an internal clock, they awakened at sunset. More eager and hungrier than the others, two males opened the steel door and stepped out into the night—a night filled with a swirling misty red fog. An instant later the males rushed back into the vault screaming and slapping at themselves as if they were on fire. Galvanized by animal instinct, some of the others had pushed the vault door closed, sealing out the red fog. By the time they looked down at the two males, they were dead. A few moments after that their bodies dissolved into nothing.

Frightened and confused, fourteen creatures remained in the vault two days and two nights. On the third night, another male, starving and desperate for blood, tried to leave. He rushed out into the red mist. Even with the vault door closed, those inside could hear the screams of the one outside as radiation ate through skin, flesh, and bones.

Trapped in the vault by a power they did not understand, the creatures attacked the smallest of their kind on the sixth night. Driven by an unquenchable thirst, they took the small

58

one down and fought each other in a desperate struggle for blood. What they took was able to sustain them for four days. A creature that had once been a chubby woman in her mid-thirties was the next to die.

The ghastly pattern continued for the next six weeks—nights of relentless pacing and fighting, snarling and deaths, until there was only one left.

He had been the biggest of them. His strength and cunning had allowed him to survive, exist, and kill until he . . . it . . . was the only one left. And now it was desperate. Almost nothing remained of the others except for bones and desiccated flesh. There was nothing in the vault that could sustain him any longer. It knew that if it did not take blood soon, it would dissolve like those who had walked into the red fog.

In life it had been a shy accountant in Seattle, content to lift weights, jog frequently, and adhere religiously to a vegetarian diet. In death it was a hulking beast with huge arms, long needle-sharp teeth, and a fierce, unquenchable thirst for blood and existence. Its eyebrows had grown together. Its body exuded an odor identical to ammonia, and its eyes glowed fiercely in the black vault, like road flares.

At that moment it was overwhelmed by an all-encompassing rage. A rage to survive. To kill. A rage to slack its thirst. And it was this blinding all-consuming rage that drove it out into the night.

It stepped out of the vault and walked cautiously across the bank lobby. It couldn't see the red fog, but it knew it was there, all around, on the ground, in the air, on anything it touched. It didn't know why it knew this, but it did.

It walked out onto a dark boulevard. The island resort town was deserted. The night was dark. A low bank of clouds covered the moon. It began to walk down the boulevard, and as the wind whirled around it, something began to happen. The creature didn't notice the sensation of warmth at the beginning, but after several blocks, it realized its skin was beginning to burn.

It broke into a run, a panicked run, and at the same time it began slapping at its face and neck in a useless effort to put out the fire on its skin. It ran faster, harder, as if to leave the burning fire behind. The hideous burning sensation continued to grow.

At the edge of town, it ran up a steep hill. By now, the radiation-saturated air and soil was beginning to take a terrible toll on the creature. It was running blindly, with its eyes clenched shut and its hand outstretched in front of it. It crashed into a tree and tripped over logs and rocks, then scrambled to its feet and continued to run.

Suddenly it was no longer running. It was falling, and the creature dimly realized it had run off a cliff. It screamed and flailed out with its hands.

The creature crashed into the thick boughs of an old pine tree growing out from a cleft in the face of the cliff fifty feet above the cold waters of Puget Sound. The impact of the falling vampire and its weight were too much for the ancient tree and the fragile roots holding it in place. With a loud ripping sound the entire tree broke away from the cliff, and with the creature still clinging to it, the tree plunged into the boiling surf.

The outgoing tide carried the tree out away from the island. Then the currents took over and the tree began to drift in an easterly direction towards the mainland twenty-six miles away. Within minutes the creature's pain subsided and its vision returned as the cold salt water washed the radiation particles from its body.

Four hours later the sun came up, but the tree's thick overhead branches shielded the creature from the weak cloud-covered sun. As it continued to cling to the tree, it grew content. Its pain was gone. It was protected from the sun. And somehow it knew that, with each passing wave, it was being carried closer to the mainland and to that place in its memory, that place where people existed. It could not recall the name of the place, but if it could have, it would have called it Seattle.

4

THERE WAS NO END TO THE DESERT. IT STRETCHED OUT INTO THE horizon forever, an endless sea of gray sagebrush, boulders, high cliffs, and an ever-changing climate. One moment he was hot, the next cold. It didn't make any sense until Braille realized he had been held prisoner in the OSMS laboratory for the better part of two months. That meant this had to be November.

Braille was sweating heavily. The overhead sun was hot. He wiped his forehead with the back of his hand, then looked at his hand. It was wet with red sweat, and there were large fragments of skin on the back. The flesh and bloody sweat baffled him for a moment. Then he realized his body was possibly sweating the blood he'd taken in the night before, and his skin was reacting to the sun by falling away in thick layers. He examined the back of his hand a final time. He wasn't just peeling, he was losing healthy, moist flesh. He shook his head in disgust. He should have realized —he was a night animal, a nocturnal, blood-drinking predator. He wiped the back of his hand on his jeans, felt more flesh fall away, and swore. A few more hours of sun, and he'd look like a two-thousand-year-old mummy. Worse yet, he'd be dead as a two-thousand-year-old mummy.

As he looked around for shade he noticed a thin gray line filling the northerly horizon. He smiled. There was a storm coming down from Canada. The colder and darker the better, he thought.

An hour later the day turned dark gray. An hour after that the storm arrived. Braille found shelter in a shallow ravine. He sat with his back against an embankment, his knees drawn up to his chest, his head bowed. Exhaustion caught up with him, and he slept . . . dreaming he was with Leslie and they were walking together through the forest not far from his lighthouse. Willie, his little retarded friend of many years, was playing with his dog nearby. He and Leslie waved to Willie. Willie waved back and then waddled off in slow pursuit of his dog.

Braille pulled Leslie close. "I never knew what love was until I met you, and then you went away."

She looked at him with wide brown eyes. "I didn't go away," she whispered. "This isn't a dream. I'm here. I'm holding you." She smiled at him as a loud clap of thunder rumbled overhead.

Large droplets of rain splattered down on Braille, stinging the flesh burned and cracked by the sun. He moaned, not from the pain but at the loss of his dream and the loss of Leslie Chapel. The sky was filled with dark gray thunderheads roiling and churning in the heavens like an angry sea. He got to his feet, cursed the gods for taking away his dream, and trudged on.

Just before sunset the cloudy sky turned pink, and it snowed briefly. But then the snow melted, the sun set, the sky went black, and the temperature dropped dramatically.

Earlier the sun had been his lethal enemy. Now he faced new enemies just as lethal: the freezing temperature and the howling winds. He knew he was too exhausted to go on much farther, yet he also knew that if he stopped to lie down, he would freeze to death. He almost wished the sun would come back up. "Fuck," he grumbled. "If it's not one thing, it's another."

He came to a steep hill. Hoping to find shelter on the other side, he forced himself to move up the slope. At the top he stopped abruptly and stared down at the men camped at the bottom of the slope a half a mile away. Dropping to his knees, Braille studied the scene, his eyes taking in the Land Rovers, tents, and the four men sitting around a small fire. The men were wearing uniforms and were heavily armed. Braille scanned the area around the fire. The men from the OSMS had not bothered to post a sentry. Braille smiled at their stupidity. "So, you've come hunting for me," he whispered as he got to his feet and began moving down the hill. "Well, now you've found me."

Hunkering in the darkness just beyond the reach of the light from the campfire, Braille watched the OSMS security guards enter their tents. When he was sure everyone was asleep, Braille entered the camp. He had two choices: kill the men and take blood, or simply steal one of the Land Rovers and use it to escape. He wanted blood desperately. He was weak, exhausted, and half frozen to death. He needed the blood. He was addicted to its life-giving powers. But he hadn't arrived at the point where he could willingly kill sleeping men to get blood.

At least not yet.

He moved between a tent and the fire, planning to hotwire one of the Land Rovers. The Land Rover was unlocked. He opened the driver's door. The dome light came on. And so did an alarm-activated siren under the hood.

Cursing his stupidity, Braille slammed the door. At the same moment, four men emerged from tents behind him.

"Over by the Rover," one man screamed.

Someone cut loose with an automatic rifle. Someone else opened up with a machine gun. Braille threw himself to the ground. A hailstorm of bullets thunked into the Land Rovers.

"I got him! I got him!" someone shouted.

More bullets plowed up the earth and ripped into the vehicles as Braille rolled under a Land Rover. Three, maybe four, automatic weapons went on firing for almost a minute, then stopped abruptly. "Jesus Christ," the same man said, "I said I got him."

"Just wanted to make sure," someone else said.

The men, their voices high-pitched with adrenaline, approached the vehicles. "I thought this guy was supposed to be bad, able to take out jeeps and helicopters with a single leap," someone said. "Some bad. I dropped him with my first clip."

"You!" a different voice said. "I hit him first . . . and speaking of our man, where'd he go?"

"Rolled under the Rover after *I* hit him," said the other, sliding a fresh clip into his MAC-10 machine gun. Both men disappeared into the darkness on the far side of the Land Rovers.

The two remaining men in camp held their weapons at the ready and stared hard at the night for a long span of time. Finally a younger man said, "Where'd they go?"

An older guard shook his head at the dumb question and the tension in the boy's voice. "They're out there." He lifted his arm and pointed.

A white hand came out of the darkness, grabbing the outstretched arm. The guard was jerked off his feet, hurled through the air, and slammed down into the hood of a Rover. The guard screamed. A hard blow to his throat cut off his scream—and his life.

As the younger guard started to raise his weapon, a dark figure spun around and slapped the automatic rifle out of his hands. Then the shadow returned to the body of the dead guard sprawled on the hood of the Rover. He grabbed the man's shirt and hoisted him to his feet. Several ghastly seconds later the body was dropped, and the shadow wiped blood from its mouth with the back of its hand. Then the figure approached the boy. Too frightened to run or move, the boy just stood there. Piercing red eyes focused in on the young guard. Then a voice seemed to emanate from a space of blackness just under the red eyes. The voice sounded like rocks being crushed. "How long you been working for Cutter?"

"Cutter?"

"The OSMS," said the shape with the red eyes.

"Four months."

The eyes studied the boy for a while longer. "How old are you?"

"Nineteen," he whimpered.

"You're young."

"Yes sir," the boy said, a note of hopefulness in his voice. Maybe this man-beast wouldn't kill him after all.

The black shadow with the red eyes gestured at the boy's rifle lying nearby. "But then, if you're old enough to carry a weapon and go man-hunting, you're old enough to die." The young man began to cry.

Braille sighed at the pathetic sight. The boy continued to cry because he didn't know what else to do. "Time for you to go," Braille finally said. "I won't kill you tonight, but if I ever see you again, I will." The young man looked as if he were in a daze. "Get on the road and start walking that way." Braille pointed towards the west. "If you stay on the road and keep walking, you won't get lost and you won't freeze to death."

The boy turned and headed towards the dirt road.

"One more thing," Braille called out. The young man stopped, but he couldn't bring himself to turn and look at Braille.

"When you get back, some men will want to talk to you about what happened here tonight. Their names will be Riddick, Kendricks, and Cutter. I want you to tell them what I did tonight and how easy it was for me to do it. Then tell them that one day I'll do the same thing to them. Tell 'em I don't care where they go or how many men they have around them, I'll do the same thing to them. You got that?"

The boy headed off into the night and Braille walked over to the dead guard next to the Rover. He rifled the man's pockets and came across a set of keys. Scooping up the car keys, he started towards the Land Rovers, then stopped. The guards from the OSMS may not have hit him during the shootout, but they had shot their own vehicles to pieces.

Braille threw the keys away and headed back out into the desert. He knew that, come sunrise, search parties from the OSMS would find the man he had allowed to walk away, and shortly after that, they would converge on the dead guards' campsite. The earlier snowfall had turned the hard-packed soil into mush. He was leaving tracks a blind man could follow and the OSMS would be on his heels by mid-morning.

With a full moon shining on his back, Braille headed east. He had tasted blood and possessed its energy, and he broke into a graceful loping run, knowing that if he were to survive the next day, he would have to either find hard rocky ground or put a great deal of distance between the campsite and himself.

5

THE BAR WAS ABOUT TO CLOSE. GREGORY WATCHED THE FIVE lumberjacks leave and knew they would be waiting for him outside. Oblivious to the impatient glances from the bartender, Gregory sat at the bar and continued to nurse his drink, not because he was afraid of the men who'd just left, but because he wanted to reflect upon this new time, this new world.

And it was a confusing world.

Two months earlier, after the nuclear power plant had exploded and a cloud of radioactive steam had rolled across the island killing everything in its path—including Clementina, the woman he had loved for five hundred years and himself—it should have all come to an end. There should have been nothing, save for a black void that he had hoped to share with Clementina. But then something hideous happened. He had not been allowed to die. His body had resurrected itself. Flesh regrew over bones. Tendons and nerve endings materialized. Skin covered flesh and he had been resurrected, rejuvenated from a withering fluidless husk to what he had been before—a vampire. The Master Ancient. A being who had lived for nine hundred years and would live on forever. Alone.

No creature had ever grieved for its mate as had Gregory. For several days he had remained in the church where he and Clementina had died together. But in the end, when he could no longer feel her spirit or her energy, he had left the island on a raft he had built with his own hands. Not caring what would happen to him next, he had let the tides and the winds set the raft's course and was not surprised when the raft finally floated ashore on a beach on the mainland some miles south of a harbor town called Bellingham. He had expected no surprises, expecting to adapt easily to life on the mainland and to the twentieth century.

66

He was wrong.

The bartender reached for Gregory's glass, hoping to encourage him to leave. Gregory put one finger on top of the glass. The bartender smiled. He wrapped his hand around the glass and tried to remove it from the bar. The smile began to fade as he labored first with one hand, then with two hands to remove a glass held in place on his bar by one finger. Embarrassed after thirty seconds of effort, the bartender stepped back and studied the strange man with the black and gray hair and the cold gray eyes. He decided that this man could sit at his bar for as long as he wanted.

Gregory had only absent-mindedly noticed the bartender's actions. He was still thinking back to the changes he had experienced after coming ashore on a beach that was part of a state park. In a secluded glen not far from some picnic tables, Gregory had come across two partly clothed men lying on a blanket beneath a willow tree. One was pretty enough to have been a woman, the other old enough to have been his partner's father. Gregory would have preferred to ignore the couple, but knew he would need money to survive on the mainland without drawing attention to himself, and these two were the first humans he had come across.

Caught up in their passion, the couple did not notice Gregory until he knelt down beside them, tapping the one on top with his finger. The man rolled off his partner and looked up at Gregory. Gregory was a large man, powerfully built. The radiation on the island and the sun had burned and blistered his skin. As always, he was healing rapidly, but at that particular moment the skin on his face hung down in tatters, like strips of flapping cloth. The younger man promptly fainted.

The older man was much calmer. "What do you want?"

"Your money," he said simply.

The older man handed over a wallet heavy with money and credit cards. Gregory asked for an explanation of the thin pieces of plastic. The man explained. Gregory returned the credit cards. "Too complicated."

The man also gave Gregory the keys to his car and his friend's money. Gregory thanked him and motioned towards the young man lying on the ground. "Does he always do that?"

Surprisingly calm, the older man smiled. "He swoons a lot. But he does have some inner strengths."

"He can stay here while you show me where your car is." The older homosexual got to his feet and Gregory was surprised by the size of the man. "You and I are the same size. Do you have clothes in your car?"

"What if I said no?" the man said.

"You and your friend are alive at this point because you have cooperated and have not lied. Need I say more?"

The older man shook his head, then led Gregory over to the park's parking lot. The car was a new Cadillac. The man indicated his clothes were in a suitcase in the trunk. Gregory thanked the man, took the keys, and asked directions to the nearest large city. The man pointed. When Gregory asked the name of the city, the man said, "Seattle." Then Gregory apologized for taking the man's money, clothes, and car. The man shrugged. "I carry lots of insurance."

With the arrogance of a being that had lived for nine hundred years, Gregory climbed into the Cadillac. Two months earlier Gregory had gone for one ride with Braille in Braille's car and now he thought back to the things Braille had done to make the automobile move. He remembered Braille had inserted a key into the neck of the steering wheel. Gregory did the same, turning the key. Immediately the engine started. Pleased with himself, Gregory pushed down hard on the gas and began working the shifting lever. The transmission finally clanked from P into R and the Cadillac smashed into two cars behind it. Undaunted, Gregory went to D and the car roared out of the parking lot and into a picnic table. Disgusted, Gregory kept on going through two more picnic tables, a barbecue and over a motorcycle before he was finally able to lurch and weave his way out of the park and up the road leading to the freeway.

When he'd asked the man for directions to the large city, the man had pointed to the south. At the entrance to a huge six-lane interstate freeway, Gregory turned south. He gunned the Cadillac and pulled out onto a large three-lane road. It perplexed him that all three lanes were filled with cars coming at him. He glanced to his right. Beyond a wide grassy divider he saw another wide strip of road filled with cars going the same direction he was. South. "Oh."

Horns honked and brakes screeched while he attempted to avoid the wall of oncoming cars. A large semi-truck and a station wagon broke into uncontrolled skids just as Gregory veered off the freeway and onto the highway divider. Oblivious to the chaos he was leaving behind, Gregory drove across the median and pulled onto the southbound lanes of the freeway. Pleased with himself, he drove on—at twenty miles an hour. Seconds later he heard the now-familiar sounds of cars honking and shrieking and crashing into one another behind him. "What is it now?" he said in disgust, turning to look out the back window just in time to see a truck behind him jackknife and slide off the road in an effort to avoid crashing into the Cadillac. An instant later an out-of-control Volkswagen ricocheted off the side of the Cadillac and rolled over several times in the middle of the freeway. Gregory made a face, hit the brakes, and brought the Cadillac to a stop in the middle of the freeway.

"Better I walk."

As more cars rammed into each other or careened off the road, Gregory casually opened the trunk of the Cadillac, picked up the suitcase, and disappeared into the dense forest lining both sides of the freeway. Always keeping the distant waters of Puget Sound in view, Gregory made his way south. He was a powerful, agile man and the thick underbrush in the forest did little to hinder the rapid loping pace he set for himself.

Just after sunset Gregory emerged from the trees and found himself standing on a low grassy hill. A few miles away the lights of a small town wedged between steep forested hills and the cold waters of Puget Sound glittered in the darkness.

Gregory was exhausted. He still hadn't recovered from the huge dose of radiation he'd received on the island and knew he wasn't ready to cope with the unknowns of a strange city in an alien land. He was too weak, too ignorant. But he suspected that if he took a few weeks or months to hide out in a small town, he could use that time to gain strength and knowledge about this new time and strange land.

Still carrying the suitcase, Gregory walked down the hill towards the town, checking his appearance while he walked. The trip from the island to the mainland in the raft and the grueling ten-mile run through the forest had torn his clothing to tatters. On the outskirts of town he came across an old, deserted cemetery. He vaulted over a metal spear fence, wandered past the tombstones, and finally came upon an old mausoleum. He broke the lock and entered.

Suddenly Gregory found himself in a house of the dead, and he envied its occupants. They had completed the circle: come to life from nothing, had lived life and returned to nothing. He wondered briefly if he would ever complete that circle. Probably not. Again he envied the occupants of this place for the peace they'd finally achieved. There had to be peace in nothingness. He had never known peace, just love. He had known love for over five hundred years, but the object of that love was gone. She had died on the island, completed her circle, and was gone. At peace.

Alone in the house of the dead, Gregory opened the suitcase and found a shaving kit and a small mirror. He checked his appearance. The burns and blisters were almost healed. He trimmed his hair with a pair of small scissors and scraped his face with a plastic razor. Then he put on dark slacks, loafers, and a white shirt before going back out into the night.

The name of the town was Stanwood. It was an old town, sparsely populated and dying. Near as Gregory could tell, two lumber mills and an ancient salmon canning factory located on the slow-moving river washing out into Puget Sound were all that was keeping it alive. The downtown district was two blocks long, composed of old two- and three-story buildings. A hardware store, some bars, a clothing store, one bank, and an old Safeway market were the only surviving businesses. The rest of the buildings were vacant and boarded up.

The surrounding neighborhoods matched downtown Stanwood. The trees were old and lush and their foliage blotted out the illumination from street lamps that resembled the lamp posts Gregory had seen centuries earlier in London. The homes were simple one- and two-story affairs falling prey to harsh winds, unceasing rains, and time. No one cared. The foliage and landscaping surrounding the homes gave evidence to that. The lawns were thick and lush and untended.

He passed an old, majestic three-story home with an "Apartment for Rent" sign in the window. Making a mental note of the location he decided he would inquire tomorrow. It was too late in the evening to talk to the landlord tonight.

He returned to the cemetery, spending the night in the crypt. Early on the following evening he returned to the three-story home with the apartment for rent.

The woman who owned the home was in her early seventies; she was gray-haired, bright, and talkative and she didn't care if Gregory smoked, drank, turned up the radio, or partied all night. What she did care about was the rent.

"Payable every Friday afternoon. Sixty dollars a week."

Her name was Molly Estleford and Gregory was the only boarder in her home. His third-floor apartment turned out to be a huge sitting room that had once been her husband's library. The library was still there, along with an array of overstuffed chairs, a black-and-white TV set, and an old four-poster bed. Aside from Gregory and Mrs. Estleford, the huge home had only one other occupant—Mrs. Estleford's granddaughter. Before Gregory met her, Mrs. Estleford warned him.

"She's kinda strange. She fell in with the wrong crowd, got mixed up with drugs, and her step-father and my daughter couldn't handle her, so they kicked her out. She acts fourteen, looks thirty but is actually twenty-one. She takes a little getting used to. Her friends who come up to see her on the weekend take a lot of getting used to. I been trying, but I still don't like 'em. Anyways, under all that makeup and that funny talk, there's kind of a nice person."

"Why does she stay with you?" Gregory asked.

"Because her probation officer told her to."

Molly Estleford's granddaughter turned out to be a pretty young woman with black hair and green eyes. She wore skintight pants, shirts made of leather, several pounds of makeup, five pierced earrings in one ear and occasionally a sixth earring in a hole in her nostril. On the first night that Gregory saw Samantha, her hair was jet black. On the second night a large shock of hair dangling down in front of her face had been died turquoise. The next time he saw her, the hair was yellow, and the time after that, green. Molly Estleford had described her granddaughter as a cross between a punk rocker and a Valley Girl, telling Gregory she was occasionally hard to understand. Gregory wasn't worried about a language barrier. Over the centuries he'd mastered eight languages. Then he met Samantha Estleford, and translating what came out of her mouth was the greatest linguistic challenge he had ever encountered. Everything was "Awesome," or "Grody to the max," or, "Gag me with a spoon and coke me out to infinity."

Still, in spite of the language barrier, Gregory rather enjoyed the girl. In many ways she was like her grandmother: talkative, bright, feisty, and far easier to tolerate than she thought she was. Only one thing made Gregory feel ill at ease. Samantha Estleford was an outrageous flirt and she would go out of her way to shock him with her come-ons and sexual overtures. During his second week in the Estleford home, she trapped him in the stairway to tell him she loved men with nice asses. Gregory countered her remark with a comment about not owning any mules. Unamused, she stalked off.

During his first seven weeks in Stanwood, Gregory spent most of his time alone in his room, learning about the twentieth century by reading all the books in the Estleford home. There were a lot of books. Molly Estleford's deceased husband had been an English teacher. In between books he voraciously poured over thirty years' worth of *Life, Post,* and *National Geographic* magazines. When he wasn't reading, he absorbed the new century through the black-and-white TV in his room. It was hard to assimilate it all and put it into perspective. The books, the magazines, and the television programs all came together to form a surrealistic, disjointed collage of formless chaos: World War I. World War II. Korea. Vietnam. The atom bomb. Penicillin. Lasers. Soap operas. The electric chair. Computers. Road Runner cartoons. Neutron bombs. He thought about it, tried to put it all together, and in the end found himself more confused than ever. Still, there was one thing that could not be denied: it was an interesting world, interesting beyond his wildest expectations.

When he wasn't reading, watching TV, or avoiding Samantha, Gregory exercised to regain his strength. He went for long solitary walks and prowled the night. He enjoyed the night. The night was his home, a friend.

But on some nights the hunger came to him, and he knew he would have to take blood. He had no choice on those nights. It was a matter of instinct. Survival. He had no choice.

Stanwood was his home. He didn't know when he would be leaving, so when he went out into the night in search of blood, he took care to not draw attention to himself or the town. Stanwood was dying mainly because the six-lane interstate freeway connecting Canada, Seattle, Oregon, and California had been built twelve miles to the east. A narrow winding road, more treacherous than scenic, connected Stanwood to the freeway. On those nights that Gregory went hunting, he would follow the narrow road to the freeway. Near the off-ramp to Stanwood there was a large public rest area with motels, gas stations, and a huge grassy park. It was there that Gregory went to find blood.

The rest stop was always crowded with people and Gregory had no problem in singling out and stalking his victims. Inevitably he would select someone traveling alone, and when the moment was right, he would strike. He was perhaps the most proficient killer in the world, and his prey never knew fear or pain. One moment they were alive and walking back to their car, the next dead. After taking their blood, Gregory would bury their remains deep in the forest surrounding the rest stop.

Gregory always took care with his victims. They never felt their own deaths, and when he finished with them, there was no blood in their bodies. To leave any blood—even a minute amount—was to invite his victims to return to life in a state similar to his. He did not wish this. He did not wish to see an outbreak of vampirism spread over the mainland as it had on Chinook Island two months ago.

Earlier tonight, Gregory had left the Estleford home an hour before midnight, then covered the distance between the town and the freeway in inhuman time. He had spotted his prey, a woman at the rest stop, almost immediately. He killed her, took blood, buried her, and returned to the town.

He had not felt like returning to his room. He never did after taking a life. Instead, he had gone into one of the bars in Stanwood and ordered a drink. It was a small bar, and quiet. Just he and an unobtrusive bartender.

Gregory liked the solitude and silence. He decided to stay until the bar closed.

Then five drunk lumberjacks off for the weekend burst through the front door. The men were loud, obnoxious, and looking for trouble. Gregory didn't like them. As Gregory was the only customer in the bar it was easy for the five to pick up on his irritation and cold disdain.

After sitting down at a table, the five put their heads together and decided they'd take on the cold son-of-a-bitch at the bar. Five on one. That was the answer. Rat-pack the guy, then stomp him into the floor. The smallest man at the table, a squat man with a build like a garbage can, said, "I don't like that fucker. He's raining on my parade. He thinks he's better than us. Nobody can think they're better than us when they're on their back."

As the men started to close on Gregory, the bartender pulled out a sawed-off Louisville slugger, its hollowed-out end heavy with melted lead. He hit the bar with the stumpy bat. "Not in my place. You wanta fight, take it outside."

After the lumberjacks left, Gregory felt the bartender's eyes on him. "Mister," the man said, "it's after two. I gotta close this place down or the law'll close me down. I know you don't wanta leave, but you got to."

Gregory eased himself off the bar stool and started towards the door.

"They're waiting for you," the bartender said. "If they're not waiting for you out by the front door, they'll be hiding in the alley. Watch yourself."

Gregory nodded to the man and stepped out into the night.

He turned to his right and started down the sidewalk. Suddenly the squat man came out of the alley with a broken two-by-four in his upraised hands. Gregory lifted his forearm as the man brought the two-by-four down. The board broke over Gregory's arm and before the man could back away, Gregory reached out, grabbed the man's face with his broad hand and squeezed. The strength in Gregory's grip turned the man's skull into pulp. The other men charged. Gregory killed one with a single blow and snapped another's neck. The third changed his mind and started to run. Gregory grabbed him by the back of the neck and slammed him headfirst into a brick wall hard enough to split his skull in two.

Shocked by what he had just witnessed, the last man stood in the dark alley, a large-caliber revolver in his hand. As Gregory walked toward him, the man pointed the weapon at Gregory's chest and fired four times at point-blank range.

Gregory felt the bullets hit him, feeling the searing sensation of lead passing through his flesh, then felt an almost instantaneous relief as his flesh began to heal and close.

The man just stood there as Gregory came forward. Gotta be a bad dream, the man thought as he stared into Gregory's red eyes. Something with burning eyes had killed four of his friends, something he had just shot four times, and now that something was coming for him. Impossible. Gotta be a dream. He clung vigorously to that hope until the dream killed him.

Gregory was turning away when he heard the sound of a door opening. He glanced back into the alley and saw the bartender emerging from the bar's back entrance. Gregory sighed and began walking towards the man. He didn't have a choice. The bartender could identify him. A loud jukebox and brick walls had prevented the bartender from hearing the gunshots and while he half expected to find the stranger beaten to death in the alley, he was completely unprepared to find the lumberjacks down and the stranger walking towards him.

Gregory stopped two feet from the bartender. The man's eyes were locked on the five bodies lying twenty feet away. "Jesus Keyrist, what'd you do to them?" He lifted his eyes to Gregory's face and saw something he didn't want to see. "I won't tell," he said, suddenly cold and afraid. "Honest. I wouldn't go to the police."

"Yes you would," the bartender heard Gregory say. Then he heard his own neck snap. He did not hear Gregory say, "I am sorry."

Gregory was trying to figure out what to do with the

bodies, when he noticed a large dumpster on metal casters in the alley. A few minutes later Gregory pushed the dumpster out of the alley, across a deserted street, and out onto an old wooden pier. The river was slow-moving, its waters dark and muddy, and it took only a few moments for the dumpster to sink out of sight.

Gregory returned home and found a naked intruder sitting on his bed. In her own way, she was attractive. She had a pretty face and a mature body, but her uninvited presence in his room irritated him. He scooped up her clothes and tossed them at Samantha Estleford. Then he told her to leave.

"I don't want to. If you try to make me leave, I'll scream."

"If you stay, you'll scream anyway," Gregory warned.

"What do you mean?" Samantha asked, suddenly suspicious.

"If you try to stay, I will throw you out the window. I assume you will scream until you hit the ground." Gregory shrugged.

"We're three stories up. You're putting me on."

"You said you would scream if I asked you to leave, and I know you would scream if I threw you out the window. Either way you'll scream, so I might as well give you something to scream about."

Before he finished his sentence, Samantha was on her feet and pulling on a pair of leather pants. The pants were skintight and she was having difficulty getting them on. Gregory sighed. At this rate she would be in his room until noon. She seemed to read his mind. "I'm hurrying as fast as I can." She got her pants on, then began to work her way into a black leather jacket. "Christ," she hissed, zipping up one of the sixteen zippers that decorated the front of the jacket. "I don't know why you had to go and get violent. All I wanted to do was play sideshow."

"Sideshow?"

"Yeah. I sit on your face and you guess my weight."

"You came to my room and took off your clothes so I can guess your weight?" Gregory was thoroughly confused. "I thought you wanted to have sex."

Samantha jumped down from the bed. "I know what

you're trying to do. You're trying to confuse me and piss me off. Well, it worked. I'm confused and pissed." She looked at Gregory as if she might slap him. Realizing it was a bad idea, she headed for the door. She jerked it open, started to go out, then turned back, a sad look on her face. "I don't understand this. I've never had trouble getting any man I wanted . . . 'til you. Why don't you like me?"

The abrupt change in Samantha caught Gregory off guard. Earlier she'd been as pushy as a French whore. Now she looked like a broken-hearted little girl. Gregory sighed. "Samantha, long before you were born, I fell in love with a woman. I loved her very much and loved her for longer than you would ever believe. She's dead now, but not to me. She is always with me and will be for all eternity. That's why I won't let you stay."

"That's the most beautiful thing I've ever heard," Samantha wailed, more tears streaming down her face. "Can I stay and hold your hand?"

"Out," Gregory ordered.

After she left, Gregory walked out on the balcony at the back of the Estleford home. The town was dark, the night pitch black. He had told Samantha the truth and it surprised him that he'd talked to Samantha so openly. Maybe he had done so because he'd felt sorry for the girl. Or maybe it was just the outcome of an unnecessarily bloody night. He had taken a life for blood. Then five more because he'd been attacked—or simply because he'd enjoyed the sport. Then there had been the bartender. He had regretted that death. He had never liked killing even when it was necessary for him to survive, and the bartender's death bothered him greatly. It had been an ugly night. Ugly for him. Uglier still for seven human beings, and how many more before that during the nine hundred years he had existed.

When will this hell end? Gregory wondered, as he put his hands on the railing. Then he remembered. He was the Master Ancient. This hell would not end. It was eternal. Without realizing it, he tightened his grip on the wooden railing so hard it began to splinter in his hands.

At the same moment Gregory's power was crushing the railing, the creature from the island finally drifted ashore on a deserted beach sixty miles north of Seattle. Sensing the sun would soon be up, it prowled the rocky beach, looking for shelter. At the base of a nearby two-hundred-foot-high cliff it found a small cave, crawled inside, and fell asleep.

While the creature slept, it stirred because its dreams conjured up humans and the coppery metallic scents of their blood. It did not awaken, but it might have, had it realized its dreams were real. There were humans nearby, two hundred feet above on a wide green pasture at the top of the cliff. Sixty people, all sleeping the night away in an assortment of RV's, tents, trailers, and station wagons. Sixty human beings who made up the entire cast and crew of a porno movie company.

During the previous day's shooting the movie company had captured on videotape eleven hours worth of screwing, lesbian activities, and twenty-one cum shots. It was an all-time production record for the California crew who hated the Pacific Northwest. They'd been on location for two days. Tomorrow they'd wrap it up, and they'd be on their way back to Los Angeles the day after that.

Even by current porn film standards this particular movie was a big-budget production. The film's writer, director, and producer had made three other fairly successful porn films. Hoping to come up with the world's first "epic" porno film, the man behind all this, Winston Slade, had high hopes for his current production. He had to; he'd invested every cent he'd made off his previous films into this one, believing that this one would be the one to make him wealthy and give him the chance to do what he really wanted to do: write, produce, direct, and star in less lucrative films—gay porno films.

Near as Winston could tell, he'd covered all the bases. He'd hired all the popular male stars, including John "Mr. Fourteen" Rock and almost all the D-cup actresses in porn films, including Cindy Sin, the fastest-rising, biggest-boobed actress to hit the X-rated film screen in ten years. She was young, incredibly stupid, and a bitch to work with, but Winston didn't mind. The woman had presence on the screen and every film she'd ever made had done well at the box office, even better in video release.

He glanced at his watch. Six a.m. Time to get the production on the road. He grabbed his megaphone. Kicking open his RV door, he pointed the megaphone at the trailers, RV's, and tents. "Rise and shine, my pets. It's show time."

Her real name was Thelma Pushkin. Her stage name was Cindy Sin. She was nineteen years old. She'd been making porno films since she was fourteen. She got away with an early start in the business because at fourteen, she had the face of a twelve-year-old and the body of a Greek goddess with silicone implants. Only, in Cindy Sin's case, the breasts were real, and they were immense. She had run away from home five years earlier, knowing she could make a fortune in porno films if she could get to Hollywood. She did, and now she was making over two hundred thousand dollars a year. She was a contented woman. The work was easy and sometimes enjoyable, and the only time she felt uncomfortable was when a director had the gall to insist she memorize more than four lines of dialogue and then deliver them on camera without cue cards. Up since 5:30 and ready for work, Cindy Sin was in her trailer brushing her hair when she heard Winston Slade call out to his crew. She was the first one to report to Slade's RV.

Winston Slade nodded pleasantly to Cindy, then barked into his megaphone. "Come on, boys and girls, we've got a movie to wrap up. Report to the set immediately." In this case the set was an Indian village and a large rock constructed from chicken wire, plywood, and fiberglass. The movie's only other set, a one-sided, single-walled Royal Canadian Mountie fort, had been blown out to sea by a small windstorm on the previous day.

Winston turned his attention back to Cindy. She was wearing a Japanese kimono and thongs. "Got your Indian costume on?" he asked. She opened up the kimono to show Winston her Indian maiden outfit: a beaded necklace and a loincloth about the size of a postage stamp.

He lost his train of thought when John "Mr. Fourteen" Rock approached. John Rock was wearing his Mountie costume and carrying a copy of Winston Slade's script for the movie, all seven pages of it. Looking happier than usual,

Rock stopped in front of Cindy and Winston Slade and held up the script. "I finally remembered, Winston," he announced.

"Remembered what?" Winston asked.

"Remember me telling you I thought the plot of your film sounded familiar?"

Winston nodded tiredly.

"Well," Rock said, "I saw a movie on TV about a year ago. It starred Ann Blyth and Nelson Eddy or Howard Keel or somebody like that and it was about Mounties and Indians and maidens and it had the same story as your movie. Problem is, I can't remember the name of the movie."

Winston gave John Rock an innocent look. "The story came to me in the middle of the night. It's original, I assure you. Don't worry about it." He turned towards Cindy. "You ready for your grand finale?" She nodded. "It involves a group scene and some interesting variations in sex."

Winston draped his arm around Cindy's shoulder, and began to walk her towards the Indian village. "In the scene coming up, the Indians who kidnapped you when you were a child realize you've been seeing John on the sly and are planning to leave the tribe to settle down with this Mountie. So they're going to sacrifice you. But first, of course, they have to punish you. After John and his fellow Mounties rescue you . . ."

While Winston Slade was explaining the intricacies of the final scene to Cindy, the creature in the cave two hundred feet below the set stirred uncomfortably as sunlight filtered through the opening. It squirmed deeper into the cave. It found darkness, and just before it settled back into a dreamless sleep, it stirred slightly. It had finally picked up the scent of human blood, and it knew that somewhere outside the cave there was sustenance. Energy. Life. It smiled in anticipation of the night, then covered its eyes with its forearm and slept.

An hour after sunset Braille heard the distant thumping whine of a helicopter searching for him. The sound of the helicopter faded away into the night, but Braille did not relax. Where there was one copter there would be others. He broke into a lope, running easily amid the sagebrush and rocks, slowing only when he came to the edge of a cliff. He stopped and peered over. It was three hundred feet to the ground below.

Off in the distance he could hear the sounds of more helicopters coming in his direction. He swore and started over the side. Working by touch and feel, Braille began to slowly inch his way down the face of the cliff. He'd climbed down about twenty-five feet when three helicopters swept over the top of the cliff just above him. The sudden blast of wind caught him by surprise, catching him while he was groping for a handhold. He lost his grip, a toehold broke away, and Braille began to fall.

As he plummeted towards the rocks three hundred feet below, he had one brief thought: This is it.

"That's it," Winston Slade said into his megaphone two hours after sunset. "It's a wrap. We've done it. I love you all." And he meant it. Cindy and John Rock and the others had been superb. He'd captured a number of excellent wet shots on film, and was sure he had a smoldering million-dollar moneymaker on his hands. "Party at my RV in an hour," he added. "See you then."

As crew and cast began to walk towards their trailers, Winston smiled. Now all he had to do was put this film together. Do some editing, dubbing, correct a few mistakes, add a sound track and he had his movie and his ticket to the gay film industry. Just one more night on location, then it was back to Seattle and hot showers, toilets that flushed, waterbeds, and Raul. Raul was Winston's houseboy. The man was gorgeous. Forty-seven years old and he still had dimples. Raul was in Seattle looking after Winston's rented condo. How Winston missed those dimples and that silly accent!

A half hour later the creature emerged from the cave. It was naked. Its skin was red and mottled from the radiation on the island. It was weak, pathetically thin, but it possessed a frenzied animal strength, the kind of strength born from starvation, the need to survive, and the desire for immortality. The wind carried sounds of laughter and rock music down to the creature, along with the scent of blood. It looked up and knew instinctively that the scent on the wind would bring it energy and life and end its pain. It began to claw its way up the side of the cliff.

At the top the party was going full blast. Having brought his "epic" in on time and under budget, Winston Slade decided to give his cast and crew a party. He'd sent one of his staff off in a pickup with orders to fill the back with ice and hard liquor. Nothing was too good for his people. A half hour later, when his RV and two adjacent trailers were jammed with people, Winston broke out his own private stock of coke, hash, marijuana, quaaludes, and speed. In his RV alone there were enough lines of coke on the kitchen counters and end tables for someone to tag Winston with the nickname "the Snow Queen." Winston was just whipped enough to take the nickname as a compliment.

Hand over hand, foot over foot, the creature climbed the face of the cliff, the smell of blood pulsating in his nostrils. It was slow going. Rocks broke away. Handholds crumbled but it continued on, clawing and digging at the soft face of the cliff like a starving cat.

Winston's party was an unqualified success, so much so that it was over only two hours after it began. Surveying his empty RV, Winston Slade thought he'd done something wrong and was devastated. No one else thought that. No one else could think. The booze, pills, and coke had annihilated them.

Half an hour later things were still not going well for Winston Slade. He'd fallen in love with a young black man who was the company's grip. Winston didn't know what a grip did, but the title sounded positively intriguing, and he had gone after the man who'd come back to the RV looking for his wallet full bore, his actions fueled by a massive intake of coke and alcohol. Running on his tiptoes, practically naked, Winston ran headfirst into an open closet door. The impact knocked Winston on his butt. He fingered the growing knot on his forehead, decided he liked a challenge and chirped happily, "I love men who play hard to get." He got to his feet and charged onward. This time his heterosexual prey was waiting for him. Just as Winston rounded a corner, the grip flung open a second closet door, knocking Winston cold.

The grip stared down at Winston and hoped the man wouldn't remember anything in the morning. He needed his paycheck and didn't need to play games with a tutti-frutti director to get it. He found his wallet, tiptoed out of the RV, slipped back into his tent and the lighting girl who was waiting for him.

The creature clawed its way over the top of the cliff, got to its feet, then began to prowl the set and camp, looking for blood.

Moving by instinct, the creature entered John Rock's trailer. It found Rock and a woman in the bedroom. As it moved towards the sleeping figures, it knocked a lamp over, waking Mr. Fourteen. Rock sat up and came face to face with something straight out of hell. He opened his mouth to shout a warning and only blood came out. He tried to scream, but couldn't. He didn't have a throat. A heartbeat later he died. The creature took the rest of John Rock's blood. Still not satisfied, it turned its attention to the woman sleeping beside the dead man.

When it was finished, the creature stood up, wiped its mouth with the back of its hand, then moved out of the trailer towards a nearby canvas tent. With one swipe of its clawlike fingers, it split the side of the tent in half. It entered, dropped to its knees beside a woman in a sleeping bag, and killed her. As it started to drink her blood, the black man in the tent came awake, saw what was happening and scrambled away. The creature didn't notice. It was killing now, not out of need but out of enjoyment. Finished, it started for the other sleeping bag, but realized it was empty. The creature was not disappointed; it could smell other humans.

It slapped its way out of the tent and moved on to Cindy Sin's trailer. Unlike so many others, Cindy Sin was alone. She'd had sex with seven men that day and wasn't about to have sex with an eighth man tonight. Exhausted, she'd slipped away from the party early and before going to bed had made damn sure her trailer door was locked.

The sudden pounding on her trailer door did not surprise her. It always happened at company parties. During the filming of the movie all the male actors got theirs. At the wrap-up cast party all the male technicians tried to get theirs. No way, Cindy Sin thought as the pounding intensified. Not tonight. She was tired, chafed, and sore. No way. The pounding was beginning to sound like kettledrums inside her trailer. She tried to ignore it, but couldn't. Irritated, she flung aside the covers, reaching into her nightstand and pulling out a loaded pistol. She had no intention of using the weapon, but it had been her experience that after watching people screw for days, movie technicians would not take no for an answer.

Pistol in hand, she jerked open the door. "No—" she started to say, and then she saw the creature. Saw its red eyes and its Doberman-like teeth. Saw its radiation- and sunburned skin.

"What the fuck is this?" Cindy Sin demanded. "A Halloween joke?"

Full of blood and wanting to kill again, the creature started to enter. Shocked to numbness by its appearance, Cindy made no effort to step back. She just stood there while the creature wrapped its arms around her body and bit down on her throat. Suddenly horrified, she tensed, clenching her fists. The gun in her hand went off as she pulled the trigger. The bullet hit the creature in the foot. The creature screamed. Cindy Sin screamed. Both fell backwards. The creature landed in a heap outside her trailer. Cindy landed in a heap in her trailer with blood streaming down her chest. She fired again. The bullet plowed a furrow in the floor of her trailer.

The creature was hurt. Its foot was on fire. It hobbled off. At that moment the grip who'd earlier escaped from the tent started a generator, then hit a switch, activating some of the movie set's lights. The limping creature threw its hands up in front of its eyes as the lights flared on. Suddenly blind, it limped on.

The grip picked up a section of pipe and went after the

thing that had hurt his girlfriend. He chased it and was almost on top of it when it snarled and turned on him. He hit it once in the head, feeling the galvanized pipe vibrate in his hand. Then the creature was on him and they were rolling on the ground. The grip was strong; the creature stronger. It bit the grip viciously on the neck, then scrambled away. Still blinded by the bright lights, it hobbled on at a frantic pace, then suddenly realized it was falling. It had run off the edge of the cliff.

The creature fell almost two hundred feet, landing head-first on a large rock. The impact burst its head like a dropped overripe watermelon, splattering blood everywhere. A few minutes later the outgoing tide washed the rock clean, gently sweeping blood, brains, and the creature's body out to sea.

The gunfire and screams woke Winston. He stepped out of his RV to find his movie set in total chaos. People were screaming and running around. The generators were going, lights were on. He could smell gunpowder. "What's going on?" he shouted. Then he realized he didn't have his megaphone. He ducked back into his RV, grabbed the megaphone, and stepped back into the chaos. "What's going on?" he screamed into the megaphone.

Then, like a dream from heaven, the grip came out of the glare of lights and ran up to him. "We were attacked by a madman. He hurt Joanie bad."

"Joanie?" Winston asked, feeling his knees go weak.

"Joanie," the grip said, massaging the puncture wounds on the side of his neck. "You know, the lighting technician."

At that moment, Cindy Sin ran up to Winston. She was carrying a pistol in one hand, and like the grip, she was rubbing some cuts on the side of her neck. "Winston!" she screamed hysterically. "Something just bit me!"

The state patrol, the county sheriffs, and the police arrived an hour before sunrise.

Prodded awake by the freezing temperature, Braille came to just as the sun was coming up. Moving only his head, he checked his surroundings. He was lying spread-eagled on top of a large rock at the base of a cliff. For a moment he wasn't sure what had happened to him. Then he remembered the blast of wind from the helicopters and the fall from the top of the cliff that ended in blackness.

Still not moving, he tried to get a sense of his injuries. He wasn't in pain, couldn't feel much of anything for that matter. Good sign, he thought, using his stomach muscles to pull himself into a sitting position. He glanced up at the top of the cliff. He'd fallen almost three hundred feet and was still alive.

As he started to get to his feet, Braille put out his left arm to brace himself. The arm didn't work. He fell forward and cracked his chin, then slid off the rock. He landed on his back and slowly struggled to his feet, his eyes fixed on his left arm. It was just hanging at his side, unmoving. He willed his left hand to make a fist. Nothing. He tried to lift his arm. Nothing. No movement. No pain. No feeling. The whole left side of his body was dead. Even his leg.

Suddenly Braille felt cold and afraid inside. He reached back with his right hand and began to explore the upper part of his spine, working his fingertips steadily towards the base of his neck. At the third vertebra he found a lump of swelling the size of half a baseball and something more. There was a puncture hole in the swollen area. He explored the hole a moment more, then drew his hand away and examined his fingertips. There was blood and bone chips on his hand. He had punctured his spine when he'd fallen from the cliff and landed on the rock.

He took in a deep breath of cold air and studied the desert stretching out before him. It was crisp and sparkling in the early morning sun; a late-night frost had turned it into a sea of diamonds. Off in the distance he could see a bank of storm clouds heading towards him. He started walking as well as he could on a good right leg and a left leg that felt nothing and barely moved. Why couldn't he just be allowed to die? Braille wondered as he continued to hobble across the desert. Everything would just be so much simpler.

6

THE POLICE SPENT THE ENTIRE MORNING AND MOST OF THE afternoon investigating the gruesome triple homicide that had occurred on the set of Winston Slade's movie. The investigation took a heavy toll on the involved officers. The mangled bloodless corpses turned their stomachs and the butchery involved sickened everyone. All were at a loss to explain the conditions of the bodies and the motive of the killer. At one point a captain in the county sheriff's department phoned Seattle, the closest large city, and requested additional expertise. The Seattle police department dispatched a criminal psychologist and a forensic pathologist. The two experts arrived by helicopter. After examining the bodies, the clinical psychologist and forensic pathologist told the captain the slaughter was the work of a psychotic madman. As the two experts flew away in their helicopter, the sheriff gave the copter the finger. Why had he bothered to call the so-called experts in? Seconds after looking at the bodies, he'd figured out they had been killed by a psychotic madman.

He turned away from the helicopter in time to see the last of the campers, RVs, and sound trucks lurch down a narrow dirt road then disappear into the forest at the far end of the pasture. Good riddance to bad trash, he thought. The idea of a porno film crew invading his county appalled him. As he watched them depart, he hoped they'd all die of AIDS. All except for Cindy Sin. She was gorgeous. She took his breath away. And there was a strong chance she may have shot the psychotic madman. He liked her for that. He also liked her because she had big boobs.

"We're about done here," one of his deputies said. "We've interviewed everyone, got their names, addresses, and phone numbers, and swept the area three times. Didn't come up with a thing. If it's okay with you, the men would like to get out of here."

"Why the rush?"

"The sun'll be down in an hour. The men don't want to be here when it gets dark."

The captain raised an eyebrow. "The men want to go home because the sun's going down?"

The deputy shrugged. "Our job's done and there's no sense in staying around after the sun goes down." He glanced out over the edge of the cliff. The orange sun was sinking in the black waters. "As for being here after dark, well, some of the men don't like the idea. That rest stop where people keep disappearing from is only twelve miles from here. And I suppose you heard what happened in Stanwood last night—"

"I will fucking fire any man in the Everett Sheriff Department who is afraid of a rest stop and that—what happened in Stanwood?"

"Six men, five lumberjacks, and a bartender just disappeared from a bar last night. I guess you were talking to the M.E. when it came in over the radio. The town marshal found their cars and a lot of blood out in an alley, but no bodies. No nothing. To make it worse, somebody else disappeared from that same rest stop last night. That's seven people who just vanished, and if you want to count the three people who got butchered here last night, we're up to ten. Ten people missing or dead in one night!" The deputy's voice was starting to climb up through the octaves. He heard the fear in his own voice and brought it back to normal by faking a loud cough.

The captain turned away and swept his eyes over the crime scene. "Ten people?" The deputy nodded emphatically. "Have the men rope off the scene. We'll come back tomorrow."

7

IT WAS RAINING HARD IN SEATTLE, AND IT WAS DARK BY THE time the mismatched caravan of trucks, cars, and RV's pulled off the freeway and started into the older part of downtown Seattle. Since Winston Slade was the only one familiar with Seattle, it was his job to lead the convoy through the warren of narrow one-way streets in this part of the city to the hotel he'd rented for them.

He stopped for a red light. It was a long light. Winston looked out through the windshield. A black storm churned overhead, its low clouds obscuring the tops of the taller buildings lining both sides of the street like rock canyon walls. Lightning flashed, followed by a loud clap of thunder. The man sitting in the passenger seat across from Slade groaned as if he were in pain.

Finally, thought Winston. Finally the man stirs.

The man sitting next to him was the grip from his movie. A stunning man. Gorgeous. And boring. When the police had finally let them go, Winston had offered the grip and Cindy Sin a ride, knowing both had been through hell.

The grip's real name was Marvin Washington. He'd been fairly talkative earlier in the day, but after climbing into Winston's RV, he had become morose and silent. During the three hours it had taken them to drive down the coast to Seattle, Marvin had not said one single word. On the other hand, Winston had wanted to talk about the ordeal, purging himself in a cathartic manner. He'd tried to engage his passenger in conversation, but the grip had just sat there, staring out at the night and massaging those odd cuts he had on his neck.

The light finally turned green and Winston drove on through the dark wet streets of downtown Seattle. High overhead another clap of thunder broke loose and sheet lightning filled the sky. The storm was getting worse. The wind howling up the street buffeted the RV and threatened to turn it over. Winston gripped the wheel with both hands and was relieved to see the light in front of him turn red. He stopped and turned in his seat, looking back into the RV's dimly lit interior. Cindy Sin was sitting on a small davenport. She had been just as quiet as Marvin during the trip. And like Marvin, she too was massaging the cuts on her throat. What a pair of zombies, Winston thought as the light turned green.

Three blocks later the Casbah Hotel came into view and Winston turned off the street, drove down a ramp into the hotel's dark underground garage and stopped. A succession of vehicles parked in spaces around his RV. Car doors began to slam as the cast and crew headed for the elevator.

Winston lit a cigarette and drummed impatiently on the steering wheel while he waited for Marvin and Cindy to get out. After a long moment he glanced over at Marvin. Marvin was no longer staring out at the night. Marvin was looking at Winston as if he wanted to eat him.

Oh goodie, Winston thought. Maybe there's hope for the strong silent type after all. Suddenly Marvin's eyes began to glow like dull red coals in the dark RV. Wow, thought Winston, turning in his seat, intending to tell Cindy Sin to leave so he and Marvin could be alone. "I'll give you your paycheck tomorrow, Cindy," Winston said, pleased to see she was standing, but wondering why she was walking towards him and smiling.

Then Cindy Sin's eyes began to glow red and she brought her hands into view, her sharp red fingernails sticking out like bloody daggers. "Marvin, help!" Winston shouted, swiveling around in his chair, hoping to see Marvin moving to rescue him from this crazy woman.

What he saw was Marvin coming for *him*, teeth bared, fingers extended like claws, eyes glowing bright as Cindy Sin's. As Winston opened his mouth to scream, the creatures that had once been Marvin Washington and Cindy Sin leaped on him, smashing his body back against the steering wheel, setting off the RV's horn.

The horn blared away in the underground garage for almost a minute. Then it went silent.

In the cold silence that followed, two creatures—a male and a female—climbed out of the RV. Winston Slade's blood had only partially slaked their thirst, but there were no humans in the empty garage. They were starting up the rampway to the street above when they heard a single melodic bell go off. Both stopped instantly, whirled around, and dashed back down into the garage, weaving among the cars.

The elevator doors opened and five members of Winston Slade's cast who'd been unable to carry all their luggage upstairs on the first trip started to file out of the open doors, none realizing they would never make it to their cars.

Marvin Washington and Cindy Sin leaped on the group, the impact of their flying bodies driving all five back into the elevator. The elevator door closed automatically, muffling the shrieks of panic and terror and death. A few minutes later the door opened and Marvin and Cindy walked back out into the garage with satiated expressions on their faces.

A moment after that the elevator door automatically closed again, sealing up the hideous sight of five bloody bodies lying on the floor of a blood-splattered elevator.

The horror had begun. Infected, dead but undead, the five bodies in the elevator would rise, but not until the next night. Marvin Washington and Cindy Sin had taken all of Winston Slade's blood and he was dead. He would never become what the dead bodies in the elevator would become. He was one of the lucky ones; one of the few.

Marvin Washington and Cindy Sin ran through the night, elated, full of life and victory. It was still raining, the wind was blowing hard down the streets, and they needed a place to hide, to sleep. They ran up an alley, broke into the boarded-up back entrance to an abandoned hotel and took a rickety stairway down into the old hotel's basement. The basement was pitch black, full of cobwebs, old wine bottles, and the smell of urine. They didn't mind. Their instincts told them this was a good place, a place where they would be safe from the sun.

As Marvin and Cindy made their way through the basement, seeking the darkest corner, the rotten floorboards suddenly gave way and they were plunged into a subterranean world even blacker than the basement.

They landed unhurt on a grimy cobblestone street. Getting to their feet they found themselves surrounded by an underground city. The brick buildings on both sides of the street were old but perfectly preserved. Most of the buildings still had glass in their windows. There was a hundred-and-twenty-year-old gas street lamp on a nearby curb. Aside from a thick layer of dust, it looked almost new. Puzzled, but undisturbed by their surroundings, the couple began to investigate this city sealed off from the rest of the world by another newer city resting on a layer of steel beams and concrete forty feet above their heads.

Some hundred and thirty years earlier, the original buildings of Seattle had been constructed on a wide expanse of land sandwiched between steep sloping hills and the waters of Puget Sound. Overall, the founding fathers and early residents were pleased with their new city—until the seasons changed. Winter arrived, the rains began, high tide set in, and suddenly early Seattle was inundated with water every time the tide came in. Houses were flooded. Sewers overflowed. Cobblestone streets became creeks of mud. The citizens tried to cope, but a destructive fire in 1889 proved to be too much. The people abandoned the old city and went on to build a whole new city. They laid steel girders, boardwalks, and wooden beams over the top of the old city and built again. A new downtown Seattle began to grow, and its foundation was several square blocks of a perfectly developed, perfectly formed city with no access to the sky. It was in this vast underground city that Marvin Washington and Cindy Sin found themselves. They separated. Marvin fell asleep behind the counter of an old pharmacy. Cindy Sin wandered into a brick building that had once been a police station and promptly went to sleep in one of the jail cells. Both slept soundly with no feelings of remorse about what they had done earlier to six of their friends.

8

BRAILLE WANTED TO DIE. HIS LEFT ARM WAS STILL PARALYZED and there was no feeling in his left leg. He had spent the entire day avoiding OSMS jeeps and helicopters and now had a new problem—fever. He was burning up inside.

Throughout most of the afternoon he'd wandered aimlessly through the desert, unsure of what was going on or even who he was. Then, shortly after sunset, he came upon a large roadside rest park sitting beside a freeway that stretched across the desert.

Half delirious, he limped up to the cyclone fence guarding the back of the rest stop and knew this would be a challenge. He had never climbed a fence with one arm and one leg. He got up it, partly over the top, then his body gave out and he fell headfirst to the ground on the far side. He landed on his back, lying motionless while his strength returned. Then he got to his feet and scanned the rest area. It was huge, and in the moonlight he could see a large cement-block building for the toilet facilities, some vending machines, a couple of picnic tables, and a huge parking lot. There wasn't a car in sight. That was good, Braille thought. His head was beginning to swim and his eyes were out of focus. He was burning up inside, but he knew he couldn't stay here. He was right next to a freeway and a freeway meant patrols—more of Cutter's men. Time to go, he decided, forcing himself to let go of the cyclone fence he'd been using as support. He took a single step and collapsed in some thick bushes that camouflaged the fence from the public.

He knew he needed a place to hide and rest and heal, if he could heal, and this place was as good as any. As he lay on the ground, he realized that if he got blood, he would be all right. But could he kill another human being for his blood, a human who was not part of Cutter's army? Up until now he had killed and taken the blood of men trying to catch and kill him. But could he kill someone who had done him no wrong? Had he gone that far? he wondered, as exhaustion and fever overtook him and he fell into a fitful sleep.

9

A LOUD COMMOTION STIRRED BRAILLE FROM SLEEP. CHILDREN were crying, and it sounded like someone was beating on metal with a sledgehammer. More irritated than worried, Braille opened his eyes and found himself in a shallow ditch with bushes and high grass on one side of him and a fence behind him. It was still dark, and the night was filled with fog and a strange amber glow.

He roused himself, pushing himself to his knees with his one good arm. He'd fallen asleep at the edge of a rest stop. He hadn't slept long. It was around midnight. A heavy fog had settled over the rest area and the amber glow was coming from tall halogen street lamps in the nearby parking lot.

With effort Braille focused his eyes on the strange scene taking place in the parking lot. Twenty yards away an old brown station wagon had been boxed in by two shiny pickup trucks. Four men in baseball caps were prowling around the station wagon, pounding on it with their fists and a tire iron, trying to rip open the doors and swearing at its occupants. Weak and worried about Cutter's men, Braille remained where he was and continued to watch.

The four men milling around the station wagon were drunk, intent on getting inside, and the night was filled with their curses and threats. "Lady, we'll beat the shit out of your car if you don't let us in!"

"We won't hurt you. We just wanta have a little fun."

"Open the door, lady, or the windows go."

The light from the halogen lamps illuminated the men,

but it was dark inside the station wagon. All Braille could see were the shapes of two or three people huddled together in the middle of the front seat.

A man on the far side of the station wagon hit the passenger window with a tire iron. The window spider-webbed and the occupants in the wagon crowded over next to the driver's window. In that instant Braille caught a fleeting glimpse of a woman's face through the glass. She looked young and terrified and her screams of "Go away! Go away!" were as loud as the men's taunts.

"Lady," one of the men said, "you're making this worse than it should be. All we want's a little fun, then we'll go away."

Braille's expression was grim. The four men wanted to rape the woman. But it wasn't his problem. He had enough problems of his own. He was weak, sick, and paralyzed, and he couldn't help that woman any more than he could help himself.

One of the men broke the driver's door open with the tire iron and groped inside. An instant later he screamed and jerked his hand away. "She stabbed me," he bellowed. "She stabbed me with some fingernail tweezers."

The woman pulled the door closed, and once again Braille could see her terrified face. And he saw something more. There were two small children with her in the front seat. They were crying and as terrified as their mother.

In spite of his earlier feelings, Braille had begun to suspect he would try to help. After seeing the children, he knew he would. Somehow. He got to his feet and stepped out into the foggy parking lot.

"Eyebrow tweezers?" one of the men asked, laughing. "She stabbed you with eyebrow tweezers?" The man who'd been stabbed examined his hand. "Fuckin'-a. And it hurts." He crouched down, glaring into the interior of the station wagon. "No more games, lady. You get out here or we're coming in. If we do, there's a real good chance your kids'll get hurt when we do." Heavy fog and mist swirled around the parking lot like gray curtains while the men hunkered down around the car. Because of the fog, none of them saw the shadowy figure limp across the asphalt, stopping fifteen feet from the station wagon.

"He's right," said the large man with the tire iron. "If you make us come in and get you, your kids'll get hurt, maybe bad."

The woman unlocked the door and started to climb out.

"Get back in the car," Braille said, "and lock the door."

The woman and the four men turned, staring at Braille. Standing some ways away, Braille was a black shadow in the fog. None of the onlookers could make out the details of his face, but the glow from the halogen lights silhouetted a tall man with broad shoulders standing motionless, his arms hanging loosely at his sides.

"What the fuck you want?" the man with the tire iron asked while the woman closed her door and locked it.

"Let the woman go," Braille ordered.

That struck one of the men as funny and he laughed. "Why don't you make us let her go?"

Serves me right, Braille thought, knowing he should have dropped them all without any type of warning. But no, he had to try and talk them out of it. Now they knew about him, were getting ready for him, and somebody would probably die. Considering the shape he was in, it might well be him. "Well, hell," Braille grumbled, heading for the man with the tire iron. The others standing around the station wagon began moving to join their friend.

Braille decided to make his move before all four got together. The man with the tire iron was bracing himself, getting ready to swing, when Braille charged. Only it wasn't a charge, it was a gimping, halting walk. Bad move, Braille thought.

The man with the tire iron swung it hard at Braille's temple. Braille improvised as only a master in Tae Kwon Do, Akaido, and Shinto Ryu Karatedo can do. He pivoted on his good leg and stopped with his back to the man, reaching up and catching the oncoming tire iron in his right hand. The move caught his assailant by surprise. He tried to jerk it out of Braille's hand. Instead, Braille jerked it away from him. Before the man could move away, Braille whirled around, hitting the man in the head with his own tire iron. The man went down without a sound.

Braille heard the sounds of men coming at him from two

directions. He turned, intending to use the tire iron like a nightstick, but they were on him before he could bring it up. His bad leg buckled and he went down. The tire iron clattered across the parking lot. He thrashed over on his back with two men on top of him. Braille sat up violently, and in the same motion snapped his own head forward. He caught the closest man squarely in the face with his forehead. The impact shattered the man's nose and teeth. The man gasped, coughed, and fell to one side, trying to draw breath through a crushed nose and a mouthful of blood.

The other man got to his feet and started to backpedal away. Braille hooked the toe of his boot behind the man's legs and jerked them out from under him. The man fell back, cracking his head against the side of the station wagon.

Last man, Braille thought. He's behind me. Braille got to his feet, whirled, and before he could make a move, the last man plunged the sharp end of the tire iron into the center of Braille's chest. "Oh-ma-god," the man gasped, stepping back, his eyes locked on the shaft of metal protruding from the center of Braille's chest. "It was an accident. I didn't mean to kill you."

Braille glanced down at the tire iron lodged in the center of his sternum, then lifted his eyes and looked at the fourth man. "Get out of here," he whispered. The fourth man just stared at Braille incredulously. Braille took a grip on the tire iron with both hands and slowly pulled it out of his body. The woman in the station wagon gasped. So did the fourth man. There was no expression on Braille's face as he continued to look at the man. "Do what I said or I'll plant this in your chest." He held up the tire iron.

The fourth man rushed over to one of his friends who was trying to get up. He jerked the man to his feet, said something to him in urgent tones, and they carried the other two men over to a pickup, dropping them on the bed. Then the man who'd stabbed Braille got in behind the wheel. He shook his head in disbelief, gunning the pickup's engine before driving away.

Braille remained where he was until he couldn't hear the sounds of the pickup anymore. After a moment more he glanced over at the station wagon. Three faces were looking at him through the driver's window. A woman, a small girl, and a small boy. Braille barely saw them. He hadn't felt pain when the tire iron had been thrust in his chest. But he felt pain now; it was bad, getting worse by the second.

The tire iron slipped from his hand and he began walking slowly away from the station wagon. The desert in the distance looked cool and comforting, and he wanted nothing more than to get out of the harsh glow of the amber lights. He touched the hole in the center of his sternum and stumbled on, moving in a lurching, halting walk. The pain made it difficult to think, to see, to hear. Suddenly he stopped. There was an old brown station wagon parked out in front of him. That surprised him. He thought he'd walked away from it, but there it was, not more than ten feet away with its lights on, its engine running, and somebody getting out of it. But it didn't matter. The station wagon was turning into a distorted brown blur as though he were looking at it through the wrong end of a telescope. He felt his body begin to sag, felt himself starting to fall.

Then two strong arms grabbed him and he heard a woman's voice. "It's okay. I got you. Can you make it to the car?"

All Braille could do was nod. A small blond girl came out of nowhere to try and help her mother keep Braille on his feet. "Get back in the car, Amanda," the woman instructed. A boy, somewhat taller than the girl, came over and stared up at Braille with wide-eyed curiosity. "You too, John," the woman repeated. Then to Braille, "Lean on me."

He couldn't see her very well, but he had the fleeting impression of long, thick dark hair and a pale cameo-like complexion. She was tall and strong in a sinewy kind of way and it was easy to lean against her, trusting her as they moved haltingly towards the station wagon.

"John, open the door," she called out. Her voice dropped to a whisper. "Easy now. We're almost there. Duck your head . . . that's it."

Braille half-crawled, half-dragged himself into the back seat of the old station wagon. The woman crawled in beside him and knelt down on the floor. She turned on the dome light and gasped at what the light revealed. Braille was battered and bloody. The sun and freezing temperature had turned his complexion a dark ruddy brown. The skin on his forehead and cheeks was peeling. His shirt was in tatters and caked with old and new bloodstains. She started to unbutton his shirt, but the material parted like old cheesecloth. The skin under the shirt was the color of cream, and the perfectly round black hole in the center of Braille's chest was impossible to miss. "Dear God," the woman murmured in disbelief.

"He's got a hole in him, Mommy," piped a squeaky voice from the front seat.

The woman made a face. "Amanda, turn around and sit down."

"How come there's no blood?" asked the boy who was perched on his knees next to his sister, peering into the back seat with interest. "Think he'll die?"

The woman pulled her eyes away from Braille's wound. "Both of you turn around and sit down. And no, he's not going to die. We're going to take him to a hospital. He'll be fine."

Braille's eyes fluttered open. The woman next to him was a blur. He groped for her with his hand, found her arm, and gripped it fiercely. She winced under the strength of his grip but didn't pull away.

"No hospital," Braille rasped, struggling to sit up.

The woman put her hands on his shoulder and pushed him down. "You don't have a choice. You're burning up and you're hurt bad. Stop fussing before you hurt yourself worse."

She tried to pull away, but Braille held her firm. "I don't know how much longer I'm going to be awake so listen real hard. I can't go to a hospital." He closed his eyes and knew he had to trust this woman. He didn't have a choice. He'd be passing out soon and unless he told her *some* of the truth, he would end up in the hospital and then Cutter would have him. "Can't explain too much," he managed, "but there're people after me, not police, but people. An organization. If you take me to a hospital, they'll find me and I'd rather be dead than have that happen."

"But—?"

Braille shook his head feebly. "Then help me get out of your car. I'll be okay if I can get on my feet."

"But what if you die on me?" she whispered. "What then?"

In spite of the pain, Braille managed a feeble grin. "Then just stop the car and push me out . . . but please, no hospital . . ." Braille's eyes fluttered, then closed.

"Is he dead?" Amanda asked.

The woman shook her head. "No, sweetie. Just sleeping."

"He sure does smell," John commented. "Are we going to help him?"

"He got hurt helping us. We've got to help him," the woman answered.

"Gonna take him to a hospital?" Amanda asked.

The woman looked down at the man stretched out on the back seat of her car and wondered about him. What did he mean an organization was after him—but not the police. Who was this man? She understood the reason for the hole in his chest, but not the other injuries. Who was he? What had he been through?

"We gonna take him to the hospital?" John asked, leaning over the front seat for a better view of the hole in Braille's chest.

"No," said his mother, Mary Kathleen Stuart. She looked at the strange man again as she couldn't believe her own answer. What she was doing went against every fiber of her being. This man was unpredictable, strange, maybe dangerous, but she owed him. "He got hurt helping us," she heard herself say. "Now we have to help him. We're going to take him home."

"To the ranch?" her son asked.

"Yes," Mary Kathleen Stuart said.

10

WHILE BRAILLE SLEPT FITFULLY IN THE BACK SEAT OF MARY Kathleen Stuart's station wagon, the director of the OSMS was glaring at the other men in his office: Kendricks, Riddick, and a half a dozen other men, all wearing baggy camouflage-colored uniforms. The men looked haggard and were dirty. Hargrave Cutter turned his attention to the six men who had supervised the frantic and massive two-day search for Braille.

"I don't care how big you claim the desert is, and I don't care how crafty you claim our man is. You six have access to over seventy security personnel and Lord knows how many vehicles and helicopters. With all that going for you, you haven't been able to capture or kill one single man. I don't care what kind of toll the weather has taken on your men and equipment. You will continue to look for Braille until I say the search is over. Now get out." As the six uniformed men filed out of Cutter's office, Cutter turned to Kendricks. "Give me an update."

Kendricks took a step forward. "Golem is being modified and we've made some progress on the weapon you suggested. The major problem right now is the development of a lightweight shield that would protect the man firing the weapon." He shrugged. "The concept is workable, but we'll need a couple more days."

Cutter sat down behind his desk, lit a cigarette, and exhaled thoughtfully. "You've both read the Telex reports from the Everett and Seattle police departments?" Kendricks and Riddick nodded. "What do you think of what's happening over there on the coast?"

"Very strange," Riddick remarked, lighting his pipe.

Cutter waited a moment. When neither Riddick nor Kendricks said anything more, he looked at his men with contempt. "Strange and that's all? People disappearing from a rest stop? People disappearing from a bar not far from the rest stop? And finally, three people slaughtered on a movie set located not too far from that town or the rest stop and all you can say is strange? Jesus Christ, it's more than just strange. It's fantastic."

Cutter leaned back in his chair. "Gentlemen, I did some checking on the tides and currents in that area of Puget Sound at this time of year. Essentially what I found out is if you were to toss a piece of driftwood off Chinook Island it would eventually drift ashore in the general vicinity of Stanwood or a couple miles south of Stanwood where that movie crew was shooting their film." Riddick and Kendricks began to nod in slow realization as Cutter continued. "If I'm right, one of those New Ones escaped from the island, or Gregory's escaped. Maybe both, who knows?"

"Then that's why you sent for Kubick," Riddick mused.

"Very good," Cutter said. "If I can't have Braille and his blood, then I'll settle for catching myself a new vampire or better yet, I'll catch Gregory, the Master Ancient." Hargrave Cutter smiled. "I think Gregory survived that nuclear holocaust and somehow got off the island. I think he's alive and prowling the area where all those deaths and disappearances are occurring. I'm sending Kubick and his men out after our fabled Ancient."

"I always thought Kubick was a myth," Kendricks said, "like vampires."

"In a way he is," Cutter agreed. "But that myth and his men landed here about an hour ago." Cutter pushed a button on the intercom box on his desk. "Send Mr. Kubick in." Then he looked over at Kendricks and Riddick. "Getting him for this assignment will cost the OSMS a fortune, and I had to pull in a lot of favors at the Agency back in D.C. since they didn't want him working stateside, but I think it'll be worth it. If Gregory is as powerful as Braille said he was, we'll need the best to get him. Kubick is the best." At that moment the door to Cutter's office opened.

There was nothing distinctive about the man who entered. He was in his early forties, had closely cropped hair, a shiny complexion, and round wire-rim glasses. The man was just over six feet tall and was wearing a dark gray suit with wing-tipped shoes. There was something about the man's body and the way he carried himself that suggested he might have once been a gymnast or a swimmer, but overall there was nothing remarkable about the man. If anything, he resembled a bank teller. And that resemblance had fooled numerous people, costing some of them their lives.

Kubick was a professional killer, and one of the most dangerous men in the world. He was a master of several martial arts disciplines, was proficient with almost every killing weapon known to man. Kubick had been a professional killer for years. Occasionally he took on a solo assignment, but on most occasions he went with his team, nine battle-hardened professional mercenaries who would follow Kubick into hell if he asked them to. None of his men were as good as Kubick in the art of killing, but each one was deadly in his own right. When working together as a team, they were efficient, diabolically clever, and unstoppable.

While Kubick and his team were available to almost anyone with money, they primarily worked for two U.S. government agencies: the CIA and the NSA. Most bureaucrats in the agencies did not know about Kubick and his men. Those few who did associated the team with the deaths of Hoffa, an Italian Prime Minister, a Spanish general, a Vatican Cardinal, and a Cuban diplomat. The list was as endless as the killing techniques used. Aside from being proficient killers, Kubick and his team were brilliant at devising scenarios that always pointed the finger at someone else: Jack Ruby, Sirhan Sirhan, the Red Terrorist Brigade, the Basque Separatists, anyone and everyone but the contracting government agency. Kendricks had been right when he called Kubick a myth. His exploits were legend and almost no one knew him.

"You read everything I gave you?" Cutter asked.

"Of course," Kubick said.

"Then you understand what happened on the island and what happened to Braille after he was bitten by this Ancient. You know what you may be up against if this Ancient exists?"

"I read the reports," Kubick stated flatly. "Frankly, I think it would be more interesting to go after Braille than the Ancient. From what I can tell, this Braille took your place and your men apart single-handedly. Pursuing him would be interesting. As for the Ancient, I doubt if he even exists, but if he is out there I'll bring him back to you."

"I don't want him killed, you understand that?"

"I understand that, Dr. Cutter. If something goes wrong and we're forced to kill this thing, please know that the money you have given us will be given back to you. If you have questions, now's the time to ask." Kubick stood in front of Hargrave Cutter's desk, staring at the director for a full five seconds before turning and walking out of the room.

An OSMS jeep dropped Kubick off in front of a large Lear jet parked a quarter of a mile away from the huge old hangar. Kubick mounted the steps and entered the cabin of the specially designed jet. The front half of the cabin consisted of ten comfortable seats and a small wet bar. A bulkhead sealed off the back half of the craft from prying eyes. It was essential. Kubick and his men stored all their specialized equipment and weapons in the back half of the cabin.

Nine men were sitting in their seats, waiting patiently for Kubick's return. Without saying a word, Kubick walked directly to the wet bar and poured himself a glass of Perrier. Then he turned to face his men. He had their full attention.

"Gentlemen, you're going to find this hard to believe, but we've been recruited to go vampire hunting." One of his men snickered, others exchanged odd looks. Only Kubick's expression remained impassive. He had read Cutter's reports, read about Braille and what he had done to the OSMS complex and security personnel during his escape. If that was an example of what they were up against, they would have to take this assignment seriously, no matter how ludicrous it sounded. Still, a slight one-sided smile did cross his face. "Gentlemen, I'm serious. From what I've been able to gather and from what I've just read, there is a strong chance that there is a vampire out there, a very deadly, very powerful nine-hundred-year-old vampire. Our employer wants this creature badly and wants us to bring it in alive. Failure to do so will cost us our fee, which, as you all know, is substantial."

A strange look came into Kubick's eyes. "If this thing is

out there and if everything I heard about it is correct, we are facing an immense challenge. Moreover, I don't think it will be possible to bring it back alive." That comment got him some strange looks from his men. "I enjoy money as much as you do, but in this case it's not the fee that counts, but the confrontation. Confrontation with what may be the most powerful adversary we have ever encountered in our lives."

Kubick looked over at his team's pilot. "Plot a course to a town called Everett—it's north of Seattle—and turn on the intercom. I want you to listen in while I brief the others." The pilot nodded, got up, and entered the cockpit. A moment later the Lear's engines began to whine.

An hour and twelve minutes later the Lear jet touched down at an airport on the outskirts of Everett, an airport located thirty-five miles south of Stanwood.

At the same moment the plane was taxiing down the runway, Gregory stepped out onto the balcony at the back of the Estleford home. He put his hands on the railing and stared south into a black, cloud-filled night. He had felt the feeling for almost an hour, and now he was sure of it. Something was coming for him. A force—a collective force—knew about him, and they were coming. He did not know how he knew this, but he trusted the intuitive feeling. It had served him well for centuries.

Gregory continued to stare south. Yes, there was a power coming for him. A collection of wills and minds and energies. It was a formidable force. Whatever was out there had power. This was not a force to dismiss or take lightly. This was something to be reckoned with. So be it, he thought. Let them come. Let them confront him. Powerful as they were, they had never encountered an Ancient before and certainly not the Master Ancient. This was a good challenge, he decided. It would take his mind off his grief and give him something else to think about. This would be a good game.

He started to turn away from the night, then stopped. Still, how did they know about him and his location? Was Braille behind this? Had Braille somehow guessed he'd survived the holocaust and was now on the mainland? Gregory shook his head. He did not think that was possible.

Powerful as Braille was, he was still a human. He did not have the intuitive powers Gregory had after nine centuries of existence. No, Braille was not responsible for the force that was coming for him now.

The brief thoughts about the strange human Gregory had met on the island and had come to view almost as a brother brought an alien sense of remorse to Gregory. He and the cold and deadly human had almost been friends. But then the power plant had exploded and the radioactive cloud had destroyed Clementina, and Gregory's feelings for Braille had changed. Right or wrong, he blamed Braille for the loss of his woman and for the lonely eternal existence he now had to deal with. Someday they would come together and they would fight again. As before, Gregory would win. Only, this time he would not spare the human. But neither would he kill him. No, that was too merciful. He would inflict upon Braille the same curse he himself was forced to contend with. He would bite the human, contaminate him, then walk away, knowing that he had passed on to Braille the same curse he had to live with.

"I will give you my legacy," Gregory whispered. "I will make you like me. And I will kill the woman you left the island with, the woman you love. You will then live with your grief forever, just as I must live with mine."

11

THE SOUND OF A SMALL CHILD COUGHING VIOLENTLY BROUGHT Braille awake. He opened his eyes and tried to get a sense of his surroundings. He was in a car. It was still night. There was pain in his chest, his body felt on fire, and somewhere close, a small child continued to cough horribly, as if trying to expel its lungs. Then Braille remembered. He'd fought some men. A woman had helped him into the back of a station wagon, a woman who said she would take him to a hospital. Oh Christ, not that, he thought as he stirred, tried to sit up, and failed. And all the while, he could hear coughing, coughing he now knew was coming from the front seat.

The car was in motion, the tires making humming sounds on the pavement. He could see the back of the driver's head. It was the woman who had helped him into the car. She kept glancing to her right, dividing her attention between the road and the coughing child next to her. She was murmuring soft things, trying to comfort the child. Braille picked up the words "medication" and "inhaler" and gentle cooing comments intended to soothe the child. Somehow it worked. The child's coughing began to subside. Then he heard the child whimper and knew it was the small girl called Amanda who'd just gone through the horrible coughing fit. Some minutes later came a boy's voice. "She's asleep." The woman nodded, continuing to drive as Braille felt exhaustion and sleep coming for him once again.

Stillness and silence woke Braille like a clap of thunder. The car was stopped. He tried to sit up, but pain and weakness kept him pinned to the seat. He despised his helplessness. If at that moment Hargrave Cutter, the man responsible for Leslie Chapel's death, had walked up to the car and opened the door, Braille would not have been able to do a thing to the man. Nothing.

Then the car door opened.

Braille lifted his head, opening his eyes. It was dark, and all he could see was a shadow standing outside the open door. It was Hargrave Cutter.

"You killed her," Braille hissed through clenched teeth. He tried to sit up and tried to reach out with his hands to strangle Cutter but couldn't. "You killed her."

The shadow outside the car shook its head. Then a woman's voice. "I don't know what you're talking about. I didn't kill anyone. Now let's get you up and into the house."

Braille relaxed, lifting up his right arm. She took it in both hands, pulling while he sat up. A couple of minutes later he was on his feet, with his good arm wrapped around the woman's shoulder, trying to make out where he was. Delirious as he was, he could see a two-story farmhouse in need of repair and paint. The home was surrounded by an unkept lawn and tall, leafless cottonwood trees. Off in the distance he could make out the shape of a dilapidated barn, run-down sheds, and the remnants of corral fences. The farm and its buildings were nestled up against a dark gray foothill.

"It's not much," she said, straining under his weight as they began to move towards the house. "But at least it's not a hospital."

Locked together, they covered a dozen yards. Then she stopped. "Just a sec," she said, out of breath. She took several deep breaths, got her strength back, and took a new grip on the arm draped around her shoulder. "Look, before I take you into my house, there're some things I gotta know about you. Okay?"

Braille nodded, continuing to lean against her.

"Are you wanted by the law?"

Braille shook his head.

"Can I get in trouble if I get caught with you in my house?"

Braille shrugged. "Don't know," he managed in a whisper.

"I knew you'd say that," she grumbled. "Next question. Are you running away from a mental hospital or something like that?"

Braille cracked a slight smile and shook his head.

"Now for the most important question," she said. "Do my children have anything to fear from you?" She stopped, looking into his eyes. Braille shook his head.

They made it to the house, struggling up steps and across a screened-in porch, through the front door and into the living room. She helped him lie down on an old worn davenport, kneeling down beside him. "Listen to me carefully. You're gonna stay on the couch. My bedroom is just down the hall and so are my children's. Now, if you try to get into my children's rooms or mine, I'll shoot you. I keep a pistol in my night stand. I've never shot anyone, but I think I could if I thought my children were in danger. Understand? I haven't forgotten about what you did for us, it's just that I don't know you, so I'm trying to set out some rules."

Braille turned so he could see her. It was dark in the living room and all he could make out were wide eyes and a white face. "Can I have some water?"

She got to her feet, limping out of the living room. She returned carrying a glass of water in one hand and a coffee can in the other. Again Braille noticed the limp. She put the can on the floor, then held the glass to his lips. When Braille finished, she dabbed reluctantly at his lips with her fingertips. "I'll leave the water here next to the coffee can. I don't think you're in any shape to make it to the bathroom, so use the coffee can if possible. But if you can't, don't worry about it. The couch is as old as Methuselah. I'll get you some blankets." While she walked away, Braille angled his head so he could watch her leave. She moved into the nearby hallway, turning on a light. Just before she disappeared down the hall, Braille caught a brief glimpse of a strip of chrome that went up her right leg. It took him a moment to realize it was a leg brace.

Moments later she reemerged with some blankets, covering him up. "You going to be okay?" she asked. He nodded. "Look, what I said about shooting you a few minutes earlier, I didn't mean it. It's just that I'm real protective of my children. Real protective."

Braille motioned her closer. She sat down on the edge of the davenport, careful not to touch his body with hers. "Thanks for not taking me to the hospital," he whispered.

"You didn't give me a choice."

"Am I going to be hard to explain to your husband?"

He couldn't make out the expression on her face, but he could hear the hardness in her voice. "My husband's dead. Died two years ago. Anything else?"

"Sorry," Braille managed. "What's your name?"

"Mary Kathleen Stuart."

Suddenly they both heard the sounds of a child coughing violently. "Damn medication's not working," Mary Kathleen said, getting to her feet.

"What's wrong?"

"My daughter's sick. That's why we were on the freeway tonight. I have to take her to a special clinic in Seattle once a month. Don't know why I do. The trip's hard on her, and the doctors over there can't . . . don't seem to be able to . . ." she broke off in mid-sentence, wiping her face with the back of her hand. She sighed tiredly. "But we keep going once a month because it's the only thing we can do. It's the only place where Amanda can get treatment."

"What's wrong with Amanda?" Braille asked, immediately regretting the question because it made him feel as if he were intruding into this woman's private life.

"My daughter has cystic fibrosis," Mary Kathleen whispered, looking towards the sounds of the coughing. "I've got to go. She needs me." She gestured at him. "What's your name?"

"Braille."

"Well, Mr. Braille, I already got enough problems of my own, so don't you go dying on me tonight." She gave him a flat smile she didn't mean.

A moment later he was alone. He shifted on the couch, trying to get comfortable. The movement only brought pain, reminding him he had no use of his left arm and only partial use of his leg. Still, he was better off than Mary Kathleen's little daughter. He'd heard of cystic fibrosis and knew it had something to do with a congenital malformation of the pancreas that resulted in continual and severe respiratory infections. The disease affected children and death was common, especially in young girls. Poor child, Braille thought. Poor mother. Nearby a clock on a mantel chimed twice. Braille closed his eyes.

A ravenous hunger woke Braille. His eyes snapped open and he sat up. He knew the hunger and had felt it before. He knew food would not drive it away. The craving had come to him many times before during his weeks of confinement at the OSMS, and while he had never said anything to his captors, he had found himself looking forward to his injections of blood because blood was the only thing that would end the craving. After escaping, he'd taken blood from his pursuers, but how long had that been? One night? Two? He had not felt the craving since then, maybe because he'd satiated himself or maybe because there were no humans around. But the craving was back, hideously strong, and this time there were humans around. Three of them. He could smell their blood. They were so close.

It would be so easy.

The beginnings of a low growl rumbled in his throat as he slowly rose to his feet. The entrance to the hallway leading to their bedrooms was just fifteen feet away. It would be so easy. Just a matter of sinking teeth into flesh and drinking warm blood. Then the pain and hunger would end; his injuries would heal. The hole in his chest would close up. His body would become alive. So hideously easy. Two children and a woman. They were sleeping. They would never know what happened to them. He would make it fast; they would feel no pain. The low predatory rumble continued in his throat. He could hear the animal noise he was making, and somehow the rasping growl gave way to a quiet desperate, "NOooo . . ." Weeks of being chained up had left his fingernails long and jagged and he clenched his fist until his fingernails cut into his palm. Pain shot up his arm. He could feel his fist fill with blood, but he wouldn't stop. He remained motionless, fighting his addiction, the hunger, with pain and his mind.

He didn't know how long he stood frozen and mute while he fought his body's demand for blood, but when he finally opened his eyes, the sun was coming up. It wasn't much of a sunrise, just a thin line of silver made jagged by faraway hills.

The craving was gone. The need—the demand—for human blood was gone. He relaxed visibly, his shoulders sagging in relief. His fingernails were still deeply embedded in his flesh, and as he walked into the kitchen he worked them free, flexing his hand. This time he had conquered the alien desire. But what about the next time? It was then he decided he would leave this family as soon as he was able to travel.

He washed his face with water from the tap, then scrubbed it dry with paper towels. On impulse he opened the refrigerator. It was stocked with a standard array of staples: fruits, vegetables, milk, cheese. And a large slab of bloody red meat lying on a piece of butcher paper.

Everything he saw turned his stomach . . . except the meat. He grabbed up the meat and the butcher paper, carrying it over to the counter. He lifted it up in one fist and bit down into the raw flesh with his teeth. It was foul and repulsive, but he couldn't stop. He went at the meat like a shark in a savage feeding frenzy, tearing, ripping, swallowing, tasting the blood, tearing at the meat again and again.

Then he gagged, throwing up violently. When he was finished, he looked at the butcher paper through watery eyes. There was a white label on the paper, a label in feminine handwriting: "lean lamb." Earlier Braille had felt a sense of satisfaction over controlling his urge for human blood. But this new urge for raw sheep meat confused him, making him feel out of control again.

The butcher paper was lying in front of him, holding a large amount of blood that had pooled up from the meat. He touched the liquid with his finger, then lifted his hand into the weak gray light filtering in through the kitchen window. A single droplet of blood dangled from his finger. The droplet captured the cold rays of the sun, glistening warmly in the light like a ruby-colored prism. Instinctively Braille licked up the droplet. An instant later he lapped up the blood puddled on the paper. As before, he was appalled and horrified by what he had just done. It was almost as if he had no control over his actions or appetite. My God, he thought. What's going on now? He straightened up, noticing his reflection in the kitchen window. He was haggard and dirty. There was stubble on his face and something more: *blood*.

Picking up a wire brush and a bar of soap, he scrubbed his face until his skin was raw. Then he rinsed and looked at his reflection again. He didn't look much better, but at least the blood was gone. He was turning away from his reflection, when he heard Amanda Stuart begin one of her coughing spells. It was a bad one, and he could almost feel the pain the child felt with each explosive fit. Ten seconds later Mary Kathleen Stuart got up, padding into her daughter's room. A moment after that Braille heard the sounds of hard rhythmic slapping, flesh on flesh, as if Mary Kathleen were beating her daughter with an open hand. Then he realized she was. Amanda's mother was hitting Amanda on the back, trying to loosen the phlegm, fluid, and mucus clogging her daughter's lungs. Braille remained where he was until the coughing subsided and Mary Kathleen returned to her own room.

He turned back to look at his reflection, then shook his head at his own woeful state of mind. "And you think you got problems," he asked himself. "You just heard a little girl cough her lungs out, heard a mother beat her own daughter to help her, and you're feeling sorry for yourself because you ate some raw meat?

"You got a disease. Now fucking deal with it."

Returning to the living room, he sat down on the couch, absent-mindedly fingering the hole in his chest. It felt different. Craning his head forward, he examined the wound. It *was* different. The swelling around the outside of the hole was gone; the hole was smaller. He stretched out, wondering if there was some sort of chemical connection between human blood and sheep blood. Had to be, he decided, closing his eyes. He was healing now, just like he had in the laboratory of the OSMS after they'd hurt him then given him an injection of blood. Had to be a connection, he decided.

The thought gave him a faint feeling of hope.

12

AFTER LANDING AT THE EVERETT AIRPORT, KUBICK AND HIS men had separated. Each had gone on to rent cars or vans from different rental agencies, then checked into motels strung along a busy boulevard close to the airport. Most of the men tried to catch a few hours of sleep. In Kubick's case, he chose to assume a yoga position in his Holiday Inn motel room, meditating for four hours. At exactly eight in the morning he opened his eyes, feeling rested and refreshed. After shaving and dressing, he trotted down a stairwell to the motel's restaurant seven stories below. Then he bought a map at the front desk, returned to his room and taped it on a wall, waiting for his men to arrive.

There was a certain sameness to the nine men who entered Kubick's room. All were dressed in nondescript business suits and none had any personal features which would make them stand out in a crowd. This was no accident. Kubick knew from experience that many mercenaries—which was exactly what he and his men were—were rowdy, flamboyant individuals who enjoyed drawing attention to themselves. Not Kubick's men. They were quietly confident, highly skilled professionals.

With his men grouped around him like disciples, Kubick began. "I filled you in on the plane last night about what may have happened on Chinook Island so I won't go into it now." He turned to the map, tapping it with his finger. "About thirty hours ago, three people who were part of a movie crew were killed here and had their throats ripped out." His finger traveled half an inch to the north. "This is Stanwood, and the important thing about this place is that the night before last, six full-grown men disappeared from a bar in this town. They haven't been heard from since." Kubick moved his finger half an inch to the right. "Fourteen miles east of Stanwood is a freeway with a large rest stop. The important thing about this rest stop is that during the past eight weeks at least eight people, and maybe more, pulled in here to take a break and were never heard of again. What we have here are three interesting locations: a movie set, a small town, and a rest stop. The first thing we're going to do is forget about the movie set." That remark got him several interesting looks from his team.

"According to our employer, what we are after is intelligent, crafty, and not interested in drawing attention to itself. I don't know who or what killed those movie people, but whatever it was, it wasn't crafty and it didn't give a damn about drawing attention to itself. Instead we're going to focus our attention on the town and the rest stop. It takes a lot of work and energy to hide a body so it doesn't get discovered. Somebody or something going back between the town and the rest stop may have hidden fourteen of them. That's why I'm narrowing the focus to those two specific areas.

"We'll divide up into two teams. One team will cover the rest stop. The other will cover Stanwood. The town'll be a relatively simple matter because it's small. Current population around six hundred. It shouldn't be too hard to check around and find out if there's somebody new in town, someone who arrived around eight weeks ago and who probably doesn't have any visible means of support. If you come across someone like that, pull back. We'll assess what we have, do static surveillance if necessary, and if it is what we're after, then the team as a whole will work on containment or elimination. Gentlemen, never forget that what we're after may well have disposed of fourteen people. Do not take it lightly. Do not underestimate its powers.

"The second team will handle the rest stop. It's my understanding this rest stop has a couple of motels, some restaurants, several gas stations, and a large park-like area. Since whatever we're after is nocturnal, we'll use a static mode of surveillance: two men to a van using standard infrared devices, motion, and thermal sensing devices and some of the other goodies we brought up with us. There we have it. Questions? Input?"

The meeting broke up forty-five mintues later and the men trickled out of Kubick's room, each taking a different route back to his car.

13

BRAILLE FELT A GENTLE TUG ON HIS EYELASHES, THEN SOMEONE took his eyelashes, lifting his eyelid up. Braille focused his one open eye and found himself looking into a wide blue eye looking back at him. Small fingers let go of his eyelashes, and his eyelid closed. Awake now, he opened both eyes. This time he found himself being scrutinized by two small faces not more than a foot away from his.

"See," said a boy not more than seven years old. "He's not dead."

A small girl who looked a couple of years younger than her brother gave her brother an exasperated look. "Well, I thought he was dead. I poked him and he didn't move." She turned her huge blue eyes on Braille. "Hi," she said brightly. "Why you sleeping with your clothes on?"

Braille smiled faintly. "Didn't have any pajamas."

"You want some coffee?" the small girl asked.

It was difficult to talk. The inside of his mouth felt as if it had been layered with cotton. "Please," he managed.

The girl trotted off to the kitchen. Her brother remained behind, his eyes flicking between Braille's face and the blanket covering him. Braille could tell the boy wanted to ask him something and was working up the nerve. Finally he leaned close to Braille's ear. "Can I see the hole in your chest? I saw it last night. I just wanta see it again."

Braille brought his good hand under the blanket. All that his fingers found was a slightly raised lump of soft flesh. He gave the boy an apologetic look. "I think it's gone."

"Nawh . . . it couldn't go away that fast. You're just worried I might get sick, but I can take it. I watched Dad debeak chickens and I used to watch Joe cut the rainers off cows."

Braille sat up with slow stiff movements. "Who's Joe?"

"Joe worked for Mom, but he took off a while back. Now can I see the hole?"

"What's a rainer?" Braille asked, suspecting he knew.

"It's what cows go to the bathroom with. Now can I see your hole?"

Braille let the blanket drop and parted the remains of his shirt. They both stared at a puckered pink circle of flesh in the center of Braille's chest.

"Wow," the boy said. "It went away." He sounded disappointed.

"Told you." Braille tried not to smile. "Where's your mother?"

"She's outside. I'll get her." Before Braille could stop him, the boy dashed out the front door and out on to the porch. "Mom," he shouted. "The man's awake. And his hole's gone."

The girl came back into the living room carrying a mug of coffee in both hands. Braille pulled the blanket up around his chest and accepted the mug gratefully. "I'm Amanda," she said. Suddenly she clapped both hands over her mouth.

116

Turning away beginning to cough, Braille waited for the spasm to pass. When it did, Amanda turned around and he could see there were tears in her eyes. "I'm not crying. My eyes always get wet when I cough."

Braille nodded, studying the child. She was tiny, had short auburn hair, and the widest blue eyes Braille had ever seen.

Just then the front door opened and closed. The boy and his mother walked into the living room. It was the first time he had seen her in the daylight. Braille could see that Mary Kathleen Stuart was the spitting image of her daughter. Beautiful complexion, long auburn hair, and bright blue eyes, but unlike her daughter, Mary Kathleen limped. Without meaning to, Braille's eyes dropped to the woman's right leg. She was wearing jeans and cowboy boots. The boot on her right foot had been altered. Chrome bars bolted to the heel of the boot extended upwards and disappeared into the leg of her jeans. Realizing he was staring, he looked up at her face in time to see her expression become hard and brittle.

"Like my boots?" she asked.

Braille kept his eyes fixed on hers. "They're very nice."

Her eyes flicked over to her daughter and back to Braille. "I see you've met Amanda." She put her hand on her son's shoulder. "This is John Junior." The boy stiffened. "Sorry," his mother added, looking down at the boy. "Just John."

Braille nodded. "Lo, John."

"Show Mom the hole in your chest," the boy said excitedly.

"John . . ." Mary Kathleen warned through clenched teeth.

"But Mom, it's all gone."

She looked at Braille strangely. "What's he talking about?"

"It's just better," Braille said uncomfortably. "It's healing. There's a clot over it." He waited until Mary Kathleen looked away, then gave John a sinister look and mouthed the word "tattletale." The boy grimaced and mouthed the word "sorry."

"You feel like trying to get up?" Mary Kathleen asked.

"I think so."

"Good. I'll go get you some clothes. Then we'll get you cleaned up."

"Yeah," Amanda said, wrinkling her nose. "You don't smell very good."

"Amanda," Mary Kathleen said, smiling in spite of herself.

"Well, he doesn't," Amanda insisted.

The woman disappeared down the hallway, returning a few minutes later carrying a pair of folded jeans, a blue denim work shirt, socks, and a tan belt. There was a blue plastic disposable razor on top of the clothes. Braille struggled to his feet. He accepted the bundle and looked at Mary Kathleen questioningly.

"They belonged to my husband," she said. "He was about your size. They should fit, and I keep the razor on hand to shave my legs," she added unnecessarily and caustically.

"Thanks," Braille said, wondering if the cause of her continual bitterness was the loss of a husband, Amanda's disease, or her bad leg.

"The bathroom's down the hall, to the left. There's peroxide, Mercurochrome, and some antibiotics in the medicine chest. The pills are kind of old, but it wouldn't hurt to take some. You had a hell of a fever last night."

After closing the door, Braille peeled off his clothes and boots. He stepped into the shower and adjusted the water until it was scalding. Painful as the stinging spray was, he could have spent the entire afternoon under it. Braille then toweled dry, wiped steam from the mirror and examined his chest. It had indeed healed up, but his left arm and leg were still useless.

Mary Kathleen Stuart was making a sandwich when Braille walked into the kitchen. She glanced over at him disinterestedly, went back to the sandwich, then looked at him again as if she couldn't believe her eyes.

"What is it?" Braille asked, suspecting she was staring because he was wearing her dead husband's clothes.

"Nothing." She broke off the stare and turned back to the counter. "You just look different than I expected."

And he did. The change was startling. The man she'd sent off to the shower had resembled a battered, down-and-out derelict. Dirty hair, a five-day growth of beard, smelly, ragged clothes. The man who had just walked into the kitchen was ruggedly handsome with dark brown eyes and classic features. Unconsciously she fingered her own hair, brushing some wisps back into place as she found herself wondering if she'd put lipstick on that morning. "You missed breakfast and lunch, so I thought I'd make you a sandwich. Bologna okay?" Braille nodded. "Then sit down. I'll have it ready in a minute." Braille sat down at the kitchen table. It felt good to sit. He was still weak, and he rested his chin on the heel of his hand, closing his eyes.

Mary Kathleen looked at him again, liking what she saw and not liking herself for looking. He's just a man, she thought bitterly as a wave of ugly memories rose up inside her. "You want milk or soda?" she asked.

"Milk," Braille said, opening his eyes.

Opening the refrigerator, she stared into it for a long time, then pulled out a carton of milk. When she turned around, there was a puzzled look on her face. "I could have sworn—" She shook her head instead of finishing the sentence.

"What?" Braille asked, stifling a yawn. God, he was tired and all he had done was take a shower.

"I was going to make some stew tonight but the meat's gone. I must have forgotten to take it out of the freezer."

Braille relaxed, turning his attention to the sandwich. He had been kept alive with injections of blood during his time at the OSMS and hadn't eaten regular food in almost nine weeks. He took a bite out of the sandwich and swallowed it cautiously. The food had a bland, almost metallic taste to it, but he could handle it, he thought. And he was hungry. He finished the sandwich and picked up the glass of milk, downing it in one motion. An instant later his stomach muscles knotted up as the worst cramps he'd ever experienced threatened to tear him in two. He gasped, pushing himself up from the table. He lurched backwards, knocking a chair over as he tried not to cry out.

"What's wrong?" Mary Kathleen shouted.

Braille was in too much pain to speak. He bit his lip, whirling around and heading down the hallway. He started throwing up just before he hit the bathroom door and managed to finish heaving in the toilet. Afterwards, when there was nothing more inside him, he slowly got to his feet. He washed his face with cold water, then used the towel to clean up the toilet and floor. The commotion had woken John and Amanda and they were waiting for him as he mopped his way out into the hallway.

"Yuk," Amanda observed. "You made a mess."

"Was it the sandwich?" Mary Kathleen asked, leaning against the wall at the far end of the hallway.

Embarrassed and still sick, Braille shook his head and continued to mop the floor. He couldn't look at her, couldn't look at the children. "Flu, maybe," he finally said, shaking his head bitterly. Christ, there was no rhyme or reason to what just happened. He could drink blood and tolerate bologna sandwiches, yet milk almost tore his stomach in two.

With slow stiff movements, he got to his feet. The knotted muscles in his stomach burned, and he was exhausted. "What do I do with the towel?"

Fighting back her concern for the stranger, Mary Kathleen shrugged. "Put it in the hamper. I'll wash it later."

He did. "I'm very tired." It was difficult for him to form the words. His speech sounded slurred. It wasn't a lie. He was exhausted.

Thirty seconds later the man Mary Kathleen Stuart knew only as Braille was asleep on her living room couch, and her children were battering her with questions. "What's wrong with him? Will he work for us like Joe did? Will he run away like Joe did? Do you like him? Why is he sleeping in the afternoon? What's his name?"

All those questions and only one answer, she thought.

"He said his name was Braille."

14

THE HEADQUARTERS OF THE SEATTLE POLICE DEPARTMENT WAS located in downtown Seattle in a large modern building which stood out in marked contrast to the seventy- and eighty-year-old dark gray office buildings surrounding it. The Seattle police department was one of the most modern and up-to-date police departments in the United States. It was computerized, had high-tech laboratory equipment, consulting psychiatrists, forensic pathologists, and a myriad of other specialists on its staff, including a full-time public and press relations specialist named Perdue. Perdue generally enjoyed the press conferences he held. But not in this case. Because the department hadn't given him any information, he wasn't able to answer the reporters' questions, and when they started to heckle and shout at him, Perdue clenched his teeth and snarled, "The conference is over." He elbowed his way through the throng of reporters, escaping into the main elevator. The elevator took him to the basement. After it opened, he walked down a wide hallway to a gray door with the word PATHOLOGY on it.

Perdue entered and walked over to the young secretary. He pointed to another door. "They about through in there?"

She nodded. "They finished up about fifteen minutes ago. Go on in. They've been expecting you."

Perdue entered a large room with tiled walls, a tiled floor, and six autopsy tables, two of which were being scrubbed down by two attendants. A third attendant was pushing a gurney through a set of swinging doors into another room. Perdue was able to catch only a brief glimpse of what was on top of the gurney, but it was enough. He knew he'd just seen one of the people who had been killed in the elevator of the Casbah Hotel. He shuddered.

He walked over to two men who were leaning against a

counter, drinking coffee and talking in hushed tones. Both men were wearing surgical smocks, and one of the doctors gestured to the coffeepot as Perdue approached. "Coffee?"

Perdue shook his head impatiently. "What I want is information, answers about what happened to those people killed at the Casbah. Twenty reporters just ragged my ass and I wasn't able to tell them a damn thing, but it's about time I do. What have you got?"

"Problems and questions," said one of the physicians.

"Problems?"

"Problems," said the same physician, "as in this is Sunday and the Chief Medical Examiner's gone sailing and nobody knows how to get ahold of him."

"But you did do autopsies on the bodies from the Casbah?"

This time the other doctor responded. "Yeah, we did. But because of the rush job everybody wanted on this, the autopsies were superficial, which is to say we examined the bodies, but didn't open them up and remove any organs. Then things started getting a little strange, so we thought we'd better leave the rest of the examination to the M.E. . . ."

"But you did come up with something?" Perdue asked impatiently.

"Mainly questions," the first doctor said. "But I'll tell you what we know. Something or someone killed six people in the basement of the Casbah Hotel. All the bodies had their throats torn out."

"Say again?" Perdue asked.

"Those people look like they were attacked by a pack of wolves."

"Gimme a break."

"We're serious. We found a lot of torn and mangled flesh, bite marks, and puncture holes that resemble the canine teeth pattern you might find in a wolf."

"Jesus Christ," Perdue said. "Are you saying a pack of wolves killed these people?"

"No. We also found traces of saliva on the victims' throats, and it wasn't animal saliva."

The other doctor coughed and cleared his throat. "On the other hand, it wasn't exactly human saliva either."

122

"But it was sort of more human than animal," said the first doctor.

Perdue closed his eyes, pinching the bridge of his nose.

"Oh it gets worse," the second doctor said. "There's even more strange shit going on. You know what postmortem lividity is?"

Perdue shook his head.

"After someone dies, the circulation system quits and gravity causes the blood to settle in the lower parts of the body where it turns the flesh red or purple. It's called hemoglobin staining."

Perdue still looked confused and the physician tried again. "If a man dies while he is lying on his back, the blood settles into his buttocks and along the ridge of the spine. When that happens, the skin in those areas gets blotchy and turns purple because that's where the blood ends up and—"

"So what?" Perdue said, interrupting.

"Postmortem lividity always occurs. People die. Their blood settles. It's a fact of death. It has to happen—unless there's no blood in the body. Now, those people in the elevators had blood in their bodies. But their bodies aren't showing signs of postmortem lividity. We can't figure out why."

More worried about wolves, people imitating wolves, and the reporters on the first floor, Perdue said absent-mindedly, "So their skin didn't turn purple—so what?"

The explaining physician sighed. "You want to hear about the other weird things going on? Their body temperatures aren't going down. They've been dead approximately twelve hours and the body temperatures of those found in the elevator aren't going down. In addition, none of those bodies are showing signs of rigor mortis, and on top of that there's the problem of involuntary body movements. All dead bodies move a little. But those people from the elevator. Well, it's downright creepy. An eye opens, then closes; a hand makes a fist. And it's not just happening to one body, it's happening to all five."

"So what am I going to tell those reporters upstairs?"

Both physicians shrugged. "Shine 'em on," one said. "Tell them the people in the elevator were killed by a maniac with a four-pronged garden rake. That'll hold up for a while, at least until one of them finds out about the saliva samples or finds out the puncture wounds don't match the prongs on a rake. But maybe by that time the Chief Medical Examiner will have solved this mess."

"God, I hope so," Perdue said, walking away and shaking his head.

15

IT WAS DARK OUTSIDE AND DARK IN THE LIVING ROOM. LIGHT spilled out of the door to the kitchen, and Braille could pick up snatches of conversation while he pushed himself off the couch and slowly got to his feet. His left arm was still useless and his leg felt as if it had been injected with Novocain. The wound in his chest was still healing and his stomach muscles ached, but overall he felt all right. Not good, not bad, just all right.

Mary Kathleen and her children were at the kitchen table, saying grace, when Braille came up to the doorway. Seeing the mother and children sitting together like that made Braille feel like an intruder. It was almost as if he had no right to be there, no right to share in the warmth that comes from being part of a family. He was slowly retreating back into the darkness of the empty living room when Mary Kathleen called.

"Aren't you going to join us?"

Braille returned, joining them at the table. They were eating hamburgers.

"Hungry?" Mary Kathleen asked.

Braille was, but he didn't want to sprint for the bathroom again. "I don't trust my stomach. I think I'd better pass."

"If you're sick, you should eat chicken soup," Amanda said with all the authority of a four-year-old.

"Okay," Braille agreed. "I'll try chicken soup."

Mary Kathleen started to get up, but Braille shook his head. "Just tell me where everything is. I'll make it."

She did, and while Braille was heating the soup, he said, "I'm a little disorganized. What day is today?"

"Sunday," John and Amanda chimed.

"How far are we from the rest stop where you picked me up?" Braille tried to sound uninterested.

"About sixty miles," Mary Kathleen answered. "Why?"

"Just wondering." But it wasn't a casual question. He needed to know how far away he was from Cutter's men and helicopters. "What's the nearest town?"

"Easton. It's about ten miles from here and it's not much of a town. One hardware store, three bars, lots of trailer parks, and a chemical plant."

There had been something bitter in Mary Kathleen's voice when she described the town, but Braille didn't give it much thought. "How far to the closest big city?"

"It's around eighty miles to Spokane. Why?"

"No reason." Braille studied the soup. "Just trying to figure out where I am, that's all." He glanced over at Mary Kathleen, surprised to see her expression was bitter and hard.

"You wanta know where you are?" she asked. "Well, I'll tell you. You're on all that's left of the Double B Ranch. The Double B stands for Bill Benton, and Bill Benton was my grandfather. He started out seventy years ago with a hundred and sixty acres and twenty-one head of cattle. The ranch stayed in the family and nine years ago, when my father died, my husband and I inherited almost five thousand acres and just as many cattle. Then, in just a few short years, with help from the weather, the government, and my husband—especially my husband—the ranch died." She had been staring off at nothing. With effort she finally looked at Braille. "You want to know where you are? I'll tell you. You're on the Double B Ranch, all nine hundred acres of it, and most of that's under lease to a friggen company in Easton and they're killing the land with—"

John jumped down from his chair and glared at his mother. "I hate it when you talk like that," he shouted, his eyes full of tears. "The ranch is just smaller, that's all. You make it sound like it's dead." He bolted out of the kitchen and ran down the hall, slamming the door to his room.

"Is friggen a bad word?" Amanda asked.

"No, honey," Mary Kathleen said. "Friggen's not a bad word." She sighed and looked up at Braille. "John loves the ranch and he's afraid we're going to have to move."

"Are you?"

The bitter expression that hardened Mary Kathleen's face returned. In the background Amanda was saying, "friggen-friggen-friggen."

"There's pressure on me to move, but I'm trying to stay."

"Friggen-friggen-friggen."

"Amanda! I've changed my mind. Friggen's a bad word, now stop it." Amanda did. A moment later she began coughing. Mary Kathleen Stuart closed her eyes and buried her face in her hands. Amanda continued to cough. Braille looked on, unsure of what to do or say next. Finally, Mary Kathleen dropped her hands in her lap. "You got enough problems of your own. I didn't mean to dump mine on you." She turned to Amanda. "Come on, sweetie, let's get your medication."

The kitchen was suddenly very empty and the house quiet. Braille turned off the stove and poured out the soup. He wasn't hungry anymore.

A few minutes later Mary Kathleen walked into the living room, turning on a table lamp. Braille was sitting on the couch and he looked at her questioningly.

"Amanda's okay," she told him. "And I guess John's going to be okay." She slumped down into a chair. "I shouldn't have gone on like that about the ranch and I shouldn't have snapped at Amanda. She's sensitive and any type of tension starts her coughing." She closed her eyes, massaging the bridge of her nose. After a long moment she opened her eyes. "You want to watch some TV?"

"Sure," he agreed, more for her sake than his. She turned on the TV and the fuzzy image of a news anchorman appeared on the scene. The reporter was talking about a grisly multiple murder in the underground garage of a Seattle hotel. The man apologized for the sketchy nature of the report, explaining that the police still had not released any information about the murders.

"While you were asleep, I made up a guest bed downstairs. I guess I should show you where you'll be sleeping," Mary Kathleen said when a commercial came on.

Braille followed her down the hallway, past her bedroom and closed doors to her children's bedrooms, to the last door in the hallway.

She unlocked the door with a key and turned to Braille. "Before we go in I think I'd better explain something." She paused as if she were searching for words. "My husband had mental problems, and sometimes he would go off on tangents. He would develop an intense interest in something and go off and buy all sorts of things, equipment actually. A month later he'd lose interest in his pipe dream or whatever you want to call it, then a month after that he'd go off on another tangent. She shook her head, pushing open the door. "I can't explain it. Maybe the room can."

He followed her into a dark room and stopped while she walked over and turned on a table lamp.

Braille was in a large room with a window, a bed, lots of shelves and two large workbenches running the full length of the room on two sides. He also found himself surrounded by the strangest mismatched collection of machines, sporting gear, instruments, and equipment he'd ever seen. There was no rhyme or reason to any of it. There were typewriters, word processors, printers, and computers sitting on a bench beside a wide variety of photography equipment. Expensive rock cutting saws sat on the other bench, and sitting on the floor were several hundred pounds of rocks in apple boxes. There were more computers on the bench next to the rock grinders and polishers and beside them were three video cameras. Six expensive professional target rifles were mounted on the wall above the computers along with an array of exotic cameras, archery equipment, wood carving tools, three VCR's, several expensive portable tape recorders, stamp and coin collection display books, martial arts weapons, and of all things, a ticker tape machine. It was indeed a bizarre room with no central theme, just different and expensive pieces of equipment and the expensive beginnings to several different hobbies.

Then Braille noticed something else that was odd. Everything in the room had been damaged in one way or another.

The mechanisms of the firearms had been broken, but then glued back together to look as if they were functional. The VCR's and camcorders had been punctured by what looked like a wide-bladed knife, and tape had been put over the holes. Even the rock cutting machines had been vandalized in an unobtrusive manner. From a distance everything looked workable, functional, but up close all had been damaged in one way or another, then put back together in such a way as to suggest they were fine. Normal. Operable.

He looked at her. Mary Kathleen was standing in the middle of the room, chewing her thumbnail and looking at the floor. She sensed his questions.

"I met my husband in college. We fell in love, got married, and came back to live on the ranch. Everything went well for several years. But when I look on it now, I can remember that even then he was moody: up one week, morose the next, but nothing bad. Nothing extreme. Then Mother died, my dad followed a few months later, and the problems and responsibilities of running a ranch fell on us. I think that's when the mood problems started to get worse. The pressure and the responsibilities started to pile up. Then John was born and the added responsibility seemed to push my husband over the edge. He wouldn't say a word for weeks, then, for no reason, he would be on top of the world, full of schemes and ideas that would put us on easy street for the rest of our lives. That's when some of this began." She gestured at one of the benches. "One day he decided he was going to write a novel and he bought a typewriter, but he couldn't be creative with it because it wasn't good enough, so he bought a computer word processor, the printer, and some of the other stuff you see there. He would spend days in here typing away, going through reams of paper, but never writing more than one or two sentences on the first page of his novel. Sometimes we didn't see him for days. Then the low part of his mood swing would come on and he'd come out of his room smelling bad and talking about being a failure and just wanting to sleep a lot.

"I finally got up the nerve to tell him there was something wrong with him and begged him to get help. He refused until I threatened to leave him. I took him to a psychiatrist in Spokane and the doctor told me my husband was a latent manic depressive. He claimed the problem was easy to treat, and put him on pills called lithium. Only, they didn't work. The doctor tried other pills. Still nothing." Again she pointed to the room. "Meanwhile all this was still going on. One month he was going to be a marksman in the Olympics. The next month it was big game hunting in Africa. He met a rock hound in Easton and decided he'd supplement our income by making jewelry. One time he disappeared for seven weeks while he went jade hunting in California. Christ, there was no end to it. He was driving me crazy and driving us into bankruptcy. One day he read a *Wall Street Journal* while he was in his doctor's office and a few days later a company delivers a fucking ticker tape machine. A day later I get a phone call from our bank and find out he's put thousands of dollars into the stock market. Needless to say, we lost it all.

"That's when I tried to have him committed. A psychologist and a social worker came out here and said spending money on eccentric hobbies or getting depressed didn't make him state hospital material. Then they drove away.

"While all this was going on interest rates were going up, Amanda was born, the government dropped some of its subsidy programs, and we had another bad winter. As a result I ended up having to sell off some of the land to keep the banks from taking over and pay off some of John's bills. And he just kept on doing the same thing. I tore up the credit cards, his checkbooks, tried to get the bank to not give him money from our savings. Nothing worked. He kept on thinking up one crazy scheme after another. He brought the video equipment so he could make How-To films about farmwork. He made one film, something about how to cut the horns off heifers."

She shook her head and her eyes began to fill with tears. "He was so proud of that video. He couldn't wait to show it to me, and it was terrible. Poor lighting, out of focus, and he didn't even know how to dehorn a cow. He actually had prints of the video made up and tried to sell them to video stores in Spokane. You know, if he hadn't been so pathetic and hadn't cost us so much money, it would have almost been funny. I mean, the idea of him running around in Spokane getting mad at video store owners because they wouldn't buy his film is funny, isn't it?" She tried to smile but failed, and more anguish came into her face. "The ridicule he ran into over the video broke something inside him, and his illness went from bad to worse. The mood swings became something I still can't describe."

She gestured with her hand. "See all that martial arts stuff?" Braille nodded. "Another by-product of his illness. He went off on a heavy-duty martial arts kick, said the meditative part of the discipline would help him and he bought all that stuff, the clothes, the weapons. See that samurai sword?" Again Braille nodded. He had indeed seen the sword, but had dismissed it. It had to be a replica.

"One day he disappeared. A few days later he came back with that sword. When I asked him what was going on, he said he'd gone to Seattle and bought that sword from a man who collected 'em.

"He paid almost fifty thousand dollars for that sword. I thought I would die when he told me that. I'm selling off land to keep us going and he goes out and spends all that money for something like that. Later, after he fell asleep, I almost killed him with that sword, but I couldn't. All I could do was cry."

"Couldn't you have returned some of this stuff and gotten the money back?" Braille asked.

"I tried. One day he caught me loading the station wagon up with typewriters and videocameras, anything I could carry. He went out of his mind, started screaming about all the money this stuff was making for us and how I wasn't appreciating the royalty checks we were getting from his book and video. Only there was no book, no video. It had finally happened. He'd finally flipped out and lost total touch with reality. And for the first time he got violent. He smashed everything in this room to pieces, and when he finished he went to work on me. He even hit John when John started crying. Later I was able to escape with the kids and we spent the night in a motel. The next morning, when we got back, he was fine. He was smiling, happy, and acting as if nothing had happened . . . and he'd kind of repaired everything he'd broken. I say kind of because he didn't repair anything. He had just glued broken parts back on the rifles and stuffed the wires back in the VCR. And that's what you see here." She gestured at the room. "Nothing in this room is whole or works, but he was so far gone, he thought it would.

"I thought maybe if the people who'd refused to commit him a few months earlier saw what he'd done to this room, saw the bruises he'd put on John and me, they might reconsider. I called them and told them what was going on. They said they'd come out the next day."

Her eyes were full of tears and she looked away from Braille. "I think in a way I killed him with that phone call. I can't prove it, but I think he was in the next room listening because an hour later, he got into our pickup and I never saw him again. Least, not alive."

"You don't have to finish this," Braille said.

She shook her head. "It doesn't hurt so much anymore and he probably would have done it eventually."

"He killed himself?" Braille asked softly.

"The sheriff thinks so. It was a straight stretch of road but somehow John managed to drive the truck into the side of an overpass."

Unconsciously Braille reached out and put his hand on Mary Kathleen's arm. The woman had suffered and was still in pain, and Braille knew about pain.

She stiffened, looked down at his hand, then pushed it away, turning on him. "Don't get the wrong idea," she hissed. "You're here because you got hurt helping me and mine. So don't go thinking that because my husband is dead I'm lonely or looking for company, because I'm not."

"I didn't—" Braille said, trying to explain.

"I will be pleasant to you," she said, cutting him off. "I will feed you, I will talk to you, and I will continue to be appreciative for what you did for us. But I will not touch you and I don't ever want you to touch me again. Understand?"

"Yes."

Suddenly embarrassed by her overreaction, Mary Kathleen Stuart walked away. She returned to the living room and sat down, trying to focus on the television. But it was difficult to see the picture since the tears in her eyes blurred the image.

16

IT WAS A TYPICAL SUNDAY NIGHT AT THE SEATTLE POLICE DEPARTMENT's downtown headquarters. The upper floors were vacant and dark, most of the policemen on duty were out on the streets, and almost no one on the main floor noticed Millie Watkins come in through the front doors. She paused while she clipped a laminated police ID card on her raincoat, then used her key to gain access to an employee-only elevator. She took it to the basement, and a few moments later the pretty young secretary and receptionist from the pathology department was letting herself back into the department's outer office.

Millie Watkins was a calculating nineteen-year-old woman with a stunning face and body. She was returning to the morgue, not because she was behind in her work, but because she needed to tend to her investment. In this case her investment was a University of Washington medical student named Bill Frank. Frank attended classes in the daytime and worked at night in the police morgue as a janitor and receiving agent.

Millie Watkins inserted the key into the morgue's door, then paused, taking a deep breath and letting it out reflectively. She had met Bill Frank the first day she came to work and had not been attracted to him until she found out he was a medical student. Five months later she still was not attracted to him . . . but she was head over heels in love with the annual income he would command once he was an orthopedic surgeon. She'd done her homework and knew that orthopedic surgeons started out at close to a hundred and fifty thousand a year. She also knew that eight out of ten doctors who married in college dumped their wives within six years of graduating. Not that she minded the prospect of a divorce; she'd also done her homework in this area and knew that the divorced wives of orthopedic surgeons averaged seven thousand dollars a month in alimony payments. It made putting up with Frank's bad breath, baby fat, and inept lovemaking techniques worthwhile. Be strong, she thought. We'll be married in a month. Two years from now he'll be board certified, four years after that will come the divorce, and then it's seven grand a month forever, and life will be sweet. She pasted a large smile on her face, arched her spine, and threw back her shoulders, which emphasized her small but firm breasts, and opened the door.

Bill Frank was sitting behind a desk, typing a paper on her word processor. He smiled, standing up as she entered. Five minutes later they were naked, lying on the floor behind her desk, and he was arguing the merits of making whoopee on an autopsy table.

"Just one time," he pleaded. "The metal won't stay cold very long and then it'll be great. See, those tables are designed for comfort. They have a concave surface designed to fit your back and there are holes in the tables so you get air circulation. I want to try it," he whined. "It sounds kinky."

She definitely *did not* want to screw on an autopsy table. Those things were hard and cold, and you never knew what had been lying there earlier. "You sure they sterilize those tables when they're done, sweetie?"

"Absolutely."

"Okay, you kinky devil," she said, fixing visions of CD's, T-Bills, and a yearly income of ninety thousand dollars in her head. "Anything you want."

They entered the adjoining room and crawled up on the first table they came to. "It's got funny grooves in it," she complained.

"All the better to catch bodily fluids," he said, clambering up on top of her and deciding this wasn't such a hot idea. The table was slippery. How could he perform if his toes skidded around?

In the nearby refrigerated body room were six cadavers from the Casbah Hotel, all lying in coffin-sized drawers embedded in the walls of the room. As Bill Frank and Millie Watkins began to make love, one of the bodies from the

Casbah suddenly opened its eyes. It found itself surrounded by darkness and immense cold. It also found itself with an appetite for blood that surpassed any appetite it had ever known while it was alive. Functioning on instinct, it prodded the darkness with its hands and feet. Finding the door with its bare foot, it realized it was trapped and kicked the door open with a loud bang.

The clanging sound woke four other bodies, but failed to disturb Millie Watkins and Bill Frank. They were too engrossed in their passion to notice the sound.

"I'm ready," she said. "Put it in."

"It is in," Bill Frank gasped as he felt himself start to climax.

Millie realized her mistake and cried out, "Oh God, it's so big. You're so good."

All he could do was nod his head as his body spasmed and he emptied his seed into her, thinking he was good. He'd lasted almost thirty seconds this time. Suddenly he heard a loud clatter like a garbage can falling over. The noise seemed to come from the body storage room.

"What was that?" Millie whispered. She would have sat up, but Bill was still on top of her.

"Relax," he murmured, feeling himself shrivel and slide out of her. "Somebody's taking some trash out to the freight elevator."

"Can they get in here?"

"Nawh. Relax," he said, wondering if making whoopee on the autopsy table was all that great. His toes had skidded all over the place, making it difficult to thrust. He was considering wearing tennis shoes the next time when he heard several more bangs followed by the thunderous sounds of ripping metal.

"Don't you tell me to relax," she hissed, struggling to sit up.

He rolled off her and the table and began groping for his pants and smock piled in a heap with her clothes on the floor. She joined him and began to sort through the pile in the dark room. The loud clatter coming from the nearby body storage room still had not stopped. If anything, it was growing louder.

"What the hell," Frank muttered as he put on his pants

and smock. It sounded like somebody was tearing the body storage room to pieces. But that was impossible. There was no one in there. It had to be a janitor loading up trash out in the hallway on the far side of the body room.

"You're standing on my panties," Millie whispered angrily from down on the floor. He lifted his foot and she grabbed her panties. Getting to her feet she began hopping around on one foot as she struggled to get into them. She had a cute body and pointed breasts that bobbed up and down while she hopped. Entranced by the sight of moving pointy breasts, Frank almost forgot about the nearby commotion . . . until it suddenly stopped.

The sudden silence was frightening to Millie Watkins, but not to Bill Frank. He patted the smock's pocket and felt the keys. "It's only a janitor. Be right back." Frank padded past the other autopsy tables, unlocked the doors, and entered the pitch-black body room. As the doors closed behind him, he found the light switch and turned it on. A network of overhead neon lights turned the room white. Squinting against the brightness, Frank took one step towards the door at the other end of the body room, then stopped cold. There were five people standing in front of him, blocking his way. Five very naked people, he realized. As his eyes grew accustomed to the brightness, he realized something more: five locker doors on one wall were open. The doors were bent and mangled, hanging by their hinges as if they'd been kicked open from inside. His eyes went to the pale naked figures. They were coming for him, lumbering awkwardly across the room, their arms outstretched, their teeth bared, all five making hissing sounds like angry snakes.

Frank started to cry out, but suddenly he couldn't. Suddenly he was on the floor, buried under several hundred pounds of cold moving flesh. Bill Frank had less than five seconds to live, and he used his final moments to explain away what was happening to him. A practical joke, his mind decided as teeth bit into his throat and wrists. The guys from school were pulling a practical joke on him because he worked in the morgue. But why did it hurt so much? he wondered briefly, very briefly.

* * *

135

Millie Watkins wanted to go home and she would have, but the door to the reception room was locked and her keys were in her coat, and her coat was on her desk and her potential fiancé had trotted off to another room, leaving her alone in a dark autopsy room. "This is bullshit," she grumbled.

She crossed her arms and glared at the doors to the body storage room for almost a full minute. "Enough!" She started to work her way by touch around the autopsy tables. She was ten feet from the doors to the body room when the doors burst open and five white figures emerged.

The creatures were angry and in pain. Angry because Bill Frank's blood had only whetted their appetites, in pain because the bright lights in the storage room had burned their skin during the brief time it had taken them to savage Frank's body. They charged Millie Watkins like a pack of starving wolves.

There were no lights in this room and the creatures took their time with this human. While Millie Watkins did not have enough blood to completely satiate them, it did pacify them . . . temporarily.

When they finished, a male pushed against the door to the reception area. When it didn't move, the creature hit it with both fists and it shattered like balsa wood. Moments later the door to the hallway was split in two, and the pack moved into the corridor, up a flight of stairs, and out a fire door opening onto an alley in back of the police department.

Earlier a winter storm had rolled over the city, leaving in its wake a mixture of low clouds and dense fog. Moving silently on bare feet, five pale shadows emerged from the alley, loping across a deserted street and disappearing into the fog.

Four blocks away a man named Paul Riester was attempting the impossible in a nightclub called the Red Hammer. He was sitting on a small stage, strumming a banjo, kicking a bass drum with one foot, playing a harmonica held in front of his mouth by a modified orthopedic neck brace, and trying to goad his audience into singing along with him. All this made for a busy man, but he didn't mind. Paul Riester owned the Red Hammer.

As nightclubs went, the Hammer wasn't much. It was cramped, had a limited seating capacity, and was located in the seedier part of downtown Seattle. But that didn't bother Paul Riester. The location was what made the Red Hammer a money maker.

Two times a night the bar would fill up with strangers who would drink, sing along with Riester, and buy tickets from the bartender. Then at eight o'clock, and again at ten, Riester and another employee would lead a line of people out of the Hammer and into a boarded-up old hotel next door. After doing a head count in the lobby, Riester would lead his tour down into the hotel's basement, through a heavy metal door and out into a subterranean city called Underground Seattle.

The tour of the underground city lasted about an hour, and then it was back to the Red Hammer, where they would again count heads, collect the flashlights and say good-bye. Two tours per night with an average of thirty people in each tour. At fifteen bucks a head, most of the time it was nice. But not tonight. Tonight there were only seven people in the Hammer. Deadheads, every one of them, Riester decided as he finished the song and scanned his audience. Two married couples, a couple of college students, and a drunken salesman. Riester sighed. Drunks were always a problem on the tour.

Riester gave up trying to get the small group into the spirit of things and began his standard tour guide lecture. He wasn't in the mood to be creative or funny, and the lecture was bare bones, delivered rapidly from memory. At the same time Patty Robbins, one of his cocktail waitresses, began passing out flashlights. Tonight Patty would help him on the tour by following along behind the group.

He finished his lecture, got his flashlight from the bartender, then led seven strangers and Patty Robbins out into the fog. He unlocked the door to the deserted hotel and entered. It was Patty Robbins' job to lock the door after everyone was inside and milling around in the lobby.

Patty Robbins was overweight with large heavy breasts. The trouble with working in a bar and being busty was the drunks. They tended to regard her breasts as community property, and she was getting damn tired of having her breasts ogled and bumped into. As Robbins followed the tour into the old hotel and pulled out her key to lock the door, the drunken salesman stopped abruptly, turned, and bumped into her breasts with his arm. She snarled. He smiled. She was about to call out for Riester when the salesman realized his mistake and scurried across the lobby to where the others were waiting. Patty Robbins pulled the door closed behind her, taking a solid grip on her flashlight. She vowed she'd whack the man in the balls if he tried that again.

It never occurred to the agitated woman she'd neglected to lock the door to the hotel.

At the same moment Paul Riester was starting to lead his group into the hotel's basement, five figures moved out from an alley and stopped on a sidewalk not more than a block from the Red Hammer. They were surly, irritable, and hungry. The blood they had taken from Millie and Bill had not been enough. They wanted more. None of the creatures liked being out in the open like this. An occasional car made them nervous and the neon lights and bright lights on the storefronts agitated them. But earlier they'd picked up the sounds of a jukebox blaring away inside the Red Hammer. Fragments of their own human memories had told them the sound meant people: blood, survival, life eternal. Keeping to the shadows, keeping close to the buildings lining the street, the five crept closer to the pulsating sounds.

They were passing by the boarded-up hotel and were just yards from the Red Hammer when a gust of wind whipped up the street, rattling windows and blowing open the unlocked door to the hotel. All five stopped abruptly and sniffed the air, their nostrils flaring as they caught the scent of humans and the unmistakable metallic odor of blood. Without hesitation they padded into the lobby.

In the basement, Paul Riester was unlocking the door that opened on to the vast underground cavern that was Underground Seattle.

Patty Robbins was swearing silently. She should have known. She'd felt fat and bloated all day long, been irritable with her mother and kids. Dammit to hell, she thought. She was starting her period.

At the same moment, and for the same reason, a girl in the tour with the pink spiked hairdo was unconsciously rubbing her stomach and trying to stand up as straight as she could. Sometimes that helped the cramps, sometimes it didn't. Right now it wasn't. The cramps were still bad. She'd gone through more Midol than she could count in the last forty-eight hours. The only reason she was out tonight was because her boyfriend had given her some of the Demerol he'd gotten from the weight-lifting team's doctor.

The line of people started through the doorway into the blackness of Underground Seattle. Patty Robbins was the last one through the door. This time she remembered to lock it when she pulled it closed behind her.

The pack of New Ones in the lobby had no problem tracking the scents left behind by the two women, and by the time Patty Robbins had finished locking the door, they were already making their way down the stairwell.

Paul Riester opened a panel box and hit a number of switches, turning on long strings of overhead lights. He always liked this moment. When the lights came on, the people in his tour finally got their first view of the underground city. He enjoyed seeing the awe and delight in their faces. Tonight was no exception.

But there was no delight in Cindy Sin's face or Marvin Washington's.

The sudden glare from numerous overhead naked lightbulbs brought Cindy Sin to her feet. Hissing like a trapped cat, shielding her eyes with one hand and reaching out with the other, she whirled around in the jail cell of the old Seattle police station, groping desperately and blindly for a way out of the white inferno.

Marvin Washington had been sleeping on the floor of an old pharmacy. This building was structurally unsafe, off-limits to the tour, and only one light had come on inside the store. Surprised, but not in pain, Marvin got to his feet. Walking over to the light that illuminated the pharmacy's dim interior, he slapped the light bulb with his hand. The darkness brought instant relief, and now he could focus on the voices he could hear and on his own growing thirst.

Paul Riester led his tour down a wide cobblestone street lined on both sides by wooden sidewalks and old, deserted buildings and stores. After walking twenty feet he stopped and shined his flashlight on the brick building to his left. "This was Seattle's first police station," he explained. "The building's remarkably intact and I think you'll find the interior interesting."

As he started up the broad steps to the station's front doors, Cindy Sin lurched out of a jail cell. She still could not see, and the overhead lights were driving her crazy with pain as she groped her way past the other cells in the corridor.

Riester stopped on the top step and looked down at his group. "This building was built in—"

The door they'd just come through—the closed door to the hotel's basement—exploded open and five naked figures spilled out of the opening.

"What the hell?" Riester muttered. A microsecond later the doors behind him began to rattle and vibrate as if someone were trying to kick them open. At the same moment, Marvin Washington stepped out of the nearby pharmacy and began to approach the group, a low menacing growl breaking from his throat.

Paul Riester was more embarrassed than anything else. There were five naked people coming up the street on his right, a burly black man coming down the street on his left, and someone was trying to get out of the police station behind him. If this ever got out, the city would jerk the tour franchise from him and give it to the bar up the street faster than he could say "bankrupt."

The approaching naked people looked menacing, and the black man looked dangerous, but what was bothering Riester the most was the incessant pounding and scratching on the doors behind him.

"Whole world's gone nuts," he muttered, whirling around, grabbing the door knobs with both hands and jerking the doors open.

Cindy Sin came through the doorway like a cat on fire. She

leaped onto Riester, clawing at his face and head. He toppled backwards under her weight. They hit the stairs and rolled over several times. Still she wouldn't let go of him. As Riester shrieked and cried out for help, the huge boyfriend of the girl with the pink hair pushed her aside. He wasn't smart, but he was perceptive. Those naked people comin' his way spelled trouble. So did the black dude comin' up from behind. But Tank Roberts wasn't concerned. He was six feet seven, two hundred and eighty pounds, and already had a spot on the U.S. Olympic weight-lifting team. If push came to shove, he'd tear an arm off of one of those naked people and beat the other four to jelly with it. Same for the black dude.

"You wanta rock and roll?" he bellowed, mainly for the benefit of his girlfriend and the others. "Then let's rock and roll!" Good line, he thought. He'd delivered it well. Somebody on the tour would tell the reporters what he said to these crazy animals. It would make for good press. "Come on," he bellowed again. "Let's rock and roll."

The five skidded to a stop ten feet from Tank and began to spread out around him. Tank didn't care. He could jerk press four hundred and eighty-five pounds. Paul Riester was still struggling with Cindy Sin. Roberts threw a quick glance at the other men on the tour. "Help him," he shouted, then snapped his attention back to the five crazies.

Thirty yards up the street, Marvin Washington stopped. He had taken blood the night before and was not as desperate as the five fanning out around the huge human. Like a calculating predatory animal, he squatted down on his haunches to wait.

Driven by an ever-growing thirst, two of the males in front of Roberts charged. At the same time, Roberts was forming his own battle plan. He had the strength to kill these crazies, but knew he shouldn't. It might hurt his eligibility for the Olympics. Just maim, he decided, as the creatures leapt for him. He hit one in the face with a fist the size of a pot roast and heard bones break. He caught the other by the throat with his left hand, clamped his right hand on the creature's thigh, and hefted it high above his head. It was a show-off move designed to get him good press.

With his arms up in the air, the rest of Roberts' body was

left wide open. The other three creatures charged instantly. Two went for his throat, the other bit into his thigh, its teeth lacerating Roberts' femoral artery. Roberts had intended to toss the man over his head across the street, but all of a sudden there were people all over him. And they were hurting him! He dropped the male, grabbing the two biting his neck and jerking them away. He bellowed in pain. Bright blood spurted out of the huge holes in Tank Roberts' throat. His girlfriend's scream mingled with the screams of Riester and the frightened cries of the men trying to help Riester.

Roberts was dying, but was too angry to know it. He looked down at the woman who'd sunk her teeth into his thigh. She seemed very far away, like he was looking at her through the wrong end of a telescope. He wanted to crush her head between his fists and wondered dimly if his arms were that long. They were. "Gotcha," he gurgled. There was blood spurting out of his leg and blood spurting out of his neck. He wondered which hole he should plug up first while also wondering why he was thinking these thoughts so slowly, and why his hands moved so slowly. And why were there people screaming all around him.

He put one hand on his neck and turned to see if his girlfriend could help him. She couldn't. She was flat on her back, and one of those naked crazies was on top of her, trying to bite her throat. "Coming," he rasped, taking one faltering step, then collapsing on his hands and knees. His girlfriend was still screaming, but she sounded very far away and he was too tired to lift his head to see where she was. The strength in his arms gave out and he toppled over on his side. Just before he closed his eyes, he noticed someone was standing beside him, looking down at him. With effort Roberts focused his eyes and saw a black man standing high above him, glaring down at him. He looked like he wanted to hurt Tank, but Tank didn't care. Like his girlfriend's faint screams, the black man seemed to be standing a million miles away. Too far away to hurt Tank Roberts, Tank thought as he closed his eyes—and died.

Randy Charter jerked a tray of steaming hot glasses out of the dishwasher and set them on top of the bar. While he waited for the glasses to cool, he checked his watch, smoked half a cigarette, then checked his watch again. Where were they? he wondered as he walked over to the front door of the Red Hammer. He pushed open the door, looking out into the street. All he could see was fog. He shook his head and glanced at his watch again. Twenty minutes after twelve. The tour should have been back an hour and a half ago and the Hammer should have been dark at midnight. Christ, where were they?

He finally decided to go looking for them. He locked up the bar and went into the lobby of the derelict hotel, trotting down the stairs to the basement and to his death.

Ten more people were dead . . . temporarily. But nine would not be missed for several days. Riester was divorced, lived by himself, and took Mondays and Tuesdays off. The Hammer would be open during that time, run by an assistant manager, but the tours would not take place. This was the off-season for tourists, and tours of Underground Seattle were scheduled only for Fridays, Saturdays, and Sunday nights.

Like Riester, Randy Charter was divorced and lived by himself. He'd worked at the Red Hammer for only a few weeks, and when he did not come to work the assistant manager would assume he'd quit and moved on without giving notice. The two married couples on the tour were friends and they had taken the week off to go skiing in the Cascade Mountains. No one expected to hear from them until the following Sunday. Tank Roberts and his girlfriend lived together off campus and had no close friends. While he was officially registered for several classes, his professors wouldn't miss him. Tank Roberts never went to class, never handed in assignments, never took tests, and had never received a grade below a B during his entire college career.

The salesman had just returned to work for his company after being discharged from a treatment center for alcoholics. When he didn't keep any of his appointments during the coming week, his superiors assumed he had fallen off the wagon again and sent a letter of termination to his home.

The next morning, when Patty Robbins' mother reported her daughter's disappearance to the police, she was told to wait twenty-four hours then file an official missing person's report. She did, and when the police finally decided to act on the report, they would make one fatal assumption: they would assume that whatever happened to Patty Robbins happened after she got off work at the Red Hammer, not while she was at work.

17

AFTER THE HOUSE WAS DARK AND EVERYONE WAS ASLEEP, Braille began to examine John Stuart's collection of martial arts weapons. Mostly it was a collection of mail order junk, purchased from supply houses that advertised in the backs of karate magazines. The shurikens or throwing stars were from Taiwan, made from cheap metal and painted black. The rest of the equipment was just as junky. Near as Braille could tell, Mary Kathleen's husband had picked up his knowledge of martial arts from magazines, Bruce Lee videos, and the hundreds of low-budget chop-and-kick movies from Japan that turned the art into a choreographed menagerie of flashing hands and whirling exotic weapons.

Poor John Stuart. He'd read the magazines, seen the movies, and sent away for the weapons, and like most, never realized that the fighting disciplines that came from Japan, Korea, and Okinawa were religious and spiritual in nature. The high kicks and slashing hands were part of the disciplines, but only a small part. Knowledge, meditation, philosophy, and discipline were the major components.

Braille shook his head and with a kind of breathless excitement turned his attention to the sword he'd noticed when he and Mary Kathleen had first entered the room. His eyes were immediately drawn to the sword's distinctive tsuba or handguard. There was a small dragon engraved on one side of the round guard and a tiger on the other. The engravings were the signature of Musashi, one of the finest swordmakers in the world. The man had practiced his craft in sixteenth-century Japan, and though he had crafted swords for forty years, he had probably never made more than a hundred, and what few existed today were on display in the Tokyo National Museum and considered priceless.

Amazing, Braille thought, as he continued to run his eyes over the sword lying on the shelf in front of him. Shurikens worth a dollar ninety-eight sitting next to a sword of incomprehensible value.

It was a katana, the long sword carried by Samurai warriors. It was over three-and-a-half feet in length with a ten-inch-long handle and a blade measuring up to thirty inches in length.

The blade, Braille thought, remembering with great fondness the conversations he had had with his adoptive parents when he was a teenager. There was no blade in the world like a katana blade when forged by a master such as Musashi or Masumune or Hoshimitsu; there was no finer sword in the world.

The secret to the blade's cutting edge and strength was its creation. Laminated strips of steel for strength, and iron for flexibility were placed on top of one another, heated, stretched, and pounded until the metals melded. Then the process was begun again until the metal had been folded hundreds of times, and the final creation was a blade that was both flexible and capable of maintaining an impossibly sharp cutting edge.

After a moment's hesitation Braille took the sword in its black lacquered scabbard off the shelf and laid it on the bed. With his good hand he worked the scabbard off the sword, then picked up the katana and brought the glimmering long blade into the light. The blade was exquisite, and it gleamed like diamonds in the dimly lit room. Even in the low light he could make out the wood grain-like pattern in the steel, a pattern brought about by the repeated foldings of strips of steel and iron. Braille reverently laid the sword down on the bed and wished his parents could share this moment with him. Both had been skilled in the art of the long sword and both would have felt the same sort of reverence he was feeling now at the sight of this magnificent weapon.

With difficulty he worked the scabbard back on to the blade and put the weapon back on the shelf. Then, out of respect to its maker and the family who had taught him so much about this magnificent weapon, Braille bowed to the sword.

He sat down on the edge of the bed and wiped his forehead with the back of his hand. He'd begun to sweat. His mouth was dry. His joints were beginning to ache. It was returning, coming back tonight just as it had the last night and all those other nights back at the OSMS. *The craving*. The insidious hunger for human blood.

It was late, close to two in the morning, and Kubick had put in a full day, but he wasn't tired. If anything, he was hyper-alert while he drove slowly through Stanwood. At the westerly edge of town he drove out onto a deserted pier, parked, and got out. His men were in place now. Five had taken rooms at the motel at the rest stop next to the freeway. The others were in Stanwood.

Oblivious to the rain and wind, he leaned against the car and folded his arms. Somewhere out there in the night was a being . . . a beast the likes of which he had never hunted before. Kubick smiled at the prospect of meeting this mythical being that Hargrave Cutter had called an Ancient.

"Be there," he whispered almost prayerfully. "Exist."

Gregory stepped out onto the balcony at the back of the Estleford home, staring out into the rain and darkness towards the westerly side of Stanwood. The collective force he had sensed the night before had arrived and were searching for him now.

He tried to visualize in his mind's eye what was hunting for him. The images that came were blurred and distorted, but he could feel their interest in him, and their united desire to destroy him.

Most of the images dissolved away gradually until only one powerful source of energy was left. This man was the leader, Gregory thought. This was the one who wanted him the most.

The man was near. Gregory could feel him, and it was not by accident that he continued to stare towards the westerly edge of town and the docks that lined the river. This man is a formidable force and he wants to destroy me, Gregory thought. Not because he hates me, but because I am a game to him.

Come for me, Gregory thought. Find me. Let us make your game a reality. Gregory smiled in the darkness and his eyes glowed red at the prospect of the coming challenge.

Braille was in agony. His mouth was dry. He was sitting on the edge of his bed, his right fist clenched and his clothes soaked with sweat. He was freezing to death. "Jesus Christ!" he moaned. Every muscle in his body was cramping, his joints burned and it took forever for him to get to his feet in a room filled with the sweet coppery odor of human blood . . . the blood of Mary Kathleen Stuart and her children. The scent clawed at his senses; the craving was overwhelming.

Sickened by the appetite and by his own thoughts, Braille stumbled over to the window, opened it and slipped out into the night. He was at the back of the Stuart home. A hundred yards away were the dark shapes of a large barn, several outbuildings, and the black slope of a steep hill just beyond. He started walking, intent on putting as much distance as possible between himself and the Stuart family. He didn't trust himself, didn't even know himself when he was like this. He passed old trees, a picnic table, a dilapidated swing set. A creek guarded by a fence marked the end of the back yard. He limped across a bridge and moved on into the working part of the Stuart ranch. There was a burned-out bunkhouse to his right, cattle loading chutes to his left, and a barn and a maze of corrals in front of him.

There was neglect everyplace. The buildings hadn't been painted in years. The loading chutes were rotting away in the winter night, and the corrals were in the same shape. Railroad ties braced the slanting buildings. The tires on a tractor and old flatbed truck had disintegrated, and the rusting bodies were sinking slowly into the earth.

A cold wind lashed Braille as he crossed the work yard, heading towards the barn. Opening the door to the barn, he found an old-fashioned porcelain light switch on the wall. He turned it and two naked light bulbs hanging down on long cords came on. It surprised him to find animals in the barn. There were several steers, a couple of pigs, a small flock of chickens that clucked and scrambled to get out of the cold wind blowing in through the door, and some sheep penned up in stalls against the back wall.

The animals milled about nervously in their stalls as he passed. It was as though they could sense what he was and were afraid of him. Maybe they had good reason, he thought, stopping in front of the sheep. Memories of the previous night, when he'd chewed on raw mutton and ingested the blood from the meat, came to him. The blood had helped him. The hole in his chest had closed up; the perverse appetite for human blood had passed.

He looked at the sheep and hated himself for what he was thinking. But at the same time he was trying to rationalize the act he was contemplating. He had a disease. This would help.

"No choice," Braille muttered aloud, his body knotted in pain. He was still sweating. He could not continue to exist this way, to be afraid of himself, afraid of what he might do if the beast inside him took over. There was no other way.

Noticing a small workbench jutting out from a wall, he went over to it and found what he needed: a chisel, a file, and a Kerr glass jar. He filed the end of the chisel until it was as sharp as a scalpel, then returned to the sheep pen with the jar and chisel, kneeling down beside the largest sheep. The animal was trembling, looking at Braille with wide brown eyes. Braille soothed it with soft words and the trembling passed. A heartbeat later he made a shallow incision in its neck. It was a small cut, not much more than a nick. The animal didn't seem to feel it, and it continued to stand quietly beside Braille as blood began trickling out of the cut. Braille held the glass beneath the sheep's throat. When the jar was half full, Braille downed its contents in one motion.

The effect was instantaneous. He gagged, but at the same time felt strength and power surge through his body like electricity. The pain in his joints and muscles vanished. He was no longer cold, no longer sweating. He felt good, almost exhilarated. Once again he was in control of himself.

He got to his feet and looked down at the sheep. The animal was looking up at him with plaintive eyes and he could see it was still bleeding. "Damn," he murmured, dropping to one knee. The animal had helped him. Now he wanted to help it. He touched the shallow cut with the tip of his finger, hoping to stem the small trickle of blood.

Then something strange happened. The air around his hand crackled and there was a faint flickering light at the tip of his finger, as though he were discharging electricity. Puzzled, Braille pulled his hand away and examined his fingertip. There was no blood, but there was a small cut at the end of his forefinger. As he stared at it, it faded away to a pink line, then disappeared. Curious and puzzled, Braille examined the sheep's neck, spreading the thick coat apart. Yet he could find no signs of a cut. Nothing.

18

BRAILLE GOT UP AN HOUR BEFORE SUNRISE. HE WASHED, shaved, dressed, and slipped out of the silent house. He felt good and could move his left arm and leg a little now.

He crossed the bridge and walked past the outbuildings and sheds, heading away from the ranch and up the steep hill behind the barn. It was a fine morning. The air was cold and clean. He could make out the upper rim of a new sun off in the east. Following a rabbit path that switchbacked its way up the hill, Braille continued on, occasionally stopping to enjoy the view. Nice, Braille thought, until he got to the top of the hill.

Instantly the air changed. It wasn't crisp and clean anymore. There was a harsh ugly chemical smell in the wind. Braille looked into the wind, trying to figure out what had happened. There was something off in the distance, something over the next hill that was polluting the air. He couldn't see any smoke, but there was a greasy texture to the wind and he realized he hadn't picked up the smell before because the hill acted as a windbreak, protecting the Stuart home from the repulsive odor. He'd originally intended to use the quiet morning hour and the isolation of the hill to involve himself in the meditative discipline of Tai Chai Chuan, but not now, not in this smell.

He returned to the ranch, crossing the bridge and stopping in front of an old set of swings. Thirty years ago someone had built a magnificent A-framed swing set out of thick oak four-by-fours. Once it had been elegant, but now it was weathered and splintered. The bolts holding the frame together were rusted. The swings' ropes were frayed. The handles on the teeter-totter were broken and the entire framework leaned precariously to one side.

The Stuart house was still dark. He guessed no one else would be up for another hour and a half. Why not? he thought. He found everything he needed in the barn and an adjoining tool shed, and while the sun slowly made its way up in the eastern sky, Braille resurfaced the swing set's oaken frame with a plane. He fashioned new handles for the teeter-totter from pine dowels and sanded down the seats and slide with coarse sandpaper. After a while Braille started to get into the project and enjoy himself, and when John Stuart stepped out on the porch to call him for breakfast, he found himself not wanting to quit.

During breakfast John complained bitterly about having to go to school. Tears came to his eyes twice as he tried to describe to his mother the way some of the other kids in class treated him. Whatever was going on seemed equally hard on Mary Kathleen, but in the end she shook her head. "You don't have a choice. It's the law. You have to go to school."

After breakfast she asked Braille to keep an eye on Amanda while she walked John down to the road so he could catch the bus. Braille nodded and started clearing the table. Fifteen minutes later Mary Kathleen and her son walked back into the kitchen. There were tears streaming down John's face and Mary Kathleen looked close to tears herself.

"The bus just drove right by us," she snapped, snatching the car keys off the counter. "Didn't even slow down. It's been happening two to three times a week lately, but today was the last time. The very last time. I'm going to drive John to school and talk to the principal. Be back later." She took Amanda by the hand, started out of the kitchen, then stopped abruptly, turning towards him. "I forgot to ask how you were feeling this morning."

Braille shrugged. "Fine. Hope you can work out whatever's wrong."

After she left, Braille went outside to putter around the swing set some more. He finished up around noon and was pleased with his work. The swing set looked as if it would last another thirty years. He was walking away when he caught sight of the Stuart station wagon off in the distance. A couple of minutes later Mary Kathleen pulled up beside the house and stopped. After telling Amanda to go in, she pulled out a pack of cigarettes, lit one and leaned against the side of the car.

"I didn't think you smoked," Braille said as he walked over.

"I don't, at least not in the house. The smoke would kill Amanda. I usually smoke out on the porch." She took a long drag and noticed Braille's interest in her cigarette. "You smoke?" He nodded vigorously. She gave him one, lit it, and he exhaled, saying, "I take it things didn't go well in town?"

"Oh, I talked to the principal and he was full of apologies. But he won't do anything. Fucking Calchem owns him just like it does everybody else in town."

"I don't get it. John's afraid to go to school, the bus won't pick him up, and the principal's owned by a Calchem?"

Mary Kathleen examined her cigarette as if she were trying to collect her thoughts. "After my husband died things were real tight around here. He'd put the ranch into the red, and the strain of losing her father affected Amanda badly. She spent a lot of time in hospitals. I sold off a lot of the ranch to pay off the bills, but it wasn't enough. So I ended up leasing what land I had left to a corporation that was building a large plant by Easton. At the time I thought it was like a miracle from heaven. All of a sudden I could put food on the table and make ends meet. See, up until about two years ago Easton was dying. Then the Calchem corporation came to town and built this huge plant. They hired lots of townsfolk, brought in more labor, and all of a sudden Easton wasn't dying anymore. People had paychecks. There were trailer parks everywhere. Calchem donated money to the school system so it could expand. Damn corporation even built a medical clinic. Everybody was happy. I was happy. The checks from Calchem were rolling in on the first of every month and the money was nice. Then the plant Calchem built went on line, and that's when things got bad. See, Calchem makes insecticides and fumigants. They're even doing genetic experiments with bacteria to see if they can alter it and use it as a pesticide."

She ground out her cigarette with her heel and looked at Braille. "A plant the size of Calchem creates a lot of waste, and guess where they dump all that waste?"

"On the land they leased from you," Braille stated, knowing now what caused the odor he'd smelled earlier. "But can they do that with leased land?"

"They can if it's in the contract." She managed a rueful shrug. "And it was. Dumb, huh?"

"I take it you've tried to break the lease?"

She nodded. "I saw a lawyer in Seattle. He told me that Calchem wasn't just a chemical plant. It was a big-time corporation with lots of lawyers. He said if I was lucky it wouldn't take more than fifteen years to run this mess through the courts. It wouldn't cost much more than a half a million in legal expenses and even then Calchem would probably win."

At that moment Braille heard a faint rumbling that sounded like distant thunder. Mary Kathleen heard it too. "Speak of the devil," she observed, lighting another cigarette.

The rumble continued to escalate as if a thunderstorm were heading for them at breakneck speed. Braille turned towards the sound. It looked like a black dot when it first came over the top of a low hill, starting down the road leading past the Stuart ranch. But then the dot turned into a huge semi truck pulling two massive tanker trailers. The driver was pushing his rig hard, and a few moments later a black truck with CALCHEM emblazoned in large yellow letters on the sides of two tanker trailers roared past.

Squinting against the dust and wind kicked up by the speeding truck, Mary Kathleen pointed at the hill behind the barn. "Twenty minutes from now that truck'll be dumping everything it's carrying in a reservoir on a plateau behind that hill, and a few minutes from now another truck will be coming along to do the same thing. It goes on that way twenty-four hours a day."

Braille nodded. "But I still don't understand why the school bus doesn't pick up John or why the principal is giving you a hard time."

She brushed her hair away from her face and tucked it behind her ears. "After I found out I couldn't do anything about the lease, I gave up and just decided to live with the problem. Calchem has a pretty good reputation. I figured they knew what they were doing. But I was wrong. Some of my cattle died after a rainstorm. Then the sheep started dying. After that the tap water started tasting funny and the kids started getting sick. I had to put in a three-thousand-dollar filter system to clean it up. Even now I'm not sure it's working that well." She shook her head. "I'm not an ecological nut, but I know when something's gone wrong, so a couple of months back, I called the EPA.

"They came out like they're supposed to, probably spent a whole forty-five minutes out at the dump site, then went away . . . back to the Calchem plant, I guess, because later that night a whole bunch of cars came out to the house, and then maybe twenty or thirty men cussed me out and threw rocks at the house for almost an hour. They broke two hundred dollars' worth of windows and scared Amanda so bad she almost died. After that it got worse. I had a man named Joe Morris working for me at the time. He took off the next night after some good old boys from Calchem set fire to the bunkhouse where he was staying. I called the fire department and it took 'em eight hours to get out here. Then John's classmates started bullying him and the school bus started forgetting to stop. The principal keeps saying he'll do something about it but he doesn't. Hell, Calchem probably pays his salary.

"I grew up on this ranch, went to school in Easton, and used to have a lot of friends there. Not anymore. Now I'm the dragon lady that tried to close Calchem down. Shopping in town's a real experience. People don't talk to me and some of the local toughs still come out here at night and throw rocks at the house. I don't know why they're still picking on me. I'll never call the EPA again. Sometimes I think if I could find someone stupid enough to buy what's left of the ranch, I'd sell in a minute and be gone in an hour."

The front door opened and Amanda crossed the front porch, starting down the steps. She was wearing a tiny red cowboy hat and had a chrome cap pistol stuck in her belt. "Gonna play in the back yard," she said, walking away.

Mary Kathleen gave Braille an odd look. "I think our conversations are getting out of balance. You know a lot about me and I don't know anything about you. Don't you think it's time you tell me who you are and what you're running from? I still don't know what you were doing out in the desert and why you didn't want me to take you to a hospital."

Braille had been expecting her questions and had been trying to come up with something plausible. He knew he couldn't tell her the whole truth. She'd never believe it, especially the part about vampires on Chinook Island or his own need for blood. But maybe he could tell her some of the truth. She deserved to know part of it, especially the part about the danger she and her children were in as long as he was around. Part of the truths, and fill in the rest with lies, he decided.

"What do you know about Chinook Island?"

She looked at him with surprise. "I know everything about Chinook Island. Hell, it was in the newspaper and on TV for weeks."

Braille hadn't been near a TV or a newspaper for weeks. "I don't know what the media said. Tell me."

She noticed his expression and realized he was serious. He really didn't know anything about the tragedy. "One of the world's worst nuclear accidents happened on Chinook Island. Several thousand people were killed when the Can-Am nuclear reactor exploded."

Several thousand *vampires* were killed, Braille thought, still listening to her.

"Because of the radiation, nobody can get near the place to find out what happened but they're guessing that the Can-Am disaster was a repeat of what happened at Chernobyl."

"What'd they say about survivors?"

"The newspapers said that five people got off the island, but they all died from radiation poisoning."

Braille sighed and shook his head. "That part about them dying from radiation is a lie."

"How would you know?"

"Because I was one of the five people who got off the island."

She frowned. "But the newspapers said—"

"The newspapers printed the story the government gave them. I had a home on the island, and about a week before the power plant exploded a strange disease broke out. In order to get infected you had to come into contact with someone who had it. This disease spread like wildfire and most of the residents and tourists were dead by the time the power plant exploded. There were a few of us who didn't have this disease, and we hid out on a deserted part of the island, waiting for a break in the weather. When the break came, the five of us who were left headed for the mainland in a power boat. Not too long after that the Can-Am nuclear reactor was blown up by a man named Warren. He blew it up on purpose because he was afraid the virus that had killed all those people on the island would get to the mainland. He figured he could sanitize the place with radiation, and he did. He also killed himself in the process."

Braille studied her expression, looking for signs of skepticism, but saw none. "We got to the mainland and were taken to the hospital. Then the government took over and packed us off to a very special hospital, only they didn't treat us like patients, they treated us like prisoners. At first we thought they were treating us that way because they thought we might be infected with that disease. But we were wrong. What they were doing was holding on to us while they figured out how they could get rid of us." Here comes the big lie, Braille thought. "See, I think that whatever broke out on the island was the result of a fouled-up government experiment. I think the disease was manmade, and the agency that had us didn't want to let us go because they were afraid we'd tell the world what really happened. When we figured out what this agency was up to and what they had in store for us, we tried to escape. One made it. The rest were killed."

"Killed!" she gasped. "By the government?"

He shook his head. "By an agency of the government. An independent agency that's gotten out of control and is doing things the government doesn't know about."

"Dear God," she murmured. There was no expression on her face and Braille didn't have the slightest idea whether she believed him.

"What were you doing out in the desert?" she asked.

"The hospital where they kept us was in the desert. I'm not exactly sure where. When I finally broke out, it was at night and I couldn't see much. I know I had to run across what looked like a huge airplane runway and I saw some dilapidated buildings in the background. Kinda reminded me of a military base."

"There's an old abandoned Air Force base near Arron Lake. It's not too far from where I picked you up."

"Arron Lake is a town?" he asked, filing the name away in his memory for later use.

She nodded. "When we were driving here from the rest stop, you called out the name Cutter several times. I didn't pay much attention to it. You were pretty delirious."

"Cutter is the head of the agency that held us prisoner," Braille told her.

"After we arrived that night, you said something like, 'You killed her.' Did he kill someone you love?"

"Cutter killed some people who were friends of mine."

"Are my children in any danger from this Cutter or his agency?"

Braille lit a cigarette and exhaled bitterly. "If Cutter ever figured out where I was, all three of you would be in danger. I don't think there's any problem right now, but if I stayed, he'd eventually get a line on me. I'll be gone before he does."

His last words startled Mary Kathleen Stuart, making her feel hollow inside. "Then it's probably best that you do leave when you can."

Suddenly she found herself regretting the words. She swore to herself and wondered what was happening to her. He was just a man. He had helped her. Now she was helping him. One day he would leave and that was best. The last thing she needed in her house was a man on the run from the government.

Confused and irritated, she started to reach for another cigarette, then stopped when Amanda ran up to her and tugged on her jeans. "Mommy, can I swing on the swing?" the little girl asked.

Mary Kathleen shook her head. "You know better than to ask that. The swing's dangerous."

Amanda smiled and took her mother's hand. "No it's not. It's all fixed and new."

"Don't make up stories, Amanda," she warned.

Tugging hard on her mother's hand and suddenly close to tears, the little girl tried one more time. "Please come and see." Mary Kathleen gave in reluctantly, allowing her daughter to drag her off to the back yard.

Braille was fairly satisfied with what he had told Mary Kathleen Stuart. He had stretched the truth, yet given her a semi-accurate picture of what had happened to him and what he was running from. Mary Kathleen had left her purse on the hood of the car. Braille scooped it up, walking around the side of the house into the back yard. The conversation about the Calchem plant and Hargrave Cutter had left Braille in a cold bitter mood. But what he saw in the back yard brought a smile to his face.

Amanda Stuart was sitting in one of the swings, giggling and squealing. "High-er . . . higher!"

Laughing as hard as her daughter, Mary Kathleen was standing behind Amanda, pushing her high into the air. Braille stopped, not wanting to intrude on the joy the mother and daughter were sharing, but Mary Kathleen called out to him. "When did you do this?"

Braille smiled. "Did it this morning. All it needed was some ropes."

"Baloney. I know the shape this swing was in." She left Amanda to swing on her own and walked over to Braille. "My dad built that swing for me thirty years ago. I used to think it was the neatest swing set in the whole world. I used to ask my husband to fix it for the kids so they could have the same feeling about their dad that I had about mine when I played on it. But he didn't get around to it—"

"Get on the other swing," Braille said. "I'll push you both."

The sounds of the mother and daughter's laughter

blended in the cold crisp air until another black Calchem tanker rolled past the front of the house. Braille stepped away from the swing, watching the tanker disappear into the distance. When he could no longer see it, he turned back to Amanda and Mary Kathleen. Both were sitting motionless in the swings. The laughter and magic was gone.

Maybe I can fix this, Braille thought, glancing back at the trail of dust the tanker had left in its wake. This family had helped him. Maybe he could help them. He was about to suggest he push them again when Amanda shouted, "Here comes the bus."

Mary Kathleen jumped out of the swing and started towards the road as the bus drove past and never stopped. "Son-of-a . . ." Mary Kathleen hissed, whirling around to face Braille. "They left John at school. Just left him there." She scooped her purse up off the lawn. "I'll be back soon as I can."

"Take me," Amanda said loudly.

"Me too," Braille said.

Easton turned out to be a dry tumbleweed of a town with one main street and lots of newly created trailer parks filled with shiny double-wide trailers. John was waiting for them out in front of the school. He clambered into the back seat with Braille, protesting his innocence and wailing something about the principal keeping him after school for starting a fight with some fifth graders. The boy had bruises on his neck and temple, scratches on his chin and a cut on his lip. Mary Kathleen turned in the seat, studied her son's injuries, then glanced at Braille.

"My son's in the second grade and he's going to start a fight with some fifth graders. Give me a break." She reached out and put her fingers on John's cheek. "You okay, sweetie?" He started to shake his head, noticed Braille was watching him, and nodded stubbornly.

As his mother turned back to start up the car, Braille leaned close to the boy and whispered, "How many?" John Jr. held up four fingers. "You do any damage to them?"

John shook his head. "Too big," he whispered back.

"Good move," Braille said. "When you're outnumbered and they're bigger than you, it's smart not to make them mad. Then they really whale on you." He gave the boy a look of approval and John smiled.

Mary Kathleen was about to make a U-turn when Braille leaned forward in the seat. "Drive by the Calchem plant. I want to see what it looks like." She shrugged, pulled out on the main street and headed east. At the top of a small hill two miles outside of Easton she pulled over to the side of the road, gesturing at the plant sitting below them in a sprawling cup-shaped valley.

The Calchem plant stretching out before them was bigger than Braille had expected. A fourteen-foot-high cyclone fence topped with concertina wire surrounded more than eight hundred square acres crowded with large metal buildings, eight-story-tall storage tanks, and a fleet of semi trucks and tanker trailers.

Mary Kathleen pointed out the windshield. "That two-story cinder block building is the plant's laboratory. That's where they invent new poisons and play genetic games with bacteria. The fancy brick-and-wood building is the plant's administrative headquarters, and see those expensive house trailers off to your left?"

Braille looked. On the far side of the compound, out beyond the fenced enclosure, were a number of house trailers built into the side of the hillside all surrounded by huge trees. "That's where the bosses live. Most of 'em live in Seattle or Spokane and commute home for the weekends, but while they're here that's where they stay. Those trees around the trailers were all imported from California, hauled up here in big trucks and planted just so the bosses could have some instant shade in the summertime."

"Who's the head of the plant?" Braille asked, studying the buildings spread out below, committing everything to memory.

"A man named Lanterman, and he's more than just the boss. He's the Northwest Regional Director for the whole Calchem corporation. Seen enough?"

Braille had, and as she pulled away he glanced out of the station wagon's rear window at the house trailers up on the side of the hill. The biggest one—the triple-wide—probably belonged to Lanterman, he decided, settling back in the seat with traces of a smile on his face.

Braille pushed Amanda and John in the swings until their mother called them to dinner. On the way to the back porch Braille noticed a canvas tarp covering something next to the house. Curious, he lifted the canvas and found an antique Harley-Davidson motorcycle resting on its kickstand. It was clean and looked in good running condition. Another one of John Stuart's hobbies? he wondered. Over dinner he asked about the motorcycle and was told it belonged to the handyman who'd taken off after the bunkhouse fire. When he asked why the man hadn't driven away on the motorcycle, Amanda gave him a you-are-so-dumb look and said, "He didn't know how to ride it. He just worked on it and washed it a lot."

Mary Kathleen smiled at her daughter. "She's right. He was trying to restore it. He called me a few days after he took off and asked me to look after it. Said he'd come back for it one day. Probably will. I just hope I'm here when he does."

After dinner Braille helped John with the dishes. The boy washed, Braille dried. John handed Braille a wet plate, then focused his eyes on the dishwasher. "Would you teach me to fight? I don't know how to. I lose all the time." He handed Braille another plate.

"What makes you think I can fight?" Braille asked.

"I saw you fight at the rest stop."

"You also saw me lose."

"You didn't lose. You were great. You were knocking them to pieces and you would'a won 'cept you got stabbed with a tire iron. Now, will you teach me to fight?"

Braille knew what was going on in the boy's head. He'd had similar experiences with bullies in orphanages. Braille felt sorry for John but knew he couldn't teach him the moves he knew. All he knew was how to kill people. But after a moment's more deliberation Braille decided to compromise. "I won't teach you to be a good fighter, but I could teach you a couple of things that might help you if you ran into some of those fifth graders."

John looked at him with a faint ray of hope in his eyes. Braille shrugged. "It's not much. Just a couple of moves that might make them leave you alone."

"Anything," John answered prayerfully.

Braille knelt down on one knee so he could look into

John's face. "There's nothing neat about fighting or being tough. Fighting is bad. But defending yourself is okay. You have a right to not be hurt. You have a right to go to school and not come home like you did today. So I'll teach you a couple of things that might make some of the other guys stop picking on you. But what I teach you isn't supposed to make you a tough guy. It's just supposed to make some of those bigger guys leave you alone."

"When will you teach me?" John asked.

Braille held up his hand. "There's one more thing. You have to ask your mother if this is okay with her."

"But she won't understand," the boy protested.

"You have to ask her," Braille repeated. He got to his feet and noticed Mary Kathleen standing in the kitchen doorway. Her arms were crossed and she was looking at Braille sternly. He knew she'd overheard every word of the conversation. I'm in deep shit, Braille thought.

"Mom . . ." John said. She shook her head, cutting him off in mid-sentence. Her eyes moved to Braille's. "Mom," John said, trying again. "Braille said he would—"

"I heard him. I heard everything," she said, her eyes still locked on Braille's. Then a faint trace of a smile broke across her face. "You have my permission. Now, I'm going to watch TV with Amanda."

For the next hour Braille taught the boy some basic moves designed to make an opponent think twice. John was a quick learner, picking up the moves rapidly. Braille liked that. But what he liked the most was that John did not view the moves as weapons he could use whenever he wanted to. They were just ways to say "leave me alone" to a group of bullies.

Braille smiled at his pupil. "Okay, try it one more time." He reached for the boy with both hands. John grabbed Braille by his little fingers, then quickly let go. "Good," Braille encouraged. "Now for another one." Again he reached for the boy. This time John's right hand shot out. He grabbed Braille's nostrils. Braille felt the edges of the boy's fingernails start to sink into the cartilage and stop abruptly.

"Those plus the other moves should help," Braille said. "They won't turn you into the village tough, but if you use them the way I showed you, the fifth graders should leave you alone after this." The boy nodded seriously. "One more thing: if somebody comes for you, what's the best way to win the fight?"

"By not fighting. By talking them out of it, turning away, or bluffing like hell." Braille nodded approvingly and sent John off to watch TV. Then he took a flashlight from a drawer, went out in the back yard, and studied the old Harley-Davidson motorcycle. It was in mint condition. There was gas in the gas tank. The battery still held a charge. Now he had transportation, he thought, as a bit more of his plan for the Calchem plant fell into place.

19

IT WAS JUST PAST ELEVEN O'CLOCK WHEN KUBICK PULLED INTO the large park-like rest stop and drove slowly past grassy picnic areas, cinder-block restrooms, and a gray van with darkly tinted side windows. Two of his men were in the van, monitoring this part of the rest stop for anything out of the ordinary. They had more than enough equipment to do the job. Both had high-tech infrared binoculars that zeroed in on the heat a human body gives off. There were two suitcases strapped on top of the van, each one containing a parabolic microphone capable of picking up a muted conversation a mile away.

In addition, the two men had placed motion sensors in the forest and had set out more than two dozen tiny wireless microphones, each about the size of a pencil eraser. Because there were so many sensing and listening devices, the monitoring responsibilities were being handled by a portable Tay-Croft Mark IV computer. The sophisticated computer had been set up to receive and separate input from the sensing and listening devices, and had been programmed to detect vocal stress patterns in the conversations it overheard. The computer was capable of listening in on and sorting out upwards of thirty conversations at a time. As long as the conversations were simply an exchange of words, the men in the van were not alerted to tune in on any of the conversations. However, if an argument developed and someone's speech pattern began to reflect stress, then the computer would signal the men with a blinking light and a beep and the conversation would then be channeled through to a speaker or headset.

It never occurred to Kubick to stop and check on his men. His men were professionals. If one was sleeping, the other was not and it was highly likely that both were hyper-awake and currently aware of his passing presence. It also never occurred to him to worry about his men. All were experts in hand-to-hand fighting, and all had access to the most up-to-date firearms in the world. Each of his team's vans had been stocked with two FIE Franchi Spas-12 assault shotguns. Since the team suspected that whatever they were after would require immense stopping power, the nine-shot shotguns had been chambered with alternating rounds of number four buckshot in which each shell contained twenty-seven .25-caliber balls and Remington "sluggers," three-inch-long Magnum shells that fired a heavy one-ounce lead slug. The withering firepower created by these alternating rounds could turn a human being into nothing, a car into litter in just under two seconds.

Aside from the shotguns, each van contained two FN-LAR-HB FALO 50.42 assault rifles, grenades, and tear gas canisters. In addition, each of his men had brought his own personal weapons and handguns.

Kubick rarely carried a firearm. He was too deadly with his hands. But because he did not know what he was up against, tonight he was carrying a .45-caliber Detonics Scoremaster modified with a special barrel and bushings that would allow him to fire high-Magnum .45 bullets. In addition he carried a kubikiri, an ancient Oriental knife, strapped to his spine. While he was proficient with firearms, he preferred to kill with his own hands or the knife. He liked the closeness and the smell of his victims' fear. He also liked looking into their eyes when they knew they were going to die. But most of all, he liked looking into their eyes when death came to them. And if his victims put up a struggle or proved to be challenging, then the ecstasy he felt during the intimate encounter was all the more exquisite.

Kubick drove out of the park-like setting and into the business area of the rest stop. He passed between two gas stations, drove past a Denny's restaurant and a small trucker's cafe. Then he pulled into a large motel parking lot. His unit's second van was sitting in the shadows on the edge of the parking lot where it had a fair view of the restaurants' parking lots and the gas stations beyond.

Pulling to a stop in front of the motel, Kubick got out and glanced back at the rest stop. Everything was in place, the equipment was operational and his men were ready. There was nothing to do now but wait for Cutter's mythical beast. Off in the west sheet lightning erupted; another winter storm was moving in off the ocean and the sudden change in weather irritated Kubick. He knew that almost no predatory animal hunted in a storm, and was sure this Ancient was no exception. As more lightning flashed in the east, he considered calling everything off for tonight but then changed his mind. He couldn't take the chance. His men would have to remain on full alert.

He could smell the rain coming and the wind's strength increasing with each clap of thunder.

"Come *now*," he whispered aloud, the wind tearing the words from his lips. "It's time we met. Time you died." Kubick was starting to enjoy the power of the oncoming storm, but it was time to check in with his men. Reluctantly he turned away from the storm and entered the motel room.

A half a mile away a dark figure loped across the deserted lanes of the wide freeway. Then, with the languid graceful moves of a large predatory cat, it climbed an embankment just beyond. At the top, Gregory stopped. Ahead of him, on the other side of four hundred yards of thick forest, was the rest stop. He glanced back at the oncoming storm, which had followed him like a giant shadow during the easy run from Stanwood to the freeway. It was almost on him, and as a bolt of lightning ripped across the sky he smiled. He enjoyed storms, reveling in their power and majesty.

He liked to hunt in storms.

Lightning flashed, bleaching the forest in front of him blindingly white with its brilliance. Gregory laughed with a kind of savage joy he rarely felt anymore. On the other side of the trees was the rest stop and something more, something that knew about him, something that wanted to destroy him. The storm was directly overhead now, releasing its full fury. Gale-force winds whipped the trees back and forth, and rain cut the foliage like hard, wind-driven hail. Still smiling, Gregory started into the forest.

John Kramer adjusted the dial on a powerful radio transmitter that filled most of the open suitcase lying on the motel bed and spoke into the microphone. "Come in . . . I say again, come in." He cupped his hands over his headset, listening for almost a full minute before glancing at Kubick. "Sorry, sir. We won't be able to raise the men in Stanwood until the storm passes."

"Fucking storm," Kubick murmured, his words barely audible over the din. "Okay, then raise V-1 and V-2." V-1 was the van sitting out in the park. V-2 was parked on the edge of the motel's parking lot. Kramer adjusted the transmitter's frequency. "Come in, V-1."

Kramer's voice crackling through the speaker irritated the two men in the van. Jackson Reber and Jim McCabe already had their hands full, and they didn't need to be bothered by a radio at that moment. Hard gusting winds were rocking the van back and forth on its springs, making it difficult to get around. The rain splattering against the van was louder than small arms fire and the overhead thunder sounded like an artillery barrage. In addition, the on-board Tay-Croft computer, which the men had nicknamed Hal, was going wild. Every time thunder exploded or a gust of wind rattled a microphone, Hal decided this was a conversation worth listening to, and it was alerting the men by turning on the red lights on its control panel and throwing out a screechingly high-pitched series of beeping sounds.

"I say again, come in," Kramer said, his voice almost lost in the confusion of beeps and lights Hal was creating inside the van.

Reber was in the front of the van and closest to the radio.

"Better get that," McCabe shouted. Jim McCabe was a demolition expert and a big man with a barrel chest and an Irish temper. McCabe liked things he could control—things that were predictable, like explosives. He also liked knives and always carried two, one under each arm in specially designed sheaths that resembled shoulder holsters.

Jackson Reber, McCabe's partner, was the unit's jack of all trades. The tall, lanky man had degrees in physics, chemistry, and psychology. He did not have McCabe's size or temperament, but in his own right, he was just as deadly. Jackson Reber was an expert in wing chun kung fu. He could kill as fast with his feet as McCabe could with a knife.

"Come in, V-1," Kramer snapped over the radio.

"I got it," Reber said. He leaned between the two bucket seats, snatching the microphone off the dash. "This is V-1. Over."

"A little slow in the response," Kubick said. "Over."

"Sorry. It's just that this storm's driving Hal crazy. We're talking malfunction city here, boss. Almost everything is useless. Over."

"Understand, V-1. Suggest you shut everything down and go to visual."

After Hal had been shut off, McCabe sat down on a stool beside one of the large windows at the side of the van and picked up his infrared binoculars. He turned them on, scanning the park. Everything he saw through the binoculars looked as if it'd been spray painted with a shimmering green paint. He heard Reber sit down beside him and knew his partner was scanning the other side of the van with his binoculars.

"I don't know what we're doing out here," McCabe said, touching a button on the binoculars that adjusted the automatic focus. The rain had lessened a little and he was able to zoom in on the edge of the forest a hundred yards away. "A fish wouldn't come out on a night like this, let alone the thing we're after."

Reber shrugged. "That thing we're after's called an Ancient and it might come out."

"Hope springs eternal," groused McCabe. "You think this Ancient is as bad as Kubick said it might be?"

"No. But even if it was, it wouldn't matter. Between your knives, my Uzi, and the other weapons in the van, we got enough firepower to drop a dinosaur."

Gregory stopped at the edge of the forest, surveying the large park spread out in front of him. Off in the distance he saw a couple of cars in a parking lot and then he noticed the van. . . .

A hundred yards away McCabe shifted uncomfortably on the stool as he focused the binoculars in on the distant tree line. For a second he thought he saw something moving among the trees, but it was nothing. Eyestrain, he decided, rubbing his eyes with his fingers. "You got any Visine?"

"No," Reber replied, staring through his binoculars. "You got any aspirin?"

"No," McCabe said, lifting the binoculars back to his eyes. "Christ, this is gonna be a long night."

McCabe saw something dark moving across the landscape and focused in on it. "What the fuck?" he muttered. There was something heading towards the van, something human-shaped, but the infrared wasn't picking it up. Everything was shimmering in lime green hues as it was supposed to be, except the black shape coming towards him. A shape that didn't have body heat. Then it hit him. "Bingo," he whispered, "we got us a visitor."

"Where?" Reber asked, looking out McCabe's window.

McCabe pointed. "I make it to be ninety yards out and coming at us slow and easy."

"I see it. Christ, no body heat. Anything that cold's gotta be a walking corpse."

"Raise Kubick on the radio," McCabe said. "Then we take it."

While Reber scuttled forward to the radio, McCabe ripped open a large cardboard box sitting beside the van's back door. Inside was a folded-up net made from steel mesh and two stun grenades. He stuck one into the pocket of his jacket. Behind him Reber was talking excitedly into the radio. "It's heading in our direction, but walking slow. And it's weird. Fuckin' trees give off more heat than this thing."

Kubick's voice filled the van. "V-2's on its way. I'll be there in three minutes. Leave your mike on. I want to monitor what's going on."

Reber clicked on the mike's transmit button and turned up the volume, then scrambled into the back of the van. McCabe was taking one last look out the van's window with binoculars. "Whatever it is, it ain't worried. It's sixty yards out and coming towards us like somebody on a Sunday walk."

Reber reached under his jacket, checking his Uzi. Then he picked up the other stun grenade. "Ready?"

"Born ready," McCabe answered. He got to his feet, pulling the stun grenade out. He put his foot on the top of the cardboard box while Reber took hold of the van's back door handle.

"Say when," Reber said.

McCabe smiled. "When."

Reber pushed the van's heavy door open. McCabe kicked the cardboard box out of the van, then both men followed it out into the parking lot. The moment they landed, both were pulling pins from their stun grenades. It was too dark to see the target, but both knew its approximate location, and a microsecond later two hard-thrown concussion grenades sailed into the night.

Three seconds later the grenades exploded at the same time. The earth shook, the night turned white, and for a moment even the overhead storm seemed stunned by the brilliant flash. Then the night and wind returned.

"Bingo," McCabe said, straightening up.

"Let's take names and kick ass," Reber shouted. The men dashed over to the cardboard box. They jerked out the heavy metal net and started across the grass, heading into the park. Reber pulled out a flashlight, shining it ahead of him, but the darkness and heavy rain cut the beam to almost nothing. "Should be around here," he remarked pointing the beam at the scorched grass where the grenades had gone off.

"Well?" McCabe asked.

Reber raked the area with a flashlight. Nothing. "I don't like this. That thing's gotta be here . . . but it's not."

McCabe felt suddenly cold. "Let's get back to the van and wait for backup."

They threw down the net and sprinted back to the van. As they arrived both could hear the faint sound of a car horn being honked in anger.

It was Kubick's car horn. Kubick and Van-2 had pulled out of the motel, rounded a curve and almost collided with a huge semi truck and trailer trying to pull out of the gas station. The driver had miscalculated the turn, and his rig was blocking the road while he backed up, cranked the wheel, inched forward, then repeated the whole process again. Though they'd been stopped for only thirty seconds, that span of time seemed almost like a lifetime to Kubick.

While McCabe stood guard at the back of the open van, Reber climbed in and scrambled up to the front. The microphone was still dangling over the seat, its transmit button on.

"We checked the area," Reber shouted. "Nothing. The grenades didn't work. Require assistance. Need backup now!"

McCabe was scanning the parking lot with his infrared binoculars when Reber jumped down beside him. "Maybe that thing's stunned and just wandering around someplace," he said hopefully. At that moment McCabe picked up a black human shape out in the parking lot, a shape coming at them through a curtain of rain tinted green by binoculars. "Bingo," he whispered. The Ancient was right in front of them, not more than fifteen yards away. He reached under his jacket and pulled out one of his huge combat knives.

"Where?" Reber asked.

"There," McCabe said, throwing the knife hard, knowing with grim satisfaction that the heavy flashing blade would bury itself right up to the hilt in the target's chest. "I got it," he shouted, but then the shout died on his lips because his target had caught the whirling knife by the blade with his bare hand. Impossible. It was a combat knife, made from stainless steel, its serrated edges as sharp as a scalpel.

Gregory snapped the knife in two, starting towards the men, noticing one was aiming something at him. Suddenly the night erupted in gunfire as Reber cut loose with his Uzi.

Gregory backed away while all around him bullets cut through the air making whizzing sounds. One creased his neck, another caught him in the shoulder, a third in the arm. Reber panicked when his quarry disappeared into the night and opened up with a second burst of machine gun fire, shooting wildly, blindly in an aimless pattern until the gun went empty. No time to reload, he thought, trying to fight off the terror overtaking him. He threw the Uzi away and reached for the FIE SPAS-12 shotgun inside the van. At the same moment, McCabe pulled out his other knife and drew out his own heavy caliber pistol. No sense in taking chances, he was thinking. What they were after had just broken a twenty-two-hundred-dollar stainless-steel knife in two.

"I hit it," Reber said breathlessly. "Hit it in the shoulder and arm. I saw its shirt explode when the bullets went in." He pushed a button located in the forestock of the shotgun, then pushed the forestock forward an inch. The shotgun was now on full automatic. The two men were now standing with their shoulders touching and the van directly behind them. Each had a full field of fire into the parking lot in front of them. Over his shoulder, Reber yelled back into the van, at the microphone. "Did you hear that, Kubick? I hit it, hit it twice. Then it disappeared." He scanned the darkness. "Where are you? We need you, Kubick."

"Easy," McCabe said softly. "Kubick'll be here soon."

"Who is this Kubick?" a voice asked from out in the darkness.

Jackson Reber whirled to his right, thought he saw two glowing eyes, and cut loose with the Spas, firing off five rounds as he moved the shotgun in a rapid arc, not caring if the van's door blocked part of his field of fire. One-ounce lead slugs and .25-caliber balls ripped the night open, blowing the van door to smithereens.

"I hit it," Reber screamed. He still had four shots left in the Spas, but wasn't about to check out the parking lot. Not on a night this dark. Not when something with red eyes might still be out there.

As Gregory moved around to the front of the van, he fingered the large hole in his side made by a one-ounce rifled slug. The pain was intense, but the bloodless gaping hole was already beginning to heal. In spite of the pain, Gregory was enjoying the game. He hoped to find out more about these men and their leader, a man whose name he now knew to be Kubick, before the game was over.

The driver of the truck blocking Van-2 and Kubick's car finally backed his truck far enough into the gas station's lot to create an opening between the front of the truck and the building on the left side of the road. Immediately the two blocked vehicles took off like rockets. Kubick was beside himself. He no longer cared about the creature they were after, just the two men trapped out in the park two miles away. Something was playing with them, toying with them, and they were alone. He pushed the gas pedal to the floor and skidded around the van in front of him.

McCabe and Reber heard nothing but the overhead storm, but Gregory had picked up the sounds of two vehicles heading towards him. A clap of rolling thunder muffled the sounds Gregory made as he vaulted on to the hood of the van.

"Kubick's coming," McCabe whispered. "I can feel it." He had a combat knife in one hand and a .44 Magnum pistol in the other.

"Hope so," Reber said, holding the Spas by its pistol grip so tightly he thought the grip might break.

Gregory stood on top of the van, looking down at the two men below him. Off to his left he caught a quick glimpse of a set of headlights coming around the curve a half a mile away. Time to end the game, he thought, leaping down to the ground and landing just behind McCabe and Reber.

Sweet Jesus, Reber thought as he realized that what they were after was behind them. Panicked, he whirled to his left and fired the Spas without thinking. Everything in Reber's world went into slow motion. He felt the gun recoil in his hands and saw four brilliantly white muzzle flashes. In that blinding light he saw McCabe's head and chest explode. He dimly realized he'd just killed his friend.

Then the Spas was gone, ripped away by something standing beside him. Something with demon eyes. There then came a voice from hell. "Why are you hunting me?"

"Money," Reber gasped. The thing was gripping his arm. He couldn't move. Couldn't kick at it.

"Who pays this money for me?"

"A government agency!"

Tires screeched as two vehicles skidded into the parking lot. Gregory glared at the intrusion, then glared at the man he was holding with one hand. The two oncoming vehicles were only a hundred yards away now. "This Kubick you talked to, he leads the hunt for me?" Reber nodded. "Is this him coming in the vehicles?" Again Reber nodded. "If he does not find me tonight will he continue to hunt? Still try to kill me?"

Reber looked over at the remains of McCabe, then at Gregory's face. "You can count on it," he said, bracing himself for his own death.

"Good," Gregory said. "I will count on it." He let the man go, glancing over at the parking lot. The two vehicles had skidded to a stop and armed men were clambering out of them. Gregory's side was still tender, and he'd developed a healthy respect for the weapons these men carried.

Jackson Reber watched the Ancient turn away and start into the darkness. He's just a man, Reber thought, stronger than most, but just a man. I can kill him.

Gregory sensed Reber's move. Looking back he saw Jackson throw his body into a tight spin while kicking out with his leg in a flying roundhouse kick. His target was the Ancient's temple. Gregory caught the human by the ankle with both hands and jerked savagely. Thirty yards away, running hard, Kubick saw what was happening.

"NOOooo!" he screamed.

Jackson screamed too, his shriek mingling with Kubick's as his leg was ripped off at the hip. Then he was on the ground, going into shock, bleeding to death and looking at his own leg lying on the asphalt, a leg with a shoe still on it.

20

IT WAS TWO HOURS BEFORE SUNRISE. KUBICK HAD PULLED ALL his men in and they were with him now in the motel room. He motioned for them to sit, then walked over to a light switch on the wall and nodded to Kramer. Kramer pushed the play button on a small cassette tape recorder sitting on the bed. A moment later Kubick turned off the lights in the room.

For almost a minute no sound came out of the tape recorder, but then the men heard a dead man say, "Bingo." Then another dead man said, "Let's take names and kick ass."

The men sitting in the darkness knew they were listening to the last minutes of Reber and McCabe's lives. The men in the dark room heard it all: the gunfire, the panic, the screams for backup. Then they heard the beast they were after talk. "If he does not find me tonight, he will continue the hunt, still try to kill me?"

Then came the shuffling sound Reber made when he started to kick out, the ghastly sounds of a leg being ripped off at the hip.

The tape caught the dying sounds of Reber, then there was nothing but silence. Finally Kubick spoke. "Shut it off." Kramer did. Kubick kept the room in darkness. "You just heard two men die. They came up against something they did not understand, could not kill, and they died because of it. They also may have died because I wasn't there to back them up.

"You now have a choice. You can stay with me and hunt this beast or you can leave. If you leave, I won't hold it against you. Anyone who walks out of this room tonight will continue to be a part of my team when future assignments arise. Take your time, think it over, then make your choice."

Kubick kept the room in darkness for almost a half hour. During that time, no one walked out. "So be it," Kubick said, turning the lights back on. He gestured to a man named Larson. "You and Hodge bury McCabe and Reber in the forest. Mark the graves. When this is over with, we'll take them home."

Kubick turned to Kramer. "I want you to take one of the vans, go back to the plane and pick up St. Jude." Several of his men nodded approvingly at the mention of the weapon nicknamed after the saint of lost causes. "I underestimated what we're after. Capture's out of the question. I want this thing and I want it dead. One more thing. We're not going to sit around and wait for it to come to us. Next time around we'll go for it. I'm pulling out all stops in Stanwood. I want you all to take that town apart during the daylight hours looking for a stranger, someone who just recently moved there. I'm confident we'll find this Ancient, and when we do . . ."

There was no reason to finish the sentence.

21

A SHARP BLAST OF COLD MORNING WIND FOLLOWED MARY KATHleen Stuart and her son as they came through the front door and into the living room. Braille was leaning against the doorway to the kitchen, a cup of coffee in his hands.

"I don't believe this," she said. "Damn school bus just drove right by. I don't think it would have stopped if I'd been standing in the middle of the road." She glanced over at her daughter. If she hadn't been so mad, she would have laughed. Amanda was leaning against the wall, holding her mug of milk with both hands. She looked like a miniature replica of Braille. "Get your coat on, honey. We're going to take a ride."

Amanda made a face. "Can I stay with Braille?"

Mary Kathleen turned to Braille. "You want to look after her while I take John to school?"

Braille stirred uncomfortably. "What if she starts coughing?"

"Just pat me on the back," Amanda said. "Not hard, just firmly."

After they drove away, Braille looked out the kitchen window. The wind was blowing hard. A slate-colored sky was threatening snow. Going outside was out of the question. He gave Amanda Stuart an uncomfortable look. "What now?"

Amanda pointed to a dollhouse and a tiny set of tables and chairs in the living room. "We play dolls."

Braille, a professional killer and one of the deadliest men in the world, agreed.

When Mary Kathleen Stuart returned, she found her daughter and the stranger who had come into her life sitting at a tiny play table having tea with two of Amanda's favorite dolls.

"No," Amanda was saying, with strong insistence. "First you ask Dolly if she would like some tea. You can't hear her when she talks, but she will say yes and then you pour her some tea. It's really easy." She stared at Braille expectantly.

"Want some tea?" Braille grumbled.

"Be nice," Amanda ordered.

Mary Kathleen burst out laughing. Braille threw her a stern look. "Be nice." She nodded, cupping her hand over her mouth to stifle her laughter. It was a charming scene. Her daughter, the dolls, the plastic teacups, and this man she knew only as Braille. She still hadn't been able to figure him out and that bothered her. On the one hand, he was gentle with her children and both of them idolized him. But there was another side to him, something just below the surface that frightened her, making her think this man was capable of extreme violence. Who are you? she wondered as she stared at Braille. How can I watch you serve tea to dolls and still think you are capable of immense violence, even killing?

Braille was sitting cross-legged in front of the play table. All she could see was his profile. But suddenly he was looking at her, his face impassive, his eyes staring intently into hers as if he knew what she was thinking. She looked away abruptly. "Do you want to have a cigarette with me out on the porch?"

"Sure," Braille answered.

And why did he have to be so goddamn attractive? Mary Kathleen Stuart thought as he went off to get the coffee and cigarettes.

A thick cloud cover hid the sun and it was dark out for ten o'clock in the morning. Mary Kathleen put her coffee cup on the window sill and zipped up her ski parka. Then she lit her and Braille's cigarettes. "Don't you ever get cold?"

"Sometimes." Braille was distracted by the roar of a huge Calchem tanker truck rolling past the Stuart ranch. He stared hard at the truck until it disappeared over the next hill, then turned to her. "I think I can help you. I think I can fix some of the problems you have with the Calchem plant."

She made a face. "Sure," she sarcastically laughed. "What're you going to do? Have a heart-to-heart talk with Lanterman, maybe politely ask him to move his dumpsite?"

"Something like that."

"Just what do you have in mind?"

Braille's face was impassive. "It's best you don't know."

She knew she didn't want to. Once again the suspicion that this man was capable of more violence than she could ever imagine began to well up inside her. "If you did what you're thinking about, could you promise me that my children wouldn't be harmed if something went wrong?"

"Long as I'm around, nothing will happen to you or your family. And if something happened to me, if I had to go away, I think I could set something up so you'd still be okay."

She picked up her cold cup of coffee, walking slowly to the far end of the porch, looking out at the gray hills. "I want to say yes, but look what happened to me when I tried to change things before."

"You went about it wrong."

"How's that?" She turned to look at him.

"You didn't get Lanterman's attention first. I will."

After a long moment she shook her head. "No. I can't take the chance. All I did was to try and get them to take some waste off my property. They turned on me and came down on me like a mountain. Companies like that are ruthless. I didn't even hurt them and they terrorized my children, battered my house with rocks, and set fire to one of the buildings. If you do what you have in mind, they'll really get mad and I think this time somebody'll get hurt . . . maybe killed. So my answer is no. Please don't help." Her head dropped forward and she started to cry. Braille walked across the porch to her. He wanted to comfort her, but remembered what had happened when he'd touched her on the arm when she'd cried once before. "You're probably right," he whispered softly. "I won't—"

Amanda opened the front door. "Telephone, Mommy," she shouted.

Mary Kathleen Stuart wiped her face with the back of her hand and walked into the house, leaving Braille alone in the cold and wind. A couple of minutes later she and Amanda walked out on to the front porch. Amanda looked up at Braille. "Boy, is John in deep shit," she piped up.

Mary Kathleen didn't seem to hear Amanda's assessment. "That was the principal." She sounded stunned. "I guess there was a problem at school. He wants to see me now." She looked at Braille. "You wanta come?"

"Wouldn't miss it," Braille said.

Braille and Amanda waited in the car for almost an hour while Mary Kathleen did whatever mothers do when they get a summons from the principal. Just before noon, mother and son emerged from the school's main doors and walked down a long sidewalk to the station wagon.

When John opened the door and got in the back seat, Braille got a close-up view of two black eyes, a bloody nose and a better view of a big wide smile. Confused, Braille looked at Mary Kathleen, who was climbing in behind the wheel. She draped her arm over the seat, turned and looked at her son. Like John, she too was smiling.

"He's a mess, but he *won*. Gimme five." She held out her palm. John slapped it affectionately.

Braille turned to the boy. "You look like that and you won?"

"My boy kicked ass," Mary Kathleen gleefully exclaimed. "When I was in the principal's office, I saw some of the fifth graders who did this. They all got splints on their fingers and funny bandages on their nose and they all have to go over to the medical clinic for x-rays and everything. Gimme five."

Mother and son clapped hands together again.

She turned and looked at Braille. "I don't know what you taught him last night, but it worked. He didn't kill anybody and the nurse didn't think there were any broken bones, but right now there's a lot of dislocated fingers in that school and a lot of sore noses and ears."

"Gimme five," Braille said, holding out his hand. John Jr. slapped it playfully.

"Yeah," Mary Kathleen said. "Gimme five, Braille." Braille held out his hand. But instead of slapping it, Mary Kathleen took it in hers. "Thank you." Then the exultation began to fade from her face. "Can I talk to you for a minute outside the car?"

They got out of the station wagon. Braille leaned against the car as she turned up her collar. "While I was in the nurse's office, the father of one of the other boys came up to me. The guy's name's Mac and he told me my son would get it. It didn't seem to matter that his boy and the others were older and bigger and now just because John defended himself, there's this King Kong ape creep out looking for him."

"Sorry," Braille said. "It's my fault."

She locked her eyes on his. "No. It's not your fault. It's the emotional climate out at that damn plant. See, Mac works for Calchem. He's a supervisor out there.

"What he said made me realize that no matter what I do, whether I play dead, roll over, or beg for mercy, those people out at Calchem'll continue to make our lives miserable for as long as we stay. So," she said, still staring into his eyes, "I'd like to take back what I said earlier. If you think there's something you can do to make things better for my children, I'd like to ask you to try. If it works, fine. If it doesn't . . . well, hell, at least we tried, and things couldn't get any worse than they are now."

"You sure?"

"Yes," she said softly, standing there, framed by a dark sky.

On the outskirts of town they passed a tavern sitting off by itself in a dust bowl of a parking lot. John Jr. pointed out the window. "There's Mac's car." The fear in the boy's voice made Braille look. A big black pickup with oversized tires stood out in the crowded parking lot. The truck had a rollbar, four spotlights mounted on top of the cab, three rifles on display in the back window, and a customized license plate that read: IBAD.

"Mac's not a nice man," John said. "He's one of the men who threw rocks at our house. I saw his truck. Jake said his dad was mad at him for losing today and mad at me for hurting his finger." The boy gave Braille a worried look. "Mac's a big man. Maybe even bigger than you, and Jake says his dad ain't afraid of anything."

"John," Braille said, settling back in his seat, "anybody who drives around in a truck with three rifles in the back window is afraid of something."

An hour later, while Amanda and John were taking naps, Braille approached Mary Kathleen in the kitchen. "I need to borrow your car for a while, and I need to borrow some money."

She stopped putting the dishes away and gave him a strange look. "You need to borrow some money?"

"Don't have a penny to my name," Braille honestly stated. "If I'm going to try to help you, I'll need some money."

She whirled away from him and hit the counter with her fist. "I should've known. I should've guessed there was a catch to it. I give you my car, my money, and you go off and help me . . . right?"

Braille made a helpless gesture. He hadn't quite figured out why she was so upset this time. "Kinda."

"Just how much money do you need to take with you when you drive off in my car so you can help me and my kids?"

"Fifty cents."

"Fifty cents?" she sniffed.

He nodded. "I have to make a phone call." She pointed at the phone on the kitchen wall. Braille shook his head. "From a phone booth."

She gave him the keys to her car and some quarters. As he was starting out of the kitchen, she called to him. He stopped and she walked up to him, handing him several ten dollar bills.

"What's this for?"

"While you're in town, get a carton of cigarettes for you and a carton for me."

Braille counted the money. She'd given him forty dollars. "There's too much here."

"I know." She walked back to the counter. "It's just that I think it's hard for you to ask me for things like cigarettes." She shrugged with her back to him. "Hell, call it an advance. Everybody should have some walking-around money."

In Easton Braille found an isolated phone booth in the parking lot of a new supermarket. He got ahold of the operator and had her place a long distance phone call to Atlanta, Georgia. Braille gave the man who answered the number of the phone booth he was in. "Tell Colonel McKlean to call as soon as possible."

Three minutes later the phone rang. Braille picked it up. "How are you, D.W.?"

"Jesus Christ," retired Colonel D. W. McKlean said. "I thought you'd bought the farm when that island of yours went up."

"Close, but no cigar."

"Well, welcome back."

Braille knew that McKlean meant it. Braille had been McKlean's best behind-the-lines assassin in Vietnam. Later, as a civilian, McKlean had set up a private business somewhat similar to what he had done overseas. He had recruited Braille, and Braille had gone on to become McKlean's best hit man. Over the years Braille had taken on the tough assignments—the ones no one else wanted to handle—and then pulled them off. In the process he had made a lot of money for himself, and a lot of money for McKlean.

"Have I got a honey of a job for you," McKlean was saying. "It's in Italy, and with your sense of justice, you'll love it. The Red Terrorist Brigade is trying to make a comeback. Some of its old leaders are resurfacing. The families of two of the judges they killed last month want—"

"Slow down, D.W. I can't take on any assignments right now."

"How come?"

Braille took a deep breath, then filled McKlean in on everything that had happened to him since the power plant had exploded, but since the truth was too hard to believe, he used the same improvised story he'd told Mary Kathleen. Only, in this case he brought Mary Kathleen Stuart, her children, and their problems with the Calchem plant into the picture.

When Braille finished, a bit of McKlean's humanity came out. "Sorry about the survivors. Sounds like Chapel and the other two had become friends of yours." There was a pause, then the skeptical businessman in McKlean emerged. "So if you're planning on a leave of absence, why the phone call?"

"I owe this family a lot," Braille said. "They saved my life, and they're hiding me now. I want to help them. I'm thinking of fucking with the Calchem plant, and if the OSMS shows up, I won't be able to finish this. If something like that happens, I want you to step in and send up your best men to make sure nothing happens to the woman or her kids. If need be, help them relocate."

"That could get expensive."

"You want access to my Canadian bank account?" Braille asked.

"Just a second," McKlean said. In the silence that followed, Braille could hear the faint clicks of a computer keyboard. McKlean came back on the line and cleared his throat. "You remember that Bahama job two years ago?"

Braille did. A newlywed couple honeymooning on a yacht off the Bahamas had been killed by drug runners interested in stealing their yacht to smuggle drugs. The dead couple's East Coast family were wealthy and they'd tried to get the Bahamian government to take action against the smugglers living openly on the island in a huge fortress-like estate. Corrupt as the Colombian dope ring living under their noses, the Bahamian government had done nothing. In desperation the two families had finally contacted McKlean, and in turn McKlean had offered the contract to Braille. Braille had gone in, spent seven days on the island, then taken a plane back to the States. An hour after his plane left the ground, an explosion of incomprehensible magnitude had leveled the Colombians' thirty-six-room mansion and all the outbuildings of the walled-in compound. Forty-two people perished in the explosion, including five highly placed Bahamian government officials. "Well, I'm still holding your fee for that job and you're covered," McKlean said, giving a low whistle into the phone. "You got lots of money down here. I don't think we need to worry about expenses."

"How much?" Braille asked curiously.

"'Round two hundred thousand."

"Like I said," Braille repeated, "I want them covered, and if necessary, relocate them."

"How will I know if they need help?"

"Either I'll call you or she will."

McKlean agreed. Business was business. He had two hundred thousand dollars to play around with. "Anything else?" he asked.

"Don't think so."

"You realize you're turning into a Good Samaritan, don't you?"

"Never happen."

"You think there's a chance you might come back to work for me one day?"

"Always that chance, D.W."

There was an awkward silence on the phone for a moment. Then McKlean asked: "What about this OSMS? You planning on taking it down?"

"Yes," Braille answered firmly. "Someday."

Two thousand miles away a man named D. W. McKlean, a deadly man in his own right, shivered at the tone he heard in Braille's voice and was glad he didn't work for the OSMS. "You really care about this woman and her two kids, don't you?" he asked, feeling the need to change the subject.

"Yes," came Braille's response.

McKlean looked at the phone he was holding. This wasn't the Braille he knew. The Braille he knew was a cold, indifferent man with no emotions. A man who didn't care about anything, not even his own death. McKlean shook his head, clearing his throat. "If you care about them, then I care about them. If something happens, give me a call. I'll send up the best I have and probably come myself."

"Take care, D.W.," Braille said as he hung up the phone.

22

Braille returned to the Stuart ranch just before sundown. Mary Kathleen Stuart was waiting for him out on the
porch, trying hard not to look relieved as he mounted the
steps. He smiled, handing her the car keys and her cigarettes. "Sorry I didn't get back earlier." He wanted to
explain it was a long telephone call, but was too tired. The
conversation with McKlean had exhausted him.

Or the lack of something else had left him exhausted. He
entered the living room and the heat radiating from the
fireplace was oppressive and overwhelming.

"I think I'll grab a quick nap," he said, heading for his
room.

"You okay?" she called out.

Braille didn't have the energy to answer. He locked the
door behind him and sat down on his bed, gritting his teeth.
The pain, fever, chills, and sweating had come back. The
lust for blood. He felt weak and disoriented, and knew he
had no choice. Opening the window, he slipped out into the
darkness and made his way to the barn.

Once inside, he went through the same ritual he had the
night before, using the same chisel and the same glass jar.
Afterwards, he touched the bleeding cut, wishing he could
make it better. Suddenly a focused surge of energy that
crackled in the air like miniature lightning jumped from the
tips of his fingers to the injured flesh of the sheep. An instant
later the animal was no longer bleeding. Its cut was healed
and it was looking at Braille as if it were wondering why this
human was fretting over it.

"Jesus," Braille whispered, getting to his feet and examining the unexplained cut on the tip of his finger. He felt
better, immensely better. He was no longer feverish and the
desire for human blood was gone. But he was baffled. All

he'd done was to touch the sheep and in that instant, the animal's cut had disappeared, then reappeared on his own hand. "Jesus," he said again. This power to heal was as baffling and as frightening as his own need for blood.

Suddenly he heard a rifle shot. It was close by, and Braille was out of the barn, running towards the Stuart house before the explosive report had stopped echoing off the hills. He jumped the creek, ran past the swing set and heard the sounds of breaking glass and two more rifle shots as he rounded the side of the house, skidding to a stop. There was a pickup truck and two cars in the Stuarts' front yard. Six men were grouped in front of the pickup. One had a rifle. The rest were throwing rocks. The pickup behind them was black. The spotlights on top of its cab were shining on the Stuart home. Its license plate said: IBAD.

Braille could hear his name being screamed from inside the house. John and Amanda were crying for him. The men outside were mimicking the children, calling out in high-pitched voices, "Braille, where are you?" More rocks were thrown. Windows shattered. The man with the rifle fired it into the air.

Braille headed for the mob of men, moving silently and menacingly through the night like the devil's shadow.

A man picked up a large rock and drew back his arm to throw it. Suddenly he found his hand and the rock crushed to pieces.

Another man leaning over to pick up a rock, felt something touch his spine. Then he felt himself paralyzed in a stooped-over position.

Sensing a threat, another was reaching for his pistol when something grabbed him by his shirt and belt and he saw the hood of his own car coming at his face.

Someone came for Braille with a baseball bat. An instant later the bat was splinters and the man was flying through the air. Landing on the cab of the IBAD pickup, he took out all four spotlights with his body and crashed down into the pickup's bed. A microsecond later another man flew through the pickup's windshield.

The man with the rifle whirled on Braille and was aiming at the approaching shadow when suddenly the rifle was snatched from his hands. Just as suddenly, a hand came out of the darkness, slapping him hard across the face. The blow slammed Mac back against his pickup. He started to recover when an open palm slapped him again, rocking him back against the hood. Mac collapsed to his knees. Shaking off the pain, he then got to his feet. Clenching his fist, he looked for his opponent and saw nothing. But again the open palm came out of the night, clubbing him hard, sending him reeling to his knees. This time Mac did not get up, he stayed on his knees and brought his hands together as if he were praying.

"No more," Mac pleaded, praying to something he couldn't see. "Please don't hit me again."

A figure that blended with the night and shadows stepped in front of him. All Mac could make out was a silhouette hovering above him, a silhouette with broad shoulders and red eyes.

Then the black shape spoke. "Try this again, try to hurt this family in any way and you'll die. Understand?"

Mac didn't say anything until a hand slapped him hard enough to make a sound like a pistol shot. The blow jarred his head. One of his teeth flew away. "Yesh," he said through lips that felt like mush.

The black shape hunkered down in front of him. Mac still couldn't make out the man's features and didn't want to. "If you ever come near this family," the shape warned, "you'll die. No bluff. Just fact. You'll find yourself on your back with pennies on your eyes and no place to go but hell. Understand?"

"Yesh!" Mac croaked through swollen lips.

"Now get outta here."

After the men had driven away, Braille stepped quietly through the back door. John and Mary Kathleen were waiting for him. "I saw that!" John exclaimed. "Saw some of it anyway. Mom kept making me duck down. You made men fly." He turned to his mother. "One just flew right over Mac's pickup. I saw it!"

Mary Kathleen gave Braille a surprised look. "This was *Mac's* doing? I thought those men were out there because you'd done something to the plant."

Braille shook his head. "Haven't done anything, at least not yet."

"But the phone call?"

"I'll tell you about that later," Braille said.

She glanced at the clock on the kitchen wall, then at the food sitting on the table. "Seems later than seven. Seems like it should be midnight." She rumpled John's hair affectionately. "Go get your sister. Tell her it's time to eat."

The boy disappeared down the hallway and Braille said, "There's some plywood in the barn. I'll use it to seal up the broken windows and—"

"Amanda's sick!" John shouted. "She's not breathing!"

Braille followed Mary Kathleen down the hallway, heard her say, "She was okay just a minute ago." But she wasn't now. The girl lay on her side on the bedroom floor, silent, limp, her eyes closed. Her lips blue. Mary Kathleen dropped to her knees and gave Braille a stricken look. "There's an oxygen tank in the bathroom and in the medicine cabinet you'll find a bronchodilator called Prestadone. Please—"

"No," Braille said, jerking Mary Kathleen to her feet. "You know where everything is. You get it. I can do CPR." She nodded, rushing out of the room.

Braille rolled the lifeless child onto her back, cradling one hand under the back of her neck. Then he touched the side of her throat with his fingers, feeling for a pulse. It was there: weak, sporadic . . . and fading like the heartbeat of a dying bird.

It started first in his hands, hands that were cradling and touching Amanda. He felt warmth, a kind of surging energy that started at the tips of his fingers, then began to radiate through his hands and up into his arms. At the same instant, his hands began to give off a flickering blue light. It was as if his hands had been transformed into hollow glass and filled with blue neon gas that glowed brightly and seemed to push back the black fog-like mist that had come from nowhere and was now swirling around him and Amanda.

Time stopped and both he and the child seemed to be caught up in a void of peacefulness. It was like being trapped in the eye of a swirling black storm and all the while the light coming from Braille's hands and arms continued to shimmer with the brilliance of sheet lightning.

Then the peacefulness ended and Braille could feel pain

rushing into his body. Suddenly his lungs were on fire. He couldn't breathe. His heart was beating wildly. Dimly he realized that he was taking into his body the disease which was killing the child. And he welcomed it, welcomed her agony and knew he was about to die. She would live. Then death stepped through the churning mist into the quiet void he shared with the child.

Braille glowered distrustingly at the shapeless apparition. It was his time to die. Not hers. He had taken her disease and dying into himself. Death was coming for him. Not her. He would have it no other way. "The child is not yours," he said to the shapeless specter, then gasped in pain as a vise closed on his heart and lungs. "You have no choice in this," he managed. "The child lives. I go with you . . ."

He heard coughing from far away. Then a close voice said, "I'll take over."

Braille emerged from the black mist. Mary Kathleen was kneeling beside him and her daughter with an oxygen mask in her hand. Amanda was coughing and flailing out with her hands like someone in a bad dream.

"At least you got her breathing again," Mary Kathleen said, trying to put the mask on her daughter's face. Amanda pushed the mask away. As the mother struggled with the child, Braille dragged himself across the floor. He leaned back against a night stand, massaging his chest as he labored to catch his own breath. The room was very quiet. Amanda was no longer coughing, not even wheezing. She was sitting up, looking at her mother with wide eyes. Then she slowly turned her gaze on Braille and stared at him hard. The color was back in her face and lips and her expression was one of puzzlement.

Mary Kathleen studied her daughter disbelievingly. Moments before, Amanda had been comatose, close to death. Now she was sitting up, looking like she'd just awakened from a nap. She had seen her daughter go through spells like this before, and always the recovery had taken days . . . sometimes weeks of hospitalization, oxygen, massive infusion of antibiotics . . .

Not sixty seconds worth of CPR.

She shook her head in wonderment at the miracle. Her

daughter was breathing and smiling and she couldn't seem to take her eyes off Braille. "You sure you don't need anything?"

Amanda smiled. "I can breathe real good," she said. With her eyes still riveted on Braille's, she asked very quietly, "Can you?"

The vise crushing his heart and lungs was easing up. The fluid that had formed in his lungs seemed to be draining away. His heartbeat was returning to normal. He gave Amanda a forced smile and nodded.

Mary Kathleen's eyes darted from her daughter to Braille then back again. "I don't understand this. Not any of it."

There weren't words to describe her daughter's recovery. It was a miracle.

23

KUBICK WAS WAITING FOR THE VAN AT THE EXACT SPOT WHERE Reber and McCabe had died. Kramer braked to a stop and climbed down, unlocking the van's back door. Then, sensing Kubick's need to be alone, he walked away.

Inside the van, Kubick could make out the vague outlines of St. Jude. His team had purchased St. Jude a year earlier but had never used it, never had any reason to use a weapon of this magnitude before. But then, they had never lost a man before, never been up against anything like the Ancient before.

What he was looking at was a GAU-2 7.62mm mini gun. The weapon looked somewhat like a thirty-caliber machine gun, but instead of one barrel protruding out of the firing chamber, the GAU-2 7.62mm mini gun had six barrels grouped together in a tight circle. Though not a newly invented weapon, the introduction of high test lightweight plastic and metal alloy parts had reduced the size and weight of the mini gun so that now one man, one very strong man, could carry and operate the weapon. In Vietnam the gun's nickname had been "Puff the Magic Dragon." Kubick's men had nicknamed the mini gun after the saint of lost causes.

Maybe the Ancient could stand up against shotguns, knives, and Uzi's, but there was no way anything could stand up against a weapon such as St. Jude. Not a weapon that could fire upwards of six thousand rounds per minute. A man carrying St. Jude could cut a giant oak tree in half or reduce a house to confetti within a matter of seconds.

A truly remarkable weapon, but he knew he wouldn't have anything to do with it. St. Jude was for his men. The deaths of McCabe and Reber had shocked and demoralized them. St. Jude was theirs. It would be good for their faltering morale. If they killed the Ancient with the weapon, all well and good. But if he had his choice, if there was a way he could pull it off, that would not be the way this creature would die. No, he would meet this creature, this man-beast face to face and kill it with his own hands. Kill it the same way it had killed Reber: violently and in hand-to-hand combat.

24

BRAILLE COVERED THE BROKEN WINDOWS WITH SHEETS OF rough-cut plywood. While he worked, Mary Kathleen sent Amanda and John to bed, then cleaned up the broken glass scattered throughout the inside of the house. He finished up around eleven and joined Mary Kathleen in the living room. There was a fire in the fireplace and the TV set was on with the volume low. Mary Kathleen was sitting in a big over-stuffed chair, wearing a quilted bathrobe and cowboy boots. Without her jeans covering her boot, Braille could see the full extent of the orthopedic brace built onto her right boot, a brace she needed, according to her son, because she'd had polio as a child. It was a cumbersome contraption of buckles, leather straps, and heavy chrome bars starting at the heel and ending in a wide leather cuff just below the knee. She had put her hair up into a ponytail and wasn't wearing any make-up. Her skin was shiny; it gleamed in the light of the fire, and she looked elegant in an unassuming way. She hid herself a lot, Braille had come to realize. Hid behind make-up, bulky clothes, and hairstyles that hid her features. But when she didn't hide, when she allowed the planes and angles in her face to show, she was stunning.

She appeared preoccupied and was in one of her silent moods. Though she occasionally glanced up at the television set, her major interest was on something she was holding in her lap.

Braille turned his attention to the television and the eleven o'clock news that was just beginning. In an effort to keep the audience tuned to the broadcast through a pending commercial, the news announcer was talking vaguely about the deaths of two people who worked in the Seattle police department's morgue, the disappearances of five bodies from the same morgue and a new mysterious phenomenon: people were disappearing off the streets of downtown Seattle at night. Then the reporter promised more details following the coming commercial. It worked. The reporter had Braille's attention. He was about to turn up the television when Mary Kathleen spoke.

"I checked Amanda a few minutes ago."

"Is there a problem?" Braille asked, suddenly concerned. For a brief period of time he had lived with the disease Amanda coped with every day of her life. He now knew intimately the power of cystic fibrosis. He now knew the kind of courage it took for Amanda just to get out of bed every morning.

She shook her head. "No. She's fine. Matter of fact, she's more than fine. She's perfect. I just checked her lungs with this." She lifted the stethoscope in her lap up for Braille to see, then raised her eyes to Braille's. "I've never heard her lungs so clear. It's like she doesn't have a disease. I don't understand it. I don't understand what happened. I go into her bedroom and she's comatose. Then you take over, I leave, and when I come back I find her coming out of it and you looking like you can't breathe. What happened while I was gone?"

Braille fixed his eyes on the fire. "Nothing happened. I gave her CPR. Ask your son. He was there."

"I did. He said all you did was to hold her and she started to get better. At the same time you started to get sick. He said you stopped breathing and he was more worried about you than about his sister. Please, I've got to know. What happened while I was gone? How did you make her so much better?"

There was something about the way she was looking at him, something in the tone of her voice that made Braille feel like a freak, a contaminated oddity. But what was worse was that he couldn't answer her questions. He didn't even know himself what had happened to him and Amanda.

"I don't know what happened in there. Maybe Amanda wasn't as sick as you thought or maybe I just give good CPR. But whatever happened, it wasn't magic, and I am not some sort of faith healer or witch doctor. Let's just drop it." He got to his feet. "It's been a long day. I'm going to bed." Before she could say anything, he walked out of the room.

He closed the door to his room, opened the window and sat down on the sill, lighting a cigarette. He blew the smoke out into the night. He'd been too abrupt with Mary Kathleen, almost rude. All she'd done was to ask him some questions about a power that baffled him, frightened him. As he continued to smoke, he heard Mary Kathleen step into the bathroom. A few minutes later she went into her own room and closed the door.

When he was sure she was asleep, he stood up and stretched. It was time to deal with the Calchem plant. He started to slip out the window, then stopped and swore. In all the confusion, he had forgotten to give her Colonel D. W. McKlean's telephone number. He rummaged through the nightstand, came up with a ball-point pen and an ancient *Reader's Digest*. He opened the *Digest* to the first page and in the margin wrote the Atlanta area code and the number for McKlean's answering service. He didn't want to wake her, didn't want to give her the number now, but he had no choice. There was no telling what might happen to him once he left the house. If something did go wrong, she would need the number. Still grumbling and hoping she wouldn't shoot him with the gun she said she kept in her room, he opened the door.

He found Mary Kathleen standing out in the hallway, her hand raised as if she were about to knock. She looked as surprised as he did. For a long moment, they faced one another in an awkward silence. Finally she broke the silence. "I wanted to apologize. I didn't mean to interrogate you earlier. I also wanted to thank you for helping Amanda." She started to turn away.

"Wait," he said softly. She stopped. "I'm sorry too." She nodded, and he held out the *Reader's Digest* to her. She took it and looked at it, then gave him a look that was half-smile, half-puzzlement.

"I wrote a telephone number at the top of the first page," he explained. "It'll connect you to a kind of answering service. Tell whoever answers you want to speak to a man named McKlean. Then leave your number and he'll call you back."

The smile faded. The puzzlement remained. "Why?"

"Depends on what you need. If you want security guards, tell him. If you want to relocate, tell him. He'll do anything you want."

"I still don't understand."

"Earlier I said I'd try and help with the Calchem plant. I also promised that no harm would come to you or your children. If something does go wrong and if I have to leave, McKlean will back up my promise. You and your children will be safe."

"Do you expect something to happen to you?" she asked.

"No."

"Are you planning on leaving?"

Braille looked away. "We both know that one day I'll have to leave." She started to say something, but he cut her off. "Point is, that telephone number is something you can use if I can't keep my promise."

She was visibly upset now, but ever practical. "But . . . but relocation costs money."

He smiled at her, and knew what she was thinking. This was a man who had to borrow fifty cents to make a phone call, and he'd just promised to relocate her and her children if she needed it. "Just know that if you need to move, you'll be able to."

"But what if I don't want you to leave?"

"Good night, Mary Kathleen," Braille said, wanting to say more, but knowing he couldn't. She had what was important, she had the telephone number. All he could do now was close the door.

When he heard her close the door to her room, he slipped out the window, dropping to the ground. He found a plastic half-gallon milk container in a garbage can on the back porch and decided it would have to do. He then set off for the waste site on the Stuart ranch. It wasn't hard to find. He returned a half hour later, and moments after that he was pushing the old Harley-Davidson motorcycle across the lawn and towards the road.

A half a mile from the Stuart home he mounted the thirty-five-year-old Harley and keyed it up, hitting the kick start. The big engine throbbed to life. It was a huge bike with an engine powerful enough to rattle his teeth when all it was doing was idling.

Twenty minutes later Braille stopped at the top of the hill overlooking the Calchem plant. The plant was well into its late night shift. There were floodlights and spotlights everywhere, and in the harsh glare Braille could see workers inside the buildings and several Calchem tankers waiting to be loaded up with waste products. He didn't have anything against the plant or the chemicals it manufactured. But what galled him was what the corporation and its regional director were doing to three people he liked.

Now it was time to pay a visit to that regional director. Sitting motionless astride the old motorcycle, Braille turned his attention to some trailers sitting on top of a level slab of land carved out of the side of the valley. Time to change some corporate policies, Braille thought as he kick-started the bike to life. Time to go see somebody named Lanterman.

Judging from what Lanterman had done to the Stuart family and the way he'd handled the EPA, the man had power and played the game by dirty rules. But that was okay, Braille decided. This wasn't a game and he didn't believe in rules. None whatsoever.

25

WILLIAM LANTERMAN WAS THE REGIONAL AND CORPORATE director of eight Calchem chemical plants all located in the northwest. He pulled in an annual yearly income in excess of seven figures and lived well. He owned a palatial estate on Mercer Island in Seattle, a gentleman's ranch outside of Spokane, a condo in Aspen, and a beachfront home on the island of Martinique.

As regional director, Lanterman practically lived at a new plant during its first year of operation. Once it was established, Lanterman would back off and visit the plant and the other plants he oversaw two or three times a year. When he did, he would make the trip in either one of the company's Lear jets or his own.

Lanterman enjoyed luxury, took pride in the way he lived and his surroundings. His office at the Easton Calchem plant reflected a love of luxury. So did the way he lived when he oversaw the construction of a new plant, no matter how isolated its location.

Lanterman was a workaholic, liked his responsibilities, and jetted home to see his family only on the weekends. The rest of the time he lived in a trailer park on a hill alongside the plant. But it was by no means just a trailer park. It was a specially designed and beautifully landscaped park surrounded by a security fence. The trailers inside the fence were intended for the Calchem administrators. None of the trailers looked like trailers; they all looked like well-done expensive homes with wooden shingles and brick exteriors. All of the trailers were double wide and nicely furnished except for Lanterman's. His was triple wide and expensively furnished with ultramodern chrome and plastic furniture, crystal chandeliers, overstuffed chairs and davenports imported from Paris, and a pure white rug with a three-inch-deep pile running throughout the entire home. The trailer had four bathrooms, a Jacuzzi, three fireplaces, a weight room, and a sauna. Of all the rooms the master bedroom was Lanterman's favorite. It was huge, had a white rug, white walls, and a white ceiling. The focal point of the bedroom was the bleached white polar bearskin bedspread, complete with snarling head.

William P. Lanterman was a hard-driving, articulate executive who was very good at his job. He was comfortable in front of the corporate stockholders and just as comfortable when he rolled up his sleeves, put on a hard hat and went toe to toe with tough-talking union stewards. Though not particularly liked by the stewards or his fellow executives, he was respected, and that was all Lanterman cared about.

It was late. Lanterman had put in a full day's work and he was almost asleep in his trailer when he began to detect the faintest traces of a foul odor. At first he had the feeling he was smelling warm spoiled milk, but the intensity of the odor grew until it began to resemble the scent of old, soiled baby diapers. For a while Lanterman stirred restlessly beneath his polar bear bedspread, thinking this was part of a vivid nightmare. That had to be it. Nothing in the real world smelled this hideous. But when he rolled over on his stomach and tried to bury his face in his pillow, he realized he was awake and the odor was real.

He sat up. Groping for the reading lamp next to the bed, he turned it on and saw a large man sitting in a director's chair just beyond the range of the light. "Who are you and what the hell is that smell?" he asked calmly.

"My name doesn't matter," the large man said as he uncoiled from the chair and got to his feet. The man picked up a jug and started across the bedroom towards Lanterman. Lanterman was too shocked to do anything but stare as the intruder put the plastic jug on the bed stand beside him, then returned to the director's chair. "As for the smell, you ought to know," the stranger said. "Your company makes that stuff." He gestured to the plastic jug on the night stand.

Lanterman shook his head in confusion. "I don't know what you're talking about."

"Your company makes chemicals, pesticides," the stranger said, speaking to Lanterman as if he were a child. "And while you're making that stuff, you're creating waste and then you're dumping it in the back yard of a friend of mine. I want you to stop."

"Just like that?" Lanterman asked.

"Just like that," Braille said.

"I take it you're a friend of Mrs. Stuart?" It wasn't a question. It was an accusation, and Braille didn't bother to answer it.

"I'd like to help you," Lanterman said, "but Mrs. Stuart signed a lease with Calchem."

"She didn't agree to have her sheep and cattle killed, her ranch destroyed, and the health of her children ruined." Braille gestured with his hands. "I don't have anything against your plant or the chemicals it makes, but a big badass corporation that takes advantage of a woman and two children irritates me." Lanterman started to say something but Braille didn't give him the chance. "Know what else I think? I think you and that corporation of yours came out here with efficiency experts, computers, and engineers and you all decided you didn't want to be hauling your wastes fifty or sixty miles away from the plant to someplace where there were no humans. No . . . that's not cost effective. Instead you took a good look at the people and used your computers to check out their financial records. You found a woman down on her luck, hit her with a contract and some money and the end result? Your corporation has a convenient dumping site. No problem, no sweat, no mess, no conscience . . . and that irritates me."

"That's not quite the way it was done," Lanterman protested.

"But I'm close, damn close."

"It was all legal and there's not a damn thing you can do about it." Lanterman smiled flatly.

"But there's something *you* can do about it," Braille

quietly stated. "That's why I'm here." He pointed to the container on Lanterman's night stand. "I think you ought to take a look at that. That stuff I scooped up from your company's waste site is melting that container. You're probably married, probably have children. How would you like to have a lake of that stuff in your back yard killing your family?"

"The EPA said that waste site was safe—"

"You know as well as I do that you and your corporation bought off those EPA investigators. Now what I want to know is are you going to do anything about the problem you've dumped on the Stuart family?"

"You mean like move the waste site? Clean up the dump?"

"Yes," Braille said softly.

Lanterman took a moment to assess the intruder sitting in the chair four feet away. The trespasser was a big man, but then so was he. Lanterman shook his head. "No."

"So much for fruitful dialogue between reasonable men," Braille grumbled, more to himself than Lanterman.

Lanterman leaned back against the headboard. He folded his arms and smiled. "I assume that now you'll try and get me to change my mind by getting violent? That would be foolish. I have a black belt in karate and my hands are registered as lethal weapons." As if to prove his point, he held up his hands while glaring at Braille.

Braille resisted the temptation to smile at the solemn warning. The Oriental couple who had adopted him as a teenager had worked with Braille, training him in the art of martial arts. By the time he was eighteen he had fourth degree black belts in three different forms of martial arts. After that he had stopped keeping track. Now, twenty-five years later, no belt existed that could summarize Braille's abilities in the martial arts. Poor Lanterman. Comparing what he had to what Braille had achieved was like comparing a choirboy to the pope.

Braille stirred and Lanterman took it as a sign of aggression. He leaped out of bed, landing on his feet with his arms out in front of him, his fingers straight and stiff in what looked like something out of a kung fu movie. "No more talk," Lanterman hissed to the intruder still sitting in the director's chair. "I should've whipped your ass the minute you came in. Now get up."

"Put some pants on," Braille said, yawning. "I never fight anybody who's naked."

Lanterman slipped on a pair of purple bikini briefs. "On your feet."

Braille had no intention of hurting the man. He needed Lanterman alive, healthy, and capable of making some changes within the corporation. If he had to hurt him, he would later on, but for right now, Lanterman needed to be rattled. Braille figured fear and terror would do the trick. He motioned for Lanterman to hold back, slowly rising to his feet. He looked hard at the man. "Black belt notwithstanding, if you try and fuck with me, I'll kill you and I'll do it with about as much thought and energy as I give to a sneeze."

Lanterman gave Braille a skeptical look. Braille sighed and glanced around the huge bedroom, looking for something he could prove his point on. He noticed a huge piece of modern sculpture sitting off in a corner. An artist with no talent and a blowtorch had cut a large human-shaped figure out of a section of old boilerplate, then gone on to mount the sculpture on a large black boulder.

"What's that?" Braille asked, wondering why the trailer floor hadn't caved in under the sculpture's weight.

"It's a work by Chez-Mann. It's called 'Man on the Mountain.' " Lanterman put his hands on his hips as if the answer should have been obvious.

"Do you like it?"

Lanterman snorted. "I paid thirty thousand dollars for it and had the floor of my trailer specially reinforced so I could have it with me. Of course I like it."

"Good." Braille turned away, walking towards the sculpture.

"What are you up to?" Lanterman asked puzzledly.

"I'm just out to prove that registered hands and black belts don't mean a thing." Braille moved closer to the "Man on the Mountain." "And I think it's time you got to know a little bit more about me. I'm not getting the attention from you I deserve."

Lanterman began to laugh. "I don't know what you're

planning, but there's not much you can do to three tons of rock and cast iron."

Braille barely heard what Lanterman said. Stopping two feet from the sculpture he remained motionless for a heartbeat, then his eyes focused on the abstract metal figure, then focused through it to a whole different dimension.

Suddenly Braille seemed to explode. He whirled his body around in a tight circle and kicked out with his right leg at the same time, slamming the edge of his boot into the middle of the metal sculpture.

For a brief moment Lanterman thought the stranger had missed the statue with his kick. The man had moved too fast for Lanterman to make out the details, and he hadn't heard anything. Then, on the other side of the room, he heard the sound of something heavy crash into the wall, clanging to the floor with a resounding thud. He glanced towards the noise, seeing a hole in the middle of one of his white walls and something large and black lying on the white rug below the hole. Confused, he glanced back at his Chez-Mann, his mouth dropping open in awe as he realized what had happened. The man had cleaved his statue in two with a kick and now the upper half of the statue, a slab of metal that had to weigh two hundred pounds, was lying on the other side of the room. Lanterman felt sick. He felt weak.

"It's going to cost a fortune to move that waste site," Lanterman said.

"Pass the cost on to your stockholders. That's what corporations do."

"I don't know if I can pull this off."

"You don't have a choice."

Lanterman regarded himself as a straight shooter and hated to lie. But in his mind he could see half of his body flying across the room just like the sculpture. "I'll stop the trucks first thing in the morning."

"And the dump site?" Braille asked.

"I'll have clean-up crews out there within the week."

"And the cattle and sheep your chemicals killed?"

"The Calchem corporation'll replace every one of them with prime grade stock," Lanterman said with visions of half his body sailing across the room still dancing in his head.

Braille didn't buy it. Lanterman was going down too easy. Still, he didn't have much choice. He had to take the man at his word, at least for the time being. He picked Lanterman's telephone up off the night stand, handing it to the man.

"What's this for?" Lanterman asked.

"Call your security guards and tell them there's an intruder in your home."

"You crazy?" Lanterman asked, his voice registering as much disbelief as his expression. "If I do that, a dozen armed security guards will come for this place like bats for blood. They could kill you."

Braille sat down in the director's chair. "I'm just making a point."

"Which is?"

"If I can walk away from this place with your security guards looking for me, then you'll know damn well that I can walk back into this place when they're not. I want you to know how defenseless you are. I want you to know I can get to you if you break your word or try and hurt the Stuart family. I'm doing this so you realize I can come for you any time I want. You can surround yourself with guards. You can put them in a circle around you, and I'll still get to you. But I don't think you believe that so I thought I'd show you."

Lanterman called the supervisor of security at the plant located less than half a mile away. "This is William Lanterman. Somebody's broken into my trailer. Get your men up here and tell 'em the intruder's armed. Hurry, for God's sake!" He hung up the phone.

"Nice touch," Braille said, "that business about me being armed."

Lanterman put on a full-length bathrobe. "If you think you're about to come face to face with a bunch of fat old ex-policemen, you're wrong. The company providing security to Calchem hires only the best. There isn't a man on the force over fifty and all have police experience."

"All the better," Braille mused.

Lanterman could hear the faint and unmistakable sounds of sirens now, growing louder with each second. Knowing there were at least a dozen Calchem guards on their way dissolved his fear of this stranger. Suddenly he was no longer afraid of the man, no longer felt the need to keep his promise. "Naturally, I'll keep my word and begin moving the dump site tomorrow, but out of curiosity, what would you have done to me if I hadn't gone along with your request."

Braille shrugged with his hands. "I would have killed you, and leveled your plant." He pointed at the plastic jug he had put next to Lanterman's bed. The caustic waste had eaten through the plastic and was now eating through Lanterman's night stand. "By the way, if you're thinking about breaking your promise to me, you might want to consider what would happen to you if I tossed you into your own dump site. In less than five minutes you wouldn't have any body parts. No skin, muscles, fingers, or testicles. Best think about that, William."

Lanterman did, but only briefly. The sirens were extremely loud now, and he knew there were security cars screeching to stops out in front of his trailer. Then he heard what sounded like a dozen car doors opening and closing. He smiled at Braille. "I think your game just came to an end and maybe your life, if you don't surrender."

Braille got to his feet, looking hard at Lanterman. "One more thing," he said softly. "The Stuarts didn't have a thing to do with my coming here. It was strictly my idea, mine alone." There was a loud pounding on the front door. Braille didn't seem to notice. "So your problem is with me, not them. Mess with them in any way, and I'll come back and kill you."

The pounding on the front door continued to escalate. It sounded like the men were trying to get into the trailer by using battering rams. It was so loud it was scaring Lanterman and he couldn't believe the stranger was still standing in front of him, looking totally at ease. Then he heard the stranger say: "A long time ago another man hurt someone close to me. I went after that man, caught up with him in Switzerland, and it took him twenty days to die. He died in agony in a hospital and nobody could help him. Not the doctors, not the priests, not God. The same thing'll happen to you if you try and hurt the Stuart family—understand?"

Lanterman heard the double front doors to his trailer explode open and knew his men were rushing into the trailer. But he was still frightened. "Yes," he screamed over the din, then realized he was screaming at no one. He was alone.

Braille came face to face with four uniformed guards clustered together near the shattered front doors. It was dark in this part of the trailer, and one of the men was trying to find a wall switch. The men were all heavily armed and confident in the belief that an intruder would be going out a back door. Braille took advantage of their confidence and the darkness. He snatched a sawed-off shotgun from one man, then holding it horizontally, he slammed it into the heads of the two nearest guards. Both went down without a sound.

"Who fell? Is there a step down?" one of the two remaining guards asked, still groping in the darkness. The man found the light switch and lights came on. The two men caught a fleeting glimpse of movement, then the room exploded in blackness for both.

Braille moved out onto a dark front porch. Out in front of the trailer were five black Chevy Blazers with blinking lights mounted on their cabs. There were also four more security guards with sawed-off shotguns. "He's trying to get out the back window!" Braille shouted.

To his surprise, it worked. The guards took off at a dead run for the back of the trailer. Shaking his head at the ease of it all, Braille scaled the cyclone fence surrounding the small trailer park. He mounted the Harley and drove off.

Lanterman filled a second glass with straight Scotch and downed it in one motion. "Tell me again how many men you brought to my trailer," he said to the night supervisor of security.

"Twelve, counting myself," said the other man.

Lanterman killed the second glass of Scotch. "Twelve," he said, turning slowly to glare at the supervisor. "Twelve highly trained, heavily armed security guards, and one man—just one man gives four of them concussions, fools the shit out of the others, then walks away from this place easy as you please. Christ, I got a bunch of pussies guarding the plant."

The security supervisor gritted his teeth. "He took the men by surprise and you yourself said he was tough, had some martial arts training."

"I said he kicked a statue in two. I didn't say he was tougher than God." Lanterman turned his back on the man and began pouring Scotch into his glass. "How many men are guarding my trailer right now?"

"Eight, and I've called in the day shift. They should be here in about fifteen minutes." The security supervisor paused before speaking. "I still think we could nip this in the bud if we send a dozen men out to the Stuart ranch. You said your intruder knew the woman. He might be staying out there. If he is, we could catch the man and end the problem here and now."

Lanterman could still recall what the stranger had said he would do if Lanterman or his men messed with the Stuart family. "No. I want her left out of it. Nobody's to go near that place." Lanterman realized he was starting to get drunk in front of one of his employees and pushed the glass aside. "I want you to call Jason Sanders. Tell him I want more security up here, tell him I want more men guarding the plant, more men around my trailer, and more men on the trucks going out to the dump. If he hasn't got that many available men, then tell him to pull some of the guards away from the other plants."

The security supervisor nodded, walking over to the phone.

26

IT WAS TWO O'CLOCK IN THE MORNING. THE BARS IN DOWNTOWN
Seattle were closing and there should have been people on
the streets, customers walking to their cars. But there
weren't. This upset and angered Otis Jamal Piedmont as he
brought his twenty-seven-thousand-dollar Toyota Supra to a
stop at a red light. Otis was a businessman, and while he
normally made good money through the evening hours, it
was that magical hour after the bars closed that was his
bread and butter. After the bars closed, the streets were full
of drunks, horny drunks who wanted to get laid. That was
where Otis came in. He had a stable of five girls. Two worked
on the streets, the other three worked out of an all-night
acupuncture massage parlor out near the freeway.

Otis Jamal Piedmont was a pimp, but in his mind's eye he
wasn't. No, he was a professional. And he had the trappings
to prove it. He drove around in imported cars, favored
high-topped Reeboks, cotton slacks, and all his shirts had
foxes or alligators on their pockets. He'd even gone so far as
to buy a computer, and he was going to use it to keep track
of his women's earnings just as soon as he learned how to
turn it on. No, Otis Jamal Piedmont *was not* a pimp, he was
a preppie. Maybe even a yuppie, except he wasn't quite sure
what a yuppie was.

The light turned green and he drove deeper into downtown Seattle. Two blocks later he stopped for another red
light and looked around. Nobody was on the sidewalks,
hardly any cars moving in the streets. He'd seen the local
news shows on TV, heard the special reports about all the
people disappearing without a trace in downtown Seattle
like it was some sort of Bermuda Triangle, but he didn't buy
that mysterious hype business. Far as he was concerned,
there was probably a freako serial killer out there bopping

winos and bag ladies and throwing their bodies in the harbor. But that was no reason for people not to come out and play, Otis thought.

The light changed. He slipped his Supra into gear and started off. He could make out four women down the street, standing on a corner under the yellow glare of a porno theater's marquee. Seeing four women on that corner irritated Otis. That was his corner, reserved for his two women. What the fuck were the other two women doing there standing next to his women. That wasn't right. If they were independent hookers, his girls should have taken care of the matter. If they belonged to another pimp, they still should have taken care of it, then let him take care of the other pimp. It also irritated him that his women were standing there. When they weren't there, it meant they were off with customers, earning money—for him.

As the yellow neon glare from the theater's marquee splayed across his windshield, Otis guided his car over to the curb. He stopped, pushing a button that lowered the passenger window. "Yo, Carmen, Gloria. Git your motherfuckin' asses over here!"

Even before he'd stopped, the two women had started towards the curb, but their high spiked heels and tight leather skirts made walking almost impossible. As his women crabbed towards him, Otis Piedmont glared at the competition. One was a teenager with peroxided white hair. The other was an immense black woman known on the streets as Ms. Mountains. Otis recognized both. They were Leroy Smiley's hoes and Otis knew he'd be having a serious talk with Leroy soon. This wasn't professional. Otis had his corner. Leroy had his. Sending Ms. Mountains and the white-haired chick over into his territory was a serious breach of ethics.

Carmen and Gloria knelt down beside the Supra, looking at Otis through the open window with pleading, terror-stricken eyes. Good, Otis thought, observing the frightened expressions on his women's faces. They knew when to be scared, knew when a beating was coming their way. "You better have good money in yo' pockets. Then maybe I'll understand why you be just standin' around here with yo' thumbs up yo' asses while the competition's takin' space on mah corner."

"You don't understand," Gloria sobbed. "It's bad out here, screams, people dying, people disappearing. Terrible scary noises!"

"She's right!" Carmen added hysterically. "Otis, there's somethin' out there, somethin' killin' people, somethin' killin' taxi drivers and hoes and bag ladies and *everybody.*"

"What you talkin' about?" Otis asked, angry now because his women weren't afraid of him but of something out there in the night.

"We think it's a gang," Gloria said breathlessly. She was wearing a tight Danskin and his view of her cleavage was turning Otis on.

"Yeah," Carmen said. "A gang." She squirmed into the small opening beside Gloria and now her bosom was hanging down inside the car and *her* cleavage was turning Otis on. With effort Otis tore his eyes away from the bosoms. He looked out the windshield, scanned the street in front of him, then turned to his women.

"What gang?" he asked. "Ah don't see no motherfuckin' gang nowhere. Now, ah see buildings. And ah scc lights, and ah see two women who ain't made no money fo' me tonight. Ah also see two other women who shouldn't be standin' on mah motherfuckin' corner. But ah sho' don't see no gang no place." He shook his head as he heard the words coming from his mouth. He was starting to sound like an L.A. pimp again. He always sounded like an L.A. pimp when he was horny or mad. Right now he was both. "What gang?" he pointed out. "I do not see any gang anyplace."

"They be hiding," Gloria said. "They don't come out into the light. But you can see 'em sometimes when a car goes by or when they run out of one alley and into another."

Carmen nodded. "They stay in the dark, but you can hear 'em. You can hear 'em when they attack. Sometimes people scream and sometimes you can hear . . . hear growling." She tried to gesture at Leroy's women, who were standing on the sidewalk next to the fender of Otis' Supra, but she was too squeezed in and all she could do was move her head. "That's why we all together."

Suddenly Ms. Mountains rapped loudly on the Supra's

fender with her knuckles to get everyone's attention. "Oh oh," said Gloria. Carmen grimaced and Otis' eyes grew wide in disbelief.

"Leroy's hoe just struck mah car," he gasped. He opened the door and got out. "Say, woman. If'n you wanta keep that hand, you best not be touchin' mah auto-mobeel."

"Shut up and listen," said three hundred and ten pounds worth of woman while she cupped one hand behind her ear to hear something far off in the night.

Otis had driven by Ms. Mountains, seen her from afar, but had never realized how really big she was. "Okay," he said, cupping his hand behind his ear . . .

And heard a man screaming "NO! . . . NO!" followed by pistol shots, two women shrieking, more pistol shots . . . then nothing but an abrupt silence.

"Lord," Otis said to himself as he heard a glass window shatter off in the night. "What is going on out there?"

"See what we mean?" Carmen asked.

"Yeah," Gloria added. "There's been stuff going on like that off and on for the past two or three nights, only tonight, it's worse, really bad."

"Gang war?" Otis suggested hopefully.

Ms. Mountains shook her head. "There's somethin' bad out there in the night, somethin' evil. It's killin' people. And it's growin'."

"So what's Leroy say?" Otis asked.

"Ain't seen Leroy since last night."

"Yeah," said the blond teenager standing beside Ms. Mountains. "He came by around ten, said he'd be back by three and he never came. We had to take a taxi home."

"Won't be that lucky tonight," Ms. Mountains said. "There's no taxi drivers around. The cabs be there, all parked along the curbs, but they're empty. No drivers." She shook her head again. "There's somethin' out there and it's killin' people. If'n I get home tonight, I ain't comin' out no mo'. Even if Leroy is alive and comes for me with a baseball bat, I ain't comin' out no mo'." She started to say something else, but the sound of someone firing a shotgun cut her off.

Close by, Otis thought. Not more than two blocks away. Then everyone heard the faint voice of a frightened man shouting. "I said hold it! Come any closer and I'll blow you all away . . . I'm a cop, goddammit! I said hold it!" The shotgun went off several more times. Silence followed the shotgun blasts, but in his mind, Otis could still hear the man screaming. The silent death scream terrified him. He wanted to jump in his car, drive away, but he couldn't. His women were watching him. He knew he had to be cool, a tower of power for his women.

"See you later," he said calmly as he started to slowly ease himself into the Supra.

"You're not leavin' us, are you?" Gloria squeaked out.

"You be okay," he said comfortingly.

"We need a ride out of this part of town," Ms. Mountains said, glaring at Otis. She tried to fold her arms across her chest, but her massive bosom got in the way.

"Yeah," Carmen agreed.

Otis Jamal Piedmont was trying to figure out how to get himself out of this mess and this part of town when he heard a loud clank. He looked into the street in time to see a two-hundred-pound manhole cover fly up into the air like a tossed coin. A long moment later it crashed down on the sidewalk thirty feet from the hole in the middle of the street.

"Lordie!" he whispered in awe of the power that could have done that to a cast-iron manhole cover. He said "Lordie" again as he saw one of the most beautiful women he'd ever seen climb so gracefully out of the hole in the street it almost seemed as if she were floating. The woman was stunning, had blond hair, an hourglass figure, and boobs for days. Like a majestic lioness, the strange woman studied the four women standing beside Otis' car. Then her eyes came to rest on Otis. She didn't smile, but she licked her lips. Good sign, Otis thought. She likes me.

The blond woman started towards the five people, moving slowly, gracefully, like a big cat. Good moves, Otis thought. Good moves and boobs for days. This woman could make him rich.

The woman had hooked him, mesmerized him. He was under her spell and he didn't see the other figures emerging from the hole in the street. But the women standing behind Otis did.

"Shit," hissed Ms. Mountains.

"Otis, start your car," Gloria shrieked.

"Huh?" Otis said.

"Start your car!" Ms. Mountains shouted. "That thing don't wanta make love. It wants to eat your heart!"

Otis came out of the spell. He saw four figures behind the blond goddess and saw more climbing up out of the hole in the street. Then he noticed something odd about the woman. Her clothes were ripped. There was dirt and blood on her face and as she came into the light of the theater marquee, he could see her teeth. They were long and sharp and belonged in the mouth of a Doberman.

Eight or nine people had come up out of the hole now and Otis had the feeling he and the women behind him were being stalked by a pack of dogs. Fighting off a growing sense of panic, he slowly lowered himself into the driver's seat. At the same moment, the women beside his car were getting ready to fight. Each was holding a knife or straight razor and for a brief instant, Otis felt pride in the way the women were handling the threat.

"Cut 'em to pieces," he murmured softly, looking out the side window at the blond woman. There was something familiar about the blonde, like maybe he'd seen her in the movies, but he couldn't put his finger on it. It didn't matter. They were almost on him. He could see their teeth, their fingernails, their red eyes. It was rabbit time.

He closed the door and hit the gas. The Supra shot away from the curb. Otis didn't look back, didn't even glance up into his rearview mirror. Ten blocks later Otis got control of himself, hit the brakes and swung the car around. He couldn't leave Carmen and Gloria back there. If it ever got out that Otis Jamal Piedmont had run out on two of his hoes when they were in danger, no woman in Seattle would ever work for him again. He'd have to relocate. Or worse, get a job. Besides, it had come to him that he could use his car as a weapon. If those weird people were still on the street, he'd just run over them and that would make him a hero and some of Leroy's women might come over and join his stable.

Otis floored the accelerator and the Supra shot down the deserted street. Might be kind of fun, he thought, feeling brave, almost heroic, while he checked to make sure the doors were locked. The car had sturdy bumpers and a high-powered engine. He'd just squish those people—if they were people—flat.

He slowed up a half a block from the porno theater, more out of surprise than caution. There wasn't anybody there, nobody on the sidewalk, nobody in the street. No bodies, no fighting. He slowed the Supra to a crawl, then braked it to a dead stop. But there was something going on in front of him, just out of range of his headlights. Otis sucked in a deep breath, turning on the lights to high beam.

"Oh Lordie," he whispered softly at what the high beams captured.

Two of those things that had come up out of the hole in the street were down on their hands and knees, tugging at the limp remains of Ms. Mountains. They'd managed to drag the body over to the hole in the street. Now they were trying to push the woman through the hole, but Ms. Mountain's massive frame wouldn't fit and the creatures were irritated, not only with their problem but with the bright lights shining on them from Otis' car. As Otis sat behind the wheel, dumbfounded by the animalistic sight, the creatures got to their feet and suddenly charged the Supra.

Otis squealed. The Supra's tires squealed. The power steering squealed as Otis wheeled the car around in a cramped U-turn. The Supra hit a curb, bouncing up on the sidewalk and back onto the street, then took off like a bullet. Otis glanced into his rearview mirror. The two things—creatures—were still behind him, coming hard, but he was leaving them and their red eyes behind. Up ahead a light turned red. Otis didn't even slow down as he raced through the intersection.

Two blocks later he turned the Supra onto a wide boulevard lit up by a long stream of halogen lights. He could see more figures now, all staying away from the lights, but they were out there. Shapes moving in the night. Shapes running past a deserted McDonald's, shapes out in a Wendy's parking lot, shapes milling around in front of dark motels. Christ, they were all around him.

Something came out of the night, running for his car. It smacked into the side of it. He caught a fleeting glimpse of a body rolling over and over on the boulevard behind him. Good, he thought. I hit one. He drove on and tried to figure out what to do next. He had no doubt now that those things had killed Carmen, Gloria, the teenager, and Ms. Mountains, taking the bodies down below the city, but why? And what should he do about it? Tell the police? The newspapers? The TV people? Would anybody believe him? His stomach was churning and he knew he would throw up any minute now, but there was no way he would stop his car. No way.

The police would never believe him. They knew what he was and had his record on file. Going to the radio or the newspapers was a so-so idea. But doing a television interview had some appeal. They might just believe him. After all, they'd been doing reports about the strange goings on in downtown Seattle, ending their reports with questions. Based on what he'd seen earlier, he was the one person in the world that could give the TV people answers to those questions. The idea of being on TV sounded good to Otis.

"It was a bad fight. We fought them. Then we ran for the car," he said aloud, practicing the speech he'd just made up for the TV camera. "I got to the car first, and my friends were just behind me when a mob of them people-things overwhelmed us. I fought as best as I could, killed some, and then when it looked like I would be pulled down through the hole in the street, I broke free and just barely got away.

"There's something bad and evil in downtown Seattle, somethin' living under the streets. It's there, waiting for people like my friends, Gloria and Carmen. I hope the world believes me when I say that downtown Seattle is not a safe place to be."

Pleased with himself and his story, Otis Jamal Piedmont pulled onto the freeway and headed off towards the television station.

27

BRAILLE JOINED THE STUARTS FOR BREAKFAST. MARY KATHLEEN was quiet. John Jr. was in high spirits because he knew none of the older boys at school would pick on him today. Amanda was in a good mood because she'd never felt better in her life. Her lungs were still clear and she'd slept the entire night without coughing, oxygen, or slaps on the back. Only one thing bothered Braille, and that was the way Amanda kept staring at him. At one point he felt her eyes on him. He looked at her, then watched her silently mouth the words "Thank you."

What is it you know about me, child? Braille wondered. Last night you were sick and somehow I made you better, somehow I took your illness into my body, but did you take something from me? Did you take my secrets? Do you know about my past, how I earned my living? Do you know what I am now? Do you know about the animal part that needs blood to exist?

Amanda neither nodded nor shook her head. She just continued to stare at him over the edge of her two-handed mug, her eyes wide and innocent, curiously accepting about what she saw.

After breakfast Braille went out on the porch for a cigarette. Immediately he caught sight of the school bus off in the distance, heading towards the Stuart home. He was about to call out to Mary Kathleen and John when he realized the bus was barreling down the road and the driver had no intentions of stopping. After it passed, Braille opened the front door and shouted inside, "Bus just went by."

"So what else is new," came Mary Kathleen's response.

Lighting a cigarette, Braille trotted down the steps and walked out onto the front lawn. The air was crisp and clean and he was appreciating the early morning silence when an ominous but familiar sound snagged his attention. He turned and looked down the gravel road fronting the Stuart ranch. A black vehicle was coming over the top of a hill off in the distance. A moment later a truck pulling two huge tanker trailers came into view. Not wanting to draw attention to himself, Braille moved over behind a large cotton-wood tree in front of the Stuart home and stood behind it as a black Chevy Blazer with flashing lights and a massive Calchem tanker trailer rig rumbled by. After both vehicles disappeared, Braille angrily flipped his cigarette away. It was easy to see what was going on, easy to tell what Lanterman was up to. Not only did he have no intentions of stopping the trucks, but now the trucks had an escort vehicle, complete with two armed guards inside.

"Serves me right for bluffing," Braille said softly, knowing he had underestimated Lanterman, had gone in too nice and easy. Now it was up to him to stop the trucks and the only way to do that was to make Lanterman a believer. Next time he wouldn't be bluffing. Next time he wouldn't be nice.

Mary Kathleen came out on the porch followed by John and Amanda. "I'm going to take John to school," she shouted. "Then I'm going to take Amanda to the medical clinic. Be back late." Braille nodded, waved, then wandered into the back yard while they drove off. There wasn't anything he could do about the Calchem plant for the time being. Tonight was a long ways off.

Kubick's team spent the morning and the early part of the afternoon canvassing Stanwood. Wearing suits, carrying briefcases, and armed with impeccable credentials that identified them as advance men for a Seattle corporation interested in building a pulp mill in the town, the men had had no problem getting the residents to cooperate and answer loosely structured questions about the available work force, unemployed members of the household, and newly arrived renters and boarders.

At two-twenty in the afternoon, John Kramer, the team's communication specialist, rang Molly Estleford's doorbell. Twelve minutes later he climbed back into his car and raised

Kubick on the radio. At three-fifteen the team joined Kramer in the parking lot of a 1950's drive-in restaurant on the outskirts of Stanwood. The drive-in had been closed and boarded up for years. Kubick's men parked their cars and vans at the back of the parking lot next to a stand of old trees and rotting picnic tables.

Kramer was strangely quiet as the other members of the team gathered around him. He remained silent until Kubick emerged from his car, walked up to the group, and motioned for Kramer to begin.

"I found him . . ." John Kramer said simply. "Earlier this afternoon I interviewed an old woman named Estleford. Seems that not too long ago she turned the third floor of her house into an apartment. The man who's living in that apartment is the one that killed Reber and McCabe."

"How do you know?" asked one of the team members.

"The man arrived out of nowhere eight or nine weeks ago. No car. One suitcase. He's never talked about where he's from or what he does. He doesn't work and has no visible means of support. He doesn't go out much in the daytime, has no friends and never gets or makes phone calls. He's totally a loner."

"So?" asked another team member.

Kramer smiled. "It gets better. The man is paying for room and board, but never seems to eat. He'll sit with the old lady and her granddaughter at dinnertime, but he just sits with them for the company. He doesn't eat. The Estleford woman likes him, thinks he's smart, but also thinks he's a little strange and ignorant of the basics. At his request she taught him how to drive her car, and when a light bulb burned out in his apartment, he didn't know how to change it. She had to teach him how to change channels on a TV set, and she also said he had an accent when he first arrived, but the accent's gone now." He broke off and continued to look at Kubick expectantly.

Kubick scratched his throat. "Could be our man, but I don't know."

Kramer smiled. "I was saving the best for last. The Estleford woman's granddaughter is living with her. I guess the kid got into trouble with drugs and a bad crowd in Tacoma and the probation department sent her up here to live with her grandmother so she could get away from the people she was running with. Seems some of this girl's friends found out where she was and came up here looking for her. The grandmother called them hooligans, but judging from the way she described them, a pack of bikers arrived one night and just walked right into this old lady's house. She tried to get them to leave. They wouldn't go. When she started to call the police, one of the bikers tore the phone out and threw it through a window. It was a real mess.

"Then, all of a sudden, this boarder of hers comes down the stairs and asks the Estleford woman if she wants any help. She says she does and the next thing she knows these biker guys—and she figures there's maybe seven or eight of them—plus their girlfriends are gone. Most are laying out in the front yard, and the rest are crawling out the front door as fast as they can. She said you had to see it to believe it and when it was done, her boarder wasn't even breathing hard. It all fits from the time when this man surfaced to the strength it took to handle the biker gang. We've found the man who killed McCabe and Reber."

"You did well," Kubick said. Kramer nodded. A compliment from Kubick was almost as rare as a smile.

"What's the layout of the house?" Kubick asked.

"The house is old and big. It's three stories with dormers on the roof, so it probably has a sizable attic. Lots of foliage and old trees on all four sides. I couldn't check out the back yard without drawing attention to myself, but I did get some photos of the place." He handed Kubick some Polaroids.

Kubick scrutinized the photos. There was a lot of foliage and trees, but there weren't that many trees in front of the house. "That's good," he said, passing the photographs on to his team. "We have a clear field of fire from the street."

"What about the civilians in the house?" Kramer asked.

Kubick gave him a withering look. "That thing killed Reber and McCabe and you're worried about an old lady and her granddaughter?" Kramer started to protest; Kubick didn't give him the chance. "I want this beast, and if I have to level the entire town to get it, I will. I don't intend to get caught off guard like Reber and McCabe. That means we go in hard core."

Kubick picked up a small stone and set it on the fender of

his car. It was just a piece of gravel, about the size of a bottle cap. Kubick's men looked at the rock, then at Kubick in puzzlement. Kubick almost seemed to smile as he stared straight ahead, staring at nothing. Then like a snake striking, his arm flashed out and he brought the edge of his hand down on the stone like a hatchet. His men strained to see what had happened to the pebble, but couldn't because it was still under Kubick's stiffened hand.

"One more thing," he said flatly. "There is nothing in this world that can't be destroyed," then he moved his hand away.

The stone was gone. All that remained was a small pile of dust, fine as flour.

28

BRAILLE FINISHED PATCHING THE BARN'S ROOF WITH NEW SHIN-gles just before sunset. He was pleased with his handiwork, but the blend of new shingles and old shingles looked a little odd. He decided to solve that problem tomorrow by painting the roof with a dark waterproof stain. Slipping the hammer into a loop on the carpenter's apron he was wearing, he walked down to the edge of the roof to the ladder leaning against the side of the barn. He sat down next to the ladder, letting his legs dangle off the edge of the roof. The winter sun was setting and the hills and pasturelands were covered with long shadows. Braille sat in silence, watching the shadows darken and the colors of the world go from violet to a dark gray.

He was lighting a cigarette when he picked up the sound of an oncoming car. He smiled. That gutsy rumble could belong only to Mary Kathleen Stuart's worn-out station wagon. A few minutes later the smile broadened as the station wagon pulled up beside the house and two small children clambered out and started yelling for him. He shouted back, and the two sprinted across the back yard, crossing the bridge and running up to the barn. Craning back their heads, both shouted in unison: "Whatcha doing?"

"Sitting on the barn," Braille answered.

"I saw some doctors today," Amanda shouted up to him.

"Did you now," Braille said.

"I got them all confused."

"How so?" Braille asked.

Amanda Stuart moved back, cupping her hands like a megaphone. "They said I don't have the disease anymore. They might even send me and my x-rays to someplace in Kansas. How about that? I might get to go to Kansas."

"Kansas?" Braille said bleakly, then smiled because he was delighted with her delight.

"Can I come up?" John asked, tired of competing with his sister.

He was about to say yes when the children's mother materialized behind them. "Looks like you've been busy," Mary Kathleen said, resting her hands on her daughter's shoulders and gazing up at Braille.

"I had a good day," Braille said.

"Some day," Mary Kathleen observed. "You leveled that burned-out deathtrap of a bunkhouse, reposted the corrals, and fixed the barn roof." She jostled Amanda. "Come on, sweetie. You can help me with dinner." Amanda protested, but followed her mother away from the barn. They were over by the remains of the bunkhouse when Mary Kathleen whirled around and looked up at Braille. "The place has never looked better. You did more work in one day than my . . . my husband and some of those hands he hired did in three years. Will you be ready to eat in a half hour?"

Braille nodded, knowing she could see his movement in the dusky darkness.

"Can I come up *now?*" John Jr. shouted.

Braille shook his head. "I'll come down to you." He was starting down the ladder when he picked up a faint familiar sound that conjured up hate and dread. He glanced up into a now-dark sky and spotted its blinking lights immediately. The helicopter was heading straight for him. Impossible, he thought, remembering the days and nights in the desert with

OSMS helicopters all around him. There's no way they could know. Not yet. Not this soon.

Standing high up on the ladder, Braille remained motionless as the copter swooped in over the Stuart ranch, hovered overhead, then continued on, its running lights blinking ominously as it flew on towards Easton.

"Wow! That was cool," John shouted.

"Yeah, cool," Braille said absent-mindedly, starting down the ladder. He had not seen numbers or a logo on the side of the ship, but that didn't mean a thing. The copters that had hunted him in the desert hadn't had logos or numbers on their fuselages either. "John," he heard himself say. "You'd better go get ready for dinner. I'll be in in a minute."

Braille remained on the ladder, waiting. Less than two minutes later it happened. A second helicopter came out of the night and swept over the Stuart ranch not more than a quarter of a mile from the barn. Braille waited a few minutes more, then climbed down the ladder and started walking back towards the Stuart home. He didn't know what the helicopters were looking for, didn't even know if they were from the OSMS, but if they were, if Cutter was zeroing in on him, his presence was jeopardizing the lives of Mary Kathleen Stuart and her children. At that moment Braille knew he would be leaving in the morning.

The realization he would be leaving tore at him, giving him more pain than the OSMS ever had. The house he was walking towards had become a home for him. He'd become comfortable here, grown fond of Mary Kathleen Stuart, Amanda, and John. He wandered over to the swing set, sitting down on one of the swings and staring at the back of the Stuart home. The house was lit up and the kitchen lights were on, casting light out into the back yard, squares of light that stopped just short of the swing, leaving Braille in the darkness.

Always the darkness.

He had to leave. It was a righteous decision, but why did doing the right thing always hurt so deeply? he wondered. John burst out on the back porch, calling Braille's name.

"It's on the table. Mom says move it, or lose it." He disappeared back into the kitchen.

Braille used the swing's ropes to pull himself to his feet,

starting towards the house. Then he stopped for a moment to wipe his face with the back of his hand.

Braille stepped into the cheery kitchen, surprised by the elegance. There was a tablecloth, china plates, and special silverware on the kitchen table. Amanda was wearing a dress. She looked delightful and knew it. John was wearing slacks and a tie. He looked good, but didn't like it. Braille grinned, then glanced over at their mother. His expression dissolved into open-mouthed awe.

Mary Kathleen Stuart was wearing earrings and makeup. Her auburn hair was pulled back in a kind of french roll. The hairstyle and makeup accentuated the woman's classic beauty. She was wearing a turquoise-colored dress with a flowing neckline and a long skirt, and the overall effect was devastating. Mary Kathleen Stuart was stunning.

Braille was wearing jeans, boots, and a white shirt with sleeves rolled up to the elbows. "What's the occasion?" he murmured, feeling out of place.

Mary Kathleen walked towards him. She was wearing high heels. The brace and cowboy boots were gone and without the support, she was limping, but trying to act as if she weren't. Braille tried not to notice her withered right leg. And it was easy. The overall effect of the makeup, the dress and the hairstyle all served to take his breath away.

"We're celebrating Amanda's health," she announced, smiling broadly. "We went to the clinic in Easton. I had her checked out. The x-rays show no signs of cystic fibrosis, and there's more. The doctors at the clinic ran tests on her pancreas and the tests came out normal." She smiled broadly. "My daughter doesn't have cystic fibrosis anymore." Mary Kathleen stopped just inches from Braille, looking up at him.

"They're going to hug," Amanda whispered.

"Bet they won't," John said.

"Yes they will," Amanda insisted.

Mary Kathleen Stuart and Braille stood for a long moment longer looking at one another, then slowly separated. "See," John said, smiling at Amanda.

Mary Kathleen explained over dinner. "The doctors said it was a miracle. They don't understand it. It's like she never had cystic fibrosis. They want to send her to a special medical clinic in the Midwest to see if those doctors can explain it. Maybe she has something in her blood that can help others with C.F." She looked intensely at Braille. "You should've seen those doctors at the clinic. They were flabbergasted. Isn't that right?" She beamed at Amanda, but Amanda didn't look back. The girl was picking at her food, her eyes downcast. "What's wrong, honey?" Mary Kathleen asked.

Amanda finally looked up at Braille, looked at him seriously with her wide eyes. "Will you say good-bye before you leave?"

Braille was dumbfounded. How could she know? How could she even suspect? He turned to Mary Kathleen. The delight and merriment had gone out of her face, and now she was looking at him with stunned disappointment.

"Are you leaving?" she asked, closing her eyes as if she anticipated the answer.

"No," Braille said. It was a lie. But he didn't want to tell the truth. They were celebrating Amanda's health. The truth could come later.

Braille watched joy return to Mary Kathleen's face. Then he glanced at Amanda. Their eyes met.

You know I just lied, don't you, Braille thought, knowing somehow that Amanda would not mention his leaving again. The child continued to stare at him, and finally Braille silently mouthed the words, "Thank you." Amanda nodded and began to eat.

After dinner Braille started to clear away the dishes. Mary Kathleen stopped him.

"No way," she insisted, motioning for him to sit down. "For the first time in my life I have two healthy children sitting in front of me. They can clear the table."

Amanda looked shocked. Her brother smiled like a Cheshire cat at Amanda. "Looks like you finally have to help out around here," he said.

While the children worked, Mary Kathleen walked over to a kitchen cabinet, pulling out a bottle and two crystal glasses. She put the glasses on the table and filled them with an amber liquid. "It's Drambuie," she said. "The bottle's been in the cupboard for years. Never broke it out before because there was never anything to celebrate. She sat down and picked up her glass. "To health," she toasted. "Now that my daughter has that, I have everything."

They touched glasses and Braille sampled the Drambuie. It was good, and the liquor didn't seem to throw his system into shock. Nice to know, he thought. Thank the gods for small miracles.

"How about we finish our drinks and have a cigarette on the porch," Mary Kathleen suggested.

The TV set was on in the living room, and while Braille was waiting for Mary Kathleen to get her coat, the Spokane programming was suddenly interrupted by a television news reporter.

"This is a special news bulletin update. We now take you to the studios of our sister station in Seattle, KOMO." The scene changed and another man appeared on camera sitting behind a news anchor desk. The newscaster was sweating and visibly upset.

"Earlier this evening KOMO reporter Misty Ying conducted an interview with a man who claimed to know what was happening to the people who have been mysteriously disappearing off the streets of Seattle. Following the interview, she, her cameraman and soundman entered Underground Seattle, hoping to clear up some of the statements made during her live interview. As you will soon see, the results were catastrophic for the young KOMO news reporter. We will be showing segments of the tape her cameraman filmed, and I must add that not only is the language during the upcoming interview explicit, but the footage taken in Underground Seattle is extremely graphic. This is not suitable viewing material for children and some adults may not want to view what we are about to show."

Suddenly a pretty Eurasian woman appeared on camera. "Good evening," the woman reporter said to the television camera. "I am Misty Ying and I'm coming to you live from the heart of downtown Seattle. Currently I am standing on Cascade Way, normally a very busy boulevard, but not tonight. Tonight Cascade Way is deserted. Traffic is sparse, there are almost no pedestrians, and those that do venture out on the sidewalks run to their cars. Why? Because very strange things are happening to the people of downtown Seattle.

"To put it simply, they are disappearing.

"Tonight I would like you to meet a man who believes he knows why the people are disappearing." She motioned with her microphone, and a tall thin man dressed in preppie clothes stepped up beside her. The man had Band-Aids on one eyebrow and his temple. He looked uncomfortable as he stared into the lens of the camera.

Misty Ying continued. "As we reported to you earlier, the city and health department feel that a new and virulent form of flu is affecting the residents of this area and that is their explanation for why people like the city's bus drivers, taxicab drivers, and policemen are not reporting for work. The city would like us to believe these people are home, ill, and incapable of phoning in. But the man standing beside me, Mr. Otis Piedmont, has a different view because last night a group of people attacked Mr. Piedmont and several of his friends." She turned to Otis Piedmont, shoving the microphone into his face. "Please tell us what happened to you and especially your friends."

Earlier when Misty had questioned Otis in the studio, he'd presented himself in an articulate and convincing manner. But now with the cameras on him and a woman he considered almost as famous as Jane Pauley asking him to say something, Otis froze, choked up, and managed to blurt out: "A muther-'bleep'-porno queen just floated up right outta that manhole cover over there in the street an' then she an' her muther-'bleep'-friends came over and ate mah friends."

Misty Ying started to pull the microphone away, but Otis grabbed the mike with both hands, staring wide-eyed at the camera. "Cindy Sin, that's who it was, Cindy Sin the porno actress. I seen her on my VCR. She just floated right up out of that hole over there and then she and her red-eyed friends came for us. Ah fought 'em, fought 'em with everything ah had, but there were too many and they drug mah friends over to that hole there and commenced to eat on mah friends even while they was pulling 'em down into the hole. Would'a taken me 'ceptin' ah fought. Ah fought that Cindy

Sin with those red eyes burnin' into mah face and finally she and her red-eyed demon friends left me cuz ah was fightin' too hard. But they kilt mah friends and drug 'em down into that hole over in da middle of da street." Otis tried to point with the microphone, but Misty was holding on to it with both hands.

The tape ended abruptly; the man behind the news desk appeared on the screen.

"Coming up now is the remainder of the earlier live broadcast Misty Ying made. Again, I would like to warn the viewing audience that what you are about to see is graphically violent and viewer discretion is advised."

The scene opened with a serious-looking Misty Ying looking into the camera. Behind her there was nothing but dark shadows and strange-looking buildings only partly illuminated by the camcorder's bright light. "My news crew and I are deep in the heart of Underground Seattle. The city street and the manhole Mr. Piedmont referred to is thirty feet above us." She smiled mischievously at the camera. "While we have only been down here a little while, we have yet to encounter any of the red-eyed people Mr. Piedmont claims are lurking down here, but it is still early." She beckoned for the camera to follow her down a narrow street. "In an effort to substantiate Mr. Piedmont's story, I intend to interview some of the residents who live in this subterranean city." The camera zoomed past the television reporter and focused in on what looked like several figures sleeping on a wooden sidewalk out in front of an old building. "I rather doubt if Mr. Piedmont's story will be substantiated by these people, but if not, we might obtain a new perspective on the plight of the homeless forced to live in this underground city."

With the firm determination of a crusading reporter, Misty Ying walked over to the dark shapes sprawled on the sidewalk. She knelt down beside one of the figures, a man lying on his side, his face and shoulders covered by a jacket. She tapped the man on the shoulder. "Sir—Sir, can you hear me?" The body stirred. "Sir, my name is Misty Ying and I'm a roving reporter for Station KOMO and I'd like to ask you some questions—"

The creature who had once been Paul Riester sat up,

ripping the jacket away from its face. The camera caught it all: the snarling expression, the needle-sharp teeth, the fiery red eyes . . .

Misty Ying gasps, tries to back away. The creature reaches out and grabs her with claw-like hands. The soundman rushes over to help while the stunned video-camera operator continues to capture the scene on film. The creature sinks its teeth into Misty Ying's throat, releasing a spray of blood that splatters the soundman. More blood dots the camera lens. The soundman tries to separate the woman from the creature and does not see the dark human shapes rising up behind him, but the camera does. Only, the camera is going out of focus now and the blurred images of Misty Ying and the soundman being overwhelmed by a pack of creatures recedes into darkness because the cameraman is backing away from the gruesome horror. Suddenly the images are gone, lost in a blurred surrealistic swirl of black-and-white confusion.

The cameraman has dropped his camera, but it's still attached to his body by straps and it is slapping against his hip as he runs down the underground street towards a ladder embedded in a cement wall, a ladder leading up to the manhole in the street above. The still-filming camera bangs against a ladder rung. The cameraman is climbing the ladder now and his camera is swinging wildly against his body. The lens angles down and shows red-eyed shapes milling around on the floor just below the cameraman's feet. The light on the camera blinds them. They snarl and turn away. The cameraman continues to climb the ladder and the television screen is filled with nightmarish surrealistic images: red eyes, claw-like hands, wolfen faces, a cement wall, the cameraman's shoe. Now something is coming up the ladder below the cameraman, something with hideous teeth, long fingernails, and eyes the color of hell. It reaches for the cameraman's leg. The camera catches the image of a ghastly hand grabbing the leg of the cameraman. Suddenly there is an explosion of jarring white brightness as the light on the videocamera shatters against the ladder. Blackness engulfs the screen.

A moment later new images come on the screen. The cameraman has climbed out of the manhole and is lying on the street, gasping for breath. The camera is lying on the street beside the man. Someone rushes up to help the man. The camcorder catches a close-up view of a tennis shoe and jeans. Hands grip the cameraman, but he pushes them away, picks up his camera and focuses it on the open manhole. There is a withered hand coming out of the hole. It is gripping the edge of the pavement. A policeman and one of the film crew's production men drag the heavy cast-iron manhole cover up to the edge of the hole and let it fall. There is no sound. There has been no sound since the soundman rushed in to help Misty Ying, but the viewer can feel the thunderous clank as the cover crashes into place and the viewer can feel—almost hear—something else: a wailing silent scream of pain. There are severed fingers laying on the asphalt next to the manhole. Suddenly the fingers and manhole cover disappear. Someone has driven a car onto the manhole cover. A tire is resting on the top of the round plate.

There is one final shot. It is of a man with Band-Aids on his face. He is screaming at the cameraman and the production crew emerging from the KOMO news van. There is no sound, but the camera captures his words. He is swearing, telling them they should not have gone down into Underground Seattle. He is cursing, telling the world he's leaving the city, then he climbs into a Toyota Supra and drives away.

The scene changed to the Spokane news center and the news reporter. "That tape was supplied to us by our sister station, KOMO, in Seattle. We still have no word about what has happened to Misty Ying or George Loomis, her soundman, but we do know that the Seattle police department has sent a SWAT team into Underground Seattle to search for the missing news team members. Currently the police are telling the citizens of Seattle there is no reason to panic. In their opinion, Ms. Ying and her soundman were attacked by a group of discharged mental hospital patients living under the city. We will update this story as events occur. Recap and details on news at eleven."

"Christ, that was horrible," Mary Kathleen whispered.

Braille had been so caught up in the news report he hadn't heard her come into the living room. The death of the newswoman and soundman had been horrible but what had frozen Braille's soul were the videotaped images of the red-eyed shapes that had done the killing. A sense of déjà vu welled up in him. He had seen those fiery eyes before, when vampirism had broken out on Chinook Island. Now it was back. The disease was breaking out in Seattle like a virulent rampant plague. He was too stunned to speak, too sickened to do anything except gape at the TV screen.

"What do you think's happening in Seattle?" Mary Kathleen asked.

Braille took in a deep breath and turned to look at her. She saw the horror in his face and knew it was not a reaction to what he'd just seen on TV. "What is it?"

Braille realized he was still holding the glass of Drambuie. He downed it in one motion, took Mary Kathleen's glass from her hand and downed that too.

"Do you want me to go get the bottle?" she asked.

He shook his head. "Let's go have that cigarette."

It was cold and dark out on the porch. Braille lit Mary Kathleen's cigarette, then his own.

"Okay, you mind telling me what's going on?" she asked. "I know that program was horrible, but there was something else going on, something even worse. I saw it in your face."

Braille took a long drag on his cigarette, blowing the smoke out into the night. "Remember when I told you about how the people on Chinook Island came down with a strange disease? Well, when they caught the disease, they became like animals. Everything about them changed: their appetites changed, their teeth changed. Even their eyes changed."

"Like those things on TV?"

He nodded. "Same red eyes, same teeth. It's happening again. Only this time it's not happening on an island, it's happening in the middle of a huge city."

"But how?"

"I don't know," he said softly. "Maybe one of those things survived the radiation on the island and somehow got to the mainland."

"Are you going to go to Seattle and try and stop what's happening?" He nodded. "How can you stop something like that?"

Braille looked into the darkness. It was beginning to snow lightly. "I don't know," he said, shaking his head. "Radiation worked once, but there's no power plant anywhere near Seattle."

"But you'll leave and try anyway."

"I don't have a choice. I've lived through this once. I know things the authorities don't know. Maybe I can help, maybe I can't, but I've got to try. That disease killed almost everyone on the island and I don't want to see that happen again. What you saw on TV was just a preview. The disease turns people into red-eyed creatures and they spread the disease like wildfire. Just one of those creatures can contaminate three or four people in a single night. And the next night those infected people go on to spread the disease to others. Each night gets more hideous. If it can't be stopped in Seattle, there's no telling where it'll stop or if it will stop. Nobody would be safe. Not even people in Easton. I've got to go. Maybe somehow I can help."

"The kids don't want you to go."

"I know," Braille said.

"I don't want you to go," she murmured.

Braille closed his eyes and nodded.

She waited for a response, but it didn't come. "Then I guess there's nothing else to say except . . . please say goodbye before you leave."

The front door opened and closed. With the closing, Braille felt the aloneness he'd felt for most of his life. There had been times when his existence had not been solitary: those years he had shared with his adoptive parents. Those few weeks he had shared with Leslie Chapel, and now this brief time with Mary Kathleen Stuart and her children. Each time something had happened to bring the aloneness back. A car wreck had killed his parents. The OSMS had killed Leslie Chapel. Now the door to a house had closed and he was alone again, and it was dark out on the porch. Always the darkness.

A Calchem truck and its Chevy Blazer escort drove past the front of the house. Both the Blazer and the truck honked their horns tauntingly as they passed. The blaring sounds were intended to irritate and insult. And it worked. Braille glared at the passing car and truck and felt hate well up inside him, a hate that pushed aside his feelings of self-pity. He stared furiously at the passing vehicles, his hate and anger growing until his eyes were as red as the taillights fading in the night.

29

GREGORY WATCHED MISTY YING INTERVIEW OTIS PIEDMONT and then go into Underground Seattle and die on the six-thirty news update. It was the second time he had seen the woman die. The actual descent into Underground Seattle had taken place on an earlier news program, but the event had been so sensational that the station had pre-empted "Entertainment Tonight" in order to show the gory piece a second time.

Molly Estleford and her granddaughter, Samantha, were sitting in the living room with Gregory. Mrs. Estleford was waiting for her favorite program, "Wheel of Fortune," to come on at seven. Samantha Estleford was in the living room because Gregory was in the living room.

"Far out," observed Samantha. "That lady reporter is history."

"All fake," Molly Estleford commented. "That station's just trying to up its ratings. That Ying woman'll be back on the news tomorrow, claiming she got lost in the darkness, and broadcasting like nothing happened." She glanced at her watch. "Mr. Gregory, would you turn the TV set up? Vanna's about to come on."

Gregory turned up the TV, returned to an overstuffed chair, and looked at Molly Estleford. He had become fond of the old woman during the past two months, and had come to consider her as a friend. His eyes traveled over to Samantha Estleford. She was sitting on the davenport next to her grandmother, eating grapes. He had even grown fond of her. She was still following him around, trying to seduce him, still outrageous, but he liked her. Like her grandmother, Samantha Estleford had become a friend of Gregory's. The realization that he had friends, human friends, brought a faint trace of a smile to the nine-hundred-year-old Master Ancient's face.

But the smile faded as his mind went back to the TV news program. Based on what he had just seen, he now knew that a New One had escaped from the island and somehow gotten to Seattle. Now the disease the New One had was beginning to spread through Seattle. He did not know if he could stop the disease from spreading, but he knew he would try. This was not a benevolent gesture on his part. Gregory had witnessed what vampirism had done to Europe in the fourteenth century and had no wish to see that happen again. Historians now called the plague that swept through Europe the Black Plague. But Gregory knew better. He had been alive then, witnessing the chaos, the insanity, the deaths, the burning of bodies all brought on by the spread of vampirism. He did not want to see that happen again.

Suddenly Gregory sensed something was wrong.

They were close; Kubick and the group of humans who wanted to destroy him had found him. He sat back in his chair, trying to push the feeling away. They couldn't have found him, he thought. He had covered his tracks too well, been too careful, too cautious.

But they were out there—he could sense them. They were close, and closing on him.

Kubick, Kramer, and a man named Hodge had been parked in a van in front of the Estleford home for almost a quarter of an hour. Kubick was sitting in the front seat. Kramer was behind him, his hands cupped over a headset connected to a highly sensitive parabolic microphone aimed at the Estleford's living room.

"What's happening now?" Kubick asked, looking back at Kramer.

"The girl, the old lady, and the man we're after are still

watching TV. The old lady's trying to guess a three-word phrase . . . wait, somebody just bought an 'O' . . . and the middle word is 'of.' "

Kubick glared at Kramer, shaking his head and glancing towards the back of the van to see how Hodge was doing. Robert Hodge was a powerful man with broad shoulders and thick legs. He would be manning St. Jude tonight. He had already strapped the metal box containing the belt of ammunition onto his back like a backpack. Now he was slipping on a cumbersome shoulder harness, attaching the straps hanging down from the harness to the heavy six-barreled weapon. Strong as Hodge was, it was almost impossible for him to carry and fire St. Jude without help. The straps attached to the shoulder harness would allow the bulky weapon to swing freely next to his right hip. With the straps and harness bearing most of the weight, the man would then be able to aim the barrels with his left hand, and activate the firing mechanism with his right. Because of the confined space in the van, Hodge was working on his knees. He picked up the GAU-2 7.62 mini gun, connecting the straps and pulling a belt of ammunition out of the backpack. Then he shoved the belt into St. Jude's firing chamber, turning on his knees and nodding at Kubick. He was ready.

"Buy a vowel, you stupid ass," Molly Estleford said to one of the "Wheel of Fortune" contestants.

Gregory got out of his chair, walking over to Molly Estleford and sitting down on the arm of the davenport. "Molly, this is important," he said softly. "Has anyone come by recently and asked a lot of questions?"

Mrs. Estleford leaned forward, staring at the TV. "Buy an 'A,' you ass."

"This is important, Molly," Gregory said, raising his voice. "Has anyone come around asking about me?"

In the van Kramer pushed the headset tight against his ears. "Oh-oh. That guy's asking the old lady if somebody's been asking about him. I think he senses something. But how?" He gave Kubick a stunned look.

Hodge was crouching in the back of the van, next to the rear door. Kubick's and Hodge's eyes met. Kubick nodded,

Hodge pushed the door open and stepped down on the street, carrying a weapon capable of firing six thousand rounds per minute.

"Stand by," Kubick said into a handheld radio. The men sitting in two cars parked on the street near the van checked their weapons. So did the three other men standing in Molly Estleford's back yard.

"It's important," Gregory said to Molly Estleford.

"Dammit, I've almost got it," she said, looking at Gregory in irritation. "And yes, a man came by today and asked a lot of questions. Said he was interested in you because you didn't have a job and might be interested in working in a pulp mill plant." She went back to looking at the TV.

Gregory stood up. So you have come for me, he thought, almost smiling in anticipation. But then the smile disappeared as he glanced at Molly and Samantha. This game was between him and the men outside. It didn't involve two innocent women. A low growl broke from Gregory's throat and his eyes began to gleam red.

"What is it?" Samantha asked, jumping to her feet, then backing away when she saw the expression on Gregory's face.

"I got it!" Molly Estleford screamed.

"Sit down!" Gregory shouted at Samantha. He rushed over to the front window but his view of the street was blocked by trees. He would have a better view from upstairs, he realized.

"It's 'INVASION OF PRIVACY!'" Molly Estleford shouted. Then the excitement in her voice died. "Why are you shouting at my granddaughter?" she asked, looking up at Gregory and seeing only blurred movement as he ran into the hallway and started up the stairs.

Don't do this, Kubick, Gregory screamed silently. This is between me and you. The women have no part of this.

"What's going on?" Molly Estleford asked loudly. "Where are you going, Mr. Gregory?"

Kramer jerked off his headset and turned to Kubick. "He knows! He knows something's up."

"Do it now," Kubick said into his radio.

Out on the street two men shouldered L.A.W. rocket

launchers. Hodge leveled St. Jude at the Estleford home, all six barrels. In the back yard, two men took aim at the house with M-79 grenade launchers while the third took a grip on an M-16 machine gun and pushed the safety off.

A heartbeat later everyone opened fire.

Two rockets screamed towards the front of the house, leaving smoke and sparks in their wakes. In the back, two men fired their grenade launchers, one aiming at the kitchen, the other at Gregory's upper story apartment. The third set up a withering field of fire with the M-60 machine gun, pumping hundreds of rounds into the back door and the kitchen, while his two companions reloaded the grenade launchers.

Robert Hodge pressed the firing lever on his GAU-2 (7.62 mm) mini gun. The weapon came to life, spitting out six thousand rounds per minute. St. Jude did not make a tat-tat-tat sound like an ordinary machine gun. St. Jude was anything but ordinary. The sound it made was a continuous roar, like everlasting thunder.

Gregory was halfway up the stairwell when a rocket blew away part of the front porch and a second rocket swooshed across the living room, into the dining room and exploded, kicking broken furniture, dust, and plaster out into the living room. In that same instant, something like a high-speed chain saw began cutting through the front wall of the Estleford home, chewing everything in the living room in two.

"NOOooo," Gregory screamed, his cry drowned out by an explosion in the kitchen. Then something exploded above him, and the house trembled. Plaster dust rained down on him.

Again the chain saw began to cut the house apart as St. Jude spat out a nearly endless stream of lead. Bullets sawed through support beams, studs, and walls. Part of the front porch collapsed. Part of the front wall began to collapse, began to sag along with the living room ceiling as the weight of the upper floors pushed down on the first story of the house. Another rocket flashed through the living room, exploding in the dining room. More explosions in the kitchen and above him. Still the chain saw continued.

Gregory leaned over the bannister, looking down at the

two women lying on the living room floor. He knew there was nothing he could do, knew both were beyond help.

Thirty seconds later Kubick spoke into his radio. "Enough." As if by magic, the grenade and rocket explosions and St. Jude's withering blast of fire stopped instantly.

Kramer was the only man on the team who had not fired a weapon. He stepped down from the van, standing beside Hodge and Kubick, surveying the devastation. "Jesus Christ," he murmured. The house had been reduced to kindling. It looked as if an earth mover had run over it.

"What about the neighbors?" Kramer asked. Houses lined both sides of the street. People were coming out on their porches.

"Kill anyone who gets too close," Kubick informed Hodge.

Several neighbors were out on the street now, cautiously approaching the devastation. "Get back," Kubick shouted. "Police business. Drug raid." Hodge turned St. Jude on the elderly people and they scurried back to their homes.

Kramer, Kubick, and Hodge stepped up on the sidewalk in front of the Estleford home and stopped. "Christ," Kramer said, "how we gonna explain all this?"

"We don't have to," Kubick said. "Let the authorities explain it. They'll come up with something for the newspapers." He lifted the radio to his lips. "Move in."

The two men who'd fired rockets into the home traded their empty rocket launchers for automatic weapons and sprinted across the street, each heading for a different side of the ruined home. Both stopped when they had good views of the side windows and took up firing positions. At the same time, the men in the back yard began making their way towards the gaping hole where the back porch and door to the kitchen had once been.

Kramer, Hodge, and Kubick began walking up the brick pathway leading to what was left of the front porch. "Take it slow," Kubick said into the radio, "and remember, this is a body search, one particular body. And I want to see it before we bag it up and take it back to Cutter." In his mind he could see Cutter's fury, hear him scream, "You were supposed to bring the Ancient back alive!" Kubick could hear his own response, "Calm down, Cutter. A dead body's better than nothing. Besides, there's no charge. This one's a freebie. Our pleasure."

Kubick came back to the present, finding himself holding the radio and staring at nothing. He stepped up on the front porch with Kramer and Hodge. Oddly, the porch light was still on, but it was difficult to see Hodge, who was standing just a few feet away. Several small fires were smoldering inside the home and the drifting smoke was mingling with plaster dust and a rising mist. "Stay out here," Kubick said to Hodge. "You won't be able to maneuver inside with St. Jude. Keep the citizens away, and if the town marshal shows up, keep him away too—any way you can."

Hodge slapped St. Jude. *"No problemo,"* he said, his eyes wide with giddy excitement.

That's the last time you get to handle St. Jude, Kubick thought, noticing Hodge's eyes. Some people could handle the godlike power St. Jude offered, some couldn't; Hodge was one of the could-nots.

The heavy mist was growing thicker, rapidly turning into dense fog. The smoke oozing out of the shattered windows and door seemed to be thickening too. "Let's get this over with," Kubick said, pushing open the shattered door. Kramer worked the action on his FIE Spas 12-gauge shotgun, setting the weapon for automatic fire, and following Kubick into a wide foyer.

In front of them was a bullet-riddled stairway leading to the upper floors; to the left, the living room. Moments earlier the room had been paneled in dark oak and furnished with overstuffed chairs, davenports, and antiques. But now it was a shambles. The paneling had been shredded, furniture shot to pieces, and chairs blasted over. A fire was smoldering in the davenport and a second fire was burning in one corner of the room. The air was thick with dense gray smoke growing heavier by the minute.

Kramer could barely see past the end of his shotgun. His eyes were watering, but he felt safe. Kubick was close. He inched forward, working his way through the debris, then the toe of his shoe bumped into something soft . . . soft and spongy. He pulled out a flashlight and knew before he knelt down what he would find.

"Over here," he called. Instantly Kubick was kneeling beside him. Kramer turned on the flashlight.

From the waist up Molly Estleford looked relaxed, comfortable, peaceably asleep. The same was true of the lower part of her body. Her slippers were still on and her bathrobe was still modestly buttoned up. The problem was that a blizzard of bullets from St. Jude had caught her in the mid-section and now her upper and lower halves were separated by six inches of carpet and a growing pool of coagulating blood.

"Jesus," Kramer murmured as he and Kubick got to their feet.

Both men could hear the sounds of other men making their way through the house. A moment later they could see faint shadowy figures enter the dimly lit, smoke-filled dining room that opened onto the living room. Kubick and Kramer separated and resumed their search. Then Kramer said, "Found another."

"I don't like it," Kramer grumbled. "He was in the living room, talking to the old lady when we opened up. He should be here."

"I'm going upstairs," Kubick decided.

"You make it sound like you're going up by yourself," Kramer said.

"I am." Kramer's observation about where the body should have been had stirred up queasy feelings in Kubick. He didn't think anything could survive the holocaust that had hit this house, but something was wrong, and it was up to him to find out what. If the creature was still alive, now was the time to meet it face to face. He had been looking forward to this since receiving the assignment from Cutter. More so since the deaths of Reber and McCabe. Maybe now it would happen: a death battle with this thing that could not die. He motioned at his men. "I want you two to search the back of the house again." Then he pointed to Kramer and a man named Larsen. "You two stand by. If I need you, I'll call."

"And we'll come," Kramer said softly.

Kubick paused with his hand on the splintered banister. "I know that." He then disappeared up the stairway.

But the upper floors were deserted. After watching Samantha and Molly Estleford die in a maelstrom of shrapnel and bullets, Gregory had continued up the stairs. During that brief time he had been hit four times. Bullets had caught him in the chest, neck, and heel. At the top of the stairway, in kind of an alcove, he had rested briefly, fighting off the pain. The bullet holes in his upper body had healed rapidly. The shattered bones in his heel had taken longer to mend, and agony had stayed with him while he moved down the hallway and into Molly Estleford's bedroom. Oblivious to the bullets and shrapnel whipping through the air like hail, he moved across the room to a shattered bay window at the side of the house. Suddenly the rockets, gunfire, and explosions had stopped. In the strange silence that followed, Gregory slipped into an old tree growing up beside the house. A moment later he was standing on a thick limb twenty feet off the ground, waiting to see what would happen next, waiting for the right time for him to begin exacting his vengeance on these humans who killed harmless women.

It was a brief wait. A man carrying a weapon came around the side of the house. He ran over to the tree Gregory was in, dropped down on one knee, and brought the weapon up to his shoulder as if he had a keen interest in shooting some nearby rosebushes.

It was time to kill these animals who kill women, Gregory thought. He dropped out of the tree, landing in front of the man. Gregory slapped the rifle away, then rammed his hand into the man's chest, intending to rip out the human's heart. There was a loud thunk as Gregory's hand crashed into the man's chest. The power behind the blow ruptured the man's heart. He died without making a sound.

Puzzled, Gregory looked at his hand. His outstretched fingers were numb and vibrating as if he'd rammed his hand into a block of steel. Confused, he turned the body over and stared at the man's Kevlar bulletproof vest. There was a large dent in the material where Gregory's hand had almost pierced the vest, but nothing else. Gregory ripped off the vest. These killers of women come prepared, he thought, slipping the vest on over one shoulder, intending to examine it later. With his eyes searing the night like the fires of Gehenna, Gregory started toward the back of the Estleford home.

Charles Maas was the team's long-range sniper. He was also one of the best marksmen in the world. While he liked what he did, it never seemed like killing to him. Instead, an assignment for Maas was basically an issue of wind velocity, weapon selection, bullet trajectory, body posture, breathing techniques, motion analysis, temperature, humidity, gravity, and distance. Maas was a professional, good at solving the complex problems involved in his specialty. At times he viewed himself more as a physicist, mathematician, and engineer rather than a mere master sniper. There was also one additional benefit to Maas' specialty: he was always too far away from his target to see the death he was bringing to another human being.

And that was fine with Charles Maas. Maas did not like the close-up work, did not like to see blood gushing out on the sidewalk, did not like to see what one of his specially designed bullets could do to a body. That was why Charles Maas had to go to the bathroom. He was in a house filled with death, looking for a body he did not want to find; he was scared, and when scared, he usually had to go to the bathroom. He'd been okay when he was out in the back yard, manning the M-60, and okay during the search of the house. But then Kubick had told him to go back and search the house again, and suddenly Maas thought his kidneys would explode. Instead of following Kubick's orders, Maas headed off for a bathroom located at the back of the house. Walking with his legs together, Maas scurried through the kitchen, past a utility room, a sewing room, and into the bathroom. It was as empty as the first time he had searched it. Smiling, he slung the M-60 over his shoulder and stepped up to the bullet-shattered gurgling toilet. He aimed and let go. God, it felt better than sex.

Having finished, he zipped up, turned and started out the doorway. Then he walked into a wall that had not been there earlier.

A wall with red eyes.

Charles Maas felt cold hands grip his chin and the back of his neck. Then he heard a sound like someone breaking a broom handle in half. Suddenly he was looking back at the toilet. But that was impossible, because he knew his feet were still pointing out into the hallway.

Charles Maas made the same sort of gurgling sound the broken toilet was making, then died. Gregory released the body and it toppled backwards, landing on its shoulder blades and nose at the same time.

One of the other men who'd come in through the back with Maas was leaning against a wall in the kitchen, eating a peach he'd found in the bullet-riddled refrigerator. He had done his part, searched and re-searched the back of the house. Now he was waiting for Maas to finish up. Damning the thick smoke wafting around him, he wolfed down the peach, slipping the pit into his pocket. Suddenly he saw a pair of red eyes staring at him through the smoke and darkness.

The man was off balance, still leaning against the wall, when a large hand came out of nowhere to cover his face. It all happened too fast. He couldn't shout, couldn't breathe or see. The hand blotted out everything—except the pain.

Gregory stood in the kitchen doorway, scanning the dining room and distant living room. Peering through the darkness and smoke, he could make out two figures standing in the living room and a third out on the porch. But which one was Kubick? Gregory wondered as he continued to push the man's face towards the back of his own skull and the wall. The wall wasn't giving. The man's skull was. Blood spurted out of the man's ears. Gregory didn't notice. Blood spurted out of the top of the man's skull. Gregory still didn't notice.

After a time Gregory looked at the man, intending to ask him which one was Kubick, but he knew it was a waste of time.

Gregory heard someone kick some planks, then the back porch creaked and Gregory knew that the man who'd been observing the other side of the house was curious and coming in to find out what was going on.

The man's curiosity brought him face to face with a red-eyed apparition, the kind of apparition small children conjure up in their worst nightmares. Only, in this case the apparition was real, and it killed him.

"I don't like it," Kramer said, talking to the only other person in the room, a man named Larsen. "Maas and the others should've finished up by now. It doesn't take that long to search a house, especially the second time through. And why haven't the guys outside checked in? I'm telling you, something's wrong. Something's happened to the other guys. Something's going on and it's bad."

Larsen wasn't worried, but his irritation with Kramer was growing fast. He was about to tell the communications specialist to shut the fuck up, when he heard a floorboard creak in the dining room. Suddenly Larsen was worried. Real worried. There were seven heavily armed professional mercenaries searching the smoke-filled house. The last thing any of those men would do would be to sneak through a room dark as the world's last night. There was someone in the dining room, someone trying to be quiet. Without a word to Kramer, Larsen reached under his jacket and pulled out two MAC-10's, slipping quietly into the dining room. He was ready. Both machine gun pistols were set on full automatic. The second he sensed or heard something he would open up with both, and fill the black void in front of him with a barrage of bullets.

Ten feet away Gregory studied the men with the eyes of a predatory night animal accustomed to hunting in the darkness. The human was working his way through the dining room, testing the darkness with his weapons the way a blind man might use two canes. Standing motionless, Gregory remained in the murky mist until the human was in front of him. Then he stepped between the outstretched weapons, clamped a hand around the man's throat and lifted him off the floor. Everything happened so fast that Larsen never had a chance to cry out. He simply died twelve inches off the floor. The only sound he made was when one shoe slipped off his foot and clumped to the floor.

"What was that?" Kramer asked, squinting his eyes against the smoke and staring hard into the darkness.

Silence.

He could hear Hodge outside, patrolling what was left of

the front porch, but knowing St. Jude and Hodge were close wasn't comforting. Larsen hadn't answered him. "I said, what was that?"

Silence.

"Don't play games with me, Larsen. You know I'm on edge about Maas and the others."

Silence.

"Lar-sen," he called out cautiously. "I know all my talking made you mad, but don't take it out on me this way. I promise I won't talk anymore if you will just say something to me. Anything."

Silence.

"Okay . . . if you're that mad at me for talkin' so much, you can hit me. But when you're done, you gotta talk to me." Kramer closed his eyes, jutting out his chin and bracing himself for a rush of pain.

The pain came from a blow out of the blackness. The power behind the blow shattered Kramer's upper and lower jaws, breaking his neck and sending him flying across the living room into a wall next to the stairway.

Gregory looked down at the man he'd just slapped, almost by invitation. Once again he decided that humans were a silly lot.

At that moment Hodge stepped into the foyer with St. Jude. "What's going on?" Hodge asked. As Gregory started towards the man in the doorway, a gust of wind blowing in through the open door and shattered windows, pushed the smoke towards the back of the house. In that one brief instant Hodge caught a glimpse of Kramer lying dead on the floor, and of a black shadow coming for him. He brought St. Jude to bear on the shadow. Gregory was ten feet from the human when the man pointed the strange-looking weapon at him. The weapon was heavy and had six barrels protruding from its huge maw. Instinctively Gregory knew this was the weapon that had torn through the house like steel lightning. He wondered if he could survive its awesome power.

A microsecond before Hodge opened fire, Kubick started down the stairs into the living room.

Screaming savagely, Hodge pulled the firing handle and St. Jude began spitting out nearly a thousand rounds per minute. Hodge's scream was one of relief. Whatever was in the room had nearly been on him, but now it was dog meat. He continued to scream as St. Jude bellowed violently, the rounds the machine was firing escalating now towards its maximum output: six thousand rounds per minute.

The brilliantly white muzzle flash spewing out from St. Jude was like a continuous lightning flash, and what Hodge could see in that pulsating light cut off his scream, freezing him like a statue. St. Jude was still firing, still belching out a withering blast of bullets, but Hodge didn't seem to know it. What he did know was that he could see something coming for him, could see a shape almost on him. The terrifying part was that he could see St. Jude's bullets crashing into it in an endless torrent of devastation.

"Impossible!!" Hodge screamed, the word lost in the thunderous roar of St. Jude. Bullets were hitting this thing, ricocheting off, pinging all over the house, and it was still coming. Hodge could see chunks of flesh and pieces of shirt flying from its body, and still it kept coming and coming and this was: "IMPOSSIBLE!!"

Then the thing was in front of him, reaching for St. Jude, grabbing the barrels with both hands as if it were nothing but a fencepost. Hodge felt the canvas straps cut into his neck and shoulder. The thing was trying to take St. Jude away from him. He tried to hold onto the weapon, but couldn't. Then the straps snapped and St. Jude was ripped away from him. The weapon fell silent. The blinding muzzle flash died.

Darkness and silence crashed down on Hodge. He began backing away from the shape that was holding St. Jude. He bumped into the splintered doorframe and couldn't move. All he could do was stand there and make kitten-like mewing sounds as he watched the shadow in front of him heft St. Jude high up over its head with both hands. Petrified with fear, Hodge watched the figure stagger and almost drop the weapon. It's dying, he thought. Finally dying. He almost giggled, but didn't. Because he saw the shape take a new grip on St. Jude as if it were a harpoon, then plunge it downwards.

Hodge felt no pain, just a violent whump as if he'd been hit by a car. He reached out in front of him, touching the thick metal shaft protruding from his stomach. He knew he was touching St. Jude, knew the huge muzzle with its six barrels had just been rammed through his body into the wall behind him; he knew that because now he was beginning to feel pain from the heat of the barrels radiating through his entrails. He lifted his eyes to the figure in front of him. It was still on its feet.

"Im . . . possible," Hodge said, and died, still pinned to the wall.

Gregory remained standing for a moment longer, then his strength gave out and he slumped to the foyer floor, leaning back against the wall. He was badly hurt. Part of his neck had been shot away along with his collarbone and the top part of his left shoulder. His shoulder joint and upper arm had been shattered, pulverized to splinters and chopped meat. Blood was spurting out everywhere and he was weak. But he still had the strength to turn his head and look at the figure sitting halfway up the stairs at the end of the foyer. So that is Kubick, he thought.

Dazed and hurt, Kubick sat on the steps, staring back at the shadow below him. He had heard Kramer die and was starting down the steps when Hodge opened fire. He had seen it all, watching Hodge fire St. Jude point-blank into the figure coming for him. He had seen the bullets hit the shape and saw the bullets start to ricochet, then felt himself get hit by several stray bullets. One had caught him in the jaw. A second had torn away his left ear, and one had hit him in the temple. The temple wound was the worst. He'd been knocked unconscious and had come to in time to see Hodge die and the Ancient crumple to the floor.

Kubick checked his injuries. His face was a mess. Most of his left ear was missing, as was the jaw muscle on the left side of his face. The bullet had caught him on the hairline, skimmed along his skull under the skin, then exited at the back of his head. His face felt on fire, but the pain and the disfigurement were inconsequential. What he could not dismiss were the lingering aftereffects of the temple wound. The bullet that had knocked him out had left him disoriented, lethargic, and partly paralyzed. His body was not responding to his will, and he had never experienced such a helpless feeling before. He stared down at the creature he had come to kill and took some pleasure in knowing that it too was badly hurt, battered, and helpless. But it bothered him that the creature was staring back up at him.

Gregory felt no pain; his injuries were too extensive; there was too much nerve damage. But he did feel tired and helpless. It was all he could do just to keep himself sitting up. He found himself wondering when the human would get to his feet, come down the stairs and kill him. The prospect did not produce fear; just irritation. He had set out to kill the humans who had killed Molly and Samantha Estleford, and had killed them all but their leader. All he could do now was sit on the floor with his hands at his sides and feel irritation with himself over his inability to move.

At that moment he felt something warm touch his hand. He looked down at the floor. Blood from the human he'd pinned to the wall was pooling up at the dead man's feet. The pool had grown increasingly wider, seeping across the floor and finally touching Gregory's hand. He scooped up some of the warm coagulating liquid into his palm, bringing his hand to his mouth and lapping it clean with his tongue. He smiled faintly as he scooped up more blood, again licking his hand clean.

What is it doing? Kubick wondered as he labored to control his fear, labored to make his body move. His efforts were beginning to pay off. The paralyzing effects he had suffered from the temple wound were wearing off. Strength was returning to his body; he could move his fingers now.

Gregory was beginning to heal, was beginning to get faint traces of his strength back. The dead man's blood was working its mystical magic on his body. But with the healing came the agony of having the shattered parts of his body begin to rebirth from the inside out. The agony of having nerve endings come back to life. The agony of having skin and muscle grow at an incomprehensible rate of speed. The Ancient clenched his jaw, sucking in air through his teeth as red-hot pain welled over him.

Wanting to distract his mind from the pain, Gregory broke the silence. "Why did you kill the old woman and her granddaughter?"

It surprised Kubick to hear the creature speak. He'd heard its voice on the tape recorder, heard the recording hundreds of times, but it still surprised him. He found he could shrug with one hand. The movement pleased him. "We were after you. They got in the way."

Gregory gritted his teeth, looking down at his shoulder. What was happening to his flesh looked like something out of a special effects horror movie. The shattered, splintered bones in his arm and shoulder were mending at an incredible rate. A clear jelly-like substance interlaced with blue threads materialized over the bones. A moment later the clear substance turned to pink flesh, the threads to blood vessels. Gregory shook off the pain and considered Kubick's answer. They got in the way? And for that they died? This human and his men were more violent and evil than he was . . . maybe. "Why were you after me?"

Tell him the truth, Kubick thought, keep him talking. The longer they talked, the more chance he had to get the full use of his body back. "A government agency wanted me to find you. They wanted me to bring you back so they could study you, find out why you never got sick, why you were so hard to kill. But you killed some of my men at the rest stop, so I decided to kill you."

"How could this agency know about me?"

"They had another one like you and they were studying him, but he escaped."

"Impossible," Gregory said, looking down at the dead human's blood he held in his hand. "There are no others like me. I am the last Ancient."

Kubick shook his head. He was still weak, but feeling better with every passing moment. "No. They had a man like you. They kept him alive with blood and they injected him with diseases and he did not die. They shot him and his wounds healed. He had strength, incredible strength, but like I said, he escaped."

This time it was Gregory who shook his head. Impossible, he thought, as he continued to stare down at his healing flesh, continuing to experience the pain of flesh rebirthing itself. Some of his flesh and skin was beginning to grow over part of the clothing he had taken from the man he had killed outside. He pulled the strange vest away from his wounds, grimacing as a new wave of pain washed over him. When it passed he said, "I do not believe you. There are no others like me. But I am curious how you found me."

"It was easy," Kubick said. "People kept disappearing from that rest stop. One night six people disappeared from a bar in this town. Who else but you.

"I don't understand it. I saw my man turn his weapon loose on you, saw the bullets hit you and turn your flesh into pulp. Most of you should be spread all over this room. You should be dead. But you're not. Why?"

In spite of the pain, Gregory smiled in the darkness. "I think this had something to do with it." He threw the remains of the Kevlar bulletproof vest over to the foot of the stairs.

Kubick lifted his gaze from the vest to Gregory. "But you were still hit, hit many times."

"Of course. That's why you are still alive, Kubick."

"And my men?"

"What do you think?"

Kubick closed his eyes. "Why did you kill them? Why not me?"

"Because they got in the way," Gregory said. It felt good to give Kubick back the words he had used to explain away the deaths of Molly and Samantha Estleford.

"And I'm next?" Kubick asked, his voice free of emotion.

"Yes."

"I think not," Kubick hissed. He forced his numb hand to grope for the pistol he carried in a shoulder holster. The hand found it, pulling it from the holster. But then dropped it. The heavy automatic thumped down the stairs, disappearing into the darkness of the Estleford living room.

Kubick moaned. He only had one weapon left, a knife he carried in a sheath strapped to his upper back. It was a kubikiri, a "head cutter." It had a curved nine-inch blade, was razor-sharp at the tip and on the in-curved side. The knife was over seven hundred years old. Centuries earlier it had been used by warriors in Japan to sever the heads from the corpses of their enemies. It was the perfect fighting knife. The sharp tip was perfect for a straight-arm thrust, but even better was the deadly edge of the in-curve of the blade. More than once he'd eviscerated an adversary while looking into his eyes. He had never used the knife for its original purpose, but he would now. He would sever the creature's head and bury it a thousand miles from its body. That was the only way to kill a demon and make sure it would not rise again.

He reached back for the knife hidden under his shirt. He touched the wooden handle with his fingertips and tried to grip it, but his hand didn't respond. More fear began to consume Kubick. He knew if he tried to pull the knife out, he would drop it just like the automatic. Below him, at the bottom of the stairs, the creature continued to heal at an incredible rate. Kubick knew that in moments it would be on its feet and coming for him. He had no choice. With every ounce of strength, Kubick forced his body to respond, and it did. Slowly he got to his feet and started unsteadily down the stairs. Gregory looked up at him with interest as Kubick stepped onto the foyer floor and started for the front door. Then Kubick stopped, his battered sense of balance causing him to weave back and forth as he glared down at Gregory.

"One day I will kill you. And then I will cut off your head and send you to hell, and you can sit at the feet of my men and be their straw dog—a headless straw dog." He began laughing. It was a maniacal kind of laughter. It was the laughter of a man who'd slipped into madness and didn't know it.

Still laughing softly, with his eyes locked on his enemy, Kubick started for the door, edging his way around Gregory. Gregory's eyes turned red and he reached out, trying to grab the man by the leg. Kubick lurched back against the wall and Gregory missed, toppling forward onto his side.

Kubick stepped into the doorway, turned and looked back at Gregory. "We will meet again," he hissed, "when both of us are whole. That is when I will kill you."

Kubick wanted to say something more, something that would erase the shame and embarrassment he was feeling at that moment, but no words came to him. All he could do was limp out into the night and head for the van. He was relieved to find the keys in it. He started it, hoping he had the strength and coordination to drive the van to the airport in Everett where the team's jet was parked.

Gregory heard the van drive off. He did not know where Kubick was going, but knew they would meet again, probably in Seattle. He did not know what he would do when he got to Seattle, did not know if there was anything he could do to stop the outbreak of vampirism, but he knew he had to try. He also knew that by going there, he would come face to face with Braille.

Seattle, he thought. That is where this will all come to an end, finally and forever.

30

THE STORM THAT EARLIER HAD LACED THE AIR WITH SNOW flurries had moved on, leaving behind a clear night sky and a thin, glistening layer of wet snow on the hills and flatlands. The air was cold, but not cold enough. The snow had already melted off the road, and Braille was able to make good time on the motorcycle.

He geared the old Harley down as he started into the outskirts of Easton, slowly driving past the Long Branch Saloon, the school, dark hardware stores, and a used car lot. He caught sight of an interesting-looking car sitting in the lot, slowed briefly, then continued on.

He idled the bike into the parking lot of a Safeway market, stopping beside some deserted phone booths. After calling Atlanta he hung up. Five minutes later Colonel D. W. McKlean called him back.

Braille said he would be leaving in the morning and explained what he wanted. "It's basically a stand-by service for a few weeks. I just want to make sure nothing happens to the family. If possible, be discreet. Have your men stay back.

Maybe they can pull this off and the family'll never know they're around."

"I'll fly six of the best men I got out tonight," McKlean said. "And I'll come myself. We'll try and do it the way you want, but the family's gonna know we're there. There's no way I can guard anyone from a half a mile away. Agreed?"

"Agreed."

"You know this is gonna cost you an arm and a leg."

"I don't care. Just keep them safe, D.W."

"Do my best," McKlean said, and that was good enough for Braille. McKlean's "best" meant he'd give up his own life to keep Mary Kathleen and her children safe.

"Where will you be if I need to get ahold of you?" McKlean asked.

"Seattle, but I don't think you'll be able to get ahold of me."

"Seattle? Christ, you seen the TV? There's a lot of crazy shit going on in Seattle. 'Cording to the news, a whole police SWAT team went down into a manhole and never came up."

Braille nodded grimly as if McKlean could see him. "Take care of yourself, D.W."

Braille kick-started the Harley, starting back through Easton. Then he turned off the street and pulled to a stop in the middle of the used car lot, his eyes locked on the vehicle he'd noticed earlier.

He was looking at an old 1978 Dodge Ram Charger. Intrigued, Braille dismounted, walking over to the big machine. It had a heavy boxy body somewhat like a Ford Bronco, only larger, and someone had put a lot of money into the machine. It was equipped with oversized radial all-terrain tires and special heavy-duty shocks. The shocks and tires elevated the chassis and Braille figured it was a good seven feet from the top of the cab to the ground. For some reason a previous owner had mounted a cage-like system of welded black pipes to the front bumper and grille. Braille popped the hood, checking the motor. The V-8 engine was stock, but powerful—around four hundred horsepower, he guessed. He closed the hood quietly, checking the street. It was deserted. Blending with the shadows, Braille continued to check out the car. He almost had to stand on his tiptoes to peer through the driver's window. Stick shift, four-wheel drive. He tested the door. Locked.

He took a couple steps back, studying the car intently. It was big and powerful, perfect for whatever was going on in Seattle. And for what he had in mind for the OSMS, if he lived that long.

A moment later Braille stepped out of the business office with the key. He unlocked the vehicle's rear door, picked up the heavy motorcycle, and wedged it into the rear compartment. As he scanned the street a final time, he unlocked the driver's door, grabbing the steering wheel and pulling himself up into the cab. Fifteen minutes later Braille pulled the Charger into a stand of trees a quarter of a mile from the Stuart home.

After making sure the car could not be seen from the road, he unloaded the motorcycle, pushing it back to the Stuart ranch. He slipped in through the back door. The only light in the house was coming from the living room; it was the flickering light from the television set. Mary Kathleen was on the couch, bundled up in a quilt. At first he thought she'd fallen asleep, but then he noticed the near-empty bottle of Drambuie on the coffee table. He leaned close to her. "You alive?" he whispered. She stirred, opening one eye. Then she nodded and went back to sleep.

Braille smiled at her, then walked over to the TV set and started to turn it off. But he didn't. The eleven o'clock news was on. The camera was focused on two worried news broadcasters sitting behind a desk. Not wanting to disturb Mary Kathleen, he adjusted the volume so only he could hear, hunkering down on his haunches in front of the screen.

A local station in Spokane was broadcasting a late-breaking update from Seattle. Apparently a second twelve-man SWAT team had gone into Underground Seattle an hour earlier and hadn't been heard from since. A woman reporter read from an official-looking news bulletin:

"The police feel there is no need to panic, and to quote the Chief of Police, 'Faulty communications equipment is the problem. I do not believe that either SWAT team has met with foul play.'" Glancing up from the news bulletin, the reporter continued. "The police are advising that the residents of downtown Seattle stay off the streets. According to the police, they feel there is a problem with some people who have taken up residence in Underground Seattle. These people may be drifters, transients, or a group of discharged mental patients from some of Washington State's mental hospitals. Whatever the case, the Chief of Police is advising that evacuation is not necessary. Neither is panic. He has stated emphatically that his men have the problem under control and expect to resolve the issue before sunrise. Let me repeat . . ."

Braille turned off the television and slumped down on the floor. It was already out of control. There was no way of knowing how many new vampires were living under Seattle at this moment, but without meaning to, the Seattle police department had just created twenty-four more creatures; two twelve-man SWAT teams meant twenty-four more vampires. Within a matter of hours the men on those SWAT teams would rise and become exactly like that which had killed them. What a mess, Braille thought. He didn't have the slightest idea how to stop it. On the island, when vampirism had broken out he had learned that the new creatures could be killed if they lost enough blood. A bullet in the shoulder would not stop them. The loss of a limb would not stop them. But a bullet through the head or heart would bring death to them, reducing them to ashes as the last of their blood poured out of their body.

Braille got to his feet and walked over to Mary Kathleen. It was cold in the living room. He could see his breath. Scooping her up off the couch, he carried her like a child down the hall towards her bedroom.

"Wha's goin' on?" she asked, her words slurred with sleep. She didn't seem to be upset about finding herself in Braille's arms.

"I'm putting you to bed. You'll freeze to death in the living room."

"Was cold in there," she managed. "You didn't fix the windows."

"I didn't do a lot of things," Braille said sadly. He bumped the wall switch with his elbow. A lamp on a nightstand came on. The covers on her old four-poster bed had already been drawn back and he laid her down on the sheets. Her eyes were still closed and she looked as if she were asleep, but Braille sensed she wasn't. Maybe she hadn't drunk as much Drambuie as he thought. He leaned over, pulling the blankets up around her neck, turning off the lamp. A weak shaft of light from the hallway filtered in through the open door. Her face was very close to his, and as he looked down at her, she slowly opened her eyes.

They both could feel it—the need, the wanting, the loneliness. She started to push the covers away, started to reach for him . . . and a Calchem truck rolled by the house, the driver mocking and taunting the Stuart family with the truck horn.

The moment . . . the magic was gone. Mary Kathleen sighed. Braille started towards the bedroom door. From behind, Mary Kathleen said, "I take it back."

He stopped but didn't look back at her. "Take what back?"

"A long time ago I told you never to touch me. You did what I asked, and now I want to take it back. Every word."

Braille didn't know what to say. There was nothing he could say. The Calchem truck's horn had shattered the moment, renewing the rage inside him. It was time to finish this business with Lanterman.

"Good night, Mary Kathleen," he said softly, pulling the door closed behind him.

Braille entered his own room, closed the door, and slumped back against it.

It took him a long time to compose himself and push his emotions aside. After he did, he walked to the center of the room, stopped and closed his eyes, bowing his head and willing his body to relax. He stayed like that for several minutes, maybe longer. He felt no sense of time, no sense of place, just a kind of peacefulness coupled with a growing sense of purpose.

When he finally felt ready, he opened his eyes, looking at the Musashi sword resting in its scabbard on the shelf on the far side of the room.

With the sheathed long sword in his hand, Braille stepped out of his bedroom, moving through the house to the enclosed back porch. He picked up two propane gas lanterns and unlocked the storm door, starting away from the Stuart house. The night was clear and the stars cast down a light as bright as a full moon. He broke into an easy loping run, heading east towards the road leading to Easton and the Calchem chemical plant.

Thirty seconds later a small barefoot figure in pajamas scurried down the back steps and onto the lawn. It was easy for John Stuart to catch sight of Braille. Braille was wearing a white shirt, and the shirt gleamed in the starlight as Braille ran along the shoulder of the road. John drew in a deep breath, hoping he could keep up with Braille. He hoped his friend wouldn't look back and see him following.

Lanterman glanced at his thin diamond-crusted Omega wristwatch: 11:30. Almost twenty-four hours had passed since the strange man had broken into his trailer and demanded that he stop dumping waste at the disposal site on the Stuart ranch. Lanterman had promised the man the trucks would stop. They hadn't. They still left the plant every half hour on the hour, only now each truck and its two tankers was accompanied by an escort vehicle with armed security guards.

Lanterman was not frightened. But he was tense, tense enough not to want to sleep in his trailer tonight. Instead he'd decided to spend the night in his office. He felt safe in his office. It was located in the middle of the Calchem plant, surrounded by armed guards and a tall cyclone fence topped with concertina wire. If that were not enough, Jason Sanders, the director of the agency that provided security to the entire Calchem corporation, and six of his best men were currently in Lanterman's office, all grouped around a two-way radio that allowed them to stay in constant contact with the trucks and their security vehicles.

A loud static-filled transmission came in over the radio. Lanterman was too far away to understand what was being said. He snapped his fingers at one of the guards. The guard turned and said, "The 11:00 truck just got back from dumping its load. The 11:30 truck's on its way."

Lanterman smiled.

* * *

Four miles from the Stuart ranch Braille found the ideal spot. He was standing on the road to town, and stretching out on either side of him were vast expanses of gray sagebrush, sand, gray hills, and huge boulders. The road stretched out in front of Braille for almost a mile, then angled up the slope of a steep hill, disappearing over its crest. Any truck or car coming out of the Calchem plant intending on going to the dump site behind him would have to come down the hill, then straight at him. It was the perfect place. Whatever would happen here would not affect anyone or anything. It was an arid and primitive slash of land, desolate as a lunar landscape, and just as uninhabitable.

Braille knelt down on one knee. Holding the katana upright with the tip of its scabbard resting on the road, he waited under a black sky.

A moment later John Stuart scrambled to the top of a low hill. He spotted Braille on the road below and ducked behind a clump of sagebrush, hoping Braille had not seen him. His friend was kneeling, holding the black stick in his hand and with his eyes fixed on the road. There was no expression on Braille's face, no emotion in his eyes. Then, for no reason, Braille turned, looking up at the hill off to his right. His eyes took in the clump of sagebrush at the top, and for a moment it seemed to the boy that a faint sad smile came to Braille's face. But then the smile faded and Braille focused his eyes once again on the road.

The boy and man remained where they were, quiet, unmoving. One waited with infinite patience. The other, the small one, waited with suppressed excitement and a new and growing feeling—dread. Earlier he had been excited over whatever Braille was up to. But now he was worried. There was something out in the night that wanted to hurt Braille. Why else would Braille be carrying that strange black stick? Suddenly John didn't want whatever was going to happen to happen.

But it was already too late. It was already happening. John could hear it now, the low rumbling sounds of a distant storm heading in their direction, coming closer with each heartbeat. Only, it wasn't a storm.

Braille heard it too, and he could feel it. The road beneath him was trembling and he knew that on the other side of the hill in front of him, a huge truck was making its way slowly up the grade, coming ever closer.

Rising to his feet, Braille lit the propane lanterns and set them out on the road in front of him, one in each lane. The lanterns cast out bright white circles of light that illuminated Braille. Illuminated the katana. The boy gasped in recognition. It wasn't a stick. It was the sword his father had bought for no reason and had never touched.

At that moment a set of headlights appeared at the top of the hill off in the distance. The headlights turned into a boxy-shaped vehicle with blinking red lights on its cab. As the Chevy Blazer started down the hill, a second set of bigger headlights appeared behind the Blazer. These headlights were powerful; they cut the night like lasers and they were part of a truck that had a face like a huge hideous beast. A Calchem truck, John thought . . . and then he knew, knew what Braille was up to, knew what the lanterns and sword were for. He tried to cry out to Braille, but no sound came. All he could do was look down at the scene slowly being played out below him. The black Blazer, its lights on high beam, started down the hill. Twenty feet behind it, the monstrous semi truck snorted, roared, and changed gears as it labored to pull the two massive tankers behind it up the final few yards of the slope.

The Blazer's driver hawked up a wad of tobacco juice, cranked down the window, spat, then noticed the two bright specks of light on the road a mile and a half away. He hit the brakes so hard the monstrous truck behind them came within inches of crushing out the Blazer's rear window with its huge front bumper.

"What the hell are those lights down there?" the Blazer driver asked, looking at his partner, an older security guard. "What should we do?"

"Radio it in," the older guard said, shaking his head. He was a forty-nine-year-old ex-Newark, New Jersey policeman who normally liked his job with Calchem security. But not tonight. Tonight he'd been partnered up with a twenty-one-year-old redneck cowboy security guard who had shit for brains and who hit the brakes of the Blazer every time something out of the ordinary happened. Never mind that there was the world's biggest truck behind them. Never mind that the truck was hauling tons of waste so hot that men in space suits loaded it into the truck. He turned, looking out the back window. The truck behind them was so big, all he could see was the lower part of its front bumper. Shaking his head, he glanced at his partner. "I said radio it in." The rednecked twenty-one-year-old cowboy driver agreed. He picked up the microphone. "We got us an obstacle. Somebody's put two lanterns on the road 'bout a mile or so out in front of us. Come on."

Jason Sanders picked up the microphone. "You see any people at your obstacle?"

"Don't see nobody by the lights," the twenty-one-year-old redneck driver said. "Wait! Somebody just stepped between the lanterns. It's just one man, and he's just standing there on the road."

"Ask him to describe the man," Lanterman insisted.

"Too far away to see his face," said the Blazer's driver. "But he's tall. Broad-shouldered. Carr'in' a black stick. He's just standing there. Looks relaxed."

"It's him," Lanterman said softly.

The director of security nodded. "Any sign of weapons?"

"Nothin', 'ceptin' the stick."

"Then clear the road," the director of security said.

"My pleasure," the twenty-one-year-old driver answered.

"Leave the microphone on transmit. We're interested."

"Understand," said the driver of the Blazer, turning to his partner. "That fool's mine."

Knowing what was coming next, the ex-New Jersey policeman strapped on his seatbelt and put both hands on the dash.

"All mine," said the younger guard, revving up the engine while his partner checked the Blazer out for a roll bar, saw one, and was grateful.

"Gonna turn that man into bug juice," the driver howled, spitting out a wad of tobacco juice and popping the clutch. The Blazer's rear tires spewed gravel onto the diesel truck behind him as it bolted down the hill.

"Fucker ain't moving," the driver said, the open microphone picking up the words. He shifted into second, then third. The Blazer was rolling hard down the hill. "If'n he don't move, he gonna be vapor," the driver screamed.

The Blazer bottomed out on the flat straightaway and headed straight for Braille.

Lanterman smiled. The director of security smiled. The driver smiled.

Braille picked up a fist-sized rock. He waited until the Blazer was thirty yards away, then got ready to throw.

"What's he doin'?" the driver shouted.

The ex-policeman leaned forward. "Looks like he's going to throw something."

"Big fucking deal," the driver shouted back.

Braille threw a rock at the oncoming Blazer.

"Rock!" shouted the older guard.

The Blazer was rocketing down the road at better than eighty miles an hour. The redneck cowboy grinned. "Big fucking—" The rock hit the windshield.

The windshield turned milky white as a million tiny cracks spiderwebbed its surface.

"Can't see!" the driver screamed. The ex-policeman braced himself. The driver hit the brake, throwing the Blazer into a violent four-wheel skid. Still braced, the ex-policeman looked at the driver. "Big fucking deal, huh?"

Skidding sideways, the Blazer slid off the road, hitting the shoulder. It rolled three times and came to a rocking stop on its top.

Perched in his huge, idling truck on top of the hill, the truck driver stared down at the scene for a long moment then picked up his microphone. "We got a problem here, but I think you know that already. Please advise."

Lanterman snatched up the microphone. "This is Lanterman. Who am I talking to?"

The driver of the truck sat bolt upright. Lanterman was the main man at the Calchem plant. "Peterson," the driver said. "Bill Peterson."

Lanterman had a good memory for faces and names; he remembered Peterson as being a big man with a barrel chest and a handlebar mustache. He was reputedly one of the better drivers on the payroll. "What's going on there now?" Lanterman asked.

"The guy who took out the Blazer went over and helped the two guards out. Good thing too, cuz there's smoke coming from the Blazer. Nope. Scratch that. There's flames coming from the Blazer now. Probably blow up pretty soon."

Sanders took the microphone from Lanterman. "What about my men?"

"They look a little shook up, but they're okay. Right now they're sitting on the ground, watching the fire. Not much else they can do. That guy took their guns and threw 'em away."

Lanterman took the microphone back. "Bill . . . what do you think of the truck you're driving?"

"It's a real mover and a stomper."

"You think one man with a rock can take it out?"

"No sir," Peterson said, laughing softly.

"I like your style, Bill," Lanterman said. "Here's the deal. I want that load dumped at the waste site and I'm willing to give you and your partner a bonus if you pull it off . . . say a thousand dollars apiece. If that guy down there gets in your way because he thinks he can stop you, and you go ahead and do your job anyway . . . well, all I can say is the bonus triples. For each of you."

"Amen," whispered Peterson. He pushed the transmit button on the microphone. "Consider the load . . . delivered, Mr. Lanterman." He revved the diesel's huge engine. Exhaust filtered out of the twin pipes jutting up on both sides of the cab. As he revved the engine again, the security guard sitting beside Peterson pulled out his pistol.

"You won't need it. This isn't your average Kenworth truck," Peterson said. "This here's a special edition, put out especially for companies like Calchem. This baby's bigger. Engine's bigger too. Has a supercharger and a body made from steel, not tin. This truck's a big, bad motherfucker, and if that guy down there gets in our way I'll turn him into a six-thousand-dollar smear."

The guard checked the man below them with binoculars. "He's holding a stick."

"Stick, rock, or fuckin' cannon. Don't make no difference to me. He ain't stoppin' this truck. Not this one." He revved the Kenworth again. The engine bellowed like some extinct beast. "Let's go make six thousand dollars." He eased the clutch out and the huge truck started down the slope of the hill, pulling behind it two massive stainless-steel tanker trailers, each tank holding more than six thousand gallons of waste. Peterson double-clutched again, shifting into higher gear and pushing down on the gas. The engine's supercharger cut in, the truck lurched ahead, and both men's heads were snapped back against the headrests. "See what I mean?" Peterson shouted over the roar of the supercharger. "This baby's got an engine that'll break your neck and eat you alive."

The huge Kenworth had just started down the hill and already it was rolling hard, fast, and gaining speed with every passing second. It was like riding in a runaway rollercoaster; a lesser driver wouldn't have been able to keep it on the road, but Peterson was a skilled driver, one of the best, and he was in his element.

"Christ," the security guard murmured, in awe as centrifugal force pinned him back against the seat. The roar of the engine and the wind was deafening.

A half a mile away, far below them, the Blazer exploded into a huge ball of flames that lifted up into the sky. At the same moment, thunder exploded from a new storm moving in from the east. Suddenly lightning bleached the night, turning the stark landscape white and gray. "Oh Christ," the guard murmured, as if the unexpected storm was an ominous omen.

The light from the lanterns and the flames from the Blazer burning nearby highlighted the intensity in Braille's eyes as he stood in the center of the road, watching the monstrous truck come for him. He was holding the Musashi long sword in both hands, and while the roar of the distant truck filled the night, he began to unsheathe the great sword, bringing the shimmering blade into the light. Lightning flashed. The blade caught and reflected the white brilliance with a power that matched the storm. To the small boy standing up on the hill, it looked as if Braille were holding a shaft of lightning.

Braille backed out of the light of the lanterns, kneeling down and placing the black lacquered scabbard on the shoulder of the road before rising back up.

The flat stretch of road at the bottom of the hill was

coming up rapidly, incredibly rapidly. "Hang on," Peterson yelled. The mammoth truck roared onto the level stretch, its shocks straining under the impact, its fender skirts scraping along the pavement and creating a storm of sparks as bright as lightning. Peterson looked out beyond the range of his headlights and saw the man a half a mile away coming back into the light of the lanterns. Doesn't he know he can't hurt us with a rock? Peterson wondered.

Braille came into the light, holding the katana in his right hand. The truck wouldn't be on him for another thirty seconds. Suddenly the gleaming blade whirled in the night in a complete three-hundred-and-sixty-degree circle, then stopped with the back end of the blade lying flat against his back, the tip jutting up past his right shoulder blade and ear. It was a resting position, a stance a samurai warrior might take while he waited for his opponent to come for him.

"Wow!!" John shouted in total awe. He had just seen the sword flash in the night when Braille whirled it, bringing it to rest behind his back like a slung rifle. It was like something out of the Ninja movies. It was magic. "Wow!" he whispered, "Do it again."

A slight smile came to Braille's face as if he'd heard the boy. As sheet lightning battered the sky, he stepped forward, the katana flashing in an arc of pure silver. Suddenly Braille was holding the sword out in front of him in both hands. Up on the hill a small boy shook his head in speechless wonderment.

"What's he got?" Peterson shouted as the truck's headlights began to give substance to the man standing on the road.

The flawless steel reflected the truck's light back at the truck like a great diamond. Both men in the cab squinted. "I think it's a harry-karry sword," the guard said. Peterson didn't hear him. He was too involved in lining up the hood ornament on the man standing in the road out in front of him. Peterson shook his head. At this speed his truck's front bumper would hook the man in the chest and tear him into two parts, and then eighteen oversized tires would turn whatever was left into a smear. Stupid fucker was just asking for it. Just for the hell of it, Peterson pushed down on the horn. The noise was deafening. The horn blended with the growl of the engine and the rumble of thunder. The truck was ten seconds from Braille, traveling at a hundred and six miles an hour.

The magic was gone for the boy. The truck was almost on his friend. He screamed . . .

. . . Seventy yards away and the guy was still standing there, Peterson thought . . .

. . . Fifty yards away. "What's a harry-karry sword?" asked the director of security . . .

. . . Thirty yards away. "Get out of the way!" the small boy screamed as he started running down the hill. He tripped and went down hard. Then he scrambled to his knees. There was nothing he could do. His friend was too far away . . .

Braille tightened his grip on the katana's long handle. As the truck's lights and grille began to fill his vision, he turned slightly so his left shoulder faced the oncoming truck. Then slowly, almost majestically, he raised the sword high above his head.

The truck was almost on him. When it was twenty yards away, he twisted at the waist. In the same instant, he cocked his arms and the sword drew back. His body was poised, tensed.

The horn sounded, thunder rolled, a boy screamed, and the road trembled under the power and weight of the truck. Braille heard nothing, felt nothing. There was just the long sword he was holding, the night, and a monstrous truck. Only it was no longer a truck, it was a hellish giant animal that had to be brought down. . . .

Then the truck was on him.

Sitting up high above the road, Peterson lost sight of the man on the road as the outer edge of the hood seemed to engulf him. Peterson winced in anticipation of the coming thud and splat.

At the last possible instant Braille took two steps back towards the shoulder of the road. As the truck loomed high and huge over him, he unleashed the violence and the power of the Musashi sword. Swinging out in a savage, yet controlled motion, he brought the blade down. The four-hundred-year-old blade sliced through the right edge of the huge truck's bumper and fender, then slashed the truck's front tire. As the truck continued past, its mass not more than eighteen inches from his body, Braille followed through with the swing, and the blade slashed through the fuel tank mounted under the cab. The truck roared on, and Braille spun his body in a tight three-hundred-and-sixty-degree circle. In the same motion he brought the sword high above his body for another assault on the truck. The first tanker was just starting past Braille when the sword came down. The oversized radials exploded like ninety millimeter cannons as the blade sliced through them. Again Braille whirled and again the sword came down. This time the tanker trailer's rear tires exploded. Again Braille whirled, the sword came down and the double set of tires on the second trailer were cut to ribbons.

The great truck rumbled on like a giant beast that didn't know it had been mortally wounded. But Peterson knew.

"What'd he do?!" he screamed as the cab pitched violently to the right like a capsizing ship. It was still barreling down the road, but it was drifting off to the right and the steering wheel was frozen. He tried desperately to crank the wheel to the left with both hands and nothing. The high beams no longer shone down on the road, now they were aimed at the ditch that ran alongside of the road. He hit the brake with both feet and screamed again. "What'd he do to us?"

"Sword," his passenger croaked. "Got us with the harrykarry sword."

"Sword?" Lanterman gasped. He looked at his security director. "Sword?"

To the men in the truck, the black-and-white world they were looking at through the windshield was going crazy. They were careening ever closer to the edge of the road, but the angle was all wrong. It was like some giant god had taken the flat road they were on and tipped it at a crazy angle. The security guard looked out his window, saw rocks and dirt, and knew the truck was going to tip over. "I don't wanna die," he wailed.

Peterson stood on the brake with both feet. He could feel the truck slowing down, but not enough, not nearly enough. The runaway truck lumbered off the pavement and onto the shoulder. And still it rolled on, jolting and groaning along the side of the ditch until it finally just seemed to give up. With almost monumental slowness, the great machine and both tanker trailers slowly toppled over, crashing down on their sides at the bottom of the ditch.

A moment later both tanks ruptured like dropped eggs.

Up on the hill the boy had seen it all. He had seen the huge truck bear down on Braille and watched as Braille had disappeared when the truck had rolled over him. The truck had gone on another hundred yards then toppled over in a ditch, and the boy knew that was Braille's doing, but it didn't matter. Braille was dead. John tore his eyes away from the truck, looking back at where Braille had been standing earlier. The truck had obliterated the lanterns, and the fire consuming the Blazer was dying out. The stretch of road he was looking at was covered with darkness, and that was good because he couldn't see his friend. But he would remember him, remember the way he had stood there and hurt the car bringing down the truck. He would hold on to those memories and he wouldn't have any memories of something lying all crumpled on the road.

The boy couldn't believe Braille was dead. It had all seemed like kind of a game up until the truck had come. . . .

"Why'd you have to die?" he whispered as tears filled his eyes. Suddenly he was crying. He didn't want to, because he knew if Braille saw him he would tell him only babies cry. Then the boy shook his head because that was wrong. His real dad would say that, but Braille wouldn't. Braille would understand, would say it was okay to cry. Tears began to stream down his face and the dark night went out of focus.

The oncoming storm was close. Wind gusted around the boy and the sporadic thunder was growing louder. The boy buried his face in his hands, but even still, he sensed— almost saw—a vivid flash of close lightning. Instinctively he braced himself for the loud explosion of thunder to follow. As he did, he cupped his hands over his ears. In that eerie silence between lightning and thunder, he saw a shape looming up before him. He looked up and as lightning and thunder filled the sky, he saw Braille. Braille with his hair blowing in the wind, his eyes gentle and full of compassion as he looked down at the boy. Braille was holding the long samurai sword in one hand. He extended the other and the boy took it in both hands, feeling himself being pulled to his feet. Thunder exploded all around them, but John didn't notice it. He just felt Braille's hand and heard Braille's voice. "You okay?"

The boy knew he was all cut up and bruised from the falls. His bare feet felt frozen and were bleeding too, but it didn't matter because he didn't hurt at all, not even a little. He nodded fiercely.

Braille shook his head. "Looks like you took on the truck."

"I fell down," John sniffed. Braille wiped the tears from the boy's face. "I've got a couple of other things to do," he said softly. "Then we'll go home. Okay?" All John could do was nod. Braille started to pull away, but the boy wouldn't let his hand go. Braille smiled. "I'm not going far away, John. I'll be back." He handed John the sheathed sword.

Braille walked down the hill and over to the truck and tankers lying on their side in the ditch. A vile gray-colored liquid was seeping out of both tanks, pooling up around the ruined vehicle. There was a heavy acid smell to the liquid spilling out of the tanks; the odor burned the membranes in Braille's nose and he knew if he didn't get the men out of the truck soon, they'd die from the fumes.

He vaulted onto the side of the truck, looking down through the window. The driver and the security guard were lying on top of the passenger door. Braille jerked open the door of the truck as if it were a submarine hatch. The smell that exuded from inside the cab was hideous, and he knew that some of the waste from the tanks had already seeped into the cab. The driver, who was lying on top of the security guard, stirred and spoke into the microphone he was clutching. "The help's here." He broke off as a racking, fitful cough tore at his chest.

An instant later a voice burst out of the radio's speaker. "Impossible. Help's on its way, but it just went out the gate."

The driver looked up at Braille. "Dear God, it's him, the one that tipped us over. He's here. He's come to kill us . . ." He tried to say something else, but the choking fumes inside the cab brought on another coughing fit.

While the driver continued to cough helplessly, Braille

lowered himself into the cab. He grabbed the driver by the jacket and belt and with incredible ease lifted the man to his feet, pushing him out the open door and onto the side of the truck. The unconscious security guard followed. Then Braille climbed out beside them. He wrapped an arm around each man and stood up, leaping from the cab to the road, carting both men over to where the two security guards from the Blazer were sitting, still trying to recover from the shock of their car wreck. After he put the two men on the ground, the driver coughed, rolling over on his back and looking up at Braille. "I thought you were gonna kill us."

Braille shrugged. "Who were you talking to on the radio?"

The driver broke into a fit of coughing, then managed: "The director of security and the plant boss."

"Lanterman?" Braille asked.

"The one and only Lanterman," observed the young driver of the burning Blazer. "He's gonna be real upset when he sees what you did to my car."

"And my truck," Peterson added. "You tipped my truck over. How'd you do that?"

"It was easy," Braille said. He returned to the truck and vaulted up on its side. Leaning down into the cab he grabbed the microphone, then hunkered down on the side of the truck. He looked at the microphone in his hand for a moment, then he said:

"Lanterman."

The name rumbled out of the radio in Lanterman's office like a growl of a predatory animal. Lanterman had been leaning on the table with both arms, staring at the radio. When he heard his name and recognized the voice, blood drained from his face. "It's him!" He began to back away from the radio as if it were a snake.

The director of security grabbed Lanterman by the arm, dragging him back to the table. "You gotta talk to him," Sanders said.

Lanterman shook his head. "You talk to him," he said, his voice high-pitched.

"This is Jason Sanders, director of plant security. How are my men?"

"They'll live," Braille said. "Put Lanterman on."

Sanders shoved the microphone into Lanterman's hand. Lanterman's mouth was dry. It took him a time to work up some spit. ". . . This is Lanterman."

The radio was silent for a moment, then came: "And you know who this is and you know what's coming next."

Lanterman was sweating, his eyes were stinging from his own salt. He felt sick to his stomach. He couldn't remember what was coming next. "Pardon?" he asked. Several of the guards in his office exchanged questioning glances at the meager response.

Eleven miles away Braille smiled at the same response. Lanterman was terrorized. It was time to push it all the way to the hilt. "In case you don't remember, I came to see you last night, asking you to stop dumping your company's waste on the Stuart ranch. It was a simple request and I made it because that waste was making the family sick and killing the ranch. You said you'd stop. You said those trucks would stop. You gave me your word, and then you broke it. Do you remember what I said I would do if you broke your word?"

Braille waited for a response. No response came. After a long moment he spoke with total conviction. "It doesn't matter. Just know you're dead. Your plant's dead. Nothing will survive 'cept maybe me, and I don't care whether I do or not. You got maybe twenty minutes. I suggest you get your men out of the plant and get yourself ready to die. I'm coming, Lanterman, and you know nothing can stop me."

Braille put the microphone down on the side of the truck and started to stand up. "Wait!!" It was Lanterman, a hysterical, screaming Lanterman. "I'll keep my word. I will—I will—I promise!!"

Braille picked up the microphone. "Too late. I don't believe you. You lied to me once. You're lying to me now." He waited for a brief span of time. "Relax. I'm good at killing. I won't give you pain. Just death."

"NOOOOoooo!!" Lanterman's scream lasted almost a minute. "I'll keep my word, I promise. The trucks'll stop, stop now. Stop this minute. I'll build a new waste site. They can dump the waste in my trailer. I don't care. I don't. Just don't come in. I'll do anything. I'm doing it now. Wait there—you'll be able to hear me. Just listen."

Over the hiss of static, Braille heard someone run across the room, stabbing the buttons on a telephone and saying frantic garbled words into the phone. Then someone dialed another number, and Braille heard more frantic words. A third phone call was placed. Lanterman was more coherent this time. He was talking to people high up in his organization, people with as much power as he. Lanterman came back on the radio.

"It's all done. The next truck out of here will go to a new dump site nowhere near the Stuart ranch. I promise. Just don't break any more trucks, don't come for my plant! Don't come for me. It's done. I'll start draining the site out at the Stuart ranch tomorrow. Tomorrow's the soonest I can start. I'll convert some of the tanker trucks so they'll be able to pump liquid out of the lake and into their own trucks. It'll all be reversed. We'll clean everything up. I promise—I promise . . ."

The radio was silent for a long moment. Then a new voice came on, a voice Braille had heard briefly some minutes before. It was Jason Sanders.

"He means it. You got to him. He won't break his word this time, and this time you have my word on it." The director of security looked over at what was left of William Lanterman and sighed. "It's over. You won. I'd bet my life on it."

"You just did," Braille remarked.

Braille walked up the hill to John. The boy was half frozen, his feet were cut and bleeding, and everything he had witnessed had left him exhausted.

Braille scooped the boy up into his arms as if he were a tiny infant, then picked up the Musashi sword. Tired as he was, John's eyes were still open and he was looking at Braille with total trust. "We going home?" he asked.

Braille nodded. "You're going home," he said softly. John relaxed in his arms. A moment later he fell asleep with his chin resting on Braille's shoulder.

31

"YOU'RE VIOLATING U.S. GOVERNMENT AIR SPACE. CHANGE course immediately or face violent reprisal." The voice coming over the radio speaker and into the Lear jet's cockpit was harsh and strident. "I repeat again! You have violated U.S. government air space. Change course immediately or face violent reprisal. Acknowledge."

Flying the jet through the night at better than eight hundred miles an hour, Kubick picked up the microphone. "Tell Cutter that Kubick is coming. Tell Cutter to get the runway lights on, and one more thing. I don't know who you are, but if you give me one more goddamn warning about air space, I'll find out who you are and I guarantee you'll never talk into a microphone again . . . acknowledge."

Thirty seconds later Kubick saw two strips of lights blink on on the floor of the black desert four miles out in front of him. He adjusted his course slightly and began cutting his air speed.

Ten minutes later Kubick was in Hargrave Cutter's office, sitting across from the director's desk. Cutter was behind his desk and Riddick was standing beside Kubick, suturing up the left side of the man's face. Riddick's hands were shaking. Kubick's ear had been shot away. All that remained were two flaps of skin that had to be brought together, then sewn up. Riddick's hands were not shaking because of the task, he was shaking because Kubick had not allowed him to use any type of anesthetic. He'd put in eight sutures so far, figured it would take another eight before he could go on to the temple and jaw wounds. Eight stitches and the man hadn't flinched, gasped, or missed a beat as he described how his men had died and what had happened during his own encounter with Gregory.

"That's the way it ended," Kubick said without emotion.

"He was healing. I was hurt, and there wasn't anything I could do, so I left."

Hargrave Cutter sat back in his chair, shaking his head in wonderment. "You say that weapon, that St. Jude, can fire six thousand rounds per minute and that Gregory just walked up to your man and took the gun away from him?"

Kubick nodded and Riddick scraped the man's skull with a needle. Riddick shuddered at the pain he must have just inflicted on Kubick, but Kubick didn't seem to notice. "I think the bulletproof vest he took off one of my men deflected some of St. Jude's firepower. But still, what I saw was nothing short of impossible."

The office turned quiet. The only sounds in the silence came from Riddick while he sutured Kubick's flesh together. Finally Cutter broke the silence. "I guess it's over."

"It's not over," Kubick vowed. "I don't care if it takes the rest of my life, I will track that thing down. When I do, I'll find a way to destroy it."

"But you don't have your team anymore," Cutter said.

"I don't need my team. This is between me and the beast that killed my men. All that matters is that either it dies or I die."

Hargrave Cutter recognized pure unbridled hate when he saw it, and he approved. He had plans for Kubick and the madness and hate that was driving him on. "But you don't know where it is or how to kill it," he said softly.

"No, but I'll find it and then I'll find a way to kill it. Or die trying."

Cutter tented his fingers. "I realize my original request that you capture the Ancient alive was impossible." Kubick snorted disdainfully. Unperturbed, Cutter continued. "However, I'm still interested in this creature's body, especially its blood. For that reason I'm not only in a position to tell you where the Ancient is, but I think I may be able to provide you with a weapon that can kill it."

Kubick's eyes narrowed. He seemed to stop breathing. "You know where it is?" he whispered. "And you know how to kill it?"

"I believe so."

"Why didn't you tell me about this weapon when you first gave my men and me this assignment?"

Suddenly Cutter knew that, if he did not answer Kubick's question correctly, Kubick would kill him. He cleared his throat. "At the time I offered you the assignment, the weapon did not exist. We were working on a kind of prototype but it was only in the planning stages."

"And the creature's location?" Kubick asked.

Cutter seemed surprised by the question. "Haven't you seen the news?"

"Where's the fucking animal that killed my men?" Kubick snarled.

"Our researchers think there's an outbreak of vampirism in Seattle. They think one of those creatures—one of the New Ones—somehow survived the radiation on the island and escaped. It's been all over the news. But that's where you'll find the Ancient . . . in Seattle, among his own kind." Then Cutter went on to explain the difference between a New One and an Ancient to Kubick and went on to describe what had been happening in Seattle. He finished about the same time Riddick finished suturing up Kubick's face. As Riddick began putting away his instruments, Kubick demanded, "Now show me this weapon."

Cutter motioned to Riddick. Riddick crossed Cutter's office, opening the door to a heavy metal cabinet and removing a metal box and a set of heavy canvas gloves. He put the box and gloves on Cutter's desk and sat down in a chair some distance from Cutter and Kubick.

Cutter unlocked the box and lifted the lid. Kubick found himself looking at a nickel-plated .357 Magnum Colt Python revolver with an eight-inch barrel, six flat-nosed bullets that had been inserted in a speed loader clip, and an oddly shaped piece of clear Plexiglas about the size of a man's fist. Kubick raised his eyes from the box to Cutter's face and said disdainfully, "I saw the creature I'm after take multiple hits from weapons twice as powerful as that Python and keep on coming. If you think that pistol of yours is going to do anything to it other than make it blink, you're either an idiot or out of your goddamn mind."

Cutter forced himself to remain composed, even managed to smile slightly. "Take a closer look at the bullets, Mr. Kubick, but before you do, put on the gloves as a precaution."

Suddenly curious, Kubick slipped on one of the gloves and was surprised by its weight. "There's threads of lead running through the material," Cutter explained as Kubick picked up the speed loader clip that held all six rounds in a circle so they could be inserted into the pistol's cylinder with one motion, and examined the bullets. They were basic .357 magnum rounds with one exception: the bullets had been hollowed out, filled with a substance, then covered over with what looked like liquid plastic. Kubick started to touch the tip of one of the bullets with a gloved finger; Cutter shook his head. "Don't. Each of those bullets has been filled with a systemic chemical compound and covered over with a water-soluble resin."

Suddenly Kubick knew. He looked straight at Cutter. "You've filled these bullets with a radioactive substance, haven't you?"

Cutter smiled. "It's something my chemists came up with. Without going into too much detail, let's just say that each bullet holds an extremely radioactive blend of chemicals—a combination of U-32, U-35, Cesium 137, and Americium 241." He settled back in his chair. "We know that radiation killed the Ancients on the island. Technically that radiation should have killed Gregory, but I have a theory about that. He was older than the other Ancients. That means he was stronger, far more resilient and that was why he didn't die when the cloud of radioactivity swept over the island." Cutter pointed to the six bullets Kubick was still holding. "But the amount of radiation in any one of those bullets far exceeds anything Gregory encountered on the island." Kubick gave Cutter a dubious look.

"The amount of nuclear material we've packed into each of those bullets is highly toxic and extremely intensive, radioactively speaking," Cutter responded. "More to the point, it's radiation that can be introduced directly into the body. If you shoot the Ancient with one of those bullets, the water-soluble resin will dissolve almost instantly. A moment later the radioactive toxins will begin spreading through his body, killing it from the inside—not from the outside, like the radioactive cloud on the island. There you have it."

Kubick was no fool. He knew that firing the weapon in the

box posed a danger to himself and he also suspected that after he did shoot the Ancient with one of those bullets, the creature would live long enough to turn on him and kill him, but it didn't matter. What mattered was that, in the end, the creature would be dead. He locked his eyes on Cutter. "What do you want from me in return for that weapon?"

"I want the Ancient's body, especially its blood. After you've killed it, I want you to bring it here."

Kubick nodded absent-mindedly, then gestured at the box holding the Colt Python. "What's that piece of Plexiglas for?"

"Radiation blowback," Cutter said neutrally. "It fits on to the pistol between the cylinder and barrel and prevents any type of radiation from blowing back on your hand when you fire it."

"Have your men gotten my jet ready?" Kubick asked, still staring at the pistol.

"Don't you want to rest or take a break?"

"No. I want the jet fueled up." He glanced down at his bloodstained clothing. "And some clean clothes. I want to leave within the hour."

"No problem," Cutter responded. "No problem whatsoever."

32

BRAILLE SAT IN THE SWING, WATCHING A PASSING STORM FOR the better part of an hour before he finally entered the Stuart home, moving quietly into his own room. It seemed odd to him. The Stuart house had become his home. This room had become his room. He would be going away at sunrise and it seemed like he should be packing, putting things into a suitcase as other people do when they go away on a trip. Dumb thought, he decided. He wasn't leaving on a trip. He was going away. And as for packing, he hadn't come with anything. He wouldn't be leaving with anything—except for some memories, some very special and very warm memories.

As he took off his shirt, he realized his skin and clothes smelled like the inside of a Calchem tanker. Scooping up a pair of clean jeans and shirt, he stepped into the bathroom and, as quietly as possible, showered and scrubbed his skin raw with soap and a bristle brush. After drying off, he buried his dirty clothes in a hamper and slipped into a clean shirt and jeans. Then he stepped out into the hallway . . . and came face to face with Mary Kathleen Stuart.

She was wearing an off-white nightgown so sheer, so translucent that Braille could see the pores of her flawless skin just beneath the garment. She had exquisite breasts, her nipples were erect, and the dark triangle of hair at the cleft of her legs was markedly visible even in the meager light of the hallway.

Braille was stunned at the sight of her, at the ripe fullness of her body. He groped for words and none came. She was looking at him intently, and Braille still could not find words. Finally, she gave words to their encounter. "If we were to make love, if I were yours like this every night, would you stay with us?"

"No," Braille said sadly, softly, not wanting to lie.

She took a step closer to him. "Then would you make love to me and hold me just for one night?"

"I'll still leave in the morning," Braille whispered.

"I know that. I know this is only for one night."

Braille looked at her questioningly.

"I already hate myself for the nights we were in this house together and I kept us apart. I know you're going away in the morning." She reached up for him, lacing her hands around the back of his neck and pulling his face close to hers. "I love you. One night is better than never."

Braille cupped her face in his hands, kissing her gently, briefly. He drew back, looked at her, then kissed her again, harder this time. She responded, meeting his tongue with hers. She rose up on her tiptoes, pressing her lips to his and kissing him feverishly, almost violently. At the same time, Braille felt his own surging need for her well up inside him. He returned her kiss with the same fervor.

She drew away, started to unbutton his shirt, then ripped it apart. A button clattered across the floor. "Wanted you for so long," she murmured, her voice deep and throaty. "So long."

They slipped into her room. With her back to him, she closed and locked the door, slipping off the nightgown. Then she took a shawl off the hook on the back of the door, pressing it to the front of her body, allowing it to drape down over her legs as she slowly turned to face him. She was stunning and beautiful. For a moment Braille didn't understand what she was doing with the shawl, but then it dawned on him. She was hiding her withered leg, trying to disguise the deformity with the shawl. Didn't she know? Didn't she realize? he wondered. She was beautiful. Her leg was deformed, but in the face of her stunning inner and outer beauty, it was no more than a blemish.

If only you could see yourself through my eyes, he thought. If only you could see what I see. She came to him in the dim muted light of her bedroom, her steps measured and precise. Braille took her in his arms, kissed her, and at the same time, he took her shawl and let it drop to the floor.

And for a span of time to come—a mystical magical span of time—Mary Kathleen Stuart forgot about her leg, forgot about everything except the man holding her, the man kissing her, the man inside her.

Braille stirred, opening his eyes. The curtains to Mary Kathleen's bedroom were open slightly. The blackness of the night had passed and the sky was the color of dark pewter; the color of the world an hour before the sun comes up.

Mary Kathleen lay beside him, her body melded to his. Moving slowly, he rolled over on his side, brushing her hair away from her face as he looked at her. The room was still dark, yet he could see her perfectly. He lay motionless beside her for a long moment, letting his eyes linger on her face and liking—maybe loving—what he saw. The night had been good for both of them, bringing release to both of them and adding a new dimension to their relationship, a loving dimension that would be very hard to leave behind.

He would miss this woman very much. The pain of his pending departure burned inside him like fire. Still, if he could work up the nerve—the courage—maybe he could turn this parting into something more than just pain . . . at least for her.

Draping his arm over Mary Kathleen, he felt her bare spine with his fingertips, then moved his hand up to the back of her neck. She stirred slightly, shivered involuntarily but did not wake up. As she continued to sleep, he began to massage the muscles at the back of her neck while he probed for two shiatsu pressure points. He had learned the art of shiatsu from his adopted father. His father also taught him the shiatsu pressure points found throughout the body. Some of the pressure points could be used to heal. Others could be used to anesthetize. Braille was searching for the two pressure points that, when pressed simultaneously, could induce sleep, but he had to be careful. There were two other similar pressure points in the neck and upper spine that, when pressed, would produce instant death. He found the first point a few inches below her left ear, then found the second point. He put his thumb on the first point and his forefinger on the second, applying pressure to both spots for a long moment.

Ten seconds later Mary Kathleen Stuart was in such a deep sleep that a physician could have taken out her appendix and she never would have felt a thing.

Braille eased Mary Kathleen over onto her back, then took a few moments to compose himself. He didn't know if he could do what he wanted to do, but he did know that if he succeeded, he would pay a terrible price.

He drew back the blankets and sat beside her, his eyes focused on her misshapen leg. When he was finally ready, he slipped his left hand under the small of her back, placing his right hand on top of her withered ankle. Willing himself to accept what would come next, Braille waited a moment longer, then closed his eyes and began to concentrate.

It began to happen a few heartbeats later. It started as a tingling sensation in his own right leg. Then the tingling slowly changed to heat, a heat that encompassed the bones and flesh in his leg. At first there was no pain. He simply felt as if he'd put his ankle into a warm pool of water, but the sensation changed, becoming more intense. Within a matter of seconds the heat began to intensify as if the water had begun to boil. Suddenly the bones in his leg and foot felt on fire, felt like liquid molten steel. He gasped at the onslaught of pain, gritting his teeth and forcing himself not to move his hands. He knew all he would have to do was pull his hands away from her body and the pain would stop, but he couldn't. He had committed himself. The pain was becoming worse, beyond description. Still Braille sat beside the sleeping woman, forcing himself not to move his hands. The agony was worse than anything he'd imagined it would be. Gasping for breath, fighting to keep himself from passing out, he opened his eyes and looked down at his own leg. He was not surprised at what he saw. From the kneecap down, his leg was glowing faintly. The skin seemed almost translucent, and below the skin, below the glowing flesh, he could see bones shifting, moving, and distorting themselves. He could see bones becoming misshapen and gnarled like the bones in Mary Kathleen Stuart's leg.

He didn't know how much longer he would last. His leg was still changing, the bones still warping, bending, and twisting, only now he could hear the sounds, grating, grinding sounds accompanied by audible clicks and pops as the bones, muscles, and tendons altered themselves, assuming the shape of the sleeping woman's deformed leg. Willing himself to last a moment longer and hyperventilating from the agony, he looked over at Mary Kathleen's withered and deformed leg. Only, it wasn't withered anymore. Like his own leg, it too was altering its shape, only, in this case it was growing. Becoming. Gnarled twisted bones were straightening themselves out. The deformed ankle joint was becoming whole again.

"That's good," Braille said faintly. He knew it was good because he was starting to sink into the abyss of pain he had taken upon himself. He knew he was seconds away from passing out, and once he did, whatever was happening would stop. "That's good," he said again as he gave in to the pain and thick blackness surrounding him, then slumped over on the bed.

Braille couldn't remember where he was or what was going on. But then the pain in his leg brought it all back. He sat up with a start. Mary Kathleen was still sleeping beside him, her body covered with blankets and quilts. Braille grasped the covers. After a heartbeat's hesitation, he gently lifted the covers up. Her legs, both of them were beautiful, perfect. He smiled, glancing out the window. The sun was just starting to come up.

He realized he was putting it off, stalling. After a long moment, he forced himself to look down at his own leg and was surprised by what he saw. During the brief time he had been out, his leg had changed from a hideous withered appendage to what it had been before. He no longer felt the pain, and everything—the agony, the grating sounds, his own leg shaping itself into a nightmare—now seemed like a very distant dream. But it had been no dream. Mary Kathleen Stuart's legs were perfect, and Braille smiled faintly at the wonder of it all, the wonder of this gift he had.

Then he remembered, and the smile faded. Through the crack in the curtains he could see the clouds being bleached by the first rays of the sun. Time to go, he thought. He slipped out of the room, washed up, shaved, dressed, and returned to her side. She was still sleeping and would sleep for hours more. He sat down beside her, pulling the blankets up around her neck and touching her cheek with his fingers. Then he got to his feet and walked out of her room, out of the front door, never looking back.

33

PILOTING THE PLANE AT TWENTY THOUSAND FEET, WITH THE rising sun to his back and the black waters of Puget Sound ahead of him, Kubick checked his instruments, putting the Lear jet into a shallow dive. The light streaming into the cabin from the sun turned murky gray as the plane entered the clouds. Flying blind now, he checked his instruments and again altered his course. Initially he had planned to land at Seattle's Sea-Tac Airport, but the transmissions he'd been picking up suggested Sea-Tac was a congested mess of unscheduled outbound flights.

The Lear jet broke free of the cloud cover and Kubick could see the lights of Seattle below him. He leveled out and flew in a westerly direction until he saw the Space Needle jutting up out of the blackness. He banked right and set a new course that would put him down at a small airport in the suburbs, twenty miles from downtown Seattle. He would land, rent a room, spend the day meditating and resting, and then tonight he would go into downtown Seattle—and Underground Seattle if he had to—to find the Ancient. To kill the Ancient.

Braille had been driving about two hours when he passed a sign that said Arron Lake, sixteen miles. Recalling Mary Kathleen's comment about an abandoned Air Force base being located near the town, he slowed the Charger, then pulled onto the shoulder of the freeway and stopped. He climbed down, walking around to the passenger side and hunkering down on his haunches, oblivious to the rain slanting down from the sky. Squinting his eyes against the weather, he studied the terrain out in front of him, noticing a distant range of familiar cliffs rising up out of the flatlands.

Still on his haunches, Braille closed his eyes, running that night through his mind, remembering their frantic race across a rutted runway towards the cliffs. So close, Braille thought. He could feel it. Hargrave Cutter and his monstrous agency were close, not more than maybe twenty miles from where he was right now. He started to get to his feet, but the memories of that night crashed down on him, immobilizing him. He remembered the sight of a beautiful woman walking towards him, smiling as she reached out for him. Braille gritted his teeth, willing himself not to remember. He failed. He saw a red laserscope dot appear on Leslie's blouse, heard a rifle shot, saw her stagger backwards and fall in slow motion. A growl broke from Braille's throat . . . and he found himself standing beside the Ram Charger being battered by raindrops as he glared at the desert, glaring at the buildings that were out there, buildings he could not see. Thunder rolled in the distance.

"I will be back," Braille said softly.

Gregory was in a foul mood. He had spent weeks preparing himself for the twentieth century, but nothing could have prepared him for freeways, traffic, and the endless confusion and congestion of a huge, sprawling city. There were traffic jams everywhere, car accidents everywhere, total chaos everywhere. He had spent most of the night getting lost or sitting behind the wheel waiting for traffic to move again, but finally, a couple of hours after the sun had come up, he had found the right exit and taken it.

Suddenly Gregory's car began making funny noises. It coughed, sputtered, lost speed, then died. As Gregory coasted down the street, his first thought was he'd broken the car. But then he noticed the gas gauge needle was resting on E. He shrugged, stopped the car in the middle of the street and got out. Oblivious to the drivers honking their horns at him, Gregory looked around. The buildings were older, made from stone. They were tall and ornate. Craftsmen had created these buildings. They were not tin and plastic like the shopping malls he had seen earlier. He was where he wanted to be: he was in the older part of Seattle, and Underground Seattle was near.

The day was overcast. In spite of the thick cloud cover hiding the sun, Gregory felt uncomfortable and found himself squinting in the diffused light. Normally even direct sunlight didn't bother him unless he was tired or needed blood. He decided to check into a hotel, rest, then, after the sun went down, he would attend to his second need.

Gregory was impressed with the Chinook Hotel. It was twelve stories high, a hundred years old, and had changed very little during its existence. The lobby was high-ceilinged, filled with antiques, faded Oriental rugs, and huge crystal chandeliers. There was an ornate fountain in the middle of the lobby. Water gurgled out of the top and lily pads floated in the pool at the fountain's base. The hotel reminded Gregory of a time when he and Clementina had lived in a similar hotel in Paris two hundred years earlier. The memories were warm and loving, full of the passion he and Clementina had shared so intensely. He pushed them aside, because remembering reminded him of how alone he was now.

The clerk behind the registration desk was as old as the hotel and he seemed shocked by Gregory's request for a room. The old man glanced around to make sure no one else could hear him. "Haven't you heard about all the trouble that's going on? Been in the newspapers and on TV." Gregory nodded and again asked for a room.

"This isn't a good place to stay, sir," the clerk said. "'Specially at night." He shook his bald head. "I've been working here for forty years and never once thought about quittin' until this trouble at night started. Now quittin's all I think about."

"Thank you for your concern," Gregory said, resting his hands on the counter. "I will be fine."

The clerk sighed, asking Gregory how long he would be staying. Gregory thought about the question, thought about Braille, and guessed that once the human knew what was going on in Seattle, he would come here as soon as possible to try and stop what was taking place. Then Gregory would find him and then the human would die. Gregory shrugged and decided to take the room for a week. If Braille did not arrive in the next seven days, Gregory would move on and search elsewhere, because that was all the time this city had left—seven days. At the end of that time there would not be a Seattle, just burned-out buildings and rubble-strewn streets, deserted in the daytime, but teeming with packs of New Ones, death, and horror at night. Gregory paid for the room, studying the old man as he gave him back his change and the key. He started to turn away, but stopped, leveling his eyes at the clerk. "If you are so worried about what is going on, why are you still working here?"

"I'd leave, but I got no family, no money. Believe me, if I'd bothered to put some money in a bank, I'd be riding a Greyhound right this minute, heading east, you best damn betcha."

Gregory checked the wallet he had taken from the man in the state park weeks earlier. It was still thick with hundred-dollar bills. He took out fifteen of them and laid them on the counter, pushing them towards the elderly clerk. He suspected the man was a little senile since he'd talked about riding a dog east, but he liked the fellow. The old man had tried to warn him and Gregory liked him for that. He pointed to the money on the counter. "Would that get you a ride on your Grey-hound?"

The clerk eyed the money. "What's the catch?"

"Catch?"

"Why you doin' this?"

"You need the money. I don't."

"There's over a thousand dollars there. I'd never be able to pay you back."

"You don't have to. Take the money, old man, and go away from this city."

The clerk slipped the money into the pocket of his uniform. Tears had filled his eyes and he started to say something, but stopped. The stranger was no longer in the lobby.

On the west side of the Cascade mountains Braille pulled into an isolated gas station. He parked beside the pumps and got out. He knew he didn't have any money and would have to steal the gas, but he pulled his wallet out anyway. As the attendant approached, Braille checked his wallet. Looking up at the attendant, he told him to fill it up, then checked his wallet again. There was money in it. Three one-hundred-dollar bills and a note:

"You worked hard while you were here and in a way what

little I'm giving you is an insult in light of everything you did around the ranch and everything you did for Amanda, John, and me. I just wish I could have given you more.

"And one more thing. If you can, if it's ever possible, come back to us. You are deeply loved. By all three of us."

Braille put the note back in his wallet. Two hours later he was driving across the world's largest floating bridge and starting into the outskirts of Seattle.

An incoming storm over the waters of Puget Sound hid the sun, but Braille knew it was setting because he could feel the changes in his own body. With the darkness came the hunting need, the blood need. He had fought the urges during his time at the Stuart ranch, been able to substitute animal blood for human blood, but things were different now. He was back in the city. There was no one to care about and no animal blood to help him overcome the craving. He gripped the wheel and began to fight off the inhuman urges and desires racking his body. At the same time he knew that within the next few hours the new vampires in Underground Seattle would be coming awake with the same urges, but unlike him, they would not struggle to fight off the urges. Not the New Ones. They reveled in their newly discovered desires and incredible strength. They would seek out blood like packs of starving animals. Braille could still remember the way Gregory had explained it to him. The New Ones were animals. They possessed two driving needs: survival and the taking of blood. The needs ruled everything, blotting out everything else: conscience, humanity, compassion, everything. All that mattered was blood and survival.

In spite of his own growing urges, in spite of his desire to get to downtown Seattle to see how bad the outbreak really was, Braille felt a heavy wave of fatigue and exhaustion roll over him. He knew the cause. He had pushed himself too hard over the past twenty-four hours, expending too much energy in stopping the Calchem truck and in healing Mary Kathleen's leg. With effort he got the car off the freeway, then pulled into a K-Mart parking lot. He turned off the Ram Charger and squinted out the windshield. Off in the west he could see a number of tall buildings framed by black clouds and faint traces of sunset. He knew he wasn't more than four miles from downtown Seattle. A moment later he was sound asleep.

"Repent!" screamed the loudest voice Braille had ever heard. Groggy with sleep, he sat up, looking out at the K-Mart parking lot. There were five cars in the lot, and a man in a raincoat was standing on the hood of one of the cars—talking down to a small group of people crowded around him—with a hand-held battery-operated loudspeaker. "And I am telling you the end of the world is upon us," the man was saying, his words as loud as artillery fire. "We did not heed the commandments of the Lord when He warned us with the AIDS plague, and His patience with us is at an end. Now He has brought forth a new plague, a plague even deadlier than the other."

"You got that right," Braille mumbled.

"I have seen what this plague can do to man. I have seen with my own eyes. This plague comes out at night, it knows no bounds, no reason, no mercy. I have seen this and I am here to tell you that the end of the world is at hand."

"You got that right," Braille repeated, starting the car.

"Repent!" the man screamed as Braille pulled out onto the boulevard, driving towards the center of Seattle. It was still early, around eight-thirty in the evening, and there were cars out on the streets and people on the sidewalks. But the closer he got to downtown Seattle, the more deserted the city became. He turned on the radio, fiddling with the dial until he picked up a local news station. The broadcaster was talking about the weather. Braille lit a cigarette and continued to drive. Then the announcer returned.

"To recap the events of the day, earlier this afternoon the governor declared a state of emergency in downtown Seattle. National Guard troops have been called in as have federal troops from Fort Lewis. A command post has been set up in the Ridgemont Hotel. General Westmore is acting commander for the troops in Seattle. Thus far the general has not made himself available to the press. However, his spokesman, Lieutenant Colonel Bragg, said during a five o'clock news conference that the problem is in hand and he issued the following statements. 'It is felt the strange behavior observed in some of the people of downtown Seattle is due to a viral infection. Those inflicted with this infection have exhibited the following symptoms: violent and hostile behaviors, psychotic trains of thought, antisocial attitudes, and fear of bright lights. A number of state and federal health agencies are now attempting to curb this epidemic. I want to again reassure the public that there is no reason to panic.'"

The radio announcer resumed speaking. "Those were the words from Colonel Bragg, spokesperson for the commanding general of the troops currently in Seattle. As I indicated earlier, he issued those statements during a five o'clock news briefing. *However*, at eight o'clock this evening Colonel Bragg again met with the press and issued the following pronouncements.

"'Effective immediately, the city of Seattle is under martial law.

"'Effective immediately, a twenty-block area of downtown Seattle is being closed off by the U.S. Army and National Guard troops. The area to be cordoned off is bordered by Pike Street on the north, Bourne Avenue to the east, King Street to the south, and the waterfront on the west. Every street leading into this area will be roadblocked by soldiers. It is hoped this action will keep the virus from spreading into uninfected parts of the streets and keep looting to a minimum.

"'Also effective immediately, a curfew is being imposed on downtown Seattle. Everyone living in the designated area is to remain indoors or seek shelter one hour before sundown and remain in said shelter until two hours after sunrise. To be on the streets during the evening hours is to risk being contaminated by those already infected with this virus. This curfew is also intended as a precautionary measure against the possibility of being hurt by government troops who have no way of knowing who is infected and who is not.

"'To repeat, Seattle is now under martial law and a curfew is now in effect. However, these are precautionary measures only, and there is no reason to panic.'"

"That was Colonel Bragg's latest press release. If there are any further announcements, we will interrupt our regular programming to bring them to you." Then the announcer's voice took on a cold, sarcastic tone. "Remember, in the words of Colonel Bragg, 'there is no reason to panic.' With that in mind, and in light of the fact that the broadcasting facilities and transmitter for KJOJ are located atop the McNeal Building in the newly closed off area of downtown Seattle, this is Rocky Black, your KJOJ disc jockey cueing up a song for all those people who told us not to panic." The deejay's voice escalated from sarcasm to anger. "I'm dedicating this song to Colonel Bragg, General Westmore, the Mayor of Seattle, the Police Chief, the Governor, and all you other fucking assholes who told everyone in Seattle not to worry. Hope you hear this song; it's coming at you with a hundred thousand watts of power and the best wishes of all us people who are now trapped in Seattle and believed all you assholes when you said don't panic." The screaming deejay cued up a hard-driving, pulsating song and Laura Brannigan began to sing "Self Control" her voice gutsy and melodic at the same time.

> Oh the night is my world.
> City lights, painted girls.
> In the daytime nothing matters.
> It's the nighttime that matters.
> In the night no control . . .

Braille had heard the song before and liked it. He glanced at the car radio as Laura Brannigan sang:

> I . . . I live among the creatures of the night.

Appropriate, he thought.

> I haven't got the will to try and fight
> against a new tomorrow . . .

In a motel room eighteen miles away Kubick was getting ready for the hunt. A radio on the night stand was playing Brannigan's song, but he wasn't listening. He was too involved in arming himself.

I said night . . . I'm living in the forest of a dream.
I know the night is not what it may seem . . .

Kubick picked up two shoulder holsters that held a
matched set of Desert Eagle .44-caliber Magnum automatics and slipped the rigging on. He picked up his kubikiri,
sliding it into the sheath located just below the nape of his
neck. Next he clipped six powerful fragmentation grenades
onto the left side of his belt, then opened a heavy metal box
lying on his bed. He removed the Colt Python, the six
bullets still in the speed loader clip and an odd-looking
holster. He slipped the holster onto the right side of his belt.
The holster weighed almost as much as the six grenades, but
that didn't surprise him. He knew the holster had been lined
with lead mesh to protect him from the radioactive bullets.
He loaded the Python, dropping it into its holster and
pulling on a black nylon parka. Finally he turned his
attention to a wide long black case with a briefcase handle
lying on the bed. He opened the case. Inside were a Franchi
12-gauge shotgun and a machine gun, in this case, an
especially altered FN-LAR-HB FALO 50.42 assault rifle.
The case also contained a bandolier of shotgun shells and a
thousand rounds of .308 bullets fitted into the specially
designed banana clips for the machine gun. Kubick checked
the weapons, ammunition, then locked the case, picked it
up, and walked out of the motel room.

In the background Laura Brannigan sang,

Oh the night is my world . . .

Looking out his hotel room twelve stories above the
streets of Seattle, Gregory listened to the song filtering
through the wall from the room next to his.

I . . . I live among the creatures of the night.
I haven't got the will to try and fight
against a new tomorrow. . . .

He put his hands on the windowsill and continued to
listen to the song. He knew it wasn't about real creatures of
the night or vampires, but he liked the song, liked the sound

of the singer's voice. A few moments later the song faded away and another song began pulsating through the wall. He didn't like this one and he refocused his attention on the streets below him. It was quiet down there, but it was still early. A dozen blocks away he could see the roadblock the Army had just set up on one of the wide streets. Glancing off to his right, he peered down through a canyon of tall buildings and saw the same kind of blockade on another boulevard a mile away. He studied the city and its blocked-off streets for several minutes more before turning away from the window. Time to go, he thought. Time to see how bad things were under the streets of Seattle.

A few miles off to the east Braille was thinking the same thoughts as he opened the door to his motel, stepping out into the night. He had picked this particular motel because it was close to the area cordoned off by the Army and because the owners had put out some effort to protect its customers from the dopers and gangs that inhabited the area. Sheets of metal reinforced the motel's doors. Deadbolt locks were everywhere and all of the windows were covered with wrought-iron bars. The place looked more like a bunker than a motel room, and it was exactly what Braille wanted. He climbed into the Ram Charger and pulled out onto the boulevard, driving slowly down the street, heading in a westerly direction. In spite of the warnings that had come over the radio, and the curfew, there were still hookers on the street, winos looking for handouts, groups of people doing drug deals.

He drove past porno theaters, empty strip joints, and some pawnshops. Abruptly he pulled off the boulevard, onto a side street, then nosed the Charger into an alley behind one of the pawnshops. He got out and walked over to the pawnshop's back door, kicking it in. Noticing the wires and magnets attached to the door frame, Braille knew he had just set off a silent alarm, and knew he would have to hurry. The pawnshop had sold off most of its weapons, but he was able to find two Colt .45 automatics in a display case, some empty clips, and a box of ammunition in a drawer.

Braille eased the Charger out of the alley, then pulled

back onto the boulevard. A half a mile later he pulled over, shut off the engine, lit a cigarette, and studied the roadblock the Army had put up four blocks away. They'd parked an armored personnel carrier in the middle of the boulevard, then flanked it on either side with two three-quarter-ton trucks. Jeeps with M-60 machine guns were parked on both sidewalks, wedged between the trucks and the buildings on both sides of the street. Concertina wire had been strung out in thick curly loops under and over the trucks and jeeps. Aside from men standing in the jeeps, manning the M-60's, Braille counted upwards of thirty soldiers—armed soldiers; most carried M-16's. Several carried M-79 grenade launchers. The men were lined up along the barricade with their backs to Braille and their weapons pointed towards the center of Seattle.

Braille looked up, studying the buildings that lined the side of the barricade. Most of the buildings were eight and nine stories tall, built close together like a massive black wall that was part of the skyline of Seattle. That's how he would get in, he thought, as he began inserting .45-caliber bullets into empty clips. He loaded up six clips, stuck four in his back pocket, and pushed the other two into the automatics. He climbed out of the Charger. He couldn't go through the barricade, or around it, but he could get into downtown Seattle by going over the buildings next to the barricade. Hidden in the shadows, he stepped into a dark alley. A moment later he was climbing up a fire escape; a few minutes after that he was moving along the roof of a tall, block-long department store.

A half hour later, after climbing down another fire escape, Braille found himself in the heart of downtown Seattle. His first reaction was to shake his head in confusion. He had come into the heart of the city expecting to find the end of the world, expecting to find himself surrounded by total chaos, blood, mayhem, and slaughter.

. . . Instead he found himself on a deserted and desolate windswept street.

Eight blocks away Gregory had the same impression as he emerged from an alley and stepped out onto a street.

Nothing. Confused by the desolation, he began to move north while, at the same time, Braille began to move west.

Braille wasn't quite sure how to get into Underground Seattle. He knew he could probably gain entrance to the underground city through a manhole cover as the TV newswoman had. But which manhole cover? On which street? He passed a sheltered bus stop, stopped, and returned to it. There was a map of Seattle mounted on the back of the shelter under a layer of Plexiglas. Various historical and scenic sights in Seattle were highlighted on the map with arrows and red numbers. After a moment's scanning, Braille found the starting point for Underground Seattle tours. The Red Hammer. Braille memorized where he was, where the Red Hammer was, then headed off.

Three blocks to the south of the Red Hammer, Gregory stopped abruptly as he picked up the scent of New Ones, a lot of New Ones, he decided. Suddenly the wind had become heavy with the ammonia-like odor of the New Ones' blood. Shaking his head in disgust, he began to make his way up the street, moving towards the source of the disgusting odors.

All the while, Kubick continued to prowl the streets as all around him people living in apartments, hotels, and lofts closed their curtains, barring their doors as they prayed for morning to come.

34

BRAILLE FOUND THE RED HAMMER BAR AND WASN'T SURPRISED to find it locked up. So much for the easy way into Underground Seattle, he thought, turning away to scan the area. He spotted a manhole cover in the middle of the street forty yards away. The television news reporter who'd gotten killed live on videotape had gained access to Underground Seattle by going down a manhole. It looked as though he would have to do the same if he were going to find out how bad the plague was, how many New Ones there were. He just hoped he wouldn't meet the same fate as did Misty Ying.

After prying away the cast iron cover, Braille used a series of metal bars sticking up from a cement wall to go down into the hole. It was pitch-black below the street. For a moment he had the feeling he was descending into a black hole full of sharks and alligators all heading for him, all planning on taking his legs off at the hip. He froze, gritting his teeth. After the eerie feeling passed and his eyes adjusted to the darkness, he checked his surroundings. He had descended partway into a huge underground tunnel some twenty feet in diameter. From his vantage point on the ladder he could see there were no human-shaped forms sleeping on the floor below him. He continued down the ladder, stepping onto a wet cement floor. Near as he could figure, he was in a drainage tunnel that channeled run-off rainwater, carrying it down to the harbor.

At that moment he heard the faint muffled sounds of thunder. Time to get moving, he thought; time to go in, count the vampires and get out. But five minutes later he was completely lost. He wasn't in just one tunnel, he was in a warren of them—a virtual maze of black holes leading off in every direction. He rounded a curve, finding himself confronted with more choices. The tunnel he was in continued straight on. But there were also tunnels leading off to his left and right. He decided to stay in the tunnel he was in and was starting forward, when he detected a Windex-like odor exuding from the small tunnel on his left. He whirled around, glaring at the opening, his memory full of his encounters with the New Ones on the island. Their blood had smelled like Windex, like ammonia. They were in that tunnel or just beyond.

Braille crouched down and crawled into the small opening. A block later he came to a vented metal door. Pushing it open, he was immediately assaulted by the overpowering smell of ammonia. Moving quietly, Braille emerged from the small tunnel and found himself staring out at what looked like a huge movie set designed to look like a hundred-year-old town at the turn of the century.

Braille knew he'd just entered Underground Seattle through a ventilator shaft. What he saw spread out before him was fascinating. He was standing at the outskirts of a century-old city whose only concessions to age were warped boards and a patina of moss brought on by a hundred years of dampness. He noticed a drugstore, a newspaper building, a funeral parlor, and an old brick police station. On the far side of the police station he could make out what looked like an open metal fire door, and beside it, an electrical panel box of switches. He doubted if any of the switches would work, but knew if he wanted to see what was going on, he would have to try to turn on the lights. He began walking towards the panel box, walking up a brick-and-cobblestone street. Then he stopped. The shapes he had been expecting all along were suddenly sprawled out in front of him like drunks in a flophouse. Sleeping shapes. Vampires. New Ones. He moved past them, offering up silent prayers that there were only a few dozen, no more than two dozen. Be no more than I'm walking by, he prayed as he continued up the street, past the police station, stopping finally in front of the panel box of switches.

He took a deep breath, holding it for a moment, then pushed all of the switches up with both hands. Turning, he looked back at the city. He could see electrical cords strung out over the streets, cords that went through one side of a building and came out on the other, cords with light sockets attached. Some of the bulbs had been broken. But many more were undamaged, and now these light bulbs lit up the underground city, giving light to what he was looking at, giving light to the horror.

"Dear Jesus," Braille murmured.

Thunder rumbled high above him, high above the street he was standing under, like an ominous surrealistic earthquake.

"Oh, sweet Jesus," Braille murmured.

He couldn't even begin to count the number of New Ones he saw lying all around him. They were everywhere—sleeping on the streets, sleeping inside old buildings. More than he could count. More than he wanted to count. And again thunder rumbled above him and the New Ones stirred. The storm was waking them up. The storm and the night.

Time to get out of here, he decided. He started through the open metal door beside the panel of switches and stopped abruptly. The door opened on what looked like the basement of an old building. In the murky darkness Braille could make out a wide stairway leading out. But he couldn't go in. The room and the stairwell were packed with bodies. There was no place to walk, no place to put his feet, and worse: the bodies were stirring, coming to life.

"Fuck," he whispered as he began running up the street, heading towards the ventilator shaft that had brought him to this place. The creatures were wide awake now. Many were standing on the street, other were coming out of the buildings. A black figure stood up in front of Braille, blocking his way. Braille pushed it aside and kept on moving, trying to pick up speed, but it was too crowded. Something slashed out at him, clawing at his shirt. He kept on going. Another one leaped at him, trying to tear out his throat. Braille rammed his fingers into its temple, continuing to wade through the mob.

He broke another one's neck. It went down and started to get up. Hissing and squalling like an evil cat, a female tried to sink her clawlike nails into his throat. Braille shot her in the head. Then he shot the one with the broken neck. He managed to kill six more with the automatic before several creatures jerked the pistol out of his grasp. He killed one with his fist, jerked out the second automatic and shot two more. The door to the ventilator shaft was ten feet away. Countless creatures stood between him and the door. Braille struggled on, killing, fighting, and shooting, knowing all the while he would never make it.

Suddenly there was an explosive roar and several screams on the far side of the mob. A head went sailing into the air, then an arm. Something on the other side of the crowd was tearing into the creatures, ripping them apart. A creature was thrown twenty feet into the air. Another one was tossed up high enough to glance off the girders supporting the street above. What was going on? Braille wondered. Who was out there? What was out there? Someone—something—was slaughtering New Ones, distracting them away from him . . . but who?

And it was working. Most of the creatures mobbing around Braille started to draw back, like a lynch mob reacting to a police siren. Braille took advantage of the distraction, clubbing two aggressive ones with his pistol and sprinting for the ventilator tunnel. He dived into the opening, scrambling around on his hands and knees as he jerked the door shut. On the other side he could hear the creatures scratching and tearing at the metal, trying to get to him.

"Fuck this," he grumbled, as he turned around and made his way back towards the main tunnel. He found it, but didn't bother to retrace his steps to where he had come in. Instead, he opted to escape from the subterranean labyrinth by scrambling up the first ladder he came to. He pushed away the overhead manhole cover, hoisting himself up on the street and kicking the cover back into place. He collapsed on the street while he labored to catch his breath.

Finally, with slow stiff movements, he got to his feet. There was a row of expensive shops on one side of the street and a large landscaped park on the other side. The choice was easy. Favoring a leg he'd injured during the fight, he limped into Kearney Park and collapsed on the first bench he came to. After a long moment he lifted his hands up in front of his face and examined them. They were trembling, just like his insides. He didn't know whether the trembling was from what had just happened to him in Underground Seattle or the number of New Ones he had seen before they woke up. He slumped back on the bench, shaking his head. He had come to Seattle knowing the city was in trouble, but never in his wildest dreams had he envisioned there would be so many of the creatures.

Hundreds. Maybe thousands.

His thoughts went back to the roadblock the Army had put up and the weapons the soldiers had been carrying. Good weapons; automatic weapons. With luck maybe the soldiers could keep the New Ones confined to the center of the city for a couple of nights, but that would be it. Eventually the soldiers would get overrun and then they would become part of what they were fighting. They would become vampires.

Say good-bye to the world as you know it, Braille thought, and welcome to hell on earth. Literally hell on earth.

A puzzled expression crossed his face as he pulled out a cigarette, lit it, and exhaled thoughtfully. Technically he should have been dead at this moment and he would have been if something hadn't distracted the creatures earlier. Something—someone—had shocked the attacking mob, created enough violent chaos to allow him to escape. But who . . . what?

He recalled witnessing something similar on Chinook Island. He had once seen Gregory wade into a crowd of New Ones and he had never seen savagery like that in his life. Bodies had been tossed up against the sides of buildings. Creatures had died where they stood. The savagery he had seen that night matched the savagery he had seen tonight, but that was impossible. Gregory was dead. The Master Ancient had died on the island in a firestorm of radiation.

But still . . . Braille's memory flashed back to when he had been picked up by a Navy destroyer. If the doctor had left him alone, he would have died, but the physician had given him plasma, bringing him back from the dead to a deadlike state, then putting Braille aboard a helicopter. It was while he was in the helicopter and delirious that he'd heard Gregory scream out from the island. Hurt as he was, Braille knew that Clementina had died, but somehow Gregory had not. Gregory was still alive and he hated the world, hated humans. Hated Braille. A moment later Braille had passed out . . . But it had been a dream, Braille thought as he opened his eyes, staring out at the park. A nightmare, a hallucination. Gregory was dead. Nothing could have survived what the exploding nuclear plant had done to the island. Nothing.

"Human . . ." a voice said behind Braille.

Still sitting on the park bench, Braille almost turned to see what was behind him, but didn't. There was nothing behind him. Only one person in the world had ever called him "human" as if the word had been his first name. That person had been Gregory. Braille shook his head. His memory and imagination were playing tricks on him, he decided, getting to his feet. And that was one hell of a flashback.

"Human . . . turn around and look at your death," something growled behind him.

Braille whirled around. The park was a mass of dark shadows and mist. There was something standing under a tree forty feet away. Lightning flashed, turning the night and park white. In that brilliant flash Braille saw Gregory and knew he had come to kill him.

Gregory began walking towards Braille. Thunder spilled out of the storm.

"Why do you want to kill me?" Braille shouted over its roar. "We were almost friends once."

"Because Clementina is dead," Gregory snarled, a hellish red light coming into his eyes. An unreasonable hate welled up in Gregory. Clementina had been his woman for five hundred years and she had died on the island, and the human he was closing in on had played a central role in everything that had happened, including his woman's death. And now the human would pay.

A New One came out of the bushes and ran for Gregory, hissing like a rabid cat. Gregory grabbed it by the throat with one hand and threw it into the air as if it were a rag doll. The creature crashed into the jagged limbs of a tree thirty feet away.

Two more came out of the darkness, charging Braille. Braille leaped into the air, kicking one in the head with his boot. It went down with a hole the size of a boot heel in its forehead. The other one lunged for Braille. Braille grabbed an outstretched arm, flipped the creature over his shoulder and sent it cartwheeling into the air. It crashed down onto a park bench a dozen yards away, limping off. The other creatures who'd been watching the fight shrank out of the park, seeking easier prey, prey that would not fight back.

As Braille turned to face Gregory, the Master Ancient said: "You still have your martial arts skills, but it does not matter. We fought once before and I beat you but did not kill you. Tonight I will."

Braille did not want to fight Gregory. He and the Ancient had always been alike in odd and deadly ways. Now, because of what had happened to him, they were even more alike. It was like fighting a brother. Braille lifted his hands in frustration. "You know in your heart I had nothing to do with Clementina's death. It was her choice—"

"I have no heart, human," Gregory snarled. "All I know is that Clementina is dead and you are one of the reasons why she stayed on the island. I want you to suffer. I want you to know the pain and aloneness I feel. I will kill you, but I will leave blood in your body and you will rise and return to life. Then you too will go through eternity alone."

"That's already happened!" Braille screamed, his words blotted out by Gregory's deep-throated snarl. The Ancient charged. Braille braced himself and knew that somehow things would be different this time. He wasn't the human Gregory had fought on the island. He was no longer human. He was an Ancient, just like Gregory.

Gregory broke into a full-out charge, intending to crush the human to pulp with his momentum and power. He had experienced the human's martial arts skills during their fight on the beach and had come to know pain for the first time in centuries. He would not make that mistake again.

He doesn't know, Braille thought, as Gregory closed on him like a runaway train. He doesn't know he's already contaminated me and that I'm as alone as he is.

A moment later they came together and the ground seemed to tremble under the forceful collision. White bolts of pain exploded in Braille's head and he staggered backwards.

Stunned, Gregory reeled backwards, his body and senses vibrating like an inhuman tuning fork. His vision was blurred. It took a moment to clear. When it did, he was thunderstruck. The human was still standing. Impossible, he thought. The human had not even bothered to lift up a hand to defend himself, and he'd taken the full force of the charge. He should have been nothing but jellied flesh and bone. But he wasn't; he was whole, still standing, and glaring back at the Master Ancient.

Gregory charged again, raising a clenched fist like a sledgehammer, intending to deliver a blow that would take the human's head off. Braille stood stock still, his hands at his sides. He didn't want to fight, and hoped if he didn't, Gregory would come to his senses. As Gregory began to swing out with his fist, Braille also decided he didn't want to lose his head. As the fist came down, Braille brought up his forearm to deflect the blow.

Gregory put all his savage fury into the swing, bringing his fist down with enough power to crush a car. Then his fist slammed into Braille's arm. Bones snapped like tree limbs. Both gasped. Both stumbled away, each injured. Braille's forearm was shattered. There were bones sticking out of his flesh. Gregory's hand was just as bad. The bones had been pulverized. The pain was intense; the shock and surprise worse. When he had fought the human before, the human had eluded his power with cunning moves, lightning-fast defensive maneuvers. But this time there were no martial arts tricks, no cunning moves. The human had made no attempt to elude Gregory's fist. All he had done was to lift his forearm. The human had changed, Gregory realized. He had always been cold, powerful, and confident, but now those traits were magnified. It was almost as though the human had become an Ancient, but that was impossible.

Gregory looked down at his injured hand, flexing his fingers. Already it was beginning, the healing. Bones were knitting; pain was fading. He turned and looked at the human.

Braille was standing a few feet away, his body turned so Gregory could not see his face, only his side and the injured arm. As Gregory looked on, the human's shattered forearm began to change, heal, the broken bones under the skin re-forming themselves, aligning themselves, becoming straight and perfect at an impossible speed.

Suddenly Gregory knew.

The pain of the injuries, the pain of the healing had

pushed Braille past the point where he wanted to reason with Gregory. And then he who had once been Braille turned slowly to face the Master Ancient, his eyes glowing red in the night as he glared at the only other Ancient in the world.

"How?" Gregory asked softly. "Only I had the power to do this to you. It was my right. How could an insignificant New One do this to you?"

"You did this to me," Braille said as the fire in his eyes slowly faded away.

"No . . ."

"It happened on the island, when we fought for the boat," Braille said. "I hit you in the mouth and cut my hand on your teeth." He shrugged. "Now you know."

Still stunned, Gregory shook his head. "And your woman, she is gone? She found out what you were and left you?"

Pain ripped through Braille's soul. He looked at the trees along the edge of the park and explained briefly what had happened to him, the Radcliffs, and Leslie Chapel after they got off the island.

"I am sorry about your woman," Gregory said, meaning it. "She had spirit and substance. What will you do now?"

"Stop the New Ones from taking over the city and the world. That's why I came here."

Gregory nodded in agreement. "Life is chaotic and unsettling when they are around. Also, they are irritating, unclean, and in sufficient number; they could end our existence."

"And they're not nice to humans," Braille added. Off in the distance both could hear the withering sounds of machine guns opening up, coupled with the high-pitched screams of New Ones or humans. It sounded as if a war had broken out on all sides of them.

"The question is, How do we get rid of them? I couldn't even begin to count the number of creatures I saw below the city. It looked like there were thousands."

"There were thousands," Gregory said. They began walking across the park, heading nowhere, just walking.

"That was you down there. You were the one that distracted the New Ones so I could escape. Why? I thought you wanted me dead, or worse."

"I did. But I did not want the New Ones to do what I wanted to do."

This time it was Braille who nodded in understanding. "Which brings us back to the original problem. There are a lot of New Ones under the city. How do we stop them?"

Gregory looked at Braille as if he'd suddenly become a moron. "It is simple. We do what you did on the island. We break a nuclear power plant. The cloud will kill the New Ones." He looked pleased with his response.

"Won't work this time," Braille said. "The nearest nuclear power plant is in a town called Hanford and it's at least five hundred miles from here."

"Bummer," the Ancient said, using one of the words he'd learned from Samantha Estleford.

"Bummer?" Braille asked, almost laughing. "The end of the world is coming and all you can say is 'bummer.' By the way, where'd you learn that word?"

"The word does not describe the end of the world?"

"Now that I think about it," Braille said, "it is a pretty good word."

They continued to walk across the park, setting a slow pace for themselves. Finally Gregory said, "Do you remember that time when I met with you and asked you why the other Ancients had died after they got too close to the nuclear power plant on the island?" Braille nodded and Gregory continued. "During the conversation you talked about radiation and nuclear power. You also told me it was used both as a power source and a weapon. You also said your country dropped two atomic bombs on two cities in the Far East. Hiroshima and . . . ?"

"Nagasaki," Braille added.

Gregory nodded. "Why don't you drop a bomb like that here?"

The suggestion almost made Braille mad. "Christ, this is a city. Millions of people live here."

"And if vampirism continues to spread, this will become a city of vampires. Millions of New Ones." He stopped abruptly, turned and looked hard at Braille. "The New Ones are still confined to this immediate area. Drop a small bomb."

Braille looked off into the dark park. "Nuke Seattle," he

said to himself. The concept was shocking, but as he thought about it, the idea took on a certain amount of appeal. If the area could be evacuated and a small warhead used, it would eliminate the New Ones. With luck, the wind would carry the radiation out to sea, not back over Seattle. He turned to Gregory. "This is crazy, but the more I think about it, the more I like it." But then he shook his head. "The government'd never go for it," he said, raising his voice to compete with the thickening gunfire. "Too many bureaucrats, generals, politicians, and red tape in the way."

"Red tape?"

Braille sighed. "We're talking about destroying the center of a very important city with a nuclear bomb. That's not exactly like flushing a toilet. It takes a lot of approval. Lots of generals, politicians, and even the President of the United States have to agree before something like that could occur. Even if it did occur, it would probably take weeks before they finally made up their minds and got the Air Force to do what we're talking about. By that time . . ."

"You give up too easily," Gregory said. "I think we should see the general in charge of the troops in Seattle and tell him what he should do. I think he would believe us. I also think that, if he did not, we could show him what he is up against, and why he and his troops and the world will die if he does not do what we suggest."

"I know where the command post is. But there'll be troops guarding the hotel where the general's staying. I don't know how we'll get in."

With the confidence of a being that had existed for nine hundred years, Gregory replied, "The general will see us. Now, where is this hotel command post, human?"

"Stop calling me human," Braille said as they neared the edge of the park. "It no longer applies."

They left the park, crossing a deserted boulevard and starting past a row of shops. As they continued on, a six-story building a block away exploded. Within a matter of seconds the building was completely engulfed in flames. A moment later the eight-story apartment building next to it caught on fire.

"Christ," Braille observed. "Maybe if we leave them alone, the New Ones will incinerate themselves."

Lost in his own thoughts, Gregory said, "I do not understand—"

Suddenly two large male creatures came out of an alley and charged. Braille caught one by the shirt, throwing it through a department store window. Gregory grabbed the other by its throat and belt, hefted it high up in the air, and slammed it down on a parking meter. The meter pierced its spine and came out its stomach, and the impaled creature slid slowly down the pole, to the sidewalk.

"Where was I?" Gregory asked.

"I do not understand," Braille reminded.

"I do not understand why your government would capture you and kill your woman?"

"It wasn't exactly the government. It was a kind of secret agency that was interested in finding out why I was immune to all the diseases they gave me, why I healed so rapidly from injuries. I think they wanted to develop a vaccine from my blood that would cure many of the diseases that afflict humans."

"I see what they wanted from you, but I do not understand why they killed your friend."

"Friends," Braille said, his face impassive, totally free of expression. "Leslie and the other two were killed because they tried to help me escape and because they could've brought a lot of unwanted attention to this agency and the illegal things it was doing. It was senseless. All three deaths were senseless."

"Have you avenged your woman and the others? Has this agency been destroyed?"

Braille's face continued to show no trace of emotion. "No," he said softly. "Not yet."

Ahead of them, three blocks away, a mob of New Ones milled about on a boulevard, trying to work up the courage to charge one of the blockades of vehicles and barbed wire the Army had put up. Occasionally a soldier would take a pot shot and a New One would squeal out in pain. Braille saw one of the creatures catch a bullet in the throat. It went down, its hands clamped over its wound. A moment later it got to its knees, one hand still covering its wound. Five seconds later it was on its feet, stunned and a little bewildered, but it was still alive. Braille glanced back at the Army blockade. The soldier who'd fired off the shot was standing on top of an APC, staring in total disbelief at the creature he had just shot. Then he took the clip out of his M-16 and examined it. Braille knew what the problem was. The man had just shot what looked like a human being in the throat. The human had gone down, should have stayed down, but it hadn't. It had clamped off the spurting hole with its hand, healed within a matter of seconds, and now the young GI was wondering if there was something wrong with his bullets.

The milling mob of creatures finally worked up their nerve and began charging the soldiers. In turn the soldiers opened up with everything they had. The withering field of fire looked like a lightning storm. The entire blockade was lit up with continuous muzzle flashes, and the night was full of withering sounds of machine guns and M-16's set on automatic. Bullets ripped into the charging crowd of New Ones, cutting the lead ones to pieces. Those were the ones who went down and stayed down. Yet, in spite of the devastation, the other creatures kept coming. Some were knocked to the ground by bullets, but they didn't stay down. For every ten that got hit and fell, eight got up. Bad odds, and depressing, Braille thought. He didn't blame the two soldiers he saw running away from the blockade, running away from creatures they couldn't kill.

The creatures were close to the barricade when suddenly Braille heard the soft whumps of three M-79 grenade launchers going off simultaneously. Four seconds later three grenades exploded at the same instant. The explosions heaved the street and shrapnel ripped through the mob of creatures. The noise, explosions, and devastation were too much for them. The creatures turned and ran away from the barricade, bewildered, limping, and hurt. At least for the moment.

Braille counted twenty-two creatures down because of the grenades. That's one way to take them down and keep them down, he thought . . . Until he noticed that many of them were moving, stirring, trying to get to their feet. Some moments later at least fifteen creatures got to their feet and staggered off. Seven out of twenty-two. The odds with grenades were almost as bad as the odds with rifles.

Braille pointed at the Army's barricade. "If we're going to get to the command post, we're going to have to get around that barricade." He turned to Gregory. "You wanta go under the street or over the buildings?"

Gregory considered the question. "I do not like heights. We go under the barricade."

They emerged from a manhole cover four blocks later on the far side of the blockade. Gregory had been favorably impressed by the sewer and told Braille so.

"It was very clean. It would seem no one ever goes to the bathroom in Seattle." Braille kicked the manhole cover back into place and smiled. "I don't think that was a sewer. I think it was a drainage tunnel."

"Not a sewer?"

"Nope."

Gregory made a face. "Just when I thought the human race had finally improved on something."

The Ridgemont Hotel was actually two separate buildings designed as a single unit. The hotel consisted of two round, high towers, one jutting upwards a full eighteen stories while its twin counterpart was twenty-four stories high. Ultra-modern in design, both round towers had skins of bronze reflective glass with well-lit, tube-shaped elevators running up and down the outside walls of both buildings. The two towers were separated by a wide street, but six glassed-in sky bridges connected the two buildings every three stories. Braille knew the two buildings were supposed to be slick, modern, and trendy, but it seemed to him he was looking at a lopsided chrome ladder.

He lowered his eyes, studying the jeeps and military policemen ringing the eighteen-story building. It wasn't hard to figure out which tower was being used as a command post by the Army. "But how to get in," he wondered aloud.

Gregory began walking towards the Ridgemont. Braille caught up with him. "You have a plan."

"There is no need for a plan," Gregory said. "There are doors to the hotel. We use those doors." He looked at Braille. "That is why doors were invented."

"And the soldiers guarding the hotel?"

"They will not stop us."

"They'll try."

"So?"

"So people will get killed."

Gregory stopped and looked at Braille impatiently. "But we will not. Do you understand that?"

"But others will die because of us. I don't want that."

Gregory gave him a puzzled look. "We are only talking about humans."

"I don't want humans to die because of us, not if we can help it."

"This is important to you?"

"Very."

"I will not sneak through the night like a rodent, but if this is important to you, I will consider another entrance to this place," Gregory conceded.

They began walking, and Gregory made a snorting sound. "Still, all we are talking about are humans." He noticed the look of exasperation on Braille's face. "Never mind," he added.

Unlike the well-guarded eighteen-story tower, the taller counterpart to the Ridgemont Hotel was deserted. They went in through a back alley loading door, taking a service elevator up through the center of the hotel to the top floor. Then they made their way through a passageway of corridors to a closed and dark restaurant that sat atop the tall tower.

After they entered, Gregory sat down at one of the tables and Braille walked over to a wide window that offered a panoramic view of downtown Seattle in flames and the other half of the Ridgemont Hotel. When Braille looked down at the other tower, he realized how large it was. The top of the smaller tower below him was large enough to support a swimming pool, a small park, a television transmitter, and a large helicopter landing pad, complete with a U.S. government helicopter. From his position he could see part of the sky bridge below him. It was glassed-in on all sides; even the roof and floor were made of glass, and he couldn't see any signs of guards or soldiers. Maybe we won't have to sneak in like rodents, he thought. He turned away and joined Gregory at the table.

They sat in a kind of comfortable and trusting silence. Finally Gregory said, "If you do not like killing humans, how do you exist? How do you take blood?"

"I killed some people who were trying to kill me, and took their blood," Braille said, thinking back to the OSMS helicopter crewman and the security guards he'd killed.

"But how do you control the hunger and the desire when you're not surrounded by enemies?"

Braille shifted uncomfortably in his chair, looking at the table. "I took some sheep blood," he grumbled in a low tone.

"I did not hear you."

"I took some blood from some sheep." Braille looked up at Gregory. The Ancient's face was free of expression; yet he seemed to be smiling. Braille looked away. "The blood lust was bad. It was take blood from a sheep or the blood from a family that was helping me."

A jagged bolt of lightning ripped out of the clouds, searing the night outside the glassed-in restaurant. A moment later thunder rattled the windows. Gregory sat back in his chair, waiting for the din to pass.

"Two centuries ago Clementina and I were trapped in a valley in the Italian Alps by a snowstorm. A hunter found us and took us back to his village. The people there thought we were like them. They gave us lodging and shared their food with us, even though they had little themselves. We were there almost two months, and during that time Clementina and I came close to dying ourselves, because we could not bring ourselves to take the villagers' blood. As it turned out, we saved ourselves by taking sheep's blood. Sometimes it is important not to kill, not to give in to the blood lust. That time in the village was one of those times for Clementina and me." He shrugged. "There is no shame in sheep blood. It has properties and substances that make it similar to human blood. It is an acceptable substitution when there is a reason—" Thunder cut Gregory off. When it was quiet again, he fixed his eyes on Braille. "This family, you met them after you escaped from the government agency?"

Braille nodded. "A mother and two children. They took

me in when I was hurt. They looked after me and gave me a place to hide until my strength returned. I think they saved my life."

"Why didn't you remain with them?"

"Because that agency's still after me, because of what was going on in Seattle, and because of what I am."

Gregory nodded in understanding. "You were wise. After I got off the island, I lived with an old woman and her granddaughter. I liked them, but now they are dead because of me." Braille gave Gregory an odd look. Gregory shook his head. "I did not kill them." Then he told Braille about Molly and Samantha Estleford, explaining how a group of men had begun to hunt him, trying to trap him at the rest stop, and how they had attacked the Estleford home in an effort to kill him. Finally he told Braille about his conversation with Kubick, while both of them were healing from their wounds. "This Kubick said he was from a government agency, an agency that sent him out to hunt for me. Is it possible this agency is the same one that captured you and killed your woman?"

Braille nodded grimly. "They learned about you from me and the others who got off the island. There didn't seem to be any reason not to talk about you. We all thought you were dead. Sorry. Maybe if I'd kept my mouth shut, your friends would still be alive."

Gregory looked down at the table. When he finally raised his head, his eyes were cold. "You were not the reason these women were killed. I was the reason. When I sensed there was a force pursuing me, I could've moved on, but I didn't. I remained where I was, played a game with the humans who were hunting for me. Now the old woman and her granddaughter are dead. This agency is more cruel than the New Ones. New Ones kill out of instinct and madness. This agency kills because people get in their way. I know you are planning on destroying this agency by yourself because they killed your woman, but there is a strong chance I may accompany you when you do this. Those women they killed were friends of mine."

Thunder and lightning exploded on all sides of the restaurant, bathing the interior with the light of an exploding sun. As the light faded, Braille said, "Let's go talk to the man about dropping a bomb."

They took the elevator to the eighteenth floor and started down a long hallway towards the doors to the sky bridge that would take them to the other tower. Braille had expected to see soldiers posted in front of the doors, and there were. As he and Gregory approached, the two military policemen brought their rifles up to a port arms position.

"Sorry," one of the soldiers said. "This part of the hotel's off limits." Braille nodded, starting to turn away. Then he clipped the soldier on the jaw with a hard right. The other soldier looked down at his buddy, starting to say something, when Gregory hit him with a fist. The man's helmet went flying down the hallway and then he collapsed in a heap.

Braille pushed open the doors to the sky bridge. He started out on it, then stopped. The raging storm outside was rocking the glass and metal span as if it were nothing more than a fragile rope bridge.

"What's holding this up?" Gregory asked, standing back by the doors and the collapsed soldiers.

"Architecture," Braille said, not sure himself.

"I see no posts or cables holding this bridge up."

"They do good things nowadays with cement and steel rods."

"I have no faith in good things," Gregory said, breaking into a hard, loping run.

"Me neither," Braille said, joining Gregory.

The sky bridge was almost a city block long. They ran the distance and hit the closed doors to the other tower full out. The doors burst in, knocking the two men standing sentry on the other side of the doors into a nearby wall.

Gregory paid no attention to the two crumpled forms, but Braille did. They weren't soldiers. These were men wearing suits and wing-tip shoes, and each had what looked like a hearing aid tucked into his ear. Curious, Braille knelt down and went through one of the men's suit pockets, finding what looked like a wallet. He gasped in astonishment.

"What?" Gregory asked.

"These guys are Secret Service."

"So?"

"These guys guard politicians and presidents."

"Good," Gregory said, pushing the elevator button repeatedly. "That means there are important people in this building."

The elevator doors swished open. There were two more men in gray suits inside it. Gregory entered, and an instant later both men were on the floor looking as if they'd been hit by wrecking balls. Gregory was studying the buttons on the interior wall when Braille entered the elevator. "Make it go down," Gregory instructed.

The elevator traveled nonstop to the first floor. The doors opened onto an oddly quiet and deserted hallway. They walked down the corridor and turned a corner. They passed two military policemen, who didn't give them a second glance.

But two Secret Service agents who had come out of nowhere did. "I.D's please," one of the agents requested.

Braille looked at Gregory; Gregory looked at Braille, and then both swung out with right fists. The agents went down like wet blankets.

Suddenly the hallway was filled with Secret Service agents, Army officers, and military policemen, but in all the confusion and noise, no one seemed to know whom to go after, whom to shoot at. For a moment the confusion worked to conceal Braille and Gregory, and during that moment Braille noticed several Secret Service agents coming out of a door down the hallway, ten feet from where he was standing. That was the door, he thought.

Gregory grabbed a large military policeman, hefting him high into the air. He threw him at the others in the crowded hallway. A half-dozen men were knocked off their feet by the flying body. Gregory turned to Braille, a "what-now?" look on his face. Braille pointed at the door down the hallway.

He and Gregory entered a large room. Braille jerked the door closed and locked it. In the split-second that followed he had time to see they were in a huge conference room crowded with computers, communication equipment, maps, and a miniature replica of Seattle.

Then two Secret Service agents standing ten yards away opened up on Braille and Gregory with MAC-10 machine guns. The sudden onslaught of bullets slapping into them caught Gregory and Braille off guard, sending both staggering back against the door.

Braille felt pain. Gregory felt pain. Each bullet was agony, pure fire, and Braille knew he was as good as dead . . . and knew he should have been dead . . . but wasn't.

Both MAC-10's went empty at the same instant.

In the silence that followed, Braille continued to feel the agony of each bullet, but he also began to feel relief as his body began to heal.

The Secret Service agents who'd just emptied their weapons into the two intruders looked at one another in stunned silence. The intruders were still standing. Both agents ejected clips from the MAC-10's, groping in their pockets for fresh clips. At the same time Braille began limping towards the two agents. A microsecond before they could jack a round into their weapons, he took their machine guns away.

"Jesus Christ!" a large man in Army fatigues with four stars tacked to his collars bellowed. "How'd they do that?"

"Yes," said an impeccably dressed man standing in the shadows behind the general. "How did they do that?"

One of the agents standing in front of Braille looked as if he were about to cry. "It was easy," the agent said, his lower lip trembling as he looked down at the weapon Braille had taken away from him. "They're wearing bulletproof vests." He reached out, grabbing the front of Braille's shirt and ripping it open.

"Jesus Christ," both agents gasped in unison, their eyes fixed on Braille's bare chest and the black bullet holes in that chest. Even as they looked on, the holes were closing up, turning into puckered circles of pink, healing flesh.

Gregory stepped up beside Braille and as the other agent reached out for his shirt, he said, "Do not rip my shirt." The agent hesitantly unbuttoned two buttons then whispered, "No vest."

The brightly lit room was filled with smoke from the automatic weapons. Braille glanced over at the general and saw a third Secret Service agent's hand creeping slowly under his suit jacket. Braille flipped one of the MAC-10's in the air and caught it by its pistol grip, aiming it at the agent.

"No more. We proved our points and I'm tired of getting hurt. If you try and pull out a weapon, I'll blast you into next week." The agent dropped his hand to his side.

"Proved what points?" the man with four stars on his uniform asked.

Braille looked at the general. "That you can't kill us. That we didn't come here to kill you. And we could have." He tossed the MAC-10 in his left hand towards the general. It clattered to the floor at the man's feet. The general looked at the weapon then lifted his eyes and looked at the MAC-10 in Braille's right hand. "How about that one?" he asked.

"Tell your men not to shoot, and I'll throw it down too."

The general nodded. "No more shooting. If they were going to hurt us, they would have hurt us by now." The other MAC-10 landed at the officer's feet.

Immediately the two Secret Service agents who'd had their weapons taken away went into action. One jumped on Gregory. The other jumped on Braille. One was thrown into a computer console thirty feet away. The other sailed into the air and crashed down on the replica of the city of Seattle, crushing the city and the table supporting it.

"Jesus Christ," the general said in awe.

"Jesus Christ is right," said the man standing in the gunsmoke and shadows behind him. "But they asked for it," he added. The general nodded.

The general looked at Braille, then Gregory. "Well, now that you're here and we're still alive, I don't suppose there's any harm in asking you what you're doing here?"

"We have come to tell you how to destroy the creatures you are fighting," Gregory announced.

Not a hint of skepticism crossed the general's face. He had just seen these two men kick in the door, get shot a dozen times each, then watched the bullet holes in their bodies heal up. Then he had seen the two men throw two full-grown Secret Service agents across the room. He was not about to cross-examine these two men. Anything they had to say was worth listening to. "You know about those creatures out there?"

Braille and Gregory nodded.

"How do you know about them? Near as I can tell,

anything that gets near them gets killed . . . or dies and then turns into whatever they are."

"In a way," Gregory said, "we are what you are fighting now." Then, as if to prove his point, he looked at the general and made his eyes glow red for a brief moment.

Gasps rippled through the room. The agent who had earlier reached for his pistol started to reach again. The well-dressed man behind the general turned on the agent.

"Pull out that pop gun of yours and I'll have your ass for breakfast." Then the man gestured at Braille and Gregory. "You saw what they went through to get here, saw what they did to the other agents. They could have killed us all and they still could. So don't piss them off. You got that, boy?" The agent nodded and the man in the shadows shook his head. "Christ, sometimes it seems I'm surrounded by shit for brains." The man turned to the general. "The reports we keep getting from your men say those things on the street can't be killed, that they heal on the spot and that they have red eyes. I don't know about you, John, but I'm interested in listening to what they have to say."

The general nodded in agreement. "What next?" he asked.

"A room where we can talk in private," Braille said. His chest still hurt, still burned, and he was not in a good mood. He noticed the stricken look on the general's face and softened his voice. "If we were going to kill you and take your blood, we would have done it when we first came into the room."

"Right," said the general. He glanced back at the man standing behind him, then pointed to a door off to his right. "It's kinda cramped, but it's private."

There was a sign on the door. It said: MEN.

"Fine," Braille said.

The well-dressed man behind the general moved out of the shadows and gunsmoke, stepping up beside the general. "I think I'd like to sit in on this, John," the man told him.

For the first time since entering the room, Braille got a good look at the man and his mouth went dry.

"You are important?" Gregory asked bluntly.

"He's important," Braille said in a low voice.

"Then you can come," Gregory said.

"Thank you," the Vice President of the United States murmured.

Fifteen minutes later General Westmore stepped out of the men's room and walked over to a communications table. He placed several telephone calls, then waited for a response to one of his calls. The response came five minutes later. Westmore's conversation was brief, and when he finished he headed back towards the men's room. Two Secret Service agents had pressed their ears against the men's room door, trying to listen to what was taking place inside the room.

"Knock it off," Westmore growled. "The Vice President's fine, I'm fine, and I want you guys and the others to stop hanging around this door like a bunch of peeping toms." He gestured at his aide-de-camp, Colonel Bragg. "Get back to the radios and make sure any other messages get to me." The colonel nodded and bustled off. The general pushed open the door to the men's room and stepped inside. It had to be the weirdest meeting he'd ever been involved in. Near as he could figure, he had spent the last fifteen minutes talking to a nine-hundred-year-old vampire, a human who had recently become a vampire, but could control what he was, and the Vice President of the United States.

The two Ancients were leaning against the bathroom counter. The Vice President had just come out of a bathroom stall. He had taken off his suit jacket, but was still impeccably attired in a white shirt, Oxford tie, pleated slacks, and suspenders. The Vice President double-checked his zipper to make sure it was up, then looked up at the general. "You do it?"

Westmore nodded. "The word has gone out to every unit and company commander on the street. Even as we speak, they're telling the men to focus all fire on the head or heart."

The Vice President nodded, then glanced at Braille and Gregory. "That part was easy enough, but as for a nuclear weapon, Christ, I don't know. You're asking me to drop a nuclear weapon on one of America's own cities." He shook his head. "You're asking me to do the impossible."

"What would you do," Gregory asked, "if one of your

cities were infested with a human killing plague that could spread throughout the entire world if you didn't destroy it with fire?"

"I'd destroy the city with fire," the Vice President said, looking at Gregory with pain-filled eyes. After a long moment he fixed his gaze on General Westmore. "What's the latest update on the casualty figures, civilian and military?"

"Currently we estimate there are between four thousand and seven thousand civilians dead, missing, or turned into those things we're fighting. As for the military, as of forty-five minutes ago a hundred and ninety-seven soldiers had been killed. The number of my men wounded seriously enough to require hospitalization is around two hundred. Currently I have sixty listed as missing in action, and at least fifty have deserted their posts."

The Vice President considered the figures. "Now that your troops know about the head and heart shots, do you think we can keep those creatures confined within the perimeter?"

"No," Westmore said, shaking his head. "I couldn't begin to tell you how much ammo my men have gone through. Those things just keep coming and multiplying. 'Cording to my field commanders, for every one they kill, three seem to take its place, and there's more of them every minute. We know they've come up from the underground part of the city, but now they're in the apartments and hotels, looking for more humans. But to answer your question again, no. There's no way my men can keep them contained." The general gestured with his hands. "And it's getting worse. Those things out there are getting smarter. Last night and earlier tonight they just charged and died. But now they've begun to throw rocks, sticks, spears, bricks, anything they can get their hands on. Some of them have taken to the rooftops and now they're dropping stuff down on the troops below them. My men are doing the best they can, but they're losing. It's only a matter of time before the blockades are overrun."

"How much time?" the Vice President asked.

"They'll be able to hold the barricades tonight and maybe

tomorrow night. But after that . . ." He didn't bother to finish his sentence.

"Would more troops help?" the Vice President offered.

Westmore shook his head. "You can only put so many men on a barricade. Put too many on one, and they start tripping over each other and shooting each other by accident. I could use extra troops so I could put up some additional barricades behind the primary ones, but if those creatures keep multiplying, if their numbers keep growing, they'll overwhelm everyone and everything we put in their way." The general looked hard at the Vice President of the United States. "I got several thousand of the best troops in the world in this city, and my best estimate is that in two to three days most will be dead and the rest'll be changed into what they're fighting."

The Vice President was amazingly composed, given what he was faced with. He made one last effort to avoid what he already knew was the obvious solution. "What do the doctors—especially the ones from the Atlanta Disease Control Center—say? I know they're over at Mercy Hospital working on two of those creatures your men managed to capture. Any progress in their efforts to come up with a cure or vaccine for what's happening?"

Westmore made a face. "I was going to update you on that earlier but I got distracted when . . ." He gestured at Braille and Gregory and continued. "Two creatures were captured and taken to Mercy Hospital. I don't know all the details, but the doctors had them strapped down and ran tests on them. They did some experimenting with drugs, primarily tranquilizers, since all those things did was fight and try to break free. They injected them with monumental doses of Thorazine, Haldol, Inderal, and Prolixin. The bottom line is that nothing calmed them down. In spite of that, the doctors did try to do some diagnostic things: brain scans, CT scans, blood work-ups. Again nothing. They're months, maybe years away from a vaccine or a cure."

The Vice President shook his head.

"Oh, it gets worse," the general said. "One of those things broke its restraints and killed a nurse. There were four military policemen guarding it at the time, and my men were able to kill it, but not before it bit one of them, and now he's becoming what it was."

The Vice President looked at Gregory and Braille, then back at the general. "Then you concur with these two? You think I should tell the President to authorize the use of a nuclear device?"

"Yes," the general said, gesturing at Gregory. "Like he said, if there were a city infected with a disease that could destroy the world and could only be destroyed by fire, you would destroy that city with fire. Well, what we got in Seattle isn't that different, only what they're suggesting is you use radiation instead of fire. I believe them. Everything they said rings true, and now I have proof of it."

"Proof?"

The general nodded grimly. "Earlier when I was in the command room, I contacted the doctors at Mercy Hospital and asked that they x-ray the other creature we'd captured. I didn't tell them why. I just told them to take an x-ray of it. And they did . . ."

"And?"

". . . And now it's a pile of dust on an x-ray table. Radiation works. Oh, goddamn, how it works."

The Vice President was silent for almost a minute. "What do you recommend? What's available to us? I don't know that much about nuclear weapons."

The general was an expert in nuclear weapons. "I recommend you drop one low-yield nuclear device right in the heart of downtown Seattle. A five- to seven-kiloton device should do the job." Though he had given his recommendation in a matter-of-fact manner, General Westmore closed his eyes and shuddered as the full impact of what he'd just suggested washed over him.

"What about the remaining humans inside the cordoned-off area?" the Vice President asked.

Westmore opened his eyes, glancing at the Vice President. "Tomorrow morning as soon as the sun is up, I'll send every soldier I have into the area. We'll do our best to go through every apartment, hotel, and building in a coordinated effort to find and bring out all survivors—human survivors, that is."

"How will you be able to tell if they're human?"

Leaning against the counter with his arms folded, Braille said, "Lead everyone you find out into the daylight. If they fight you or turn to dust, they're not human."

"How about the people outside of the perimeter?" the Vice President asked.

"I've ordered up more troops from Fort Lewis. I'll use them to evacuate the surrounding area."

"What kind of area are we talking about?"

Westmore walked over to the mirror above the sinks and pushed the soap dispenser lever. A glob of soap squirted out onto the counter. The general dabbed his finger in the soap, then made a single dot on the mirror. "This is ground zero, and in this case we're probably talking about Kearney Park, since it's easy to see from the air and right on top of Underground Seattle." He dabbed more soap on his finger and drew a circle around the dot he'd named Kearney Park. His drawing resembled a bull's-eye. "This is the blast area. This is where the maximum effect of the device takes place. Now if we use a five- to seven-kiloton nuclear device, this circle represents a perimeter of destruction approximately a mile and a half in diameter . . . which is the size of the area currently inhabited by those creatures."

He drew a larger circle around the smaller circle. "This represents the area we must evacuate with the troops from Fort Lewis. It basically symbolizes everything within seven miles of ground zero. In most cases this circle would symbolize a ten-mile area, but because we know that the creatures are hiding out underground, I am going to recommend that the bomb's fuse be set so that it goes off a microsecond after it hits. That means it would be *underground* before it explodes. This will dramatically reduce the destructive effects of the device: heat, blast wave, fireball, ground shock, and will also reduce the amount of radiation the device releases into the air. It will also allow for maximum radiation input into Underground Seattle. If we do it this way, we don't have to evacuate a wide area, and most of Seattle will come out of this in good shape. The heart of downtown Seattle won't. The concussion will be immense, and most of the tall buildings in that area won't survive, but if we do a good job of evacuating people, clear an area of five to seven miles around the impact point, we ought to be able to walk away from this with almost no loss of human life. And that's what we're talking about. Survival for as many humans as possible and a maximum death impact for those creatures we're up against."

"When are you going to do this?" Braille asked.

The general glanced at his watch. "The sun'll be up in about six hours. I'll need the entire day tomorrow to clear any surviving humans from downtown Seattle and evacuate the surrounding area." He sucked in his breath, held it for a moment, then released it with a quiet sigh. "I would recommend the bomb be dropped an hour after sunrise on the following morning. Say, seven o'clock in the morning."

"Why then?" the Vice President asked.

"As a rule, the prevailing winds tie in with the tides. At that time of the morning the wind is blowing out to sea; that would carry the radiation away from the city. Moreover, at that time of the day there's usually a lot of haze, fog, and low-hanging cloud covers. Those climatic elements will reduce the transmission of thermal energy."

The Vice President released a long, agonizing sigh. "I guess the rest is up to me. I came out here at the President's request to see how bad the crisis was and to come up with some recommendations. Now I know; now I have a recommendation. With luck, I'll be back in Washington and with the President an hour after sunrise. I'll tell him how bad it is here and I'll tell him about the only solution we have for the problem here."

He looked hard at Braille and Gregory. "If you don't mind, I'll tell him about you two and I'll tell him about how this happened once before, back in Europe in the fourteenth century. I'll do the best I can to explain how the Church covered up what happened back then by calling it a disease, by calling it the Black Plague."

The Vice President took a moment to collect his thoughts. "The President and I have been friends for thirty years. We've been through a lot. This is his last term in office. He can't run again. I was kind of thinking about running for the office, but it never held that much interest for me, and maybe that's just as well. Once it gets out that I recommended we nuke Seattle, I might as well retire and write my memoirs. Still, that part doesn't matter. My job is to help my country, and I think what was recommended here tonight is the only way we can go." His eyes were still on Braille and Gregory. "You went through a lot to come to us tonight and I thank you for that. If my thank you sounds a little stilted or insincere, I apologize. I'm trying to express what's in my heart, and sometimes that's hard to do without speech writers."

The Vice President leveled his eyes at General Westmore. "The same sentiments go to you, John. When this is over, when the dust has settled, I doubt if we'll come off as heroes. More likely we'll be remembered as the two madmen who recommended the United States bomb Seattle. This will probably cost you your career just as it will cost me mine. But I think you already know that."

Westmore nodded. "I would walk through hell and kick the devil in the face if I thought it would keep my troops safe. The decision offered up tonight may get me damned by the world, but not by the soldiers who are left when this is over."

The Vice President's last words were: "I've known the President for thirty years. We like and trust one another, and when I tell him how bad things are here and what kind of future Seattle and the world faces if we don't put a stop to this disease here and now, he will support the recommendation. He's the only person in the United States who can give permission for the United States to bomb the United States. In the end I think he will give that permission." The Vice President of the United States walked out of the room.

Five minutes later his helicopter lifted off the Ridgemont Hotel and sped towards the air base at Fort Lewis.

Twenty minutes after that, Braille and Gregory walked out of the Ridgemont Hotel with an escort of soldiers, all under orders to make sure the two got through the ring of soldiers guarding the command center.

35

A HALF HOUR AFTER LEAVING THE RIDGEMONT HOTEL, BRAILLE and Gregory found themselves walking down a deserted street. Though the earlier storm continued to rage in the sky not far from them and the Army was still fighting the New Ones with an impressive display of gunfire and explosions less than two miles behind them, it was strangely quiet on the street where they were.

Breaking the silence they had established after leaving the Ridgemont, Gregory said, "It is like we are in the eye of a storm."

Braille nodded in agreement. In spite of the din created by the Army and the storm, it was quiet and peaceful where they were. The street was wet and shiny. A thickening fog and the buildings were blocking out the sounds of violence coming at them from two sides. But in spite of the newly found quietness, something was gnawing at Braille's senses. His nerves were tingling. Something was wrong. He stopped and glanced back down the street. So did Gregory. "You sense it also?" Gregory asked.

"Something's out there."

Gregory scanned the street. "It is nothing."

They began walking again, heading away from the war being fought in the center of the city, each knowing they had done what they could and that the final outcome was now in the hands of a man in a plane flying east and a second man four thousand miles away.

Braille fished a cigarette out of his pocket. He lit it, then stopped abruptly as something tugged at his senses. His nerve endings turned cold.

They were in danger. It was behind them.

* * *

A half a block away Kubick emerged from an alley, holding the OSMS-issued .357-caliber Python pistol in both hands. There was madness in the man's eyes. He had spent the evening tracking Gregory through the hell that was now downtown Seattle and had killed more creatures than he could count. He had melted the barrel of his machine gun and used up all his shotgun shells and grenades. He had killed hundreds, maybe thousands; killed them as a god would kill. Then he had lost Gregory, only to spot him again as the Ancient and the man walking beside him emerged from the Ridgemont Hotel. He had spent the past half hour tracking them, waiting for the perfect time, the perfect place. And this was it. The street was well lit. The Ancient was close. He could not miss. He brought the pistol up, aiming it at the spine of the beast who was walking away from him . . . the spine of the beast who had killed his men.

Braille sensed it.
Gregory sensed it.
The world went into slow motion.
Braille started to turn towards Kubick.
With cold clarity Gregory sensed Kubick's presence, sensing his feelings of elation and power. He knew that something was different tonight. Kubick possessed something special: a special weapon.
Braille whirled around, seeing the figure half a block away aiming a pistol at him and Gregory. Instinctively he knew this was no ordinary weapon.
In a brief second frozen in time Braille reached for the .45 automatic at the back of his belt, his hand moving as if it were trapped by a perverse form of gravity.
At the same time, Kubick started to squeeze the trigger. In the same flicker of time Gregory shoved Braille away from him.
Kubick pulled the trigger, knowing it would be a perfect shot.
The pistol bucked in Kubick's hand. Gregory gasped as the bullet punctured his spine and exploded.
A microsecond later Kubick fired again and a second bullet saturated with cesium, iridium, and americium

struck Gregory in the spine. This time he did not gasp. He took a single faltering step, collapsing to his knees.

Gregory's push had caught Braille off guard. He stumbled into the street, rolling and coming to his knees, the .45 clutched in both hands.

Kubick wanted to shoot the Ancient a third time, but was worried about the other one. What if it was an Ancient too? Deciding not to take the chance, he snapped off a quick shot at the figure coming to his feet in the street.

The bullet cut past Braille's cheek, burning his skin.

Then Braille fired off five quick shots in succession, firing five because the man was too far away for a weapon such as the .45.

A bullet tugged at Kubick's shirt. He laughed and began to take careful aim at the man shooting at him. More bullets whipped the air around him. Still laughing, Kubick started to squeeze the trigger; at this distance he couldn't miss.

He was still laughing when Braille's fifth bullet slammed into his pistol, splattering a dusting of rarefied iridium, cesium, and americium over his face. Kubick didn't care. Having the pistol shot out of his hands was only a minor irritation. He would kill the one on the street, kill it with his kubikiri, he decided, unsheathing the four-hundred-year-old knife. His face and eyes were beginning to burn. He didn't care. He would kill the one with the .45 first, then he would take the head of the Ancient, the supposedly immortal beast now on its knees on the sidewalk. Kubick began walking towards his prey.

Braille heard the man at the end of the block laugh and watched him start forward. As the man continued to close on him, Braille glanced over at Gregory and was horrified by what he saw. The Master Ancient was on his knees, writhing in pain. Braille knew that the other human had used something on Gregory that only the OSMS could have invented. He turned his attention back on the man. "What'd you do to him?" Braille bellowed.

Something clicked in Kubick's brain and suddenly he knew who was yelling at him. It was Braille; he knew about Braille, had been briefed by the OSMS, and the demented smile on his face broadened. "Special radiation-filled bullets," he shouted out laughingly. "Compliments of Hargrave

Cutter. You remember Cutter, don't you . . . Braille? He told me about you, told me what he did to your friends, told me you were a hotshot in martial arts. Let's see if you're any good."

Kubick broke into an easy lope, then began to increase his speed. Kubick was elated as he charged Braille. The skin on his face was burning; his eyeballs were burning. But it didn't matter. He couldn't be hurt. He was a god. He had slaughtered hundreds of New Ones earlier and had just brought the Ancient to his knees. In a moment he would kill Braille and then take the Ancient's head. After that he would resurrect his team, heal their wounds and bring them back to life. Together they would set out again to hunt humans, demons, anything that was a challenge. This is good; this is right. He was immortal, unstoppable. He was a god.

The man charging Braille was screaming now, screaming incoherent words that made no sense. Braille took a two-handed grip on the old .45, took aim, and when the man came into range, fired.

The bullet caught Kubick in the chest, stopping him in his tracks. Standing in the white light of an overhead street lamp, Kubick examined the hole in his chest. Lifting his head, he smiled at Braille and started coming again. Braille gasped in shock. A man with a fist-sized hole in his chest was coming for him and worse, the man's face was melting. The flesh was oozing off his skull like hot cheese. The guy was dead and dissolving but he didn't seem to realize it. Braille shot it again, this time in the heart, and still it continued to lurch towards him like a hideous, unstoppable robot.

Kubick's mind was reeling. The madness that had started to overtake him after Gregory had killed his men was complete now. He knew he had been shot twice, knew the skin on his face was dissolving, but he felt no pain, and that was right; a god feels no pain. A god couldn't be stopped. "I am a god!!" he screamed as he broke into a halting charge.

Taking his time, Braille waited until the hideous apparition was close, very close, then he shot it in the forehead. The grotesque fleshless skull exploded and the thing finally collapsed in the street.

"Jesus Christ," Braille muttered in sick revulsion as he stood for a moment longer, watching the face and skull of whatever he'd just killed melt away into nothing on the street like a candy bar on a hotplate.

Throwing away the empty .45, Braille returned to Gregory. The Ancient was on his hands and knees. Braille dropped down beside him. "How bad is it?" he asked, already knowing the answer.

"There was something in those bullets," Gregory managed. "Some sort of poison like the radiation on the island. I can't feel my legs." He angled his head and looked at Braille with pain-filled eyes. "I cannot move."

Braille carried Gregory to the Ram Charger, driving back to the motel and carrying Gregory into his room. He put the Ancient down on the bed and turned on a weak bedside lamp, wincing at the destruction the OSMS bullets had brought to Gregory. From the waist up Gregory was as he had always been—broad shouldered and powerful. The horror Braille beheld was from the waist down. It was as if Gregory no longer had flesh or bones. There was no substance in his clothes. No flesh, no bones. His legs were shriveled sticks, barely visible through the folds of his slacks. Gregory noticed Braille's expression and pulled the bedspread over his legs. "There is nothing you can do," he said. "I'm dying."

"You have lived for nine centuries. You survived the holocaust on the island. You'll survive this."

The Ancient shook his head. "This is different. I don't know what Kubick did to me, what he shot me with, but it has spread into my body and it's killing me." There was no remorse in Gregory's voice, no sadness. It was just a simple assessment, a statement of fact.

Braille looked at Gregory skeptically. "You're immortal. You can survive any bullets the OSMS comes up with."

"This is different. There is not much pain, just an expanding nothingness moving through my body, destroying it from the inside out, killing it completely."

Braille was silent for a moment as he weighed what he was about to say. "What if . . . what if I went out and brought you blood?"

Gregory looked up at Braille. "You would kill a human being and bring me his blood?"

"Yes," Braille answered without hesitation.

"It would be a waste of a human life and a waste of time. It wouldn't work. On the island, I was burned. Flesh fell from my body, but in the end my body rebirthed itself. This is different. This is killing me from the inside out. I can feel the burning, the destruction in the marrow of my bones. This is death and I will not be reborn from this."

Braille sat down on the edge of the bed, staring down at his own hands. "I have this power," he finally said, raising his eyes to Gregory's. "I don't know where it came from, but I have the power to heal. I can take your pain and death into my body. You'll get better. I'll live with what you have for a while, then I'll get better. I know it sounds strange, but I can do it. I've done it."

The Master Ancient seemed to smile. "All Ancients have that power. I have it; Clementina had it. I have not used my power very much, but Clementina did occasionally— especially if she encountered a sick or dying child. I don't know where the power comes from but it seems to offer a balance to the horror we bring to the world."

Braille shook his head in confusion as Gregory continued. "By all the laws of man and nature, we are the most evil beings in the world. We take blood and kill to maintain our eternity. This power lessens our evil, allows us to somehow bring something other than darkness to this world." Suddenly Gregory gasped and his face became a mask of pure agony.

"Let me help you," Braille said, gripping Gregory's arm. "Let me use this power."

Irritated over his earlier display of pain, Gregory spoke without emotion. "I am dying and your power cannot save me from that."

"Then there's nothing I can do?" Braille asked, slowly getting to his feet.

An odd look came into Gregory's eyes. Braille recognized it and almost smiled. It was the look of the Master Ancient when he was angry. "An agency exists that killed your woman and your friends. It also killed my friends. Destroy this agency," Gregory said in the stillness of the motel room. "Take this agency from the face of the earth. Do it for your dead woman, your friends and mine. Do it for yourself; do it for me. And do it well, human."

Braille nodded in sad understanding. The Ancient really was dying. "I don't want to leave you here like this."

"You have no choice. I don't want you here. My passing is not for the eyes of anyone."

Braille started for the door, then stopped and looked back at Gregory.

Gregory gave him a final look. "Take care and remember the agency that has killed me also has the same kind of bullets for you. If they do kill you, consider it a blessing and accept it for the gift it is. Death is a blessing. Remember that." Gregory closed his eyes.

Braille stepped out into the night. It was late. The gunfire emanating from the center of the city was fading. Off in the east the sun was coming up. Pulling the motel door closed, he locked it, turning his thoughts on the OSMS. It seemed as though the debt he owed that agency had been a long time in coming.

And now that time was at hand.

36

IT WAS JUST AFTER TWO IN THE AFTERNOON WHEN BRAILLE pulled onto the shoulder of the freeway. He shut the Ram Charger down, climbed out, and turned towards a barely visible dirt road leading out into the desert. He did not have a weapon with him. No rifle; no pistol. Just himself, his rage, his skills, and an old Dodge Ram Charger. He knew the OSMS was waiting for him, ready for him, but he wasn't afraid. This day—this time had been a long time in coming and even if he failed, Gregory was right. Death was a blessing.

Hargrave Cutter was sitting in his office, watching five television sets at once. All of the sets were broadcasting updated news information about the disaster in Seattle.

A knock on his office door interrupted Cutter's concentration. He pushed a button, the door unlocked itself, and Martin Lopez, the head of security, entered.

"What?" Cutter demanded.

"We have an intrusion. Someone's just pulled onto the road to the base. Near as we can tell at this point, it's a big car, a heavy one, and it's coming slowly towards us."

Cutter followed Lopez down a long corridor to central security.

Central security was housed in a huge room filled with high-tech equipment and computers. One wall held nothing but television monitors. Each monitor offered a view of a building, or a road, or the desert, depending on where the security videocamera was located. Four security guards continually watched the monitors twenty-four hours a day. The back wall was the most interesting. On this wall was a huge, detailed relief map of the air base and an expansive desert surrounding the base for twenty miles on all sides. The map was to scale and was impressive. The hills stood out as if viewed in 3-D. The roads were there, the cliffs, the buildings. Everything. Even more impressive was the system of miniature lights hooked into the wall behind the map. The tiny lights were tied into pressure sensors located throughout the base, in the desert and on the roads. If anything weighing more than a hundred pounds stepped on a sensor, a light came on.

Cutter's attention was immediately drawn to the replica of the freeway by-passing the OSMS twenty miles away and a short ribbon of brightly glowing blue lights leading from the freeway and partway down the main road to the air base. It was easy to tell what was going on. A vehicle had turned off the freeway and was on the road. The vehicle had traveled about half a mile, activating pressure sensors as it moved. In turn the sensors had activated a two-inch-long strip of blue lights on the map. More lights were coming on, indicating the vehicle was still heading in their direction.

"Whoever it is, he's coming slow," Lopez said. "But it's probably a false alarm. Probably a duck hunter. He'll turn around when he gets to the first fence."

"You have a visual on this vehicle?" Cutter asked.

"Cue up fourteen," Lopez said.

Off in the desert a videocamera elevated itself out of the soil like a macabre ghost rising up from a grave. It locked onto the slow-moving Ram Charger, following it as it continued down the road.

"Is that the best you can do?" Cutter asked. The black-and-white picture on monitor fourteen told him nothing.

"It's the rain, sir," Lopez said. "It's smeared the lens."

"Any other cameras in that area?"

Lopez shook his head. "No. But by now the driver has seen the No Trespassing signs and the fence and he should be turning around about . . . now."

The lights just to the left of the lit-up road began coming on, indicating the driver had just made a U-turn and was now heading back towards the freeway.

Cutter released a pent-up sigh of relief and started towards the door.

"We got a problem here, sir," Lopez called out.

Cutter whirled around, staring up at the map. More blue lights were coming on. Lopez explained, "The vehicle made another U-turn and now he's heading towards perimeter one. He's picking up speed . . . really picking up speed!"

This is it, Cutter thought.

The gate had been designed to look like one endless expanse of heavy-duty cyclone fence topped with concertina wire. Hidden hydraulics below the road worked to lower a section of the fence into the road if the proper radio signal were activated. Braille saw the fence come into view, guessed it was a deception and knew it would be a tough obstacle to run. He pushed the gas pedal all the way to the floor.

Twenty seconds later the Ram Charger collided with the fence.

Braille was belted in, but it didn't matter. His body was thrown forward and his chest slammed into the steering wheel as the fence held and the Charger ground to an almost dead stop. At the same instant, the vehicle's nose pitched forward, its rear tires left the ground, and the Charger started into a front roll. But then the fence collapsed, poles were jerked out of cement holes, and the underground hydraulic system was ripped up through the asphalt. The Charger broke free. Its rear end crashed back down on the road and it kept on going, beginning to pick up speed as Braille accelerated again.

"He's through perimeter one," Lopez screamed, "and still coming!"

At the same time, a mechanical inhuman voice began squawking through hidden speakers. "Intrusion . . . Intrusion . . . Intrusion."

"Shut that thing off," Cutter shouted. A security guard hit a switch and the voice stopped. "You got roving patrols in that area?" Cutter asked. Lopez nodded. "Well, get 'em on that vehicle." He pointed at the map and the lengthening blue line.

Lopez said something into a radio microphone.

Out in the desert the driver of an OSMS Bronco with a high-powered engine acknowledged the transmission, gunned the engine, and sped off.

Braille was pushing the Ram Charger hard, driving it down a straight stretch of road that cut past a sloping hill. He noticed movement up on the hill to his right. Glancing up through the windshield he saw a Bronco come over the crest and start down the hill at an angle, trying to cut him off.

The Ram Charger picked up speed. The Bronco came down off the hill, jouncing onto the road and pulling up close behind Braille. There were three men in the vehicle. Two leaned out of windows and began firing with automatic weapons. As bullets spiderwebbed the Charger's rear window, Braille glanced at the speedometer. He was doing ninety miles an hour on a narrow dirt road. The Bronco was right on his tail, not more than ten feet back.

Braille hit the brakes as hard as he could. The Charger went into a controlled skid.

The other driver screamed, jerking the wheel to the left, trying to avoid the rear end of the Ram Charger. The Bronco broke into a wild skid, slid sideways off the road, then flipped and rolled over several times. Braille stomped down on the gas again and the Ram Charger began to .pick up speed. Ahead of him another cyclone fence loomed up in the middle of the road. Braille braced himself, but this time there was no need. The Charger tore through the fence at a hundred miles an hour as if it were made of spiderwebs.

"Through perimeter two," Lopez shouted, "and communication's been cut off from our patrol car. It may be down."

At that moment Riddick and Kendricks burst into the room. Ignoring them, Cutter gestured at Lopez. "I want to see that fucking car." Lopez punched out a code on a computer keyboard. A quarter of a mile off to Braille's left a surveillance camera emerged from the desert floor. It zeroed in on the Ram Charger, following it as it rolled past. Lopez tapped out some adjustments on the keyboard. The camera focused in on the Charger and captured the driver's profile.

They saw Braille.

"Fuck," Riddick groaned. "It's him."

"Deploy your men in the hangar bay," Cutter said to Lopez. As Lopez began shouting orders, Cutter turned to Kendricks. "I want Golem out there. You stay with it to make damn sure it does what you've programmed it to do."

Kendricks gave Cutter a stricken look. "Sir, there's going to be a lot of action out there, a lot of bullets. That's okay for Golem. He's bulletproof but—"

"Stay with your fucking robot," Cutter snarled. He turned to Riddick. "Go get the weapon." Riddick nodded and ran off.

Cutter motioned Lopez over. "Get me the best marksman you got." As Lopez hurried off, Cutter glanced over at the wall of television monitors. The image on the video screens had been frozen. Someone had hit the pause button. Braille's face was up on the screen, up on thirty screens. He seemed to be looking at the camera, looking at Cutter himself. There was no expression on his face. But the hate was there. Pure cold hate. It was in the eyes, eyes that seemed to be staring at Cutter.

Cutter tore his eyes from the screens and shouted to another security guard, "Any more roving patrols in that area?"

The man shook his head. "They're too far away. They won't be able to get to him in time." The guard gestured. "Hell, we never thought he'd come for us down the main road!"

"How long until gate three?" Cutter asked.

The guard looked at the map. "He's two miles from perimeter three. I make it a minute and a half 'til impact."

Riddick came back into the security room carrying an expensive European-made bolt-action 30.06.

Cutter turned to Lopez. "Who's your marksman?"

Lopez motioned for a woman in a security uniform to come over. She was tiny, maybe five feet two, with a pixie nose and freckles. Cutter knew her slightly. Her name was LaVida Andrews and she'd been with security for four years. She was close to thirty, but looked sixteen. "She's the best rifle shot in the OSMS," Lopez said.

Cutter took the rifle from Riddick. Deciding not to tell the woman anything about the cesium bullets in the weapon, he said, "There are special exploding bullets in this rifle. Those bullets may be the only way to stop the intruder that's heading our way. I want you up on top of the building. If he gets into the hangar bay, I want you to take him out with one of those bullets." He handed her the rifle. The weapon was almost as big as the woman, yet she handled it easily.

"You'll have lots of company out in the hangar. Extra security will be out there, I'll be out there, Lopez'll be out there. But as far as I'm concerned, you're the one I'm counting on the most. The bullets in that rifle will stop him. And aim for the head or spine."

"He's going to hit number three," a guard yelled.

Everyone looked up at the monitors. Out in the desert a videocamera was zeroed in on the Ram Charger. "Jesus, look at the size of that machine," said one of the guards. "Those must be thirty-five-inch tires."

The camera continued to swivel on its base, following the Ram Charger as it sped across the desert. "Christ," the same man said. "He must be doing close to a hundred. Here comes the gate."

Unlike the other fences, this one was a gate with a guard house and guards. As the camera continued to capture the scene, everyone in the security room saw the two sentries behind the locked gates. One of them was kneeling in the center of the road. The other was standing. Both were firing automatic weapons at the approaching Ram Charger, but there was no sound accompanying what the people in security were seeing. But each could see the sentries were firing frantically, the muzzle flashes from their weapons showing up white and bright on the screen. Though the camera was a hundred yards away, everyone felt the guards' surprise and shock when their weapons failed to stop the Charger.

Then the Charger hit the gates. The fence exploded. The standing guard tried to dive for cover but was hit by a flying section of metal gate. The guard on one knee simply disappeared under the vehicle. The camera continued to remain frozen on the scene: shattered gates, a crushed guard in the middle of the road, the other guard writhing in pain at the side of the road. And no sign of the Charger.

"How long 'til he gets here?" Cutter screamed.

"Four, maybe four and a half minutes," someone said.

"Everyone out in the hangar," Cutter snarled.

Braille was no longer on a disguised desert road. Now he was on a flat black asphalt road and his speedometer said a hundred miles an hour. Ahead of him he could see dark shapes framed by a gray sky. A moment later the shapes became collapsing barracks, officers' houses, and movie theaters.

Braille slowed up somewhat as he entered the deserted Air Force base and it seemed a shame. He was proud of the Charger, proud of the way the vehicle had held up. She was pockmarked with bullet holes, her windows were gone. The metal pipes welded to the front grille had saved the engine from most of the bullets. But a few had hit home. He could tell that from the clanking sound the engine was starting to make. Still, the Ram Charger showed no signs of wanting to slow up.

The road he was on took him through the Air Force base, then led him out onto an endless expanse of black runway.

Three miles away and coming up fast, the world's largest airplane hangar loomed up on the gray horizon like a massive black monolith.

Inside the huge hangar better than thirty people waited for the oncoming vehicle. Some had taken up positions behind the cars parked in front of the OSMS building. Others stood behind two Apache helicopters armed with rockets and some jeeps parked at the far end of the hangar.

Everyone in the murky darkness was armed, and the weapons ranged from laserscoped M-16's to portable rocket launchers. Cutter stood on the top step of the OSMS building, his hands in his lab jacket. Below him, crouched behind a car, Lopez stood ready with an automatic weapon in his hands. Riddick was standing beside Cutter half frozen with fear. Like Cutter, he was unarmed. They didn't need weapons. There were over thirty heavily armed men in the hangar. It was their job to handle the oncoming problem.

Cutter could smell Riddick's fear and shook his head in disgust. When this was over, Riddick would have to go. The man had been useless for months but Cutter knew he couldn't retire him. Alcoholics shot their mouths off; alcoholics didn't retire from the OSMS. Alcoholics died from complications. Then they retired.

He lost his train of thought when he detected the faint sounds of a vehicle coming hard and fast.

It was dark in the huge hangar. Its massive doors had been closed, and the halogen vapor lights mounted on the overhead girders did little to dispel the murkiness. Cutter could barely see his men; they were just shapes and shadows armed with the most powerful high-tech firepower in the world.

Braille would die in a few moments, Cutter thought. He hoped it would be a quick death. He wasn't merciful. He just wanted to have a chance to extract some of Braille's blood from his body before it went bad. Even with a small amount he could continue to experiment, continue to work towards a cure for disease and aging, and unlimited wealth for himself. Unconsciously Cutter gripped the case in the pocket of his smock, the case containing three large syringes. The sound of the oncoming vehicle was louder now, loud as close thunder. Cutter braced himself.

The huge hangar filled the speeding Ram Charger's windshield like a raging black storm. Bracing himself, Braille reached for the door handle . . .

The Ram Charger burst through the side of the hangar at better than seventy miles an hour and Cutter's men opened up with everything they had. As the Charger shot across the bay, it was hit with hundreds of rounds of ammunition. A microsecond later a rocket fired from the back of the hangar streaked across the darkness into the windshield of the Charger. The explosion ripped the roof off the vehicle, but the machine kept on coming, pushed on by its momentum and an engine that would not die. A second rocket tore into the front fender of the car, exploding just as the burning vehicle slammed into an Apache helicopter. The copter's fuel tank exploded and the copter's rockets went off, whizzing across the hangar and exploding.

"Jesus Christ!" Riddick screamed, shielding his face with his hands.

Then the other helicopter exploded into flames and more rockets went off.

Cutter was oddly detached from the scene. He could hear his men screaming in agony as rockets exploded and flames and shrapnel filled the air, but it didn't seem real. It was like watching a movie with spectacular special effects, and the special effects were taking place at the other end of the hangar two hundred yards away.

Suddenly Riddick gasped and took a step backwards. Cutter glanced over at Riddick and saw a gaping hole in the man's throat, a hole put there by a large chunk of shrapnel. Riddick was looking back at Cutter with panic-stricken eyes, pointing to his wound and desperately trying to say something. Cutter was a physician. He recognized a mortal wound when he saw one. Still detached from everything going on around him, he shrugged with his hands and mouthed the word sorry.

Desperate and terrified, Riddick tried to reach out for Cutter. Cutter pushed the hand away, looking back at the destruction inside the mammoth hangar. The helicopters were in flames. Several vehicles were burning.

And the gutted remains of Braille's car was an inferno.

Cutter stared at the burning car, straining to see through the heat and flames into the interior. It was impossible, but in his mind's eye Cutter could see Braille's blackened, charred corpse writhing and twisting on the seat as the intense heat shrank tendons and cracked bones.

Cutter released a sigh of relief. The Charger had been hit with over a thousand rounds of ammunition, rockets, then consumed by fire. There was no way Braille could not be dead.

He gave Riddick a final glance. The man was lying on the steps, his throat open, his eyes open. That was one way to retire, Cutter thought, turning to look down at Lopez. He could barely see him. Smoke from the fires had turned the interior of the hangar into a dark foggy night. He heard Lopez say, "God, that was beautiful. The way we worked together, the way everything went. God that—"

"Put out the fires and bring me his bones," Cutter said with a mixture of emotions. He was relieved because he did not have to worry about Braille anymore, but upset because there would be no blood to experiment with. Still, if Kubick could bring back Gregory's body . . . there was always a chance.

Cutter glanced out at the destruction a final time. Smoke drifted like low thick clouds through the hangar, obscuring almost everything, even the burning helicopters two hundred yards away. Some of his men were putting out the fires. Others were helping those who had been hurt during the explosions. As he started to turn away, he noticed the large ragged hole in the side of the hangar where the Ram Charger had broken through. He thought he saw a shadow move through the opening and step inside the hangar, but didn't give it much thought. "Clean it up, Lopez," he said, "and bring me his bones, as soon as you can."

Cutter was starting into the building when a shout from Kendricks stopped him. Kendricks and the robot were moving across the hangar bay towards him. Kendricks waved. "Sure was easier than we thought. Too bad." He patted the robot as if it were an old friend. "Golem was all programmed and ready to go."

That was true, Cutter thought. The robot had been reprogrammed. Not only had its offensive mode been amplified, but it also had been programmed to recognize Braille. Photographs and videotapes the OSMS had taken of Braille had been fed into its memory banks. The robot had memorized Braille's features, committed to memory the way the man walked, moved, and gestured. It was now like a giant metal attack dog with incomprehensible strength and only one enemy in the world: Braille.

Bothered by a nagging suspicion, Cutter said, "Put Golem in a scout mode and keep it in that mode until we have positive proof of Braille's death."

"But he couldn't have survived what we hit him with," Kendricks argued. "Nothing could have survived that inferno." Kendricks pointed to the still-burning Charger.

"Just do it," Cutter shouted back.

At Kendricks' command Golem turned and disappeared into the thick smoke. Its objective, to scout the huge hangar bay and search for a man with the physical characteristics implanted in its memory.

Braille moved through the thick smoke in the hangar like a ghost. The arm he'd shattered when he had leaped from the Ram Charger just before the Charger crashed into the hangar was almost healed. The pain was gone. He could move it now. Braille stopped first beside a man who had been badly burned when the helicopters blew up. The man's uniform was still smoldering and no one had found him yet because the man was in too much pain to cry out. All he could do was make soft hissing sounds like an asthmatic. Braille took the man's MAC-10 machine gun, several clips of spare ammunition, then he put him out of his misery.

He got to his feet and saw a second guard walking towards him, his hands outstretched like a blind man as he tried to make his way through the smoke. Braille hit him in the forehead with the heel of his hand and the man went down like a sack of cement.

A dim shape forty yards away shouted, "Get the hangar doors open. Get the fans going. Let's get this smoke out of here." An electric motor came on and the two huge doors behind Braille began to part like giant curtains. The doors parted ten feet, then stopped abruptly. "They're jammed," somebody said.

Braille moved out of the gray light streaming in from the partly open doors and moved on. Smoke surrounded him like wind-whipped clouds. Keeping to the darkness, and with his back to the hangar wall, he began to inch towards the huge OSMS building in the middle of the hangar. He came to some empty rubber garbage cans and worked his way around them, stopping when he heard a terrifyingly familiar sound. He whirled around and saw Golem coming for him. The robot had always been big, yet somehow it looked bigger this time as it rolled for him on its treads, its giant mechanical arms outstretched, its metal hands making pincerlike movements.

Braille had fought Golem once before and didn't want to tangle with it again. He emptied the MAC-10's clip at the oncoming machine. It didn't even slow down. Then it was on him, reaching for him with metal skeleton-like hands. Braille sidestepped the arms. The arms punched two holes in the hangar wall behind Braille.

Ten yards away Kendricks began screaming, "Over here! Over here! It's Braille!!" Golem turned on his treads, shredding the wall with its arms as it did. Then it attacked again. At the same time Kendricks fired his machine gun at Braille. Most of the bullets bounced off Golem's back. But one creased Braille's face. Braille jammed a clip into his MAC-10 and activated the bolt, starting to fire. Suddenly Golem was on him again, wrapping its metal arms around him like a giant bear. At the last instant Braille dropped to his knees, and the arms crushed nothing. Kendricks howled in frustration at Braille's escape and began reloading his own machine gun.

Braille scrambled away from Golem, stumbling into the garbage cans. Golem whirled around and started coming for him. Braille got to his feet, remembering how he had beaten Golem the last time. He'd cheated and would have to cheat again. As Golem charged, Braille picked up a large rubber garbage can. An instant before Golem was on him, Braille jammed the open end of the garbage can over Golem's fishbowl-like head.

Suddenly Golem was blind and confused. It had been programmed to shut itself down in the event of a malfunction, but it had also been programmed to destroy the shape it was attacking. The destruction program won out.

Nearby, Kendricks activated the bolt on his machine gun. Golem heard the sound and moved towards it. An instant later Golem fulfilled its primary directive: it attacked. The machine attacked Kendricks, wrapping its metal arms around the man and beginning to crush him.

Kendricks screamed, trying to tell Golem to stop. But the transmitter he used to communicate with Golem was strapped to his wrist like a wristwatch, and that wrist was pinned to the side of Kendricks' body by one of Golem's arms, and the wrist and transmitter were slowly disappearing *into* Kendricks' body as Golem continued to squeeze. Kendricks' other arm and his machine gun were pinned to the front of his chest by Golem's own chest. Both the arm and the machine gun were disappearing into Kendricks' chest as Golem continued to fulfill its primary directive.

Golem did not know. Golem could not see, but the physical characteristics of the shape in its arms matched the shape in its memory bank, and that meant it had to destroy what it was holding. That meant mechanical arms continued to crush and meld the rifle, the transmitter, and the arms of Kendricks into the torso of Kendricks.

Fascinated, Braille looked on, remembering all the things Kendricks had done to him, remembering the deaths of Louis and Jade Radcliff. He could have killed Kendricks, ended his agony with a bullet. But he didn't. Bullets began whizzing around him as others in the hangar realized what was going on and were firing off random panic shots. A bullet grazed the back of Braille's neck. Unmoving, he continued to watch Golem crush Kendricks, turning his muscular torso into an amalgam of red, shapeless flesh. Blood gushed from Kendricks' mouth, his eyes went blank, and Braille knew it was finally over. But Golem did not. The giant mechanical monster with an alien body and a rubber garbage can over its head continued to fulfill its directive, continuing to perform the functions Kendricks had programmed it to perform.

Braille disappeared into the shadows and smoke.

Hargrave Cutter stood on the steps of the OSMS building, cursing the smoke and darkness. He'd heard Kendricks shout, the machine gun fire, then heard Kendricks' prolonged screams. Now he knew Kendricks was dead and Braille was somewhere in the hangar. "Find him," he shouted to Lopez.

Lopez decided he didn't want to go hunting alone. There was safety in numbers. He jerked out his radio, ordering his men to report to him. Of his thirty men, eleven had been killed or wounded when the helicopters and rockets exploded. Six others had taken off out of small doors at the rear of the hangar and were running across the runway, heading for the desert. The remaining thirteen jumped to their feet and ran across the long hangar, almost two hundred yards, and they prayed the smoke would give them cover. It didn't. Braille cut eight down with the MAC-10 before it went empty. Lopez heard the shots, heard his men die, and decided there was more safety in leaving.

Suddenly Hargrave Cutter decided he was out of his element. He was a doctor, for Christ's sake, and the head of an agency. It was stupid for him to be where he was. He should have flown off to Washington and waited until this mess was over. He pushed open the doors, stepping into the building.

Lopez heard the door close and knew Cutter had just taken off. He felt rage and fear flutter up inside him. He turned to the five men who'd made it across the hangar. "They ain't paying me enough to stay here and die." The other guards nodded, and as if on a prearranged signal, all six crowded into a nearby jeep. Lopez started the engine, threw the vehicle into a tight U-turn, and headed for the partly open hangar doors.

It was difficult to steer. His men were crowded around him, hanging onto anything they could to keep themselves from falling out of the vehicle. The closeness made it difficult to shift, and Lopez was trying to get the jeep into third gear, when he heard a single shot and the left front tire exploded. The jeep pitched to the left and two of Lopez's men were thrown against him as he tried to bring the jeep out of the skid. While he tried to steer and push the men away, it dawned on him. That hadn't been machine gun fire. That had been a rifle shot. LaVida Andrews, he realized, and his last thought was: I shouldn't've left her behind. Then the jeep rolled over.

Braille had seen the muzzle flash come from the roof of the hospital. He raked the top of the building with bullets and waited. After a long moment of silence he set out again, moving cautiously across the hangar, up the steps, and through the front doors.

Hargrave Cutter was in his office, filling a briefcase with research material and case files. It was time to leave. Time to pack it up, head for the basement, take the underground tunnel to the staff's living quarters, and then go. There was an underground heliport there with a small Bell helicopter, a helicopter whose only purpose was to take Cutter out of there in the event of an emergency. He closed the briefcase, knowing he had enough documents and research material to make the government pay him any amount he wanted to keep his mouth shut and the files secret. He knew he would never have power or prestige again, never head up another agency. But at least he would have money, any amount he wanted.

He picked up the briefcase and ran down the hall, to the elevator. The elaborate security system used to keep unauthorized personnel out of the basement was no longer operational. The earlier system had failed to keep a doctor, his wife, and Leslie Chapel out of the basement. A new security system was in planning, but for the time being, it was just an ordinary elevator. Cutter pushed a button. The elevator complied.

The lights were out on the lower level floor. Deciding the explosions in the hangar had done something to the generators, Cutter groped his way down a black hallway, entering the dark lab. The only source of light came from computer screens that bathed the room in an eerie green glow. Everything was green except for two red dials on the wall off to his right. He moved on, working his way past the cage built for Braille and over to the door that opened onto the underground tunnel. The door was locked. Grumbling in frustration, he pulled out what looked like a credit card, inserting it into a slot in the door. Nothing happened. Frantic now, he jerked out a ring of keys, trying to push the master key into the lock. It wouldn't go in. He pulled out his lighter. Lighting it, he examined the lock. There was a piece of metal jammed in the keyhole.

"What the—"

Suddenly he remembered the two red lights glowing in the dark when he'd first come into the lab. There wasn't any equipment over on that side of the room. He dropped the briefcase, whirling around. Suddenly he found himself staring into eyes the color of hell.

"Don't kill me," Hargrave Cutter pleaded. "I can help you. I can fix what you are. I can make you rich. Just don't kill me."

Braille grabbed Cutter by the shirt, picking him up and pushing him against the door with one hand. As he glared at the man, the hate he felt for Cutter made it almost impossible to speak. Finally he managed, "Can you destroy this building?"

"The main computer can," Cutter said, rasping for breath.

"Destroy this building," Braille said softly, "help me with my disease, and I'll let you live."

Part of Cutter didn't believe Braille, but another part wanted to believe, needed to believe; Cutter was terrified of dying. "Anything you say," he gasped.

"Then do it," Braille said, throwing Cutter across the room.

Cutter landed on the tile floor, skidding into the bottom of the computer console. He scrambled to his knees and began typing on the computer keyboard. The letters appeared immediately on the green terminal screen. "Only Riddick and I know this code," Cutter explained rapidly. "When this building was built, explosives were laid next to the foundation. It was something we had to do. There was always a chance that an experiment could go wrong, maybe release a lethal virus or bacteria. Something deadly to humanity. We needed a fail-safe system in the event that happened, and we came up with a good one. Christ, I think the explosives in the foundation weigh more than the foundation."

"Just do it," Braille said, his words more growl than human.

"Almost like a doomsday machine," Cutter said nervously. "Wipe this place right off the planet."

He stopped typing. Braille looked at the console screen.

Cutter had typed in a series of numbers and letters, then added in the center of the screen: Omega Night.

Cutter glanced up at Braille. "Rather dramatic, but it gets the point across."

"Nothing's happening," Braille said.

Then Cutter pressed the enter key.

Everything immediately disappeared from the screen. A second later the digits 09:00 appeared in the upper left part of the screen.

Then: 08:59.

Then: 08:58.

"That's it?" Braille asked.

"What'd you expect? Bells? Sirens? Mechanical voices announcing a countdown?"

"Yes."

Cutter smiled. "It's a 'no warning' destruct program. If a destruct sequence were announced in the building, there'd be mass panic. Someone from the contaminated lab might escape and spread whatever was released. It's just simpler this way."

"And this place will go up in . . . ?"

Cutter pointed to the screen. It said . . . 07:54.

"Can anything stop the destruct sequence?" Braille asked.

"Only me," Cutter said. "I've got the stop code." He tapped his temple. "All I have to do is type it in the computer and the sequence stops." He looked up at Braille.

And Braille looked back at him with eyes that glowed red in the dark room. Suddenly he grabbed Cutter with one hand. He dragged him across the room, throwing him into the cage Cutter had built for him. The cage had been repaired and was stronger now than it had been when it held Braille. Braille slammed the door. It locked automatically.

Cutter scrambled to his feet. "You can't mean this. The destruct sequence is going."

The head with the red eyes turned slowly and looked at him. "I know," it said.

"But you gave me your word," Cutter screamed. "You said if I helped you destroy the building, helped you with your disease, you'd let me live."

"I lied," said the beast with the red eyes.

A silhouette framed by the green glow from several computer screens walked across the room. It studied the computer Cutter had used to institute the destruct sequence, then it swiveled the monitor around so Cutter could see the screen. The digital readout on the screen said: 07:04.

"You can't do this!" Cutter screamed. "I did what you wanted me to do!" The black shape began walking towards the door.

"Don't leave me. Not like this."

The black shape opened the door.

"Don't go! I don't . . . I can't just watch the clock count down and know that when it hits zero everything will end."

"Yes, you can," said the shape with the red eyes as it pulled the door closed, leaving Cutter alone in the darkness. Alone with a computer terminal that said: 06:52.

Braille took the elevator to the main floor. He stopped briefly in what looked like a waiting room just inside the front doors to the OSMS building. There was a desk on his right, a desk with a computer terminal on it. The screen was blank. But the screen was not blank on the computer terminal in the lower-level lab.

Cutter gripped the bars of the cage, staring at the computer terminal ten feet away. 05:40. A whining sound came from his mouth. Spit dribbled down his chin. This wasn't right. No one should watch a clock click off the minutes leading up to one's own death. No one.

Braille pushed open the front doors of the OSMS building, starting down the steps. It was finished. Riddick was dead. Kendricks was dead. Cutter would soon be dead. His revenge was complete. There was nothing else to do, no more people to kill. It was over. The Radcliffs and Leslie Chapel were avenged and he felt empty inside, like a man with no heart or soul. The desire for vengeance that had carried him on for so long was gone. Braille felt hollow and cold and tired as he walked across the hangar towards the partly open doors.

* * *

At the top of the OSMS building a kneeling woman pressed the stock of a long-barreled 30.06 against her shoulder and took aim. The man was walking away from her. She couldn't miss.

In the basement the computer said: 04:22. Cutter had beat his hands to a bloody pulp and still the bars did not give. He had screamed at the closed door until his voice was harsh and raspy. And still the beast with the red eyes did not come back to let him out. "What do you want from me?" he shouted.

His answer was silence. His answer was: 04:12.

Braille was halfway across the hangar. At the top of the OSMS building a woman named LaVida Andrews placed a manicured finger on the 30.06's trigger. She released half the air in her lungs, and her finger tightened on the trigger. At the last possible instant Braille turned, looking at the building.

Andrews fired. The cesium-laced bullet caught Braille in the back three inches to the right of his spine. It hit him in the shoulder blade, sending him crashing to the ground. He gasped at the pain, a pain unlike anything he'd ever felt before. It felt as if his flesh were burning, as if flames were licking at the flesh. Somehow he knew what had happened, knew what he'd been hit with, and now he knew what Gregory had felt.

He lay on the cold cement floor of the huge hangar, waiting for the final shot that would end this. Nothing. It didn't come. Lying motionless, he opened his eyes and looked out across the floor. There was a dead security guard nearby and there was a weapon in the dead man's hand. It looked like an AR-15. Maybe there was a way to keep the second bullet from coming, if it wasn't already on its way.

On top of the OSMS building, Andrews struggled with her weapon. There was something about the bullet she'd just fired that had screwed up the rifle, jamming the bolt. It was like the gun had rusted shut on her. It was taking every ounce of her strength to slide the bolt up and back. Just one more shot. That's all she would need. She'd hit her target, come close to hitting it in the spine, but knew she'd been off a couple of inches. Just one more shot, she prayed as she struggled with the bolt. Just one. Then as if by magic, the bolt shot back, and Andrews knew her prayer had been answered. She had that last shot.

Braille had one hand on the handle and trigger of the AR-15. The safety was off. He hoped there was a round already in the chamber.

Andrews dropped to one knee, resting the stock of the rifle on the top edge of the wall, sighting down on her target.

Braille gripped the AR-15. He rolled over on his back and fired off a full clip of .223-caliber rounds at better than six hundred and fifty bullets per minute. The bullets gouged huge holes in the building, stitched along the top of it, raising clouds of shattered stone and rock.

A microsecond away from firing, Andrews screamed, clapping both hands over her eyes and toppling backwards, leaving her rifle rocking back and forth on the wall. She'd been blinded by a spray of debris kicked up by the bullets. She knew there was no permanent damage and that her vision would return as soon as she got the grit out of her eyes. Forcing herself to relax, she pulled her upper lids over her lower lids and immediately her eyes began to tear. She could feel the debris being washed away.

The computer screen said: 01:59. Cutter dropped to his knees at the meaning of it. A minute and fifty-nine seconds to live.

It wasn't supposed to happen this way. He wasn't supposed to know *when* he was going to die.

01:51.

And the last thing he wanted to know was *how* he was going to die. He knew about the special explosives in the foundation. Some of it was plastic, but there had been special compounds added to the plastic, compounds related to napalm—oily, jelly-like chemicals whose only function was to supercharge the fire and create an intense inferno capable of destroying any virus or bacteria that had contaminated the labs.

The knowledge, the remembering brought a wild, uncontrollable fear to Cutter. He hated fire. It was the worst way to go. The pain would be beyond description. The pain could last for a very long time. Maybe he wouldn't get knocked out in the explosion, maybe he would be alive when the flames swept over the lab and burned at him as if he were some sort of mutant form of organism. He tried not to look at the computer, but did anyway. It said . . . 01:12.

Braille got to his feet, willing the pain in his shoulder away with his mind. It worked a little. Enough so he was able to throw the AR-15 away, walking out of the hangar and into the gray haze outside. He spotted two OSMS Broncos sitting side by side thirty yards away. Steadying himself, he grabbed the door handle, opened it, and looked inside. There was a key in the ignition.

It had worked, Andrews thought. The tears had swept away the grit. She wiped her eyes with the back of her hand and could see. The rifle lay on the top of the wall. It was time. Now the fucker was hers. She crawled up to the rifle, hefting it to her shoulder. She took aim at the spot where her target had been lying.

Where was the fucker?

Braille started the Bronco, accelerating it into a U-turn and driving away from the world's largest hangar.

She had hit him, Andrews thought as she knelt on top of the OSMS building. So where was he?

On his knees, gripping the bars, his mouth mouthing meaningless words, Cutter watched the green computer screen click off the time: 00:04.

00:03.
00:02.

"Where'd the fucker go?" Andrews said aloud.

00:01.
Cutter screamed: "NOOOOO . . ."
00:00.

Braille stopped the Bronco on the runway, looking back at the huge rusty hangar a half a mile away.

It began with a low rumble like the rumbling from a minor earthquake. But then the rumbling escalated, grew louder, more intense, until it sounded like a volcano were going off in the middle of the runway.

Suddenly the hangar erupted in a ball of flame as intense as a firestorm from an atomic blast. A billowing mountain of fire seized the entire hangar, dissolving it in its maelstrom. Then the maelstrom turned into something that resembled a noonday sun bursting from the earth.

The impact and heat from the blast rocked the Bronco back and forth on its springs, charring its paint and turning the inside of the vehicle into an oven. Braille shielded his eyes, feeling the searing heat burn his skin as a virtual volcano exploded and re-exploded a half a mile away.

Then it was over.

The sky and the land returned to normal. Braille found himself sitting in a charred dusty car not far from a smoldering giant crater in the middle of a wasteland of an old Air Force base.

Braille sat in the Bronco throughout the remainder of the afternoon, staring at the remains of what he had hated so intensely for what seemed like so long. A storm came down from the north, engulfing the desert before passing on. A second storm was filling the northern horizon, when he climbed slowly down from the Bronco. There was just one more thing to do.

With painful movements he brought the palms of his hands together, bowing formally to the spirits of Louis and Jade Radcliff. "Thank you."

Then, after a long painful moment, he bowed to the spirit of Leslie Chapel.

Lightning danced across the northern sky. A setting sun captured the slanting rain. There was no rainbow, but the sky was a prism of colors. The storm seemed to capture the magic of Leslie Chapel: her beauty, her moods, her majesty. Braille found something almost overwhelming in the moment. He bowed again, and straightened up. "You gave me meaning. You gave me life. Thank you."

While thunder rumbled off in the distance, he turned away, reaching out for the Bronco's door. He gasped in pain. Pain from a bullet still inside his body. Suddenly it felt as if everything on the right side of his chest and upper shoulder were on fire, and worse, the fire was spreading like poison through his body.

He managed to get into the Bronco. In spite of his pain, he almost smiled. This business of being an Ancient wasn't all it was cracked up to be. For beings who were supposed to be immortal, the only two in the world weren't doing too well. If not already dead, Gregory was dying.

And so was he.

Some minutes later Braille stopped the Bronco. Ahead of him, not more than a half a mile away, lay the interstate freeway stretching out across the desert. If he took the eastbound lane, it would carry him back to Mary Kathleen Stuart, Amanda, John, and maybe a chance at life. If he turned right, the highway would take him back to Seattle and the hell it held.

As he put the Bronco into gear and idled forward, he found himself wondering which way he would go.

37

JUST BEFORE SUNRISE THE NEW ONES DISAPPEARED OFF THE streets, and for a few minutes it was absolutely still, and the stillness was as loud as the hard-fought battles that had taken place in downtown Seattle throughout the entire night.

The eerie silence lasted some minutes longer, and during that time the soldiers remained at the barricades, their rifles trained on empty streets.

Then an air raid siren exploded in the pre-dawn gloaming. Within a matter of moments every soldier in the vicinity of downtown Seattle was in a truck or a jeep and was speeding towards a designated shelter center located miles away from the point of impact.

In the silence that followed the mass evacuation, a lone vehicle eased its way past deserted trucks and abandoned A.P.C.'s, heading slowly towards the center of the city. The progress of the vehicle was slow. Its sole occupant drove the vehicle as if he were tired or badly hurt. The car weaved slowly from side to side as it crept down the street. On several occasions it scraped parked cars. Yet it continued on as if its only purpose were to seek out the heart of downtown Seattle.

Some blocks later the car finally stopped, and its driver slowly climbed out and collapsed to his hands and knees on the deserted street. After a long moment the driver got up and began walking down the street. His movements were like the vehicle: slow, methodical, staggered at times, but with purpose.

With halting measured steps the driver forced himself to continue until he finally found himself on the outskirts of a small park near the center of downtown Seattle. The lone figure surveyed the park, noticing a man sitting on a park bench. With the last of his strength, the driver limped across the grass. A moment later he sat down on the same bench.

Gregory had aged dramatically. His skin was taut, his cheeks sunken and hollowed. His hair had turned white. He was dying.

What Braille's eyes took in did not shock him. He had caught a fleeting glimpse of himself in a store window minutes earlier. His cheeks too were gaunt, and his hair had turned white. Like Gregory, he too was dying.

"How did you get the strength to get here?" Braille asked.

Gregory was gazing across the park at the distant harbor. At the sound of Braille's voice, the Ancient lifted his eyes, fixing them on the dark clouds above the skyscrapers. "Blood," he said. "Two looters came to the motel room. They thought I was dead. While the man searched the room, the woman searched me. I killed her and took her blood. The other escaped." Gregory waited for a moment, then added: "Home delivery of blood . . . like pizza."

It took Braille a moment to realize Gregory had made a joke. When he did, he tried to smile and failed. The muscles in his face didn't seem to be working. For that matter, neither did the muscles of his body. He had used up all his strength getting here. Now all he seemed to be able to do was to sit and look at the sky with Gregory.

"The agency," Gregory said. "The agency you went to destroy, it no longer exists?"

"It's gone."

Gregory looked at Braille, noticing for the first time how hideously hurt he was. "It would seem you paid a price to destroy this agency."

A gust of wind full of smoke and ash swept through the park, picking up leaves and scattering them in a westerly direction. That was good, Braille thought. The wind will carry the radiation out to sea. He hoped that by the time the radiation touched water, it would have thinned out enough not to harm the ocean.

"Why didn't you return to the family you spoke of?" Gregory asked. "You cared for them. They cared for you." A heartbeat later Gregory gasped as a spasm of pain hit him. Braille grimaced along with Gregory. He knew what the

Ancient was feeling. The pain from the cesium-laced bullet came and went, increased and faded as it seared flesh from the inside out. Gregory's pain faded. Braille continued to remain silent.

"It was a question you didn't want to answer?" Gregory said.

"I was just thinking about my answer. I wanted to go to them, but it wouldn't have been right. I'm not like them. I'm not human. It's like I'm something from a different kind of species. In time I would've brought them pain, and I couldn't do that to them. Not them."

Gregory nodded in understanding.

"So I came here. I think I would rather die than live on this way, empty and alone . . . and evil."

Again Gregory nodded, approvingly this time. "For one so recently human, you make decisions worthy of an Ancient who has existed for centuries." He looked back at the sky. Braille too raised his eyes to the sky as he heard the sound of a plane heading towards Seattle.

"Will it be long?" Gregory asked.

"No," Braille said.

They sat in silence, a cold comfortable silence as the wind gusted around them and the noise of an Air Force jet bomber grew louder in the sky above them.

A question occurred to Braille. "Do you believe in hell or heaven?"

Gregory looked at him, but did not see him. He was blind now. "Yes. But, I don't think there is a place for us in either dimension."

"That figures," Braille said, as the sound of the jet bomber continued to grow louder.

Gregory picked up on the irony in Braille's voice. He seemed to smile as he settled back on the bench and resumed looking up at the sunrise with sightless eyes. "Bummer, huh? We don't fit on earth and are inappropriate for heaven and hell." And this time he did not appear to be smiling. He was.

The Air Force bomber overhead now, its jet engines were loud, and growing louder with each moment. Though it was thousands of feet above the cloud cover, the roar of its engines seemed to rattle buildings, and shake the earth. And still it grew louder, until the bomber's monstrous roar seemed to fill the sky, the universe.

Then, abruptly, the sound took on a tone of urgency. At the same time, the roar began to fade into the distance. Braille glanced across the barren park and he knew. The bomber had just dropped its payload, and now its pilot was guiding it away from ground zero.

As the roar faded away, a new sound could be heard. At first it sounded like a faint shriek, but moments later the shriek turned into a low-pitched mournful whistle.

"It is time?" Gregory asked.

Braille nodded. "Yes," was all he said.

Like the bomber's earlier roar, the singular mournful whistle grew louder and louder with each passing second until the very last moment. Then the sound stopped abruptly . . .

And there was only silence. Only silence.

In that brief moment of silence Gregory whispered, "Clementina . . ."

And Braille said, "Let it be now. Let it be forever." He smiled at the prospect of finally meeting death.

The silence hung on the earth for a moment longer. Then the world turned blindingly white.

Then black.

Epilogue

As it turned out, Kearney Park had not been target zero for the nuclear device.

Two dozen Air Force and Army tacticians, along with two high-speed computers, spent a full twenty-four hours poring over any and every map made of downtown Seattle. Since they were interested in pinpointing the heart of underground Seattle as opposed to modern Seattle, most of the maps they consulted were old, in some cases a hundred and thirty years old. As a result of that research the technicians and computers agreed that the bomb should be targeted in on a deserted hotel six blocks south of Kearney Park.

When the bomb was dropped, it missed the hotel by twenty feet. The warhead slammed into a wet street, penetrating the asphalt. A microsecond later it exploded with all its fury, directly in the heart of the underground city, vaporizing everything that dwelt within.

The bomb created a crater a hundred and eighty-five feet deep and three hundred yards across. The destruction was immense, but almost insignificant in comparison to what the New Ones had done to the interior of the city during their nights of death, destruction, and rampaging.

Not every New One was killed in the blast. Some hiding

out and sleeping in brick and cement buildings several blocks away from Ground Zero managed to survive.

Six hours after the blast armed men wearing strange astronaut-like garb entered the city and the final extermination began.

And continued.

And was so successful that, at sundown, nothing came out on the streets. Nothing human. Nothing animal.

After a night of extensive flyovers by helicopters armed with high-tech infrared vision systems and movement-sensing monitors, the operation was declared a success. The following day the President went on TV to explain why he had authorized the use of a nuclear device on downtown Seattle. He did so by presenting a series of Army and news network videotapes that documented in grisly Technicolor the horror taking place in downtown Seattle prior to the dropping of the bomb. An hour after the Presidential explanation the Vice President and a high-ranking Army general attempted to resign. The resignations were not accepted by the President nor by the population at large. Public opinion polls done by the ABC and NBC news networks firmly established the fact that both men had acted accordingly, even heroically, given the fact that the disease in Seattle could have spread throughout the United States.

Forty-eight hours after the blast the massive cleanup began. The damage was not widespread. But there was a great deal of nuclear contaminated waste and debris that had to be disposed of. Huge trucks and more men wearing astronaut-like garb converged on what was left of downtown Seattle and a cleanup began. Long convoys of huge trucks carried radioactive debris across the Cascade Mountains in central Washington to deposit their cargo in the desert outside of a small town known for its nuclear reactors and disposal sites, a small town called Hanford.

It was while the cleanup was underway that two bodies were found in Kearney Park under a thick layer of dust and debris.

The workers immediately backed off and allowed the supervisor and several armed guards to approach. After studying the bodies in the muted gray daylight for the better part of a minute, the supervisor said into the microphone inside his Plexiglas helmet: "Well, they ain't creatures. They're not dissolving in the sun."

He called for a Geiger counter, knelt down beside the two forms, swept the counter over the bodies, and came up with a low reading. That didn't surprise the supervisor. Most of the radiation had been confined to Underground Seattle and what little that had escaped had been swept out to sea by a strong morning wind. He got to his feet and raised his right hand over the bodies, making the sign of a cross in a parody of a priest giving last rites. "I pronounce thee human," he said, his voice muted and metallic because of the Plexiglas helmet. "I also pronounce thee safe to handle and stupid as hell for being caught in this area when the bomb went off." He turned to his work crew. "Tag 'em, bag 'em, and cart 'em over to Mercy Hospital."

"Why don't we just toss them on the truck," one of his men asked, "and dump them out by Hanford with all this other stuff?"

The supervisor had worked for the AEC for thirty years. He was a company man. Had never questioned directions or orders, wasn't about to now. "I told you about the briefing yesterday. The directive is that anything even remotely human gets bagged and shipped off to Mercy Hospital." He shrugged with his hands. "Orders from on-high," he said, shaking his head. "I never heard of the man and I never heard of his agency, but he's got clout. All the AEC director could do was go 'yes sir-yes sir' to everything the damn doctor wanted."

The supervisor glanced at his watch. The sun would be down in a half hour and it was almost time to get his men out of here. Although the Army was sure that no more of those creatures were alive, there was always the chance that the Army was wrong. Fifteen minutes to go, then it was back to the motel four miles away. Some Christmas Eve, he thought.

Seven days later . . .

Two men in pale green laboratory smocks moved up to the one-way mirror and stared through the glass. For a long moment neither doctor spoke. Finally the taller of the two said: "This has been the most incredible seven days of my life. I still don't believe it. You've pulled off a miracle. An absolute miracle."

The shorter man smiled as he continued to peer through the one-way glass. It was a cold smile, a learned response to praise. "It has been interesting, hasn't it," he observed.

"I still don't know how you knew these two were the ones. All Cutter's records and documents were destroyed in the explosion."

"Hargrave did a lot of bragging when he was in Washington. I knew what he was working on, and a lot of his test results and trial data had been fed into the agency's computer. Being the assistant director gave me open access to even the most highly classified programs."

"But how did you know that these two were the ones?"

"Simple," said the newly appointed director of the OSMS. "I had photographs of the one Hargrave had at his lab. I had one of our computers do an analysis of the photograph with an eye towards giving me an accurate representation of what the facial bone structure would look like if it were burned or partly unrecognizable. With the computer composites, it was fairly easy to recognize the man."

The other physician shook his head. "Must have been some composite. I saw those bodies when they were brought in. They looked like two-thousand-year-old mummies." He paused. "How 'bout the other one? How'd you know he was . . . was one of them?"

"Lucky guess. I knew Cutter had suspected there were two of them and when I found out there was a body lying next to the man I was after, I decided to treat it the same way." The smile faded and the small doctor began to scrutinize his two patients in the other room through the glass. Both were still comatose, both were still receiving IV's of fresh human blood and both were strapped to steel tables with wide metal straps made from space-age high-tech alloys that allowed them to be flexible as leather and stronger than steel.

The taller doctor crossed his arms. "Seems like it should be Easter rather than New Year's Eve."

"Easter?"

"It's like watching a resurrection, a twofold resurrection. Two bodies brought back from the dead." He looked down at his clipboard, then at the men in the next room. "I figure they'll come out of that comatose state in a week or two. They're responding beautifully to whole blood and Dothor. A couple more days of Dothor and most of the radiation will have been neutralized or washed out of their system. Interesting chemical. I'd never heard of it until you had it flown in."

The new director of the OSMS just nodded.

"What now?" asked the taller doctor.

"Now I pick up where Cutter left off."

"Gonna be a hell of a new year."

"That's putting it mildly," said the director of the OSMS.

Three days later . . .

The room had been constructed from cement, and the floor, ceiling, walls, and door were all painted semiglossy white. The harsh glow from the overhead fluorescent lighting added to the whiteness, as if the illumination bleached the air.

There was one window in the room, a small window with a latticework of bars running vertically and horizontally. There was no glass in the window, just a mirror. A one-way mirror.

The only furniture in the room were two large steel tables, tables with legs that had been sunk into the floor a full twelve inches so that nothing short of a wrecking ball could move them. Two figures were strapped onto the specially built tables. The straps were made of metal and they covered the figures' ankles, thighs, waists, chests, arms, wrists, and necks. Had they been awake, the only portion of their bodies they could have moved were their heads, and a U-shaped neck collar welded to each table confined the movements of their heads.

The only objects that added color to the room were the red plastic bags on hangers just to the right of each table. Red liquid oozed out of the plastic bags and down individual tubes into the arms of each figure strapped to the tables.

The figure on the table on the left stirred, moving. A moment later his eyes fluttered open. The eyes took in the surroundings with slow methodical movements, then glanced up, noticing the red plastic bag and the tube that led down into a vein in his arm. And he remembered a time when this had happened before, a time when he'd been pulled out of the waters off an island in Puget Sound, taken aboard a U.S. Navy destroyer, and been given plasma. He was dead when they had taken him aboard, but the plasma had brought him back to life.

"Fuck," he said, his eyes fixed on the bag of whole blood dangling above his head. "They did it again."

"Did what, human?" asked the other.